They chatted while they ate, and Catriona nearly forgot about the storm outside. Occasionally a jagged fierce streak of lightning would blaze through the sky. Robert said, "In Spain they call this kind of storm a *tempestad*."

"In Gaelic it is called *gailleann non sliabh*."

"Galeen-an-sli," Robert attempted slowly.

"Not exactly," Catriona said. "It is in how you form the words with your mouth." She took his hand. "Come closer." He did, and leaning forward, her face near to his, Catriona pressed his fingertips against her lips. *"Gailleann non sliabh."*

It was the most erotic feeling he'd ever known. Robert did not move even after she released his hand.

Neither of them spoke for some time. The fire crackled in the hearth. Catriona's heart was pounding. She watched his face in the firelight; when he came forward and replaced his fingers with his lips, she melted against him, taking his kiss and returning it with her own. When Robert's lips met hers, it was as if they had been swept away by a furious current, the two of them riding out the storm that had begun between them, a storm more fierce, more potent than the one raging outside.

White Heather

Jaclyn Reding

A TOPAZ BOOK

TOPAZ
Published by the Penguin Group
Penguin Books USA Inc., 375 Hudson Street,
New York, New York 10014, U.S.A.
Penguin Books Ltd, 27 Wrights Lane, London W8 5TZ, England
Penguin Books Australia Ltd, Ringwood, Victoria, Australia
Penguin Books Canada Ltd, 10 Alcorn Avenue,
Toronto, Ontario, Canada M4V 3B2
Penguin Books (N.Z.) Ltd, 182–190 Wairau Road,
Auckland 10, New Zealand

Penguin Books Ltd, Registered Offices: Harmondsworth, Middlesex, England

First published by Topaz, an imprint of Dutton Signet,
a division of Penguin Books USA Inc.

First Printing, August, 1997
10 9 8 7 6 5 4 3 2 1

 REGISTERED TRADEMARK—MARCA REGISTRADA

Printed in the United States of America

To Hilary Ross,

for knowing my capabilities,
and giving me the encouragement
to meet them.

Thank you.

*It is the image in the mind
that binds us to our lost treasures,
but it is the loss
that shapes the image.*
—Colette

Prologue

OCTOBER, 1793
INVERNESS-SHIRE, SCOTTISH HIGHLANDS

"What is taking so bloody long in there!"

Bent over the swollen and struggling body, the midwife shifted her eyes momentarily to the door. Yet even the dreadful shadows and the thick pitted wood which separated them could not keep his terrible venom from stinging sharply. Nothing could.

Wickit Deil, she thought, frowning as she returned her attentions to the young woman laboring on the tall tester bed. It was her only response to the man who waited so impatiently on the other side.

Her silence seemed only to incite him.

"I could have rooted the little whelp out with a pot hook by now!" he shouted. A momentary pause, and then a pounding on the door. "Do you hear me, you Scots witch? Get that brat out quickly 'else I'll come in there and see to it myself!"

Do it and I'll be showin' you what you can do with your bludey pot hook . . .

But Mary MacBryan bit back her response, one which would have belied her social station and would have no doubt seen her censured for it later. Her concern was more for the young woman before her than the devil's own instrument lurking outside this overheated and ill-lighted chamber, one which had never been intended for use as a bedchamber, but surely as a prison cell.

Sweat beaded at Mary's brow, slipping from beneath the worn linen kerchief that bound her hair. She wiped it away with the hem of her apron, then glanced bleakly at the small clock set beside the bed. The birthing was not progressing well. Not at all. Lady Catherine hadn't rested for more than a spell or two since the night before, and still the babe wasn't coming. Mary had been trying to get it turned round, gently rolling Catherine from one side to the other in order to maneuver the child within the womb, yet still the head lay nestled tight beneath her swollen bosom.

Mary peered at Catherine's delicate face, noticing the increasingly unhealthy murk in her blue eyes, like a candle whose fragile flame was slowly burning itself out. *She is dying,* she thought, her heart growing stone heavy inside her chest. If she didn't find some way to get the babe out soon, both it and the mother would be lost. Time had run short. She could no longer wait for nature to remedy the matter. She would need to see to it herself.

Mary leaned forward over the bed, her mouth close to Catherine's ear. "My lady?" she said, tucking a strand of dark hair behind it. " 'Tis me, Mary. Can you still hear me?"

Catherine moaned, a weak and struggling sound, more exhaustion than pain. She swallowed slowly before finally rasping out, "Aye, Mary."

And Mary knew then she was fading. "Let us get you to drink the last of this raspberry and lavender tea I drew for you. 'Twill help to bring you some easement from your pains and strengthen you for the bairn's delivery."

Mary gently lifted Catherine's head from the pillow, tilting the wooden cup to her parched lips to drain the last of its tepid liquid into her mouth. Catherine swallowed but a sparse few drops, the rest of it dribbling down her chin to the cloth Mary held there.

Smoothing a hand gently over her head, Mary studied Catherine closely in the dim candlelight that cast a gloomy and inimical glow about an already gloomy and inimical chamber. Catherine was weakening fast. Her dark hair was damp, sticking to her forehead, her cheeks and neck reddened from her exertion and the oppressive heat in the cramped room.

Behind them, a fire burned steadily in the crude stone hearth, a fire Mary could not put out, for she needed both its light and its heat to keep warm the small bit of water she had to use for cleaning after the birth. The candles surrounding the bed were burning low, one after another dimming more of the precious light she worked by. The devil had refused to allow Mary more candles for light soon after he'd refused her earnest request for additional water, stating she would work faster at delivering the child by withholding them.

But soon they would be left in darkness, for the stone walls held no torch sconces nor was there so much as a small window opening to let in a breath of the night air or the barest sliver of the moonlight from outside.

Indeed they were prisoners in this chamber, a chamber of terror.

"He thinks to bake us alive in here," Mary said aloud, though more to herself than to Catherine. "The devil he is, that one. He canna e'en fetch some bits of ice from the icehouse so I can ease this heat for you. He thinks this birthin' an easy thing. *Och,* but I would like to see him do it." She lowered her voice, pressing a damp cloth to Catherine's heated forehead. "I fear my infusions will only do so much and last so long to relieve you, my lady."

Catherine slowly raised a hand, her gold wedding ring glimmering in the soft firelight. Her fingers trembled from the tremendous effort. Mary had never felt so helpless as she watched this woman, once so strong, so vibrant, now looked as if even the task of taking her next breath was beyond her. Mary briefly closed her eyes. If only the laird had lived long enough to see his young wife safely through this night, she thought, sorrow's tears rimming her eyes when she opened them again.

They had been wed but a handful of years, the laird and his lady, yet the love they had shared had filled every moment of those years with unquestioned bliss. Catherine was his second wife, his first wife having died in childbed, and he had traveled all the way to London in search of her. He had said that from the moment he'd first seen her, a diamond amidst a crowd in some faraway fairy-tale ballroom, he could hear the angels sing. And the love he felt for her was twice returned, Mary knew; one had only to look at how Catherine had gazed so adoringly at her Charles to know it.

Catherine had once told Mary how the laird had serenaded her outside her chamber window when he had been courting her. It was a thing another man of his age wouldn't likely have done, and Catherine had known then that he was the love, the only love she would ever have. In turn, Catherine's gay spirit had brought back a youth to the laird's decades-older face that had only flourished.

Their mornings had been spent walking together or picnicking on the outskirts of the estate, their nights in each other's arms, making love with only the light of the moon through the windows shining down on them. Mary remembered well the day Catherine had told her husband of their coming child. The laird had been so happy, arranging a celebration the likes of which hadn't been seen since the clan days. Everyone for miles about had come to join in the frolic, even the laird's grandnephew, who had arrived so suddenly, so unexpectedly, the very morning of that happy gathering.

But then the sickness had come to the laird, swiftly and without warning, a curious sickness which Mary's herbs and cordials had been unable to combat. It had taken the laird's life just as swiftly, felling that great and gentle man. Catherine had been unable to attend her beloved husband for his fear that this unknown sickness might harm the bairn. She had begged Charles, sitting outside the closed bedchamber door, until he'd finally relented, allowing her to sit with him the last night. He was gone by the morn, leaving Catherine to pass the next several months living alone in this remote tower castle, awaiting the outcome of her pregnancy with her husband's grandnephew, the presumptive heir.

And now that time had come.

Mary took Catherine's hand with her own, one that was callused and worn from a lifetime of labor, willing the younger woman the strength she would need to see this night through.

"Lady Catherine, you must hearken to me. I dinna think I'll be able to get the bairn turned 'round. I've been trying for nigh on twelve hours now and its head is still up at your belly. We canna wait no longer. We've no other choice left to us. We're goin' to have to take the bairn breech first."

Catherine closed her eyes. When she looked at Mary again, tears of frightened unknowing came to her soft blue eyes. "Will it die, Mary? Will the babe die before it is born to me?"

Mary smiled, trying to keep a calm to her voice when in truth she didn't hold much hope for the babe's safe delivery. Indeed, Catherine's life was also at risk. "Nae, my lady, dinna worry yourself. I dinna believe your bairn will perish, if we can get it out soon, that is. I've delivered afore with the bairn's feet coming first. Every one of them a lad and every one of them fitter than a horse. If we take it slow, and you hearken to me well, we'll get it out fine. Then you'll have a stoussie laddie-bairn for your own."

Catherine took in a ragged breath and with it mustered up her flagging courage. "If only Charles could have lived to see his son born." She gazed up at the ceiling. "Dear, sweet Charles . . . how I have missed you . . . I love you still so very much, my dearest."

Her eyes misted over then and it was as if his lordship, her husband, gone now these five months, were suddenly there with her, kneeling at her bedside while he whispered sweet words into her ear, smoothing back her tousled hair, telling her how very proud of her he was, for a small smile touched Catherine's parched lips.

"Charles . . ."

"That's a guid lass," Mary said, echoing words she'd heard the laird speak to Catherine throughout their short time together, knowing if she didn't act quickly all would be lost. "You're goin' to feel the need to push the bairn out of you, my lady, but I dinna want you to bear down afore I tell you to. I've got to ease the bairn out a bit, to position it aright before we can take it. 'Twill pain you some my doin' so, but 'tis the only way. Now do you need some time to ready yourself afore I start on it?"

Catherine moved her head sluggishly to one side. "Nay, Mary, nay. Please do whatever you must to save my child. Quickly. I fear so for the babe's life."

Mary lifted the hem of the bloodied sheet, pushing it back over Catherine's hugely distended belly. She was so small, her hips so narrow, and the babe was so large, confining her to her bed these past eight weeks. Standing to the side and over her a bit, Mary placed one hand atop Catherine's belly, applying a small amount of pressure as she eased the fingers of her other hand inside. Catherine tensed, drawing in a sharp breath as Mary maneuvered within.

" 'Tis all right, my lady. There it is. I've found the bairn's foot. Now I just need to find the other and—"

Catherine cried out.

" 'Tis there. I've found it. Nae, dinna push yet, my lady. I know you want to, but we must needs take it slow. If you birth the bairn too quick, you'll tear and the bairn will—"

Catherine gave another cry, louder this time, cutting off Mary's last words.

"What in bloody hell are you doing in there, you witch?" rose an angry shout from outside the door. "If you damage her or that whelp in any way, I will see you punished for your incompetency!"

Mary ignored him, concentrating everything on Catherine. "That's it. You're doing fine, my lady, real fine. The bairn's feet are both out. Now, I need you to ease off and take a slow, deep breath. You musna push it, my lady, no matter how you want to. Not yet. You must let me begin to bring the bairn through myself."

Mary moved around between Catherine's raised legs. The bedding was soaked with sweat and the birth water, mixing with the heat and bringing a heavy smell to the stagnant air. Mary wiped her apron over her brow then leaned forward.

"That's right, my lady, take you in deep breaths. 'Tis hard, I know. You can push a bit now. Aye, that's it, my lady. You're doin' fine. I'll be bringing your bairn to you real soon now. And when you've done with your labor, I'll get you a nice cup of the tea I make with the motherwort and basil. I put in a bit of honey to sweeten it against the bitterness. Then after you've rested a bit and I've cleaned you well, we'll get you into a cool comfrey bath. 'Twill aid you in your healing. You will see."

Mary continued on, chattering now about whatever would come to mind, anything to occupy Catherine's attentions as she began to slip her hand inside of her. Instantly she could feel Catherine tighten around her.

"Nae, my lady, ease yourself. The bairn's head is soft, aye, but comin' out this way is most perilous. Try, my lady, try to lay yourself back and I'll pull it out slow. I've got to hold the bairn's arms down with my hand to keep them from breaking. 'Tis the only way, my lady. It'll pain you fierce, but only a moment. And I'll take it quick as I can."

Her words seemed to soothe Catherine, inducing her to slacken her taut muscles. Catherine eased back on the bed and Mary slowly began to ease the babe from her body, her eyes focused on Catherine's face, watching to see if she would expire from the pain.

Catherine was a study of concentration and self-control, biting down against the pain and setting all her energies to this one task she must perform. The laird would have been so proud of her, his English lassie. Mary waited, watching Catherine until she felt the babe's buttocks in her hands. Only then did she look down.

The babe's feet and legs were out and the skin was blue. Too blue. Mary needed to get the child out quickly, but she also knew she must take care with its neck and head. Taking the shoulders through was going to bring Catherine the most pain. And it would put the babe at the most risk. Mary placed one hand beneath the babe, between its tiny legs and against its belly, and the other inward to curve around its head. Slowly she started to pull.

Catherine screamed.

"That's it, my lady, push now. Aye, 'tis almost there. I've got it, its arms and shoulders are through, and I can see its neck now . . ."

Catherine's scream reached its highest point, echoing through the cobweb-strung rafters before it abruptly cut off to silence. Only her breathing, heavy and erratic, filled the stillness in the chamber. Mary quickly pulled the babe free, positioned it, and whacked it soundly on the backside.

There came no sound.

She turned the babe over to face her, closing her eyes when she realized it was a boy. A son. Lady Catherine had so wanted a son, to give her beloved Charles the heir he'd prayed for. It would surely break her heart to lose him now.

Cleaning out his mouth and nose, Mary swaddled the child in a thick cloth and vigorously began to rub his bluish skin. She kneaded his tiny arms and legs, massaging her thumbs upward over his weakened chest, willing him to take that first life-giving breath. She worked and worked and she'd nearly given up hope when, suddenly, the babe sputtered, coughed weakly, and began to cry. It was a fragile cry, but one that soon grew stronger. No sound was ever so beautiful.

Mary allowed herself a relieved breath. " 'Tis a boy, my lady, a fine laddie-bairn!"

A smile crept slowly over Catherine's face as Mary was making to lay the babe on her belly.

Across the room, the door suddenly burst open and the devil himself stood there, dressed in black, a sinister silhouette against the torchlight glowing from the corridor behind him.

"A boy you say, Scotswoman? Lady Catherine has given birth to an heir?"

"Aye, my lord," Mary answered, lowering her head so as not to have to look at him as she tied off the birth cord and snipped the babe free. From the first moment she had seen him, that day when he'd arrived so unexpectedly to pay a visit to the laird, his granduncle, Mary had sensed the villainy that surrounded him like a black cape. Hidden behind his polite words and timely smiles lurked the heartlessness of evil.

Mary swaddled the child and released the crying bundle into Catherine's arms.

"Congratulations, Catherine," he said, coming forward from the door, though what should have been happy words were contradicted by the wicked look that gleamed in his dark eyes. "It would seem your husband, my uncle, did see to his responsibility in begetting an heir of his blood before he died." He then snatched the wailing bundle from Catherine's arms, holding the child up for his inspection with as much care as he might a stray pup. "He looks pale, though, no doubt due to this Scotswoman's procrastination in delivering him. I'll get the lad to his wet nurse directly so we can fatten him up and assure he'll be a healthy one."

He made for the door. Mary started after him. "Nae, my lord, the bairn needs his mother now and—"

He was gone, slamming the door behind him and allowing Mary no chance to follow. Mary stood there, troubled and uncertain when she heard Catherine's sudden moan. It wasn't a moan of exhaustion or even one of subsiding pain. This was a moan of surprise.

She hastened for the bed. "My lady?"

"The pain," Catherine measured out. " 'Tis coming again, Mary. 'Tis strong once again, very strong and building."

" 'Tis the afterpains, my lady. I must needs fetch out the burthen from you, then I'll see to gettin' you some water to drink so to cool you while I draw you the healing tea."

Mary wiped her hands on her apron as she moved back between Catherine's legs. She gasped, taking in a startled breath at the blood, bright and new, that was seeping from Catherine's body, spreading fast across the bedsheets. Mary threw back the covers and took up a cloth, pressing it to her and trying in vain to stem the flow of it. None of her tincture compresses would combat bleeding this severe. This wasn't birthing blood. This was lifeblood.

Mary fought to push back her inmost fears at knowing what was to come. Catherine cried out suddenly, nearly sitting up on the bed as she clutched at her belly.

"Oh . . . Mary . . . the pain . . . it grows . . ."

Mary eased her back then pulled the cloth away. There a small head was crowning. "Oh, sweet heaven, my lady, you've another bairn comin'!"

Mary quickly placed her hand under the tiny head that nigh delivered itself to her, so much more quickly than the other. In moments, the babe was free and already squalling like an angry autumn storm. Gently Mary lifted up the babe, amazed to tears. " 'Tis a lassie, my lady. A wee lassie bairn with dark hair like yourself."

Mary cut the babe free and swaddled her in one of the blankets from Catherine's bed before bringing her to her mother. "She's a beauty, she is, my lady. A lovely little lassie."

"Mary?" Catherine's eyes were closed, her breath grown shallow. Her voice had become so weak, Mary barely heard her.

"Aye, my lady?"

"You must listen to me. Please." She drew in a slow, failing breath. "He does not know there are two babes. He must never know of it. He will take the other, my son, and he will kill him this night." Catherine paused, fighting to give voice to her words.

"Nae, my lady. He canna do such a—"

"Mary, please listen to me well. I am dying now. I feel my spirit leaving from me this moment. I am not afraid. I'm for joining my Charles in the other world, but you must promise me . . ."

"Aye, my lady, anything."

"You must promise me . . . you will take her . . . my daughter. Foster her . . . keep her safe . . . from him . . . for he would kill her . . . too . . . if he were to know she lives."

Catherine's eyes fluttered helplessly.

"Nae, my lady, please, dinna say such things. Open your eyes. Look at your lassie bairn, my lady. She's your sweet daughter."

Catherine's eyes drifted open briefly, long enough for her to see the babe, and a weak smile came to her mouth. But her lips already were losing their color, her face now frighteningly pale. She lifted a hand to lightly touch her daughter's healthy pink face. "She is beautiful, Mary . . . and she is yours now . . . there is no hope for me . . . he would kill me if I chanced to live through this night . . . it is better this way . . . that he not know the truth . . . of her . . . please . . . please just promise . . . promise to name her for m—"

Catherine's head slackened to the side and her chest stole its last mortal breath, releasing it slowly before the silence that followed. A single tear trailed down her fair cheek, disappearing behind the curve of her ear.

She was gone. Lady Catherine was with her beloved Charles at long last. A stillness came suddenly upon the room, a peacefulness that was filled with a strange and wondrous sorrow. Mary looked through the blur of her own tears and saw that the bedding beneath Catherine's body was now soaked with her blood. The babe still lay cradled in her mother's lifeless arms, staring up at Mary, her eyes, misty blue like the summer sky, like her mother's, affirming the words Catherine had last spoken.

"What shall I do?" Mary said softly, sadly to her.

The babe gurgled then let out an impatient "Wa."

Mary stood watching her, fixed with indecision.

No one knew of the lass, no one except Mary. If she left her with him, that devil, the babe would never know of her mother, of how special she was, of how much she was truly loved. Mary thought of Catherine's words, her prophecy of what that man would do with her son. If she was right, if he took the lad and killed him this night, that same fate that would befall her daughter unless . . .

Catherine's hand suddenly slipped down from where it had rested at her chest to dangle over the edge of the bed. Something shiny, glinting in the ebbing candlelight, caught Mary's eye. She reached for it. Entwined in Catherine's lifeless fingers was a chain of twisted gold, suspended from which a locket glimmered in the firelight, Catherine's first gift, her last gift to her newborn daughter.

And in that moment, Mary knew what she must do.

Chapter One

No man can lose what he never had.
—Izaak Walton, *The Compleat Angler*

Lord Robert Edenhall frowned as he worked his way through the front door into the club. Gentlemen were everywhere, standing about, their competing voices creating a consistent droning that filled the congested lower hallways.

He had hoped for a quiet supper before retiring. He realized now it was not to be.

The hour was early, not quite eight o'clock, yet the Front Parlor was filled with stylishly dressed men, and some not so stylishly dressed, vying for attention. Nearly every coat peg beneath the polished mahogany double staircase had already been taken. Brummell and his contemporaries were at their place before the bow window facing St. James, alternately snickering over some poor buffoon to whom they'd delivered a cut and pinching varying blends of snuff from elegant enameled boxes. Further inside, the Card Room was a crush, those who weren't involved in play standing idly by watching those who were, while fortunes were won and lost on the high-stakes play of the cards.

The Season, it seemed, had begun.

Robert hadn't seen such a rumpus since the Jubilee the previous June, when he, most of the army, and their distinguished commander Wellington had returned to

London to celebrate England's grand victory over the French. For a brief moment, as Robert removed his cloak and handed it to the steward, he wondered if the duke might have been named prime minister after all, the rumor having first surfaced after Wellington had left to return for the peace talks at Vienna. Although from the fragments of conversation Robert caught as he maneuvered his way toward the stairs, the subject on most everyone's minds these days wasn't Vienna, Wellington, or even Bonaparte, safely exiled to Elba, but instead the dilemma of the proposed Corn Bill.

Robert located an empty table at the far corner of the Dinner Room, one of but a sparse few remaining. He asked for a bottle of claret and three glasses with the meal from the steward who greeted him.

A celebration after all, was in order, for this would be his last night in London as a bachelor. The contracts had been signed earlier that morning, his lengthiest acquisition to date, but one that he knew would prove well worth the effort. On the morrow, Robert would set out for Lancashire and Devonbrook House to inform his father of his impending marriage.

"Well, you certainly haven't the look of a man who has just been tried in all your phases, Rob."

Robert looked up as Noah, his younger brother, dropped into the seat across from him. His chestnut hair, only a shade lighter than Robert's, was tousled as if he'd been caught in a high wind. His boots, as always, were in sorry need of a polish.

"I wouldn't say Lord Hastings made the negotiations an easy affair, but I did manage to come through with my manhood intact," Robert said, staring at the lopsided tie and telltale wrinkles in Noah's cravat. He couldn't resist the urge to shake his head, wondering if his brother would ever accomplish a clean knot. "You know there are pamphlets you can purchase which demonstrate the proper manner of folding a cravat."

Noah looked up from the news sheet he had begun perusing, the lenses of his tortoise-rimmed spectacles blinking in the candlelight. "Nothing escapes your notice, does it? You've just managed to claim one of society's most sought-after diamonds, and all you can think of is the deplorable state of my cravat?" Noah shook his head, returning to his news sheet. "And I've seen those pamphlets, Rob; Mr. Goodfellow's Latin exercises were easier to execute than they are."

Robert smiled at the mention of their childhood tutor, a man who'd made even the most fascinating subjects tiresome. Noah and Robert had passed many a spring morning making the staid Mr. Goodfellow's life a little less reserved. Actually, they had plagued the poor fellow unendingly, but his boredom never eased.

"Even Pietro was able to understand the pamphlets, Noah, and he has only begun to read English."

"Then I might as well abandon all hope for it now. Besides, I didn't come here tonight to celebrate the fact that your Spanish batman-cum-valet can execute a cravat fold better than I." He shoved the news sheet away. "Let us get back to the subject at hand—specifically, your wedding. When is it?"

"It is to be held at St. James, Piccadilly, on the fifteenth of March."

Noah sat back, raising a discerning dark brow beneath the mop of hair that fell over his forehead. "A little more than three weeks hence. You're certainly not wasting any time."

"I have been courting Anthea since my return from the Peninsula. I understand more than a few of the gentlemen below stairs have lost healthy sums, wagering I'd have hooked her long before now. Still, with the negotiations completed, I saw no reason to wait. I wouldn't want to give his lordship, or his daughter, spare time to reconsider."

"And what of you? What if you should wish to reconsider?"

Robert almost laughed at his brother's absurdity.

"What is there to reconsider? I have made a good match and not one lightly decided. As you have already stated, Anthea is a lovely girl, much sought after. She is heavily dowered, and the daughter to an earl. She knows her way about society and would never do anything untoward. She has, in short, all the requirements of a suitable wife."

Even if a reticent one. Robert couldn't help but think of the chaste kiss of her cheek and the demure smile Anthea had granted him upon his leaving her father's study earlier that day. He envisioned their first night together; every candle in the room doused, Anthea, his wife, dressed in a dainty and thoroughly proper maiden's night rail, realizing her duty to him, of course, yet shuddering at his touch.

He reminded himself then that passion wasn't one of his requirements in a wife. Passion was a thing for which one chose a mistress, and his current mistress Juliana Delafield quite enjoyed Robert's preference to have the room ablaze with candlelight when he made love to her, so he could watch the moment of release shining in her eyes as he took her.

Wives, on the contrary, were to be chosen with but three considerations in mind: their dowries, their appearance, and the social distinction they would bring to their husbands, all of which Lady Anthea had in abundance.

"But what of love?" Noah interrupted. "Passion? The uniting of souls?"

Now Robert did laugh. Heartily. Surely more than five years separated the two of them in age. A decade or two, perhaps. Had he himself ever been so oblivious?

And then he remembered that indeed he had, for he had at one time thought to become an artist who would paint the most beautiful women of the world. He would travel from country to country, committing the heavenly creatures to canvas, immortalizing them for centuries to come. It hadn't daunted him at all when his tutor had declared him unfit to even mix colors properly. When

had he lost that euphoria? At twenty? Twenty-five? It
had to have been some time ago, for he was only thirty-
two now and it seemed aeons since then.

And it was past time Noah learned that same lesson.

"One does not wed for passion, brother. And as for
love and the uniting of souls, I shall be happy to leave
that abominable nonsense to the poets. Marriages are to
be founded on like social backgrounds and a sound
financial future. Anything else is unnecessary."

Noah was grinning and at the same time, shaking his
head. "You make the choice of a wife sound as analyti-
cal as the decision about which of Christie's paintings
to bid for."

"It is not so very different, you know. You would do
well to believe me when I say I have learned that there
are but scarce few things in this life which aren't an
investment and one must always consider what the
worth of each will be in the years to come."

"So then, you are saying you believe Anthea *worthy*
to be your countess?"

Robert leveled his eyes on his brother. "You have
heard the rumor?"

"There aren't many in Town who haven't. Have you
peered into the betting books lately? Even at Brooke's
it is said it will be only a matter of time before your
earldom is declared. You certainly proved yourself on
the field of battle, Rob. Lady Anthea, no doubt, has
lent an ear to the gossips as well. It must have helped to
make her decision to wed you a simple one." He hesitated, adding, "And there is Lord Hastings' recent
acquisition from Christie's which surely helped to
make him favor your pursuit of his daughter."

Robert's expression revealed nothing. "Lord Hastings is, as am I, an avid collector. He expressed
an interest in the piece. I merely assisted him in its
purchase."

"Hastings *plays* at being a collector because it is the
thing. It is *fashionable*. You, on the other hand, are
devoted to it. That Van Dyck was yours, Rob. Father

told me of it last Michaelmas when Lord Fairchild refused to sell it to you outright. He said you paid Christie a good deal of blunt to give you first crack at it when Fairchild kicked off. Everyone knew his health was failing—I cannot recall a night when he wasn't so deep into his cups he could form a coherent sentence— but you somehow discovered that he had long been in dun territory with his creditors. You knew his heirs would be left in financial straits. They had no choice but to put his collection up for sale. Had you played that card with Fairchild from the start, you might even have persuaded him to give the piece up before he died, for a much inflated price, of course. But you simply waited. Then, for all your efforts, when you finally have the piece all but wrapped up for delivery to Father in Lancashire, you bow out and allow Hastings to take it instead. I think you will find Father hard-pressed to understand that maneuver."

Robert shrugged. "Admittedly, that particular Van Dyck work has eluded me for some time. It was no easy task either, convincing my future father-in-law to make the purchase. You see, there were two items up for bid from Fairchild's collection at Christie's that day. Of course the one Hastings took is the better known of the two. That was, I believe, the push which finally convinced him to take it. However, my private sources have informed me the other piece, a Rubens I hadn't even known Fairchild owned, was the wiser choice of the two." Robert took a sip of his wine. "And it promises to be a very lucrative purchase. The value of that piece will most likely treble in the years to come. I simply chose what I felt to be the better invest- ment of the two."

"While you arranged for Christie to sell the other to Hastings."

"He did not sell the piece to Lord Hastings, Noah. It was an auction. Hastings simply bid on the piece and won."

"And took it for a steal, from what I hear of it."

Robert revealed a wry smile. "He did pay a bit less than Christie took in on the sale."

Noah stared at his brother a moment before the realization dawned on him. "You arranged for the whole transaction, didn't you? And I'd wager you made up the difference between Hastings' final bid and the true purchase price yourself."

"I had no choice. Kinsborough's agent was set to take the piece if Hastings didn't. Allowing the piece to go to Hastings is one thing, but if Kinsborough had laid his hands on it . . ."

"Father's rivalry with the marquess in the game of collecting has become legend among the *ton*," Noah finished. "Without your efforts in acquiring all the pieces you did while abroad, Father's dream of having the grandest collection in England would never be realized. At least a collection grander than Lord Kinsborough's."

The Devonbrook collection was becoming something of a sensation, a sensation which would one day become Robert's by the terms arranged between the duke and his second son. Paintings, statuary, books, and classical and medieval antiquities comprised the majority of the collection, as well as some more pieces such as odd bits of weaponry.

During the wars, Robert's military position had played well in the acquisitions. Upon the purchase of his captain's commission with the Guards, Robert's regiment had traveled first to Spain, stationed wherever Wellington made his headquarters. The commander learned of Robert's fluency in both French and Spanish and wasted little time in giving him a new assignment, that of reconnaissance. With his dark hair and skin tanned from the hot Spanish sun, Robert—or in some instances, Roberto—easily passed as native on the Peninsula.

By Wellington's order, Robert's objective was to ascertain the French position and forward maps back to headquarters. Obtaining information for the maps wasn't the difficulty. With his batman Pietro's assistance, the Spanish peasants were all too eager to help in the hopes of ridding their country of the Bonapartes. It was the transport of the maps back to headquarters which introduced the risk, but Robert came up with a system of accomplishing this effectively.

He still remembered Wellington's fury when he'd returned to headquarters after a particularly dangerous run.

"Just what in perdition am I supposed to do with a painting of a bowl of fruit, Captain?"

Rolled and tied and stuffed into his coat pocket, it had been easy to transport. Anyone inspecting it would think it just what it appeared; a painting, no more.

But it was more, indeed, for hidden underneath the painting's false canvas backing was the map he'd been charged with bringing to Wellington.

The general's anger had immediately turned to laughter and he'd slapped Robert hard on the back, saying with noticeably less irritation, "You certainly are a resourceful fellow, aren't you, Captain?"

It had been the highest compliment Wellington could have paid him.

With his freedom of movement as a soldier and the connections he formed throughout the Continent, Robert was able to intercept a number of works before they ever crossed into England. In the beginning, Robert's father had financed the purchases for the collection while Robert had acted as his agent, performing the legwork, acquiring the specific works and pieces. Eventually it became more. Not every piece Robert pursued ended up in the collection. They were turned about and resold and the profits were divided between father and son.

And now Robert's reputation had grown to where few would question his opinion as an expert. The venture had proved a lucrative one. In the months since his return from the Continent, word of Robert's investments had gotten around. Robert had seen the betting books, the entries wagering as to his actual worth.

Not even his own father was privy to the true amount of his wealth. Only one man other than Robert knew of his success, his solicitor, Quinby, and he was as tight-lipped as if he'd just eaten a dozen lemons. It was his latest transaction, though, which brought Robert the greatest satisfaction: the acquisition of Lady Anthea Barrett.

"I leave for Devonbrook House on the morrow to inform Father and Jameson of the match," Robert said, pushing his supper plate away. "I will return to London the week before the wedding with them both, and Elizabeth and Jamie."

"Thereby excusing yourself from the tedium of wedding preparations. You certainly managed that quite well. And Lady Anthea? On the outside she is all honey and smiles. Is she truly agreeable to your sudden departure from the city?"

"Let us just say that the prospect of having a duke of our father's repute in attendance at her wedding, as well as our brother and his socially triumphant wife far outweighed any opposition to it. As you already stated, Anthea will busy herself with the preparations for the wedding, the grandest of the Season no doubt. I daresay she'll scarce notice my absence till the moment she comes to meet me at the altar."

Noah shook his head in amused disbelief. "Once again, Rob, you have brought a nearly impossible acquisition to success."

Robert spotted a man then threading his way toward them through the crowding of tables. He was dressed in an impeccable suit of navy superfine with buff trousers and top boots that shone like glass. His sandy hair was styled in the fashionable Brutus crop, and in stark contrast to Noah, his cravat was stiff, perfectly folded, and perfectly white.

"Am I to assume, Lord Robert Edenhall, by the sly grin on your face that the fair Lady Anthea Barrett has finally managed to snare you in her silken net?"

Bartholomew Archer, Viscount Sheldrake, dropped

his stylish self into one of the two chairs remaining at the table. Termed Tolley by most everyone who knew him, he and Robert had first met when at Oxford more than a decade before. Afterward they had served together on the Peninsula, and despite his dandified appearance, Robert knew Tolley to be honorable, wise with his holdings, which brought him a substantial yearly income, and keen in his perceptions of everything that went on around him. He could match wits with most anyone in Town and extracting a cut from him—something he never did unless it was thoroughly warranted—could mean social suicide.

Tolley stared at Robert now, awaiting his answer, but Robert did not have to give it. No doubt at that moment news of his impending marriage to Anthea was already wending its way through Almack's overheated and overcrowded rooms.

"I owe you my thanks, Rob," Tolley said, casually removing his kidskin gloves and dropping them on the table. "You've just won me fifty guineas from that bore Natfield. He wagered you'd not pull it off, that Lady Anthea would hold out for Whiteby and his father's marquessate, although his odds were never very favorable, given that Whiteby dances thoroughly at the ends of his mama's purse strings and she shows every sign of continuing to live a long and hearty life. Poor Anthea would never have stood a chance against that grimalkin. So now, instead, Natfield has offered to double our wager at stakes of your engagement falling through by Michaelmas."

Robert sat back with a wry smile. "Take the wager, Tolley. By Michaelmas, I expect Lady Anthea and I will be retiring to the countryside to twiddle our thumbs for the winter."

Tolley chuckled. "I'll wager the fifty guineas I already took in that you'll be twiddling far more than Lady Anthea's thumbs while away in the country. She is quite the creation, my friend." He sighed dramatically. "Have you ever seen hair so blond? Eyes so perfectly green? She floats about the best ballrooms and one would swear she even has an original thought or two running through that lovely head. I understand her father, the earl, spared no expense when it came to her upbringing. She is well educated, plays the pianoforte as if she'd been born to it, sings like an angel, and has never so much as looked at a young buck with an improper glance. And above all else, her taste in fashion is impeccable. I daresay you have done well, Rob."

Robert grinned at his colleague. "I am, after all, an appreciator of fine art."

Tolley laughed. "An appreciator who will no doubt 'appreciate' this particular piece laid out on the canvas of his bed. Perhaps I should treble the stakes on the expectation of a child by the time you return for next Season?"

Robert looked calmly at his friend. "It should prove a sound wager."

"As sound as the odds on that Portuguese beast of yours taking another win at Newmarket?"

Robert grinned. Tolley only termed Bayard a beast because Robert had refused the numerous offers he'd made to purchase the stallion. A gray Alter-Real standing sixteen hands, the horse had attracted many such offers. He'd come to Robert after the French troops had sacked the Royal Braganzan stud at Alter, killing some of the Andalusian-blooded breed for food, and stealing the rest. Robert felt it only right he should return the favor, and having come upon a French soldier snoozing under a tree on a cool summer night, he did, then bringing the horse he christened Bayard home with him to England with the plan to preserve the regal breed.

"I expect Bayard to be in top form when next he runs."

"Let us hope so," Tolley said. "And let us hope your new wife doesn't become jealous of your affection for the nag," he chuckled, adjusting his cuffs, "and *nag* you into selling him."

"And then there is Rob's love for his art and his books," Noah said on a grin. "I've yet to see a beautiful woman who would stand by and allow any man to spend his time gazing at something other than her."

Tolley roared. "Poor Rob. You know it is not too late to change your mind."

"So you can step in to take my place?" Robert countered. "Not bloody likely."

Tolley smiled, casting a sidewise glance. "Anthea is a catch, yes, admittedly, but I can assure you, my friend, I have no designs of ever stepping into your place."

"And I assure you I have no designs of leaving it. My solicitor would fall apoplectic," Robert said. "Beyond that, what would I do with the house I just purchased this morning?"

"A house? In Town? Oh, but you were confident of success, weren't you? And where is this grand domicile located?"

"Charles Street, off St. James Square."

Tolley grinned. "Impressive, and no wonder your poor solicitor looked as he did. You've given him more to fret over in the past week than your father ever had in all the years since he's worked for him."

Robert chuckled. "You should have seen poor Quinby this morning. I thought he would faint right there in Hastings' study when the earl finally signed the contracts. I swear he held his breath through the entire transaction."

Tolley raised his glass in toast. "Well done, my friend. Well done, indeed! 'May your pockets grow heavy all the rest of your life, and may you never catch a dose of the Spanish gout from your wife.' "

Tolley paused in his poetic levity only long enough so that he could drain the rest of the claret from his glass. "Not bad for the second son to a duke who just sold out with a rumored earldom awaiting him. You certainly lead the life of the charmed, my friend, but then you always have. It looks now as if things couldn't be any better for you. You have acquired everything you've ever set after: a lovely and heavily dowered wife, a prestigious address, and a rumored earldom. I ask you, what could possibly go wrong?"

Chapter Two

What could possibly go wrong?

Tolley's words, unknowingly uttered on that last night in London, thrummed through Robert's head as he sat stock-still, barely listening while his solicitor Quinby cataloged his inheritance.

". . . the Devonbrook estate with its annual incomes, the properties in South Yorkshire and in Gloucestershire with incomes, Edenhall House here in London, of course, as well as your own recently purchased property on Charles Street . . ."

The same house Robert was to have shared with Anthea. Anthea who was to have become his wife that morning.

How could it be that only a month before, Robert had felt as if everything had finally fallen into place the way he had wanted it, the way he had planned it all his life to be?

He had just become engaged to marry a young woman who most would have thought above his reach. He had purchased a house on one of the most fashionable streets in London. He'd been awaiting a rumored earldom for the role he had played during the wars. Foolishly, naively he had believed Tolley's prophecy, that nothing could mar his perfect world, this fairytale world he'd created on his own. But now everything had changed. The life he'd planned, the marriage, his entire future had vanished, destroyed by the flames which had ravaged Devonbrook House, and taking with them the lives of his family.

Robert still wondered at what had caused him to fall asleep that night, his first night back in Lancashire at Devonbrook House in the library situated safely on the ground floor and separated from the main house by an outdoor arcade. He should have been on the second floor, in his own chamber, in the family wing just down the hall from his father's suite, the rooms of Jameson and Elizabeth, and the nursery where his nephew Jamie lay sleeping.

But Robert had been up late that night, passing several hours after supper with his father in the library talking privately over brandy. They talked about acquisitions and plans for the collection. They laughed over Hastings and his purchase of the Van Dyck and its part in Robert's betrothal to Anthea. They discussed the future that night, Robert's future, a future which Robert had accomplished on his own.

Hours later, long after everyone else had retired, his father rose from his chair, ready to take his leave for the night. He said just one thing more to his son before going: he told Robert he was proud of him. They were the last words Robert ever heard from his father.

It was well after midnight when his father left the library that night, yet Robert hadn't felt tired. He was too filled with his accomplishments—the marriage, the financial independence, and the collection, his stability for the future. So he had stayed on in the library to read, he couldn't recall now even what, but either the book or the glass of port he had sipped with it had soon put him to sleep there in the overstuffed wing armchair in front of the hearth.

Sometime later, when Robert was roused by the acrid smell of the smoke, his first thought was that the chimney had closed somehow, the room filling with smoke from the fire. By the time he realized that the smoke wasn't coming from the fireplace, but from outside the room, the upper floors of the main house were already engulfed in flames, curling about the central stairway threshold like fingers reaching for him as he stood just out of their reach.

Still Robert tried to fight his way through the fire, to save the lives of his family trapped on the other side. He made it as far as the nursery door, the first chamber on that wing, where he found Jamie inside, his small body lying unconscious in his bed. Robert grabbed the boy, running with him while yelling for help, and deposited him gently on the dew-damp lawn in front of the main house where the servants were already forming a fire line.

By the time Robert made it back inside, the fire was burning out of control. He tried to find a way through, covering himself with the heavy draperies from the lower hall, and was nearly crushed when a section of the ceiling in the upper corridor came crashing down before him. It missed him by bare inches, the intense heat and penetrating light from the fire billowing against him like a tidal wave from hell. Standing there with pieces of the grand house raining down around him, Robert realized he would have to turn back. There was nothing more he could possibly do.

It was late the following day when the fire finally burned itself out. Only then did Robert realize the true damage.

The west wing and most of the main house had been gutted, the once pristine limestone shell of the Devonbrook estate indelibly stroked black by the billowing smoke and furious flames. Nothing remained of the Upper Gallery, where his father had once displayed the pieces of the Devonbrook collection and where portraits of every Edenhall ancestor from time immemorial had graced the elegant Chinese silk-covered walls. The high ballroom ceiling, fashioned by Grinling Gibbons nearly two centuries before, with its ten crystal-ornamented chandeliers and intricate painted scenery, had virtually collapsed.

Robert could remember as a child, when on the mornings before one of his mother's elaborate balls, Robert and his brothers had been at liberty to race around the vast room in their stocking feet, sliding on their bellies and breeches-clad bottoms across the Italianate marble floor. Their mother, the duchess, had always said nothing could polish a floor better than her boys' active feet. And now it, everything was lost, every chamber of the grand house devastated. Except for one.

The library where Robert had fallen asleep that night, with its thirty thousand books and ancient scripts and pamphlets, stood apart from the wreckage, untouched but for a slight smoke discoloration on its western side. It had been protected from the fire by the ivy-covered arcade which separated it from the main house and the other attached wings. Ironically, his father had planned the library specifically separate, not as a means of protection, but as a means of isolating the place, his sanctuary from the rest of the house. It stood now like a lone surviving soldier on the field of a bloody battle.

Sometime later, Robert was told that his older brother Jameson had been found covering his wife's body, a futile attempt at sparing Elizabeth's life and that of the child she carried, his unborn child, in exchange for his own. Instead, they both had been crushed by the tremendous weight of the upper garret floor falling over them. The duke had died crouched in a corner, the copious smoke blessedly his most likely cause of death. Jamie, sweet four-year-old Jamie, who was to have been the future fifth Duke of Devonbrook, had never regained consciousness, his tiny body simply too weak to combat the suffocating effects of the smoke.

And there was one final casualty who hadn't stood a chance of survival against the flames. Pietro, Robert's batman, valet, and companion for so long, had been asleep in Robert's chamber, the last room on that long corridor, when the fire had begun. This man, who had saved Robert's life while on campaign, who had stayed awake at night in the woods of Spain and in the hills of southern France, keeping watch while Robert had taken a few hours sleep, and who had fallen asleep while faithfully waiting for Robert to come up to bed that night, had died. The fire hadn't brought about his end, though. It was the fall he had risked against the odds of the flames when he'd leapt from the window while trying to escape.

The fire, Robert had been told, had started in the family wing, and the cause appeared to be suspicious in nature. And it only made the horror worse. To have had nearly his entire family taken by the fire was terrible enough, but to think that it might have been set deliberately made Robert wake in the middle of the night screaming out loud, bathed in his own sweat and tears. Who would have committed such a heinous act? Who could have wanted to obliterate an entire family?

Robert would not have been able to survive the subsequent weeks if not for his younger brother. Noah came immediately from London, and while Robert recovered from the minor burns on his hands and face and upper body, and from the smoke that had burned his lungs and throat, rendering him unable to speak for a time, Noah assumed responsibility over the arrangements which had needed to be made. It was the start of the Season, yet it seemed nearly all of London society had left town, traveling to Lancashire to attend the funeral services. Even the Regent came, somberly dressed and sincere in his sympathies.

And this only made Anthea's absence all the more conspicuous.

Lord Hastings' letter arrived the very day of the funeral, the messenger who brought it drenched from the late spring rain which had started at dawn and hadn't slowed by midday. Robert sat silently in the small chair in his room at the inn near Devonbrook, listening while Noah read Hastings' words to him, expressing his heartfelt sympathies over the family's terrible loss and wishing Robert a speedy and complete recovery from his injuries. He included his hope that Robert would understand Anthea's sudden change of heart concerning their future together.

It had been a difficult decision for her, Hastings had written before going on to cite everything from inopportune timing to female malaise in explanation of his daughter's dissolution of her engagement to Robert. The announcements, he'd finished, summing up his discourse, had already been posted in the newspapers, sparing Robert from having to see to the task himself.

Despite the multitude of words, the carefully composed sentences meant to give reason to this most unreasonable act, Robert realized Hastings had really only been saying one thing.

My daughter will not wed herself to a blind man.

Even now, weeks after the fire, anything brighter than candlelight would bring a pain to Robert unlike any other, leaving him to do nothing but recoil in agony. In the faintest light, Robert could barely see the shadows of the most prominent objects before him. In the darkness, where he was at last free from the pain, he could see nothing at all.

The physician near Devonbrook, Dr. Dunbury, who had mended Robert countless times as a child, from wrapping his ankle when he'd jumped off the stable roof on a dare to stitching his head when he'd fallen off the staircase banister, examined him first. His prognosis was that the injury to his eyes would heal in time. However, when Robert still hadn't regained his sight three weeks after the fire, even Dr. Dunbury seemed to lose hope. The nerves were damaged from the intense heat and light of the fire, he concluded, and he could not with any confidence say when, or for that matter if Robert would ever see again.

After returning to London and Edenhall House, Noah

sent for a host of physicians to examine Robert. One quack in particular suggested the direct application of leeches to Robert's eyes in order to "draw out the burnt blood." Washing out the eyes with a solution of lye was yet another prescription. Robert dismissed them all and spent his days closeted in a dark room with nothing but the nightmare of the fire and the loss of his sight to occupy his thoughts.

Finally, Noah suggested his optician, who rather than attempt to introduce all matter of foreign substance into Robert's eyes, crafted a pair of spectacles made with opaque lenses to ease the discomfort brought on by the light. They would shield the eyes, he reasoned, preventing pain and further damage, while freeing Robert from living out his days in dark seclusion. It was only while wearing these spectacles that Robert could reemerge into society, riding in his carriage through Hyde Park or sitting through a performance at the Opera House, though in doing so, the spectacles also served to mark him wherever he went.

His father's former valet Forbes, who, having been in his own chamber in the servants' quarters that night, had assumed the position of Robert's valet. Forbes wanted the position no more than Robert wanted him there. He was aloof, crusty, even insolent at times. His dislike for Robert was evident. But while he might not particularly care for his new master, he also was no fool. He realized he had little choice. At his advanced age, his chances for a more agreeable position were nearly nonexistent and the strict hierarchy among servants wouldn't allow him to accept a lesser post elsewhere.

Thus Forbes had fallen into the role and Robert had simply allowed it. Forbes wasn't Pietro, but after all, he did see to his duties. He kept Robert's clothes in good order and made certain he was shaved each day, the difference now being that in addition to shaving, Forbes was required to direct Robert first from the bed to the washstand. His duties had expanded from simple valet to constant companion. Robert couldn't go from one room to the next without assistance. He didn't know where things were kept, and couldn't see where to place them when he finished with them. Even now, at Quinby's office, Forbes was left to stand silently behind Robert's chair, like a bandog keeping watch on his invalid master.

Robert tolerated this detached sometimes disdainful manner only because he was too numb, too over-whelmed with this new life to find someone else more to his liking. He wondered once if he had ever done or said something to have made Forbes dislike him as he plainly did. It wasn't until sometime after his return to town that Robert discovered precisely why the man performed his duties as if he were performing them for the devil himself. It was a feeling shared by most everyone in the household.

Perhaps it was the loss of one of his senses which had heightened the others, or instead that Robert had been waiting for society's reaction to him, but he could not deny what had taken place on the night of his true reemergence into public life.

Nearly a fortnight had passed of sheltered excursions which served to keep Robert at a distance from the populace, affording him the connection without the necessary intimacy. But he knew he could not pass the remainder of his life avoiding all contact with society. Noah and Tolley had harassed Robert into going to White's for supper one evening. A simple meal, they'd said. A chance for Robert to take the air and adjust himself again to the *ton*. No grand assembly or ball. No gawking crowds. Just an informal meal among the men he knew—his peers—men who had known him forever.

It had sounded reasonable at the time. There would be no interaction with the female faction, that facet of society which would make a melodrama of his appear-ance straight out of one of Lane's Minerva Press novels. Beyond this, and more specifically, there would be no crossing of paths with Anthea. While their dissolution hadn't hurt his heart, for their marriage had been based solely on practicality, it had definitely bruised Robert's pride. Yet a dinner among men who knew him and knew of his accomplishments? Men who wouldn't allow the tragedy of the fire to change their manner of dealing with him? It sounded simple. Even desirable.

He couldn't have been more mistaken.

Robert's appearance at the club caused an immediate and undeniable hush, bringing to a halt the customary banter that always greeted him the moment he came through the front door. Regardless of past associations, Robert was now a duke, and his elevation in society alone would have been cause enough for such notice. Add to that the horror of the fire and his blindness, ominously advertised by the dark spectacles covering his unseeing eyes, and he went from conversation piece to phenomenon. No doubt wagers had been made as to when the momentous event of his return would occur. Now that it had, the morning papers would have a field day.

A few individuals offered quiet greetings to him, several of his father's contemporaries, former university colleagues. Each greeting was followed after by the requisite expression of sympathy as Robert and his party moved on to the Coffee Room for their meal. Once there, Robert could hear the sounds of a table clearing for them, and then after they were seated, the initial excitement of his appearance began to wane. The men returned to their brandy and cards, conversation resumed, and Robert realized the hope that life as it would be might finally begin.

It was then he heard the news of Napoleon's escape from Elba.

"He is in France?" Robert asked, hoping he had been mistaken in what he thought he'd overheard at the neighboring table.

There followed a silent moment before Noah finally

answered. "Yes, Rob, Bonaparte landed at Cannes on the first of the month."

Had he secluded himself so that even an event this momentous hadn't reached him? "The first? That was a fortnight ago. What is the response from France? From Wellington?"

"It has been reported in the papers that the French seem to be welcoming him home like some sort of resurrected war hero, not an exile who had been shamefully defeated less than a year before."

"Good God," Robert said, shaking his head. "With the defeat in America and so many having resigned their commissions, the English army has all but been dispersed."

Tolley broke in then. "Wellington is yet in Vienna." He paused. "I leave on the morrow to join him. That is why I pushed you into coming out for this meal tonight, Rob. I wanted to bid you farewell before I left for the Continent. I'm not at all certain when I'll be coming back . . ."

Or if you will be coming back, Robert finished inwardly. "Why wasn't I notified of Napoleon's escape before now? Regardless that I had resigned my commission, surely Wellington knows . . ."

Robert's next words faded into oblivion. Of course he wouldn't have been notified. Nor would he have been called back to serve. After all, what good was a blind man to a war, especially a blind man who had been relied upon for his keen sense of recording every visual detail?

Robert wanted to pound his fist in frustration. No matter how he tried to ignore it, how he tried to get around it, the fact remained.

He was naught but an invalid.

Useless.

Unnecessary.

"I will inform Wellington of what has taken place here, Rob," Tolley said. "This will all most probably be over by the time I get to Vienna anyway. Bonaparte cannot hope to think he'll manage to conquer the world this time when he was defeated so soundly once already."

Robert frowned. "I hope you are right, Tolley."

Conversation quieted then for some time as plates of food were set out before them on the table. Noah and Tolley started eating. Robert sat stone-still, his food untouched. He wasn't at all certain if he could feed himself without assistance. And he wasn't about to try.

The silence was awkward, but it also made possible his hearing the whispers around them. His attention had been focused on the talk of Napoleon. He couldn't know when the other conversation began.

At first, Robert caught only sparse words.

Fire.

Blind.

Physicians uncertain of recovery.

Everything lost.

While his father had been a very wealthy man, he had invested nearly all his ready money in his estate and in his obsession, the Devonbrook collection, a collection which was to have been Robert's inheritance. From what could be concluded, with the exception of the few pieces at Edenhall House in London, the entire collection had been destroyed in the fire. And with it, Robert's security for the future.

The cost to rebuild Devonbrook House would nearly bankrupt a man on solid financial footing. Robert's own personal wealth was ample, yes, even exceptional for a second son. But for a duke? A duke whose centuries-old seat had been destroyed by fire? Obviously Anthea's education had included the basics of ciphering, for it hadn't taken her long to tally an image of what her future would be as his wife.

And then there was that *other* speculation, which no doubt played a great part in her decision.

Robert wouldn't have believed it if not for the fact that he had heard it himself that night at White's. Voices had risen quickly, laughter erupting at a jest about some unfortunate soul whose wife had been found in a compromising position with her husband's valet. Taking safety in the background confusion, someone must have believed Robert couldn't hear when the wager was made.

Twenty-five guineas staked on the belief that Robert had set the fire at Devonbrook House deliberately.

Robert couldn't have known who uttered those despicable words, but upon hearing them, he lost all sense of reason. He stood up, flipping the table forward and sending everything atop it, the supper plates, the bottle of wine and the glasses, soaring. He began shouting accusations at everyone there, demanding to know who made the wager, threatening to call out whoever it was. A pitiful sight he must have been, this blind man seeking satisfaction in a duel, waving his fist at his invisible culprit, while not even knowing if the man stood before him, behind him, or for that matter in the same room.

Noah managed to calm Robert with a whispered, "Rob, don't do this," before both he and Tolley escorted Robert out of the now silent room, past all the astonished members, and to the nearest hackney home. Since that night, a week ago now, Robert hadn't ventured out of the town house, not until this morning, when he had been called to Quinby's office. It was a task he'd been avoiding, hearing the details of the inheritance that should have been Jameson's and was now his. He'd already put Quinby off a number of times, but there were documents which needed signing before the estate could be settled, before he could endeavor to put the unpleasantness behind him.

Quinby's voice suddenly broke through Robert's thoughts as he summed up the remainder of the holdings.

". . . oh, and yes, your grace, there is also the Scottish property."

Everything else Robert had known of, the properties, the incomes, the business ventures. Robert always made it a point to be aware of the family interests. This holding, however, was unfamiliar to him.

"Scottish property, Quinby?"

"Yes, your grace. I believe it is pronounced 'Ross-mor-eye.' It is an ancient sort of dwelling built at least five centuries ago. It came to the Devonbrooks through a wager somehow." He paused, shuffling through his papers. "In fact, I see here it was to be part of your original inheritance. It reads here that I am to inform you that your father gave it to you for its 'hidden treasures, which only you could appreciate' and apparently he found the angling there superb."

He went on. "I believe your father won the property from some down-on-his-luck Scottish lord whose finances fell into dire straits after the tobacco trade fell off during the war with the Colonies, the uh, first war. It sits in a rather remote part of the western Highlands, accessible only by packet boat. There is not a coaching road within twenty miles of it. Judging from the financial reports I have received from your father's factor there, it is not a very profitable holding either. It says here he had often suggested to your father that he sell the property and get what he might for it, but the duke said he didn't care if it turned a profit or not. He was fond of repairing there at times, to hunt and fish and take his ease in solitude. He said it was as far from his life as he could ever get. He must have grown quite fond of it, too, for his records indicate he had made five visits there in the past two years alone. If you would like, I could endeavor to see what it might fetch in sale."

Robert remembered the times when his father would mysteriously disappear for the space of a few weeks. It had always been in the fall, just after the close of the Season. The duchess and the rest of the family would retire to Devonbrook House. The duke would join them sometime later. Robert never knew where the duke had gone; even his mother wouldn't say. Learning of it now, he couldn't help but wonder why.

What had his father meant in saying this place, this *Rosmorigh,* had "hidden treasures that only Robert could appreciate?" And why would he, a duke who had other holdings which certainly warranted his attentions more than some remote Scottish estate, have visited there five times in the past two years? There had to be something there. Surely that was it. Why else would his father have kept the property a secret for so long?

Robert then remembered Quinby's words when he had been describing the property and his father's attachment to it. *As far from his life as he could ever get.* Far from curious, assuming eyes. Far from contemptible accusations.

The duke had refused to sell the place. Knowing his father as he had, Robert believed he must have had a reason. The curiosity of the frequency of his visits there might indicate it had something to do with the fire. In any case, it would be as good a place to start as any, as well as offering Robert a place to escape.

"That won't be necessary, Quinby." Robert stood, cutting off Quinby's next words. "There will be no sale of the Scottish property, Rosmorigh. In light of my father's obvious attachment to it, and given that he intended it my inheritance, I have decided to take up residence there—permanently."

above her. It couldn't be eight o'clock. Surely the faint light had played a trick on her tired eyes. She'd only just sat down, at least it seemed so, yet the sky outside the leaded casement windows had darkened, the sun's last purple–gray light barely peeking over the distant hills of Skye, signaling that in fact three hours had passed. Three hours and she'd only weeded through a handful of the other books, her notes barely covering half of one page. The Colonel, she thought, frowning, was not going to be pleased with her.

Catriona looked beside her to the open passageway from where the voice had called. It was silent now except for the sounds of the sea echoing in the distance beyond the darkness. Another hour. If she could but stay just one more hour, she would be that much closer to finding it. At least then the Colonel wouldn't know the truth, that she had spent all her time reading again and not searching as she should have been. She glanced toward the passageway again. Perhaps, if she didn't answer, Mairead would just go away.

Catriona set Malory's book aside, still open to her place should she find she might return to finish reading the rest of the passage later. She grabbed the next one closest to her and began leafing through its heavy yellowed pages. Her sister, however, stubbornly refused to oblige her.

"Catriona? Are you up there?"

Catriona continued, jotting a notation on her page before moving to the next book. She suddenly wished she had never shown Mairead the hidden entrance to the castle.

"Catriona MacBryan, I can hear your scribbling and I can see your candlelight fluttering off these moldy castle walls. Now get you out of there afore you bring us more trouble." Mairead paused. "Lest you forget, Da's coming home today. You know he warned you against coming here anymore."

Catriona hesitated, the page at midturn. She'd for-

Chapter Three

Then came king Arthur unto Galahad, and said, Sir, ye be welcome, for ye shall move many good knights to the quest for the Sancgreal, and ye shall achieve that never knights might bring to an end. Then the king took him by the hand, and went down from the palace to shew Galahad the adventures of the stone.

"Catriona?"

Catriona lifted her head abruptly from the small circle of flickering light given off by her single tallow candle. She glanced quickly around the shadowed room. Her heart was pounding in her chest, and she half expected King Arthur himself to be standing there swathed in rich velvets before her. But he wasn't. No one was.

The room was dark and she was sitting on the floor, her feet tucked neatly beneath her woollen skirts. The book she'd been reading, the Malory, lay open on her lap while others were scattered around her like fallen leaves from a grand oak tree. The quill and paper she used to scribble her notes rested somewhere among them, long lost beneath the burgeoning pile of books. No, she wasn't in Camelot, and there wasn't a knight to be found. She was in the library at Rosmorigh and she'd gotten lost in the reading again, instead of doing what she'd come there to do.

"Catriona?"

Catriona squinted against the darkness that shrouded the remainder of the room, glancing at the walnut mantel clock ticking on the carved stone hearth just

gotten about Da, which was odd really, for he was usually foremost in her mind when she came there. Angus MacBryan never lost an opportunity to warn his oldest daughter against the dangers of this old castle, the perils that would befall her should she ever be found there. He wouldn't be pleased with her when he found her gone, more than likely guessing to where. But since he would already be angry with her, Catriona reasoned, she might as well linger as long as she could. With Da having come home, it would be weeks before she'd find the chance to return, putting her that much further behind in her quest.

"I'll give you three more seconds afore I come up there to get you myself," Mairead persisted.

A moment.

"One . . ."

"Meddlesome Mairead," Catriona whispered to herself, tucking a small bit of ribbon in the crease of the page she'd been reading to mark her place. It didn't appear she'd be getting back to it again tonight.

"Two . . ."

She began picking up the other books, sliding them back into place on the shelves.

"Catriona, if you force me to come up there, I swear I will . . ."

"All right!" Catriona exclaimed. "You sound just like old Miss Grimston peering down at me with her beady black eyes while I was at my lessons. Go on ahead now and start back for home. I'll be coming right behind you."

Minutes later, Catriona was reluctantly pushing the last of the books, the Malory, onto the shelf, her fingers lingering on the aged leather binding. For a moment she thought to take it with her. Even if someone happened to come to the castle before she could return, how would they ever notice this one small book missing out of all the rest of them? They filled every wall of the room. But even as she thought this, Catriona knew she

could not take the Malory home with her. Reading the books while she was here was one thing. Taking them, even if for but a short time, sounded too much like *stealing*.

Catriona stepped back to survey the shelves, making sure none of the books looked out of place lest anyone notice they'd been moved. But that was silly, really—few souls ever came to the castle, and even when they did, their visits were scarce and far between. Many of the books lining these shelves looked never to have been read at all, still Catriona's one fear was that she would one day be found out. And were that to happen, her visits to Rosmorigh would be forever at an end, and with them her secret quest. Da might be angry with her for coming, but he would always leave for the coast again, and she would always thus return. But if the laird ever discovered that she came to his castle . . .

Catriona didn't want to think of what the Sasunnach would do to her if he ever learned of her clandestine visits. Especially should he ever discover why.

Catriona gathered up her papers and ink, shoving them into the small wooden box she kept them in, before slipping on her shoes. She turned to leave, and when she did, she caught sight of his portrait in the candlelight. As always, she found herself stopping to stare.

He hung on the paneled wall, ostensibly placed between the two towering sets of book-lined shelves that guarded his image on either side. An ancient-looking carved chest, which might have been exceptional were it not overshadowed by him, was set beneath. Catriona often thought a rich red carpet would have been far more appropriate. His image was framed in brilliant gold, which glimmered in the flickering candlelight, and the rich colors stroked over the canvas seemed to take on dimension in the shadows that moved around him.

She studied him in the candlelight. His eyes had been the feature which had first drawn her attention to him. They continued to capture her every time she looked at him. Penetrating, intelligent, indomitable, they were blazingly golden brown, the eyes of a hawk. One dark brow raised at a skeptical slant, his black hair windblown around his rugged clean-shaven face, his mouth firmly set above a determined jaw.

He wore a glorious red uniform which set off his broad shoulders, his long legs set apart, standing boldly atop the boulder he had surmounted. Behind and around him a battle raged from which he was removed and yet he still remained a part of. Every time she saw him, his image, Catriona realized an undeniable pull, a profound allure that reached out and caught hold of her. She didn't know his name, but she had invented an image of him having been a brave commander of a victorious army championing the cause of good against evil. He was her guardian when she would come to the castle late at night, her knight watching over her and protecting her in the darkness. Oftentimes she would talk to him, laughing at herself when she seemed to await his response, as if a man such as he had ever walked among mortals.

She didn't know his name, had never met him, and never would, but he was the man whose face filled her head at night.

He was, quite simply, the man of her dreams.

He was magnificent.

Original.

And she loved him.

"Good night," she said, smiling softly to him as she tucked a stray bit of her coppery hair behind her ear before turning to leave.

A chilling draft blew up around Catriona's legs beneath her woollen skirts when she slipped from the room. She pulled her worn tartan shawl more closely about her shoulders, tightening the loosened knot in front of her. Taking up her small wooden box, she

released the lever that would slide the secret door set in the walnut bookcase closed, once again shutting away that wonderful Rosmorigh library.

She could hear Mairead below on the passageway, hidden by the gathering of shadows and muttering her typical objections to herself.

"You can move on now," Catriona called to her. "I am coming."

Catriona started down the narrow stone steps that stood above the labyrinth of caves running inside the rocky cliffs beneath the castle. Torch holders jutted out from the smoke-darkened gneiss walls, ancient etchings and drawings decorating the length of them. It was a place that would have frightened most, and indeed it had. But not Catriona.

She had always felt quite at home here among the long-forgotten bones which littered the shadowy corners (she wasn't quite certain if they were animal or human), picked clean by the tiny creatures who crept through every darkened, hidden niche. The rhythmic sounds of the sea as it crashed against the rocky shore beyond echoed around her, its salty waters slipping in like a thief to fill the lower caverns at high tide.

She loved this place, dreamed of living here and spending her days and nights reading every book in that magnificent library. She imagined waking with the sun breaking through the crystalline leaded windows while the sea air drifted in to flutter over her face. She loved Rosmorigh, yet she had never gone further inside than that one room, for while her conscience might allow her to read the books, it wouldn't allow her to intrude any further. That would be too much like trespassing.

As Catriona came around the last curve in the cave's stairs, she found Mairead waiting for her at the shadowed bottom. Her sister's light brown hair, the color of the reedy grass that filled the winter fields, trailed

over her shoulder in a frazzled, wind-whipped plait. Wisps of it drifted about her stern-set face in the light of the small tin lantern she held. Dark brown eyes stared stonily at Catriona as she reluctantly approached.

Mairead was Catriona's younger sister, and curiously she stood nearly a head taller. She had their mother Mary's sandy-colored brown hair and the MacBryan brown eyes. When she had been a girl, Catriona had asked her mother why her eyes were blue, not brown like her sister's and both her parents, and Mary had told her it was because she had been born at night when the stars were bright and the moon was full. Catriona remembered wondering if the moon had colored her hair darker as well.

"Have you lost your wits coming up here like this?" Mairead said, pulling Catriona back to the present. "Da warned you never to go into the Sasunnach's castle by yourself. You know there's ghosts and the like running about through those old hallways." She glanced around them, grimacing at the shadows set to dancing by her small tin lantern. "And these caves. A body never felt so close to the gates of Hades as here."

Catriona rolled her eyes. "There are no ghosts here, Mairead. It is only a legend made up a long time ago to keep people away."

"People like you, Catriona MacBryan. And Ian Alexander tells a far different tale. He swears to me he came up here late one night and found himself nose-to-nose with one of them. Dressed like a barbarian it was, with its flesh hanging from its face and moaning like a stuck pig, saying it was going to kill him. Appeared out of a cloud of smoke, it did."

Catriona suppressed a smile. "Ian Alexander likes to spin a yarn to impress the lasses."

"Never you mind the ghosts and if they be or not be," Mairead said, taking Catriona's homespun sleeve in a tight grip. "Worse than any spirits, what if you'd been caught by the Sasunnach, Catriona?"

Catriona looked at Mairead and smiled, totally unaffected by the terror that seemed to grip her sister.

And for good reason.

"But the Sasunnach isn't here now, Mairead. No one is here, and you know whenever he's about to come, that factor of his, Abercromby, comes from Edinburgh the week before to hire the servants and set up his stores for him. And even old Abercromby surely wouldn't be finding me here at this hour. He's another who believes the tales of the ghosts at Rosmorigh. He won't come unless it's daylight out and he certainly wouldn't dare stay once it's dark."

They were at the end of the passageway and Mairead grabbed the iron handle on the small trapdoor that opened to the outside. It was the only route leading out of the caves that wasn't submerged when the tide came in.

In the haze of the thickening dusk, Mairead looked over the stretch of moor that led way from the castle toward home. A gathering of dark clouds billowed overhead, the wind whipping up with the promise of a storm.

"Och, Catriona, I'll never know why I let you drag me time and again into your mischief. We're going to have to run if we're to make it before this storm comes. Da's not going to be pleased, Catriona, not at all."

Nestled against the grassy hillside, the MacBryan croft was bordered by open moor and peat bog on its far side, stretching down to where a shallow stream whispered by its eastern facade. Peat smoke curled upward from the crude stone chimney, to blend with the low-hanging clouds and incoming mountain mist. The cottage's wattle and daub walls gleamed white against the dusk, its thatched roof held in place against the twisting Highland winds by heather ropes weighted down with stones. Primitive and even lonely to the outsider, that

perception would change the instant a person passed through the weathered wooden door to be immediately enveloped by the welcoming warmth always found within.

The wind whipped Catriona's hair from beneath her shawl, flipping her skirts about her legs as she started down the rise beside Mairead. The mingling scents of heather and peat and sea-kissed breezes filled the twilight air. As they neared, Catriona noticed her father's hempen fishing nets, which he had knotted by the light of many a night's fire, hanging to dry over the low stone fence. His boots, muddied and worn, stood just outside the door, his black oilskin rain cape drooping from the hook above.

Da had indeed come home.

Despite the scolding she knew she was about to receive, Catriona felt a warmth creep through her limbs at knowing her father had made it through yet another of his adventures. He had come home and he was safe. And that made his anger a far easier thing to face.

Catriona opened the cottage door, making to enter first, then quickly slipped back, leaving Mairead no choice but to go on ahead.

"Where the devil have you been?" their father's voice grumbled, competing with the storm that was fast brewing outside. Catriona scooted in behind Mairead, completely hidden by the shadows.

"I was fetching Catriona," Mairead said, calm as a cow. "She was off to the Colonel's to take him a firlot of meal."

Angus MacBryan came forward from the fire, his formidable body clad in linen shirt and worn kilt shutting out the light from behind him. "And so where is your sister then? Did she stay there at MacReyford's for supper?"

Mairead reached behind her and grabbed Catriona's arm, yanking her forward.

"Ah," said Angus, glowering down at his eldest daughter. "And how did you find Colonel MacReyford then, lass? In good health I trust?"

Catriona smiled unassumingly and stood on tiptoe to kiss her father on his beard-stubbled, wind-burned cheek. His white hair hung in thin stringy strands to his wide shoulders and he smelled of whiskey and his familiar blend of tobacco. When she had been a girl, Catriona had loved falling asleep in his arms with her face to his chest, surrounded by the scent of him and soothed by his thundering heartbeat close against her cheek.

"Welcome home, Da. We missed you." She started away, setting her things in their place in the small wooden cupboard near the door. "The Colonel is well. I am sorry I wasn't here when you came home. It isn't Mairead's fault. I hadn't realized how late was the hour."

"Din't you now?" said her father, watching her with that I-already-know-where-you've-been look in his dark gleaming eyes.

Catriona walked over to the fire to kiss her mother on the cheek. "Hello, Mam."

Mary MacBryan looked up at Catriona from her spinning wheel and smiled, that smile fading to an affected frown when she noticed the reproachful look given her by her husband. She checked the twist on the kerchief which covered her hair and stood, moving toward the fire to stir the pot simmering there.

"So what is it that took you so long at the Colonel's then, lass?" Angus asked, lowering himself into his chair. He sat himself down at the head of the crude pine wood table in the middle of the modest but cozy room, looking quite like the king before his subjects.

"He had some hose that needed darning. He cannot do it himself. His hands shake too much now. I told him I would see to it for him," Catriona answered, taking her seat safely on the opposite side from where her father sat.

It wasn't a lie, not exactly. She had been to see the Colonel, taking him the firlot of meal, even darning his hose, then waiting until he'd fallen asleep in his chair by the fire before slipping out quietly to go to Rosmorigh.

"Right kind of you, Catriona MacBryan, seein' to the Colonel like you do," Angus muttered, ripping his oatcake apart and dipping half of it into the broth bowl Mary had just set before him.

Catriona kept her eyes downcast. She started to reach for the basket of oatcakes before thinking the better of it. She knew that tone in her father's voice, knew well what it was leading to.

"Catriona?"

She glanced up to find Angus staring at her. Her mother and Mairead were sitting at the table, still as ancient standing stones, looking anywhere, everywhere, but at the two of them.

"Yes, Da?"

"Hold up your hands."

"Excuse me, Da?"

"I said you're to hold up your hands before you now, daughter, palms out."

Catriona glanced one more time at her mother, chewing her lower lip. Mary nodded slightly as if to say she should just comply and face what would have to be faced. She might get by with the occasional disobedience, but one thing Angus MacBryan would not abide was chicanery.

Catriona slowly raised her hands from her lap, splaying them outward. The tips of the first two fingers on her right hand were blackened from ink, her palms dotted here and there. There was no hope for it. She was caught.

"What is it you were darnin' the Colonel's stockings with then, lass? Tar?"

Catriona lowered her hands and immediately erupted into a shower of words. "Da, I was only to Rosmorigh for a little while before Mairead came to fetch—"

Mairead cleared her throat from across the table, indicating to Catriona that she had better not think to drag her into the fray she'd made for herself. Catriona wisely moved on. "Da, you know that no one is in residence at Rosmorigh now. The whole place is deserted. All those books and no one to read them. What is the harm? You wanted your daughters to be educated. That is why you had Miss Grimston come to teach us to read and write. But there is so much she didn't teach us, things I have learned from reading the books at Rosmorigh. Did you know that there is a man who has cataloged 47,390 separate stars in the night sky?"

Angus took a swallow of his ale, wiping his mouth on his sleeve. "Is that a fact?" He looked at Mary. "So that's the reason those sheep have been bleatin' like bludey fools through the night. Too many bludey stars!"

"Angus," Mary scolded, frowning, "your tongue."

"Och, woman, you coddle the lass too much. She spends her days filling her head with such nonsense when she should be home seein' to what must needs be done here."

"No one knows I've gone to Rosmorigh," Catriona argued, "and I finished all my work here at home before going. Really, Da, it's just—"

"You're trespassin' on Sasunnach land," Angus said, cutting Catriona off from further response. "That is what is wrong with it. Books or no, it'll be the toll-booth for you and me both if you're caught there. I've asked you and asked you, lass, but you refuse to heed my word. Now I'm tellin' you. You'll not go to that castle again, d'you hear? I forbid you it."

Catriona looked to her mother. "Mam, please, make him understand."

Mary MacBryan closed her eyes and shook her head. "You heard your father, Catriona."

Catriona looked from one face to the other. Mary looked away, stirring the broth in her bowl as if to cool it. Mairead looked at Catriona as if to say she'd warned her. Catriona quickly realized no one was coming to her defense.

"But, Da—"

"I've said my piece, Catriona. Now let us eat afore your mother's good supper goes cold."

And with that, Angus MacBryan effectively closed the floor to further argument. Everybody picked up their horn spoons in unison and began quietly sipping at the broth in the wooden bowls set before them. Everyone except Catriona. She just stared at Angus, hoping he might reconsider.

The room was silent as a tomb. Even the fire dared not crackle. Catriona picked apart her oatcake, nibbling on tiny crumbling bites while trying to think of a way past her father's stubborn edict.

Finally, having emptied his bowl, Angus spoke up, ending the uncomfortable silence.

"Young Ian's becomin' a fine kelper."

No one acknowledged his proclamation.

He persisted. "He'll be to settin' up his own croft soon, takin' a tentantship at Crannock under Dunston. He'll be lookin' to take himself a *guid wife*." He hesitated a moment. "Taken a fancy to our Catriona, he has. I think 'twill be only a matter of time afore . . ."

"Nae!"

All heads turned as Mary set down her horn spoon and glared at her husband.

"I winna have it, Angus. You may think on young Ian like your son since he lost his parents at the young age he did, and him being left alone to his grandmother till she passed this spring. And I know his father Callum was your dearest friend since you were a laddie. You promised Callum you'd look after the lad and you've done well by him. You saw to it he was clothed and fed and had enough peats to keep him warm at night. And when you're off to your ventures, I rest easier at night alone in our bed knowin' you have Ian with you lest you run into trouble. But I say this now and final, Angus MacBryan, Catriona winna be weddin' herself to the likes of Ian Alexander!"

Catriona stared at her mother. She had never heard Mary speak so strongly before. Even as children, when she and Mairead had bickered over sisterly things, Mary had favored calm and reason in her role as parent. She never raised a hand to her girls, she'd never had to, and she never—ever—raised her voice to her husband. Angus was the one who was prone to thundering. Even Mairead looked startled at her mother's outburst, clutching her horn spoon tight in her fist as if it were a talisman. Angus opened his mouth to argue, but Mary quickly cut him off.

"Och! I don't want to hear it from you, husband. You can forbid the lass from goin' up to Rosmorigh and reading those books, despite that she's not causing anyone any harm, but you canna stop her from what she should be. Catriona is not goin' to wed Ian Alexander. She's for far better things than bein' a crofter's wife."

Angus's face grew red. "And what the devil is wrong with crofting? Do you dislike your life with me so much, Mary?"

Catriona watched them, helpless, hating that she had brought this on between them.

"Nae, Angus," Mary said, calmer now. "But crofting isn't to be for much longer. You said so yourself. The lairds are pushing the crofters off the land for the sheep. That's why we had our daughters taught to read and write, and now they've each begun to go their own way. You're not here to see it, Angus. But I am. Mairead weaves a cloth and makes a stitch finer than any I've seen afore. Catriona's calling lies in her books and her reading. You said so yourself she can cipher better than you can." Her voice began to rise again. "A life of toilin' on another man's land is not the life for Catriona. She'll not be weddin' Ian Alexander, and she'll certainly not be weddin' anyone she has no feelin' in her heart for. Neither of our daughters will be doin' that. And as I am your wife, Angus MacBryan, I'll be havin' my way in this!"

Chapter Four

Catriona closed the door to the cottage quietly behind her, slipping out into the twilight. The hour was early enough that everyone was still asleep. With any luck, they would stay that way at least until she was too far away to go after. She waited a moment just outside, then hearing nothing, she started on her way.

Clutching the small wooden box which held her quills and papers tight against her chest, Catriona skipped over the heather-carpeted moors and hills thick with broom leading away from the slumbering cottage. It felt blissful to be out, to know again the touch of the tall grass wet and cold, tugging at the hem of her skirt as it swished against her lower legs.

Nearly three weeks had passed since her father had forbidden her to go to Rosmorigh, and for that three weeks Catriona had heeded his wish. She'd had little choice. She had passed the time on small tasks, carding the wool with her mother while Mairead saw to the cooking and the weaving. But even as she tried to avoid it, she would find her eyes straying to the window set in the wall of the cottage, and the top of the tower at Rosmorigh that rose just over the hilltops in the distance through it.

The waiting was maddening. Catriona forced herself to focus her attentions on her tasks at the cottage, and for a time she tried very hard to forget that place, with its books and promises and dreams. Until her father had announced that he would be leaving for the coast again on one of his ventures, reminding Catriona precisely why, despite his stern warning, she would have to go back to Rosmorigh.

Angus would be away longer this time, her mother had said, speaking as if she had expected Catriona to fly through the door to that forbidden place the moment she'd told her. Mary knew her daughter well. Yet Catriona hadn't gone, not at once. She had waited, passing the night with her mother and sister, spinning the wool and exchanging quiet conversation. But with the coming of the morn she rose early to resume her quest. Perhaps this time, she wished inwardly, she'd succeed.

The sun had just begun to rise pink and yellow in the early-morning sky, the low-lying valley mists shrouding the dawn in Highland mystery as she came to Rosmorigh. Catriona slipped quickly and quietly through the darkened passageways beneath the castle, skimming the steps which led to the secret library door. She had brought with her just one candle, which she had lit to guide her through the tunnels. The room was quite dark on the other side, despite the morning light and her small light. Too dark to read, surely. Too dark to do much of anything.

She moved across the room to open the draperies that were drawn on the tall windows. Setting her candle holder on the table beside her, she proceeded to yank the heavy fabric open.

"Close the damned draperies!"

Catriona nearly jumped out of her shoes. She immediately pulled the drapery closed, then stood there, her fingers still clutching the thick brocade. Her heart was pounding so hard she could feel it in her throat.

A bare sliver of light came through the window, where the fabric was still slightly parted. She stared at that light, the dust motes floating about within it, too frightened to do anything more than blink.

It had come from behind her, that thundering voice, directly behind, not ten feet away. There was no place for her to run, no way for her to hide, nor could she feign she wasn't there. What Mairead had warned her about, what her father had predicted would happen had come true. She was in the Sasunnach's castle, trespassing on Sasunnach land, and the Sasunnach was there.

Catriona thought for a moment, realizing she could do nothing other than turn and face him, and perhaps try to explain. With any luck, she might avoid arrest. But it would be a blessed miracle if her father didn't learn of this.

She turned, and when she did, she took in a startled breath at the man she found waiting behind her.

It was him, the man from the portrait that hung on the wall, the one in the uniform with the hawk's eyes that looked as if he could see straight to her soul. He had materialized somehow, magically, magnificently, sitting in the armchair before the hearth, the same one she had spent so many hours curled up in, reading into the early hours of the morn. She hadn't noticed him when she'd first come in, for no fire was lit, and no candle other than her own burned inside the chamber. With the draperies drawn so tightly closed, she could never have known anyone was there.

Catriona didn't speak. She couldn't. All she could do was stare at him. Her knight. Her guardian. And—the Sasunnach. She should be frightened, yes, for faced with him now in the flesh and not on canvas was more than a little disconcerting. Yet for some peculiar reason, from the moment she'd turned, recognizing him, her fear at having been discovered had gone. Instead her mind was filled with questions. What was he doing sitting alone in the darkness? Had he somehow learned of her previous visits to the castle and lay in wait now, hoping to catch her when next she came?

A moment passed. Then two. He didn't move, nor did he speak. Catriona fixed her eyes on him, wondering. Could he not see her standing there plain as the day before the windows? Perhaps when she'd thrown open the draperies, the light from outside beaming in so suddenly behind her had thrown her into obscurity. Slowly, cautiously, she took a step forward. The light of her candle beside her wavered with the movement.

Closer now, Catriona could see him more clearly. His hair was dark as the new moon night and tousled about his head and neck. His eyes were placed beneath deeply arched brows, his mouth set in an austere frown, punctuated by the taut and distinct line of his jaw. His fingers, long and tapered, gripped the velvet edges of the arms on his chair. The only trace of light about him was the white shirt he wore, open at the top, exposing a strong corded neck and a hint of the smooth muscular chest beneath that was visible even in the faint light. His shirt contrasted with the darkness of his breeches, black and snug and tapering down below his knees, into the tops of his boots, which were set apart and placed firmly on the floor.

His body looked tense, ready to spring at any moment. Catriona felt quite like the fox when faced with the hound, unable to escape, simply awaiting the inevitable.

He looked just like his picture—with one very noticeable exception. His eyes, the hawk's eyes which had so caught her the first time she'd seen him, were different somehow, not nearly so mesmerizing. What struck her as odd was that they weren't staring at her as they should be. Instead, they were focused straight ahead at an empty space of the wall.

"I can hear your breathing," he said then, his voice coming so suddenly it startled her. It was a firm voice, one that was meant to be listened to. "Do not think to slip away from the room. I know you are here and I will have your name from you."

It was then Catriona realized why he was staring so oddly away from her at the wall.

He was blind.

"You have precisely ten seconds in which to identify yourself, else I will find out who you are and have you dismissed from service."

He thought her a servant, and what else could he have concluded, being that he was unable to see her? Considering this, he could never know who she truly was. Catriona looked to the passage door, yet ajar. The thought to slip through it and be gone before he summoned someone occurred to her. She even made a step toward it, but as she took one last glance at him, she hesitated.

Something about him, his face, the look of anger and frustration and despair that showed so clearly in the deep crease of his brow caused her to linger. What could make a man so openly ache? Before she even considered what she was doing, she said softly, "Please forgive the intrusion, sir. I did not know anyone was here."

The crease in his brow eased a bit at her response and he turned his face in the direction of where she stood. Still his eyes did not see her, she knew, for they were focused at the center of her, at the place where her fingers were knotted before her, and not at her face, where they should be.

"You still have not told me who you are," he said, his voice softer but no less intimidating.

"I am not of the household, sir."

He was silent, then said, "If that is so, then why are you here?"

Catriona wondered if she should tell him the truth, and quickly decided it would be far less damning than anything else she might think to say. "I came here to retrieve a book I'd been reading. I did not know anyone was in residence."

He waited a moment. "This book that you were coming to retrieve. It is your book?"

Catriona hesitated. "No."

"Then it is a book belonging to the owner of this castle?"

"Yes."

"And I presume you have the owner's permission to borrow it?"

Catriona watched him, confused. Who was this man? Was he not the Sasunnach, the English laird of Rosmorigh? But then she realized he was not, for hadn't her father said the Sasunnach was older, much older than this man before her now? Perhaps he was kin to the Sasunnach and had come to Rosmorigh for a visit.

When she didn't answer, he assumed, rightly of course, that she did not in fact have anyone's permission to be there. "Most would consider your coming here trespassing, miss."

"I have not damaged anything, sir. I merely come to read the books sometimes. It seems such a terrible waste, having so many of them with no one ever here to read them. I truly meant no harm by it."

"So this is not the first, or even the second time you have come here then?"

Catriona paused. "No, sir."

He quieted a moment, most probably to decide what to do about her intrusion. Would he have her arrested and thrown in the tollbooth? She thought of the few people she had known, crofters who had gone away to that place, never to be seen again. What if they transported her away and she never saw her family again?

Lost to her thoughts, she couldn't have expected what he said next.

"Being that you are quite obviously familiar with the room, I would assume you could describe it to me?"

"I beg your pardon, sir?"

"I asked if you would be able to tell me what is contained in this room."

Catriona stared at him, uncertain. Slowly she looked

about the familiar setting. She had come there so many times, countless many, yet viewing it now with surveying eyes, she realized she had never truly looked at the chamber, never noticed what it contained beyond the walls lined with books, the table she would sit at to write, and his portrait. She nodded abstractedly.

"You cannot describe the room to me?" he asked, breaking into her thoughts. Catriona realized he would not have been able to see her nod.

"I'm sorry. Yes, I can tell you what is here in the room, but I would need to open the draperies a bit more to be able to see clearly."

His frown deepened. "Of course. A moment, if you please." He reached to the table beside his chair, knocking something from it with a clatter. "Damnation!"

Catriona went to him. "It is all right. I will get it."

She came around the chair and knelt beside him. A curious-looking pair of spectacles with blackened lenses lay beneath the table.

"You were looking for these?" she asked, placing them in his hand.

His fingers automatically closed about the spectacles, and with them, her hand. His touch was warm, nearly hot, and he didn't release her, not at first. Nor did Catriona try to move away.

Considering that his hand looked as if it could easily crush her fingers, it was deceptively gentle in the way it held hers. The touch of his skin so intimately against hers sent a strange shiver through her. Catriona looked at his face. The sadness she had seen, the frustration and guarded anger which had caused her to stay rather than flee when the opportunity had been open to her had returned to his face. He looked as if he would like nothing more than to throw the fine crystal vase sitting on the table beside him through the window. If only he could see it.

"Thank you," he finally said, letting go of her hand. The warmth that she had felt was instantly gone.

Catriona waited while he placed the spectacles over

his eyes. He nodded. "All right. You may open the drapery now."

Catriona drew the heavy blue brocade slowly aside, tying it back with the gold tasseled cord. Morning sunlight beamed through the window, filtering in through the diamond-shaped quarrels and reflecting a spectrum of bright colors that were splashed across the carpet in an elaborate pattern. It was a lovely sight.

"What do you see?" he asked.

"Rainbows."

"Rainbows?"

Catriona turned and started to walk back to him. "Yes, the sunlight is coming through the windows and is creating tiny rainbows all about the room. It is quite beautiful, really."

He waited a moment. "What do you see outside the window?"

She looked out at the view. "The sea, and beyond that, Skye."

"What color is it?"

"The sea?"

"No, the sky."

Catriona glanced at him, realizing the misconception. "Not the sky. I was referring to Skye, the island. It lies just off the mainland."

"The islands are that close to the castle?"

Catriona looked back to the horizon. The rocky, treeless strand of the Sleat peninsula rose out of the churning seawaters, green-and-yellow-carpeted hills dotted with small crofters' cottages rolling off into the distance. The waves crashed against the rugged shore, shooting sprays of seawater across the coastline. She had forgotten how lovely was the view from the cliffs at Rosmorigh, how truly magical the place could be. It was that same magical feeling which no doubt had inspired the original owner to build the castle at that spot nearly four hundred years earlier.

"Yes," she said, "Skye is very near. The sound is all that separates the lower peninsula from the mainland, though most often it is obscured by the mists. Today, though, with the sunlight, it can be clearly seen." She leaned back on her shoulder against the wall, still staring out. "It is not usually this bright in the morning. The clouds generally block the sunlight." She hesitated, drinking in the scene a moment longer, then added, "The light is reflecting off the water like twinkling stars on a murky night."

When Catriona moved back and looked at him again, his expression had softened the slightest bit. "Would you like me to describe the inside of the chamber for you now?"

"Please."

Catriona started from the windows, describing the dark oak paneling which began at the floor and covered both the walls and ceiling. Carved in a bas-relief pattern, it gleamed rich golden brown in the sunlight. Alongside were the bookshelves, crafted of the same wood and rising above an intricate ladder attached to a landing which gave access to the shelves nearer the ceiling.

"So there are quite a number of books here?" he asked.

"Oh, yes. I haven't even looked at half of them." Catriona hesitated. "I am sorry for having come without first attaining the owner's consent."

This time he nearly smiled. "It is all right. Your secret shall remain quite safe with me. I tend to agree with your opinion that books are wasted without use. I know of many people who collect hundreds of them without any thought to what they might contain. I remember reading somewhere once that a book which is never read is quite like a painting that is never seen . . ."

His voice dropped off and the sadness returned to his face once again. He was referring to his blindness, of course. Catriona wondered at it before she quickly went on with her description of the room. "The desk is immense. It is made of a wood I have never before seen. It is a honey color striped with a darker brown and rather unusual-looking."

"It is called zebra wood."

"Zebra wood," Catriona repeated, mentally recording it and thinking it quite an appropriate name. She went on. "The desk sits in the middle of the room, where the view through the windows can be seen even if one is sitting behind it."

"Would you please go to the desk."

Catriona looked at him and then did as he had asked. "All right. I am behind it now."

"Open the top drawer."

"But, sir, it isn't my desk."

"Nor is it your library. It is, however, my desk as well as my library, so please open the top drawer." He hesitated. "I give you my permission."

Robert listened as the girl tried the drawer. Even without his sight, he knew exactly what the desk looked like. He had been with his father when he had purchased it at one of the first auctions the duke had ever taken Robert to. It had originally belonged to an eccentric Prussian nobleman who had had the desk made to his seemingly queer specifications. The thing was filled with secret drawers and compartments and crafted so that they would be hidden in the naturally cryptic pattern of the wood. One of the compartments was even booby-trapped, Robert recalled, rigged to spew ink on the poor unfortunate who might try to open it.

Unusual, yes, the piece was also a monstrosity, and a genuinely ugly piece. Robert's mother, Duchess, as she'd been termed by everyone including her husband, had certainly thought so. She had even forbidden the men delivering it from Christie's to bring it into the house. Robert's father had arrived and a great battle had ensued there in the street with the men who were attempting to deliver the piece standing to the side, and every passerby slowing to observe. The duchess eventually won out and the desk had been taken away.

Robert had often wondered whatever had become of the thing, for he knew it had cost his father dearly. He figured it sold long ago, for after the desk had been taken away that day and even after the duchess had died five years ago, the duke had never mentioned it again. Now he knew why.

"The drawer is locked," she said even as Robert thought that it would certainly be.

"And there is no place for a key," he added.

"Yes, you are right. How does it open?"

"If I remember rightly, there is a mechanism of sorts that will open it, but it is very difficult to locate."

She jiggled something that sounded like a drawer.

"Be aware," he said, "if you should chance upon the wrong drawer, you might end up splattered with ink."

"Intriguing," she said. "Though I do not see any mechanism. Perhaps you can show me where to find it."

"I hardly think so."

"Why ever not?"

"In case you hadn't noticed, miss, I am blind."

He heard her coming toward him. "Does that mean you've lost your memory or the use of your other senses as well?" She took his hand. Robert was a bit startled at the intimacy and the sudden unexpected contact. Still he didn't pull away when she urged him to stand. Instead he allowed her to lead him toward the desk.

"Try to rely on what you have and not what you are lacking," she said to him. "You have seen this desk, before you lost your sight?"

"Yes."

"All right. You are standing behind the desk now. Picture it in your mind. There are two sets of drawers on either side of the center kneehole. There is one narrow drawer above the kneehole. Do you recall where the mechanism to release the lock is located?"

Robert tried to picture the desk, thinking back on that long ago day. "I believe it is somewhere under the middle drawer."

"Where?" She urged Robert to kneel beside her in front of the desk. She placed his hand on the smooth wood. "Show me."

Robert ran his fingers along the underside of the desk, searching, focusing his memory as she'd suggested to him. With his touch he could detect the lines of the desk, where each drawer was situated, and he reached back to where he recalled the mechanism was located. He stopped when he felt a small raised portion in the wood. "Here."

She leaned closer and placed her fingers next to his. As she did, her hair brushed against his face. Its touch was whisper soft and smelled of sweetness and flowers, a fresh and foreign scent that in itself seemed to characterize her. Robert found himself turning his face further into it.

"I found it," she said. "How clever the way it is masked by the grain of the wood."

Robert moved to stand, stepping away from her, more than just a little disconcerted at how the room had grown noticeably warmer from their contact. "It was designed that way so anyone who shouldn't have access to it couldn't. There is no lock that can be picked. Unless someone knew the mechanism was there, it would be imperceptible."

"Yes, but you found it without having to see it. It was just a matter of your relying on your touch and your memory instead of your sight. I would imagine it is a bit like taking your first steps out of leading strings all over again."

Robert could think of absolutely nothing to say in response.

"How did you know about the hidden mechanism in the first place?" she asked.

"Because this was once my father's desk."

"Then you are the laird's son? The heir of Rosmorigh?"

Robert stiffened at hearing the word *heir*. It was not something he'd ever considered himself to be in connection to his father. That had been Jameson's claim in life, his rightful title. Robert had never wanted the distinction, and certainly never under the circumstances in which it had been conferred to him. Yet, somehow, for some senseless reason, it had come to him and for the first time since that horrible night months earlier, Robert found he could finally admit it.

"Yes, I am Robert Edenhall, the Duke of Devonbrook and the laird of Rosmorigh."

Chapter Five

Robert had expected many reactions from her at his introduction of himself, none of them the one he would receive.

"It is a pleasure to make your acquaintance, your grace," was all she said. No ensuing sympathetic strings, no uncomfortable silence the weight of which would crumple a boulder, not even a slight hesitation in her terming him by his title. She was sincere in her acceptance of him, seeing him as nothing more than who he'd told her he was, Robert Edenhall, the Duke of Devonbrook.

But then she didn't know, couldn't know the true circumstances behind his becoming a duke. She knew nothing of him. She certainly wouldn't know of the fire nor would she have heard the rumors which no doubt yet filled every candlelit salon in London, the accusations that he had in coldblood killed nearly every member of his own family. And, yet, even with knowing what she did, that he was blind, she didn't react as if the nose had just dropped from his face.

This girl, whoever she was, had done the one thing those who had known Robert throughout his entire life had not. She had allowed him to remain himself, the person he had been before the fire, the same person after, the man and not the curiosity to be stared at and whispered after and conjectured over.

"You know," he said, suddenly wanting, needing to know who this thoroughly affable creature was, "when a person first introduces himself, it is customary for the other person to respond in kind."

She remained silent, quite obviously reluctant to confess her identity, perhaps even still a bit fearful of punishment for having trespassed at the castle.

"It is all right, miss. I will not—"

An abrupt knock sounded on the door across the room seconds before it swung open. Robert felt the sudden whisper of someone passing quickly by him before he heard the dour voice of his valet Forbes sounding from the direction of the door.

"Your grace, I have brought you your dinner and some correspondence which was delivered a short while ago from London."

Robert didn't need to have seen to know the girl had vanished. The atmosphere in the room had grown cold and forbidding the moment Forbes had come in and she had slipped away. If she had still been in the room, Forbes would no doubt have already descended upon her.

Robert thought suddenly of Pietro, and what his reaction to this lady would be, one certainly far different from that of Forbes. A consummate charmer, whenever the two of them had encountered an intriguing member of the opposite sex during their times together on the Peninsula, Pietro would immediately set out to win her heart. More often than not, he succeeded. And he would have been thoroughly bewitched by this one.

"The draperies," Forbes announced, having just noticed them. "They are open."

"Yes, Forbes, they are," Robert said, restating the obvious. He waited a moment, listening while Forbes set the dinner tray on the table beside him. He then waited a moment longer before saying, "Thank you, Forbes. You may leave now."

"But, your grace, your dinner . . ."

"I am quite capable of feeding myself without a chaperon, Forbes. The more I do the simple things for myself, the better off I will be." *Had he really just said that?* "I would appreciate my privacy now. You may return in an hour or more to collect the tray."

Forbes remained a moment before saying with ill-concealed displeasure, "As you wish, your grace." He started to leave, then hesitated. "What of the correspondence, your grace?"

Robert had known the question would be forth-coming and had expected it sooner. "What of it, Forbes?"

"Shall I open it and read it for you?"

Robert reached beside himself and searching, found the glass that stood near the plate. He was improving. At least this time he hadn't knocked it over, spilling its contents across his shirtfront. Bolstered by this small trace of independence, he took a sip of his claret before answering. "That will not be necessary, Forbes. I will attend to the correspondence myself."

Robert knew Forbes was surely staring at him as if he'd lost his wits as well as his sight, for it was the first time in their unfortunate acquaintance that the man seemed left at a complete loss for words.

"Thank you, Forbes. And leave the draperies as they are, if you please."

Robert waited until he had heard the valet leave and close the door behind him. Only then did he allow himself ease.

It took him two hours to finish the meal. A bit of it had ended up on the floor, but in the end he had accomplished it on his own. And during that time, while sitting in his chair, struggling to direct something as seemingly simple as fork to mouth, Robert had come to a decision. He could not pass the remainder of his days sitting in a darkened room while his life slipped by. More importantly, he would not.

Not since the day he had left university to serve in the Guards had he been dependent upon another person for his livelihood. Just as he had found a way to support himself then as a second son, he would learn to overcome this blindness now. He had never allowed his life to be shaped by others and their opinions of what he should be. He had risen above his planned existence before. He would overcome this obstacle now and he would find the truth. He would discover who had truly killed his family.

Robert stood and made for the window. He had removed his spectacles and his eyes now differentiated between the light of the outdoors and the darkness within. Having been exposed to the light for a time, the pain from it was nearly forgettable. *Nearly.*

Moving slowly, Robert made his way across the room toward the light. Behind his eyes he felt a painful and steady throbbing, which he tried to ignore. When he reached the window, he lifted his hand and flattened it against the glass. Cold, solid, familiar somehow. It offered him something else on which to concentrate other than the pain. He felt along the window until he found the latch that held it, loosened it, and pushed the glass outward.

Cool wind blew against his face, whipping against his skin with brisk, healing vigor. Robert took in as deep a breath as his lungs would allow, reveling in the icy feel before expelling it slowly. The throbbing in his head was still there, centered behind his eyes, sharper now because of the light, but if he concentrated his attentions elsewhere, he found he could tolerate it. Below and away from where he stood he could hear the sounds of the surf crashing on the rocks. He focused his attention on it. It was a soothing sound, offering him comfort from the pain, solace among chaos.

He could smell the salty sea and the fragrance of something which reminded him of the girl mingling on the breeze. It was a pleasant scent, exotic in its own way. He thought of her description of the view, of the sunlight shining like stars upon the water. He tried to picture the island Skye, lying just off the mainland, the unfathomable blue of the sea surrounding it. He imagined her standing at the window, her soft hair—what was its color?—blowing in the breeze as it had whispered across his face earlier.

He wished he could see the view.

He wished he could see her.

He wondered if she'd return.

He knew she would.

And he hoped it wouldn't be long.

Upon leaving Rosmorigh, there was but one place Catriona could go.

Colonel MacReyford lived in a small cottage on Rosmorigh land, the other side of the glen from the MacBryans, and directly between their croft and the castle. Catriona had known the Colonel for longer than she could remember, and even before they'd embarked on their quest together, she had gone to visit him every time she could ever manage to slip away. Even as a child, whenever Catriona's mother was looking for her, the first place she knew to go was the Colonel's, where she would always find Catriona, and where then she, too, would end up staying at least another hour or two sharing a pot of herb tea and listening to the Colonel's stories just as eagerly as Catriona.

Catriona had never heard him referred to by any Christian name, only Colonel by anyone who knew him. His age was as much a mystery as were his beginnings, although inwardly Catriona believed the Colonel at least a century old. He had to be, for he spoke of events from ages ago with a familiarity of one who had been there. No one knew from where he had come, who were his family, his clan. MacReyford was a name unfamiliar to all. Yet he'd been a part of them forever it seemed, living in his small ramshackle cottage, bouncing Catriona on his great knee when she'd been a wee babe, and telling stories of the Great '45 and Bonnie Prince Charlie by the soft amber light of the slumbering peat fire.

It was the one thing which was certain about the Colonel, his having been a soldier during that terrible time decades ago. The uniform jacket he still wore each day, tattered at the elbows, the gaping hole where he'd been hit by grapeshot fraying away its back, told it to anyone who ever encountered him.

By the time Catriona reached the Colonel's cottage, it was nearing midday, the sun high in the cloud-puffed sky. The distant sounds of the sea reached for Catriona as she came to the small, weathered door and rapped on it softly. The smell of the peat burning in the hearth filled the air around the cottage, for despite the sun, the air still held its customary Highland briskness.

"Colonel?" Catriona called, pushing the door open a bit.

Through the haze of smoke which hovered over the inside she could see him sitting with his back to her, facing the central hearth in that ancient carved rocking chair he seemed ever rooted to. His fuzzy fat orange cat Matilda, as ancient, it seemed, as he, and named for the Colonel's deceased wife, whom nobody had ever known, lifted her head at the intrusion. Seeing Catriona, she simply blinked and lowered it again, disinterested in anything that wasn't edible.

Catriona slipped silently inside the cottage, moving for the Colonel's still form from behind.

"Colonel, are you awake?" she said softly as she drew closer to him.

He did not respond.

The fire in the hearth was barely burning and Catriona retrieved a fresh peat from the peat-neuk set in the wall, tossing it on the fire and rousing up the embers beneath it with an iron poker. She noticed a crock of his favorite colcannon simmering on the fire, and stirred it a bit, testing its doneness before removing it from the fire to cool. When she turned around, Catriona saw the Colonel's peaceful wizened face in the firelight, half covered by the snow white beard that he assured her at one time had been carrot orange. His hair, thin and also white, was pulled back in its customary queue, his eyes closed, his head drooping slightly to the side.

"Colonel?"

Still he didn't answer. Catriona approached, setting her hand on his stooped shoulder. "Can you hear me, Colonel?"

She began to grow worried when he didn't respond even after she'd shaken him. She looked at his chest. She didn't detect any movement. Dear Lord, she thought, had he . . . ?

Catriona moved her hand beneath his whiskey-reddened nose. She could feel nothing, no warmth, no whisper of breath. She moved her hand away, eyes already filling with tears. She struggled against admitting it, but when he still hadn't moved moments later, she realized the truth. He was gone. The Colonel had left her. And she hadn't been there to bid him Godspeed.

A sadness began to fill Catriona's heart as she stood there watching him, so still, so peaceful, and she wondered what she'd do without him, her special friend. The Colonel had been so much a part of her life for so long; regardless of the fact that he was older than the hills and couldn't be expected to live forever, somehow she had always expected him to be there. And what made her even sadder was that he'd died alone.

Catriona bent over the Colonel, moving to press her lips to his forehead in a final farewell kiss. She shrieked aloud, jumping back when he suddenly opened his eyes.

"What the devil do you think you're doin', lassie?"

Catriona was so startled by his unexpected resurrection she could but stare at him, white in the face and trembling. "I was . . . I mean, I thought . . ."

The Colonel cackled, revealing his numerous stained teeth and the even more numerous gaps where there were none. He stroked a gnarled hand through his white beard. "Hee, hee. You mean to say you thought I'd finally breathed my last, din't you, lassie?"

Catriona could think of nothing to say to him and watched as he swept his hand outward with the swiftness of a man a third his age, snatching the bottle of *usquebaugh* beside him and swallowing down a goodly dose of it.

"Ah," he said, wiping the whiskey from the corner of his mouth with the back of his hand, "that'll certainly wake the dead." And then he chuckled again. "Aye, certainly it would. It woke me now, din't it?"

His lucid eyes, which were of no natural color, twinkled with a devilish light, the corners crinkling with his mirth. "What's the matter, lassie? Ne'er known you to be at a loss for the word. Mattie 'ere got your tongue?"

Catriona finally smiled, dropping down on the dirt floor before him. "Stop teasing me so, Colonel. You frightened me half to death." She grinned at him, realizing yet more the loss her life would have seen without him. "Not because I thought you dead, mind you, because I didn't. I just couldn't think of what I'd do without you."

The Colonel stroked the side of Catriona's cheek with his time-roughened finger. "Ah, lassie, you remind me of my sweet Mattie, my wife, mind you, not this worthless cat. God rest her soul, my Mattie. She had your spirit. And your beauty. I miss her fierce, I do. But you? That I were fifty years younger ..." He took another swig from his bottle. "Now, I must tell you something."

"Is it something to do with the treasure?" Catriona immediately asked, leaning forward even before he'd answered.

"Of course 'tis about the treasure, lass. Time's runnin' out for us, for I well could have kicked off this morn,

and then where'd we be? I'm the last that knows
of Prince Charlie's gold. The rest of them—Lochiel,
MacPherson, and the others—they all vowed to take the
secret of it to their graves with them, still believing
Prince Charlie, and then his kin, would come back yet
again to claim it. We all pledged not to dig it up till there
looked no chance of another rebellion. But when the
Stuart died, they ran like flies to the feast and took the
gold what was hidden at Arkaig."

He took a quick swallow from his bottle. His eyes
misted over and Catriona listened quietly as he lost
himself to his memories. The story was always the
same, but she didn't care. She loved listening to it.

" 'Twas the last days of April when the French
arrived at Loch nan Uamh, their ships, the *Mars* and
the *Bellona,* lugging what was to have been thirty-five
thousand in gold louis sent to the Stuart for his rebellion. Aye, but it was too late, it was. It was back in '46,
and Culloden had already been fought and lost, the
battle that dinna e'en last an hour. That bloody Cumberland sought out every retreating Highlander, showing not a whit o' mercy for a one of them, wounded,
woman, or child. Fugitives all, he called them." The
Colonel looked at Catriona, taking her fingers with his.
"Ah, lass, that you were spared that horror is the one
thing I can thank the Lord for. Innocent eyes like yours
should never have to see what the English did here."

Catriona squeezed his hand. "But the English never
took the treasure."

The Colonel smiled. "Nay, lass, they dinna take it.
They dinna e'en know of it. The Stuart was gone into
hiding, running to save his backside into the Highlands. He spent the next five months running around
these parts, waitin' for the French to fetch him. The
Jacobites heard there had been six cases of the gold
taken off the *Bellona* and that they were later buried
over on Cameron land at Loch Arkaig. What most
dinna know was that there really had been seven cases
of the gold."

"And the seventh is the one that is hidden somewhere near Rosmorigh," Catriona added.

"Would that I had buried it myself, lass, then this task I set you on would be simple, for my mind's as clear now as it was then. Nay, that bear, MacDonnell of Barrisdale, buried that seventh case when he took the others from the *Bellona*. Only he knew that there were seven cases. His thought was to abscond with it, of course, so he buried it away somewhere at Rosmorigh, where no one would be able to retrieve it but him. He knew the rebellion winna succeed. Bloody hell if he dinna take the first steps to ensure its failure. Traitorous bastard he was, that MacDonnell. But he was also a clever sot. Drew himself a picture map of where he hid the treasure, so vague none could decipher it. Then he scribbled out the words that would explain his images before hiding them away."

"But you have the picture map."

"Aye, I do, but neither is of any use without the other." The Colonel snorted, then coughed on his whiskey, his shoulders shaking with the effort. "That is why we must find that other map," he said, recovering. " 'Tis hidden somewhere in that library, woven within the text of one of those many books so one might never realize lest they knew just what they were looking for. Without those words, lass, MacDonnell's images—a burn, a cave, a forked oak—are worth less than the paper on which they are written."

Catriona stared at this man, so ancient, so wise, her eyes glazed with dreams of a life unbound by tenancy and escalating rents, a life where her father wouldn't have to involve himself in his ventures—his smuggling ventures—just to get by. The Colonel had given her those dreams, instilling in her the belief that they would find the treasure, the seventh case of gold, and with it they could help to free the poor crofters from their miserable plight.

"I fear that cough of yours is growing worse," Catriona said, fetching him a bit of water from a nearby ewer. "I'll have Mam make you up one of her herbal tinctures with the marshmallow to ease it for you."

The Colonel shook his head. "Nay, lass. This cough is nothing less than I deserve for the life I've lived. I asked the Lord long ago to take me to my Mattie. He keeps me here in like payment for the things I have done."

"You cannot mean that, Colonel. How can you say that? You have been so good to so many."

The Colonel snorted. "Tell that to the laird when he sees fit to replace me with the bleatin' tenant of the four-legged sort."

The laird. Good heavens, it was for that reason Catriona had come to the Colonel in the first place, to tell him of the duke having come to Rosmorigh. In listening to his tales, she'd completely forgotten to tell him.

"Oh, but he is here."

The Colonel took another swallow of whiskey. "Who's here, child? And whoever he be, why is he here at all?"

Catriona lifted Matilda and dropped onto the small stool where the Colonel usually rested his feet. She scratched the cat's orange head, eliciting a happy purr from her oversized belly. "The laird is here, Colonel. And he's come to stay at Rosmorigh."

The Colonel pushed himself to sit upright, peering at her closely. "The laird, you say? It canna be. He is here? At Rosmorigh? He's come back? You're certain it is him?"

Catriona nodded, wondering why the Colonel should sound so surprised by the news. The laird did come occasionally to Rosmorigh. "Yes, but it is the new laird. Colonel, the other laird's son. And from the looks of it, he seems to be staying for good."

The Colonel rubbed his fingers over his beard. "Why the devil would he be for doing that? He's young, you say?"

"Yes. Thirty years or more."

"Why would a young lad like himself be wantin' to live out here in this forsaken part of the countryside? He's no wife with him?"

Catriona hadn't even thought that the duke might have a duchess. He very well could have, and she just hadn't come with him to Rosmorigh. But then she remembered something, his hand when it had held hers. There had been no ring on his finger. "No, Colonel. I do not believe he is wed."

"And he's the laird's heir, you say? Surely he must have another place to live far grander than Rosmorigh."

"Rosmorigh is grand," Catriona interjected. "It is the grandest place I've ever seen."

"Aye, she is, lass, but there are places far grander in the south, golden palaces filled with lovely things you winna believe, and they are nearer to where people of his ilk reside. There has to be a reason for his comin'. He's traveled here for something." The Colonel looked at Catriona, narrowed his small eyes, and added, "And I can probably guess what that something is."

"No, Colonel," Catriona said, shaking her head against his unspoken thought. "I do not believe the laird has come here to search for the treasure."

The Colonel discounted her opinion. "How could you possibly know that? Did he tell you so?"

"No."

"Did you read his mind then?"

Catriona smiled. "Of course I didn't."

"Then what? What is it?"

"He is not here to search for the treasure." Catriona looked at the Colonel. "The new laird is blind."

The Colonel looked puzzled by her statement. "Blind, you say?"

"Yes, but I do not think it is a blindness he's had long, for he is still struggling with it." She thought of the duke's reaction when his spectacles had fallen from the table. "It makes him very frustrated and angry, his blindness."

"And how do you know this?"

"Because I could see it on his face and hear it in his words when he spoke to me."

"You spoke to the young laird?"

"Yes. He was there in the library sitting in the dark when I went to Rosmorigh this morning. He caught me quite by surprise, but he wasn't angry that I'd come or even that I'd been before to look at the books."

"You told him you've seen the books?"

"Of course I did."

"Och, lass, why din't you just reveal everything we know of the treasure to him then?"

Catriona frowned. The Colonel was angry, but only because he didn't understand. The duke was magnificent, just as he had seemed in his portrait. He wasn't what people thought him to be.

"You asked him if he is planning to stay then?" the Colonel asked, still irritated.

"No. I wasn't able because his man came in and I quickly left." She thought back and smiled. "Odd, though, he didn't tell his man I had been there, for I waited on the other side of the door in the passageway and listened to see if he would."

The Colonel thought a moment, frowning, then looked over at Catriona. "You must go back to Rosmorigh, lassie. You must go back to see the young laird." He took her hand, his voice grave. "And you must get rid of him just as we did the others."

Chapter Six

The library at Rosmorigh was dark when Catriona slid the secret door open, but not completely dark. It was late, the moon hovering high above the castle's lone tower, the stars tiny pinpoints blinking in the endless black sky. Catriona loved the room best when it was like this. Shrouded in shadows. Quiet. Secluded. *Mysterious*. The sort of place one might expect to find a legendary treasure. Some might have thought it eerie, even frightening, the stillness and the stygian darkness. But Catriona had always believed the Highland nights at Rosmorigh steeped in wonder and magic.

At times, when she would come to the castle at night like this, she would wait before lighting the candle she carried with her in her pocket to begin searching through the books. She would sit on the cozy cushioned window seat, knees drawn up to her chin, watching the play of the night on the water far below the castle cliffs. It always made her feel wistful, sitting there alone, and she thought sometimes of Charles, the Bonnie Prince, of the months he had spent hiding out in the Highlands, running for his life from the English soldiers. The Colonel had told her once that the prince had even passed a night once hiding out at Rosmorigh. Catriona imagined him having sat at that very spot by the window, watching out, hoping for a glimpse of the

French frigate that would take him to safety. Once or twice she had even fallen asleep there, her head resting against the windowpane, awakened by the soft colors of the coming dawn shining in through the mullioned windows.

Across the room, the draperies were open now and the moonlight spilled in from outside, casting a bluish glow about that part of the chamber. Catriona spotted the duke's chair, its deep red velvet looking nearly black in the shadowed light. It was empty, a small dip in the cushion indicating where he'd sat earlier.

A small part of her had hoped he would still be there when she returned, while the better part of her, the sensible part, had purposely waited until he'd surely have retired for the night. Catriona knew she couldn't allow herself to wonder about him any more than she already had. She couldn't allow herself to know him, to care, not when he would be leaving Rosmorigh.

Catriona looked behind the chair to where his portrait hung at its place on the wall, fully illuminated in the moonlight. While still a splendid rendering of him, having met him now, seen him face-to-face, spoken with him, the likeness had shed some of its sublimity. The man was so much more imposing, the painting simply a depiction of that. And after he'd gone, when he left Rosmorigh, Catriona knew she would no longer look on it with the same awe and wonder she had before. Instead, she knew she would look on it with regret.

Why should she feel this hesitance, this reluctance to see him leave? It hadn't bothered her before with any of the others, and she knew she would be a fool to think there could ever be anything more between them than the relationship of laird to tenant. He was a nobleman. A duke. She was naught but a poor crofter's daughter, her family entirely dependent on him for their survival. Anything more would simply have to remain in her dreams.

Still, when Catriona had first turned to see him

sitting there in the shadows that morning she had
thought she must surely have imagined him, conjuring
him up like a dream having come real. She had spoken
to him—to his portrait—so many times before, countless times, but this was the first time he had ever
spoken back to her. And when he did, his voice had
been as deep, as commanding as she had always imagined it would be.

She had been dreaming of this man for as long as she
could recall. She had fallen in love with his image,
while not even knowing his name. She had invented
tales about him, making him seem larger than life. And
now, after all that, she must send him away. It was this
that troubled her most of all.

All day thoughts of the duke had occupied her mind.
She was drawn to him as she had been to his portrait
before, only more so, for she was filled now with a
curiosity about him and his life, his true life and not
any tale she had imagined. She could not help herself.
She wanted to know how he had lost his sight. Had it
been during some terribly fierce battle, she mused,
thinking on the portrait and the scene depicted there?
She pictured him astride a great destrier, his dark hair
tousled by the winds of war as he led an army of his
men to victory. What had brought him all the way to
Scotland? Despite that they might seek out the North
Country for its isolation at times, English landlords
always grew weary of their Scottish properties. Everyone knew that, for they were too remote, too far
removed from London and all its excitement and
glories. Few English landlords ever kept Highland
properties at all, most concentrating their interests
instead along the borders where the land was rich
and fertile and where a coach could always be found
to take them south when the novelty of the north
wore away.

Turning from the portrait, Catriona moved to the
duke's chair once again. She lowered herself into it,
running her hand against the rich fabric. The seat and

the soft cushioned back of it still held a hint of his body's warmth. He hadn't been gone from the room very long, for the scent of him, a decidedly male fragrance of clove and bergamot, clung to the plush velvet covering. Catriona snuggled further into the chair and closed her eyes, wishing she would not have to do what she was about to do. Wishing . . .

Voices came then from the hall outside. She sat up. They were close. She wouldn't have enough time to slip out of the room. Whoever was there might hear her. Instead, Catriona pressed herself further into the chair, praying they didn't come inside.

"Finally took himself out of that chair to bed," said the first voice, a male voice whose tone hinted at sarcasm.

"What more can he do?" answered the other.

Catriona recognized this one as the man Forbes, who had come to the library earlier that day. "His scheme backfired on him and he lost his sight for his greed. At least there is a certain bit of justice to it, watching him submit to his well-deserved punishment."

"He is a broken man, the duke is. Sits there all day thinking of what could have been. Perhaps it is the guilt at what he done that is eating at him."

Forbes snorted. "I assure you it is not guilt the duke suffers from. His grace is far too ruthless for something as soft as that. He got what he wanted, but with a heavy price to pay for it. And now he thinks removing himself to this godforsaken place far from civilized society will serve to quiet the gossips' tongues in London. But there are some things a man simply cannot outrun."

They had moved farther down the hall and out of earshot, leaving Catriona sitting in the dark room, contemplating what she had just heard.

She had been right after all. The duke hadn't come to Rosmorigh for the treasure. He had no idea of its existence. He had come to Scotland because he had wanted to escape from something in London. A scandal, perhaps? From what she'd just heard, it seemed the likeliest reason. But what sort of scandal? Perhaps a duel he had fought to defend an insult to his honor? Or even a lady's honor? Perhaps he had killed the other man, but lost his sight when his pistol backfired. Indeed, Forbes had said something about a backfiring. But what of the other things Forbes had said. *Ruthless. Greed.* These were not words that suited the duke, not when he could easily have seen her brought up on charges of trespassing when he learned of her clandestine visits to his castle.

Catriona had to tell herself to stop speculating then. She had not come to Rosmorigh to spend the night fretting over the duke's past or for that matter, his present either. Despite his reasons, whatever they were, one thing was certain: the duke could not remain at Rosmorigh any longer. Catriona focused on her quest, the Bonnie Prince's treasure, the secret of which lay waiting for her to find somewhere in this room. She thought of her father and the danger he placed himself in time and again. Smugglers were jailed, even hanged. The Colonel was right. She must find a way to make the duke leave. She needed to resume her search for the treasure and she would not be able to with the duke here. How she wished it wasn't necessary, but there really was no other choice.

She would have to get rid of him.

Just like she had all the others.

Robert wasn't certain which he felt first, the chill which blew softly against his cheek, or the uncanny prickling that made itself felt at the back of his neck. It was the prickling that first caught his attention, the same prickling which had always proven a presage to danger during his days in the Peninsula.

"Who is there?" he asked calmly. He was less than surprised when he didn't receive a response.

He was sitting in the library, sipping a glass of port before retiring for the night. It had been a long day, and a disappointing one, for he had hoped the mysterious girl who had come the day before would return. In fact he'd waited, turning each time he heard any unexpected sound, but she hadn't come back, and he had been left to sitting alone through the day with his memories—and his questions—to keep him.

Until now.

Robert waited a moment longer. Hearing nothing more, he picked up his glass and sipped at it. Minutes passed. Except for the ticking of the clock, the room was silent. Several minutes passed and he had begun to think he had imagined it when suddenly a shadow moved close by in front of him, he could tell from the way the light from the candles Forbes had lit shifted slightly. Forbes hadn't yet come to add wood to the fire, so the light from the hearth was low, making the candlelight even more significant to Robert's shadowed and muted vision. A noise, like the dragging of something heavy on the floor, sounded immediately to the right of him.

Robert waited, sitting calmly. Whoever was there clearly wanted his attention, but wasn't getting the reaction wanted. The sound came again, closer to him this time. Louder. Still he didn't budge. Until the candlelight went out with a rush of air, leaving him in total darkness.

"Who is there?"

A silent moment and then softly he heard a noise. It sounded like a whisper, a prophetic sort of murmuring beside his ear.

Leave . . . this . . . place . . .

Robert turned toward the voice. A waft of air blew across his face. "What do you want?"

Close by to his other ear he heard the voice again, more ominous now, echoing eerily as if spoken in a tomb.

You . . . are . . . in . . . danger . . .

And then, before he could react, something crashed against the floor, something which sounded very much like glass. Across the room, an unearthly scream, and then the voice again, strident and alarmed.

Beware!

Two loud thuds, like heavy books being dropped to the floor. The windows came open and the night wind rushed over Robert's face, whipping through the room like a gale. Pages from books flipped open somewhere beside him. A whistling came from above. Still he did not move from his chair.

The voice came again, whispering.

You . . . have . . . been . . . warned . . .

Pounding, like that on a door, came from across the room. The voice returned.

Go . . . now . . . before . . . it is too late . . .

Something soft and light touched Robert's face, like gossamer cobwebs. The pounding on the door grew louder. Another crash, this time right in front of him.

"Your grace!" came Forbes's voice as a key jiggled frantically in the lock. "Why have you locked the door?"

The clamorous noise had alerted the staff. "I haven't locked it, Forbes."

The soft cobweb something brushed against his cheek again, this time carrying with it a scent, earthy and floral, a scent that reminded him of . . .

Robert grabbed at the object and yanked it to him.

Across the room the door burst open. Several people entered quickly.

"Your grace," said Forbes, coming before him. "What have you done? The windows are open. The vase is broken. There are books lying about everywhere."

Robert hadn't moved from his chair. In his hand he clutched the soft bit of fabric that had been intended, along with the rest of the macabre performance, to frighten him. Instead, he could but smile at the comedy it really had been.

"What is it, your grace?" Forbes asked, obviously agitated by the sight of his master's smile. "Do you know what happened here?"

"Yes, Forbes, I believe I do," Robert answered calmly. "I think I may have just been visited by a ghost."

Catriona knew that she had failed even before she had slipped back through the secret door leading down to the caves beneath the castle. She'd failed and she'd almost been found out, for they had unlocked the door far quicker than she'd figured. And what made it even worse was that the Duke of Devonbrook had been totally indifferent to her maneuvers.

She reached the bottom of the stairs quickly, but instead of following the path that would lead her back to home, she turned and moved even deeper into the cliff belly. It was dark and chilly, but she hardly noticed. She was too agitated by her failure. She should have used the chains, she thought, reaching the small chamber where she kept hidden all her spectral contraptions. She placed her mother's wooden mincing bowl back on the shelf which was formed naturally in the rock wall. Small and easy to carry, it gave just the right amount of a report to her voice when she spoke into it. And when she whispered into it, the effect was truly eerie.

Into the bowl she dropped the string of small seashells that sounded like chattering teeth when she shook them. They rattled softly against the sides. Catriona spotted the small bit of rusted chain she'd found one day half buried in the sand along the shore. She picked it up, shaking it. She frowned. Even the chains wouldn't have spooked him.

He was just like his father that way.

With everyone else Catriona had ever tried to scare away from Rosmorigh she had succeeded, even stone-faced, meddlesome Mairead. Catriona remembered the day she had come upon her sister in the library at Rosmorigh. She had been looking for Catriona, of course, who had been there searching through the books. Catriona had just hatched on the idea of haunting the castle in order to keep others from learning of the treasure and her hunt for it. She hadn't been at all confident it would work. Mairead, however, had quickly proven it would, making the ideal first victim.

From the moment Catriona had moaned like a dead soul from behind the heavy drapery, Mairead's face had turned positively white. The chains rattling at her from the shadows had set her feet to running faster than Catriona had ever seen her move. Afterward, anytime Mairead would come to fetch Catriona home, she wouldn't so much as set her foot on the narrow stone steps leading up to the library. She would instead stand at the bottom, calling up to Catriona while watching the shadows warily around her for any sign of movement. But spooked as she had been, Mairead had never told anyone what she had encountered at Rosmorigh that night. Instead she used Ian Alexander and his similar experience as her proof for believing spirits dwelt within its ancient walls.

When Ian had come to Rosmorigh, Catriona had used her most frightening scream, and a sprinkling of the Colonel's black powder in the hearth. At the sudden flash and cloud of white smoke rising from the fireplace, Ian had simply backed from the room. Quietly. Calmly. And he hadn't come looking for Catriona again. Even the Rosmorigh factor, stodgy old Abercromby, had wailed like a babe until one of the housemaids had come to his rescue. All of them, every one had been fooled, easily persuaded to believe otherworldly beings inhabited Rosmorigh. Every one of them except the laird, the duke's father. He had simply sat there in the dark, chuckling at each device she employed before finally breaking out in applause when she gave it up.

And the new laird appeared to be as blithe as his father—and just as determined to stay at Rosmorigh.

It wasn't until Catriona turned to leave, checking over all her implements first, that she realized she didn't have her handkerchief. She had employed it as a last-ditch effort, brushing it against the duke's cheek in hopes that since he could not see her there, standing so close to him, the touch of something so unexpected would convince him to the presence of a ghost. She thought back to the last time she remembered having it. It had been just as Forbes had unlocked the door. She had been so startled, she had snatched up her other things and had left as quickly as she could. She had thought she had it with her when she slipped from the room. Perhaps, she thought hopefully, she had dropped it somewhere in the passageway.

Or she had left it in the library.

Catriona frowned. Her mother had given her that handkerchief when she'd been a girl, telling her that a special lady had stitched the small *C* in blue at its corner. It would always keep her safe, Mary had told her, before warning Catriona she must never misplace it. And now Catriona had done just that.

She would have to go back for it, but not now, not with the others having come into the room just after she'd gone. They would need to straighten up. They would need to investigate to see if they might find a plausible reason for the occurrence. She would simply have to wait, going back to look for the handkerchief later. And when she did, she would find out just how blithe the new laird of Rosmorigh really was.

Hours later, Robert sat in the dark of the library, twisting the little square of linen in his fingers. Light as air, he might have been persuaded to believe it evidence of a ghost, had it not been for the peculiar scent it carried. He lifted the handkerchief to his face. It held the very essence of her. New. Unique. He'd known even before she had left it behind that the girl who had stolen into the library the other morning and his mysterious ghostly visitor were one and the same.

It had taken Forbes and the others quite some time to repair the room. Two vases had been destroyed, they'd said, and a good dozen books lay scattered about the room. A heavy chest had been pulled five feet from its place, the windows thrown wide. And while Forbes wouldn't dare admit to it, the idea that the intruder had been some sort of ghost wasn't completely without merit to him. Robert found that the most amusing part of it all.

Robert was indeed impressed with the effort she had made to frighten him off. Impressed and curious. She had gone through a tremendous production, and one not without some risk. She'd wanted to scare him obviously, to induce him to leave the castle, and the question foremost in his mind now was why.

Robert hadn't had the opportunity before she'd gone the previous morning to learn more about her. What was her name, her age? She was young, yes, but how young? Was she a spritely adolescent? Barely out of the schoolroom? That didn't seem likely given that she had indicated to him she had been coming to the castle for some time. And she was well spoken and intelligent enough to have masterminded this elaborate ghostly hoax, not only this time, but many times over, for several of the servants had confirmed this wasn't the first, second, or even third such "haunting" at the castle. In fact, it was becoming increasingly difficult to find any of the local people who were willing to take a position there at all, having escalated into something of a legend, this mysterious spirit who moaned on the wind, warning the wary visitor to leave Rosmorigh lest danger befall him.

Robert had to smile to himself. She really was quite clever. And bold, especially to attempt frightening off a blind man. But was it boldness, or simply desperation? What could she be after?

Robert went on cataloging the rest of what he knew of her. She came often and regularly to Rosmorigh, arriving unnoticed, which meant she had access to some way other than the known entrances into the castle. She frightened off anyone who might interfere with her visits, so her reasons for coming there were something she wanted kept secret. The "hauntings" always occurred in the library, which would indicate whatever she wanted was there.

All of this meant but one thing to Robert.

She was indeed after something.

And she had yet to find it.

Curiously though, through all her visits and after all the hauntings which had been reported not a single object had been taken from the castle. This didn't surprise him really, for she didn't strike him as a thief, not after how concerned she'd been in explaining her visits there to him. Whatever her reasons, his sudden appearance must truly have caused her a great deal of trouble.

The servants had also told Robert that the previous laird—his father—had refused to believe the castle haunted. So she hadn't fooled his father, either. That thought made Robert smile. Until he considered the possibility, the probability that his father had also been looking for something at Rosmorigh, perhaps the same something this girl was looking for, the something that might have brought about his death.

Whatever it might be, Robert could not allow this to bring harm, or even death, to another person. He had to make certain this girl didn't fall into danger. And the only way he might do that would be to keep her close by. He knew, should he ask her, she would never tell him what it was she was looking for. But it had to be something quite special for her having gone so far as to "haunt" the place in order to keep others from interfering. This only made the connection between the castle and his father's death even stronger. His father had been after something here. Robert knew it. And whatever it was, Robert knew one thing more: this girl was the one who could lead him to it.

And Robert planned to do whatever he could to make certain she did precisely that.

Chapter Seven

"Bloody hell!"

Robert yanked the tie on his cravat now a fourth time, flinging the damnable piece of fabric clear across the library. He didn't know where it landed, nor did he care. He rather hoped it had touched down directly in the hearth. But even as he thought this, he knew it wasn't an inadequacy in the cravat that had rendered him unable to tie a knot that didn't lie lopsided across his chin. He might as well accept it. He was blind.

"Here," said a soft voice suddenly beside him and he felt someone loop the cravat gently around his neck. His anger calmed the instant her fingers softly brushed against his skin.

She had come back.

He had been waiting for her two days now, since the night she'd come to frighten him off. During that time he'd thought of what he would say, how he would find some way to keep her from danger while trying to discover what it was she was hiding. The perfect solution for it had come to him just the night before when he'd been lying on his back in the middle of his father's bed.

He'd been wide awake. It had been the same every night since he'd come to Rosmorigh. He found that if he didn't sleep, the nightmares wouldn't come and then he would have only his own thoughts and memories to

combat. He could push those aside by concentrating
hard on something else through the long night hours,
even something as simple as picturing in his mind the
colors of the sunset, the many different shades of blue
found in the oceans, things he never wanted to forget
now that he no longer could see them. Then, before the
dawn, he would usually slip into a few oblivious hours
of exhaustion, where even the nightmares could not
penetrate to him.

But he would always awaken to the memories again.

To combat these, Robert had filled much of the rest
of his time with thoughts of her, playing over what he
would say to her, imagining what she must look like.
And now, when she had returned, he had been so occupied with cursing himself and his clumsiness he hadn't
even heard her enter the room.

Standing near to her now, Robert wondered how he
couldn't have realized her there, for the scent of her,
that same scent from the handkerchief, seemed to fill
the room. He wondered how long she had been there
watching his feeble attempts at the cravat, his increasing frustration, his final outburst. He suddenly felt very
foolish.

Catriona quickly, easily, tied off his cravat, then
stepped back a space. "There," she said. "It is a bit
wrinkled, not a perfect knot, but I think it will do."

Robert stood still as a stone. "Thank you. You
undoubtedly made a better effort of it than I could,
although I wasn't aware the art of tying a neck cloth
was something taught to young ladies."

"I would imagine it isn't, but I had discovered a pamphlet here in the library once giving detailed instructions. I couldn't resist the urge to try a few of them. If
you do not like that particular knot, I can try a different
one. There were several illustrated in the pamphlet."

Robert frowned, picturing instead Noah doubled
over with laughter had he been there just then.

"This one is fine." He remained standing where he

was. "Please accept my apologies for my coarse tongue. I did not know you were here."

"It is all right, your grace. Your frustration is under-standable. It will take a little time, and a lot of patience, but you will be able to do these things again. You will simply need to relearn the method of tying your cravat without having to depend upon a looking glass."

Listening to her, her simple explanation, Robert could almost believe it.

"Perhaps next time I could find the pamphlet and read the instructions given to you. It might help you to better execute the tie."

"Indeed." Robert reached behind him, found his chair, and sat. This was certainly not what he had imagined it would be like when she returned. "I am pleased you decided to come back."

"Oh, well, I am sorry for having left so suddenly the other day. I guess it is just an instinct long-practiced. That, and I wasn't quite certain how others in the household might react to my being here. It was silly of me, really. I realized that after I had gone. And I also realized I hadn't finished describing this room for you."

Robert nodded, suspecting that it was not her sole reason for returning. She'd no doubt come to look for her handkerchief, which he had even now in his coat pocket.

Catriona moved closer, sitting near to him he knew because he could feel the weight of her skirts brushing his legs as she lowered into the chair beside him. "Well, you mightn't thank me if you knew that my motives are really rather selfish. You see, despite that I hadn't finished with describing the room for you, I also came back because I hadn't retrieved that book I had come for that day either. I was hoping to finish reading it, that is . . ."

"It is all right," Robert said, perceiving her reluc-tance. "I already told you I am not angry that you have

been coming here. Your secret is quite safe with me."
He paused. "There is one other thing though . . ."

"Your grace?"

"You never did tell me your name."

She was quiet for a moment. He almost thought
she would refuse. Finally she said in a quiet voice,
"Catriona. My name is Catriona MacBryan."

A hint of lovely Scottish burr rolled from her tongue
when she spoke her name, heretofore concealed behind
concisely spoken English. *Catriona.* It was a lovely
name, dulcet, unusual. The handkerchief had a letter
stitched upon it which had felt like a *C.* Robert smiled
to have his suspicions about his spectral visitor all but
confirmed.

"You are Scottish," he said, "yet you speak English
very well."

"Yes. I spent a great part of my childhood with an
aunt who lives in Manchester and took most of my
schooling there. My father also had an English tutor to
teach my sister and me after I had returned to live here
again."

"How long have you been living in Scotland then?"

"I came back to live with my family when I was
twelve, ten years ago," she answered. And then she
added, "I was born on the same day the French
beheaded Queen Marie Antoinette."

"Indeed?" Robert was briefly surprised at her age.
He had thought her much younger. Perhaps it was
her candid honesty or her straightforward manner of
speaking such as when she had mentioned the rainbows
created by the sunlight beaming in through the windows. Not many of the women of her age in London
would have even noticed the color play of the sunlight, much less remarked upon it with such innocent
delight. Nor would many have gone to such lengths to
stage such an elaborate hoax in order to try to frighten
him off.

Now all that was left was to discover why.

"So then," she said, breaking into his thoughts, "where had I left off with describing the room?"

"I believe you were at the desk."

"Oh, yes. The zebra wood."

He heard her stand and move away. He wished he could follow, but the thought of falling over the furniture was well enough to keep him rooted to the safety of his chair. Instead he concentrated on his mental image of the room.

"Behind the desk," Catriona began, "is a very large chair fashioned from dark oak that looks more like it has been hacked with an ax than carved by any woodworker. It is covered with some sort of hide and it is huge, easily seating two. It looks as if it could at one time have been an ancient forest ogre's throne." She laughed softly. "It even has antlers sticking out the top of it."

Robert smiled at the picture of the chair which had formed in his mind's eye. Despite its rudimentary styling, he could well imagine his father's proclivity for the piece, a chair on which he could hang his hat as well as the powdered wig he'd clung to wearing, fashion be damned. The duke had always had an eye for the use of an item while completely ignoring its appearance. It was a trait his youngest son Noah had inherited. In that regard, this chair was the perfect complement to the desk.

Catriona went on. "There are books lining three of the four walls, thousands of them, and they include most every topic imaginable." She paused. "Oh yes. There is a portrait of you between the shelves."

"A portrait?"

"Yes. You are on a battlefield and you are wearing a red uniform coat."

Robert felt a chill, more of a shudder pass through him. He remembered the day he'd posed for the portrait well. His father had sent the artist all the way to Spain to find him. It had been a bloody day, and Pietro had been there with him. Pietro had always been with him.

Catriona must have sensed his sudden change of mood at the mention of the portrait and the sadness of the memory, for she quickly went on with her description of the room. "There is a rather old-looking pistol on the mantel above the hearth, and a perspective glass set on a stand beside the windows, most probably for peering out at the stars." She had come back to him and sat beside him once again. "Did you know that there is a man who has actually catalogued 47,390 different stars?"

Robert nodded. "Joseph Lalande."

"Yes!" she said, excited. "Do you know him? What is he like? I would imagine he is quite a fascinating man."

Robert smiled at her enthusiasm. "No, I'm afraid, although I knew of him, I did not know him personally. Monsieur Lalande died a number of years ago. My brother Noah was acquainted with him and from him I've heard he was a rather crusty fellow well known in the scientific and literary circles."

"I read of him in a pamphlet. There are wonderful drawings in it. It is here in the library somewhere . . ."

Robert listened as she made her way across the room. "Miss MacBryan—"

"Here it is!"

He waited to see how long it would take her to realize . . .

"Oh," she said suddenly. "I am sorry. I had forgotten."

"That I am blind," Robert finished. "Would that I could do the same." There was a moment of silence. "Is that all?" he asked.

"What? Oh, with the room," Catriona said. "No. There is also a stuffed dog sitting on the floor beside your chair."

"I beg your pardon? A dog?"

"Yes. A small one, a spaniel with brown ears, a white body, and large glassy eyes."

A stuffed spaniel . . . Robert mused on this a moment. *Of course. Crumpet.*

She had been a sweet-natured little creature and his father had loved the dog more than anything in life. She had gone everywhere with him, shooting in the oak woods behind Devonbrook House in Lancashire and driving in the park when they had been in town, her front paws perched on the polished sides of his landau. She had even gone to the duke's seat at the Lords, creating quite a stir there, a veritable fixture at his father's side. She had lived to see her sixteenth year and the duke had been heart-struck at the loss of her, weeping when he'd woken that frosty winter morn to find her unmoving at the foot of his huge ducal bed. The duchess had even remarked that she wondered if he'd be so grieved at the loss of her.

Robert remembered how he had tried to take the dog that morning to spare his father the task of her burial in the garden behind the house. But the duke had fervently refused, telling Robert he knew just what should be done with her. Robert now knew what that had been.

This place, this castle and this room, were everything his father had ever been. Like the library at Devonbrook House, Rosmorigh had been the duke's place of refuge, his means of escape. But what was it that had drawn him here? What mystery lay hidden at Rosmorigh?

Robert suddenly remembered his plan for how he would both keep Catriona safe and learn what she was looking for here. He stood and made his way to the desk. It was a route he had practiced many times during the past two days while he'd been waiting for Catriona to return, and he managed it quite without complication. Such a small victory in something he'd done previously without conscious thought, but now required all of his attention, felt wondrously huge to him. His fingers brushed along the desktop until he found the pile of letters that still lay where Forbes had left them days earlier.

"Here, Miss MacBryan." Robert held them out to her. "You will find that these are letters which are addressed to me. Private letters and some business correspondence. I was wondering if you might read them to me since I obviously cannot do so myself. I would pay you for your time, of course, and I would appreciate your continuing to do so when called for. In other words, I should like to hire you to be my eyes."

Catriona looked at the letters, wondering why the duke would want her, a stranger, to read them and not one of his servants. Surely a valet would be more likely to . . .

Catriona thought back to the conversation she'd heard in the hall that night and Forbes's regard so obviously unfavorable for the duke. Perhaps the Colonel was right. Perhaps there was something more to the duke's coming to Rosmorigh than his simply wanting to get away from London. The Colonel had told her to try and find it out. And now the duke was offering her that opportunity, as well as giving her the chance to continue in her quest, for by coming to read his letters, she would also be allowed access to the library. Now, if only . . .

"I would be willing to act as your secretary, your grace, although on a condition that you would not pay me."

"You do not wish to be compensated?"

"Not in the customary manner. I would instead simply ask that I be granted continued access to the library, and the books, only this time with your permission."

Robert nodded. "That is fine. But there is one more thing I would like to ask of you, Miss MacBryan."

"Yes, your grace?"

"I should prefer it if you would address me simply by my given name. Robert."

Catriona looked at him, wondering at a nobleman, a duke, who didn't wish to be known as one. "Yes, of course. Robert. And please call me Catriona." She looked at the letters. "Would you like me to read your correspondence to you now?"

"Yes, a ..." Robert hesitated at the approach of someone in the hall. "No. I mean not at this time. It would seem we are about to have a visitor. Please stay where you are, though. Do not leave this time."

The door opened without the formality of a knock. Catriona remained where she stood.

"Excuse me," said Forbes upon noticing her, using a most supercilious voice, "but who are you and how did you find your way in here?"

"I ..." Catriona faltered before him. He was tall and thin and looked like a long-eared owl with bushy brows, large gleaming eyes, and a nose that resembled a hooked beak. He swept his narrowed eyes over her person, her homespun skirts, and linen chemise. His upper lip even curled a bit to further demonstrate his distaste. She had never before encountered a more unfriendly individual.

"Forbes," said Robert, "I should like you to meet Miss Catriona MacBryan."

Forbes turned to regard his master. "Your grace—"

"It is quite all right, Forbes. Miss MacBryan is here at my request. She will be coming to Rosmorigh to use the library. She is to be given access to the castle and grounds whenever she wishes it."

Forbes was silent, glaring at Catriona as if she were a field mouse he wanted for his supper, but couldn't have. Robert didn't trust this man, his servant. It was easy now to see why.

Forbes looked then to the desk, at the place where the letters had been. He looked directly back at Catriona and he knew they were gone. She could see the realization of it on his querulous face. His expression then turned from annoyance to outright enmity.

Catriona remained standing while Forbes left the tray of food he'd been carrying on the desk and turned without a parting word. She waited until she was certain he'd gone, until his echoing footsteps had faded down the corridor, then said, "I don't think he was very pleased to find me here. He looked as if he had just stepped on a tack."

Robert smiled. "I wouldn't worry. It is my understanding that he has always looked like that. He is quite the crosspatch."

"Your letters. Am I to assume you would like me to read them to you in private?"

Robert nodded. "I suspect the walls have ears, which given my blindness I cannot see. I wish my business to remain my own, not that of every person in this place. To be quite frank, since you do not know me, I feel confident you will read the letters without addition or deduction. There are matters about which you know nothing, but others believe they know everything. They would therefore arrive at their own interpretation of my business."

"In light of this, I would suggest we then go elsewhere to read your correspondence, away from the castle."

"I don't see how that would be possible," said Robert. "As you know, I cannot see."

"But you can walk, can you not?"

"Of course."

"Then come with me. I know of a place nearby where we can go right now and no one will even realize you have gone."

Catriona took Robert's hand and started leading him across the room.

"A moment," she said, turning back. "You will need your spectacles, for we will be out in the daylight."

Robert had nearly forgotten the need for them. "On the table beside the chair."

She got them and pressed them into his hand. While he put them on, Robert heard the sound of something moving, sliding, scraping almost, and then he felt a chill waft over his face. The smell of the sea hit him strongly, wrapping around him. If he didn't know better, he might think he was standing on the shore, for he could even hear the sounds of the waves echoing to him.

"The stairs we are to go down are very narrow and uneven," said Catriona, taking his hand. "We will go slowly and I will lead you."

It took some time for them to reach the bottom, where the sounds of the sea had grown louder, echoing off the walls around them.

"Where are we?" Robert asked.

"There are a series of caves which run in the cliffs underneath Rosmorigh. They were made centuries ago for purposes of defense when the castle was first constructed. They were to be a means of escape in times of siege, leading to the shore. I thought we would go there to a small stretch of beach that lies far below the castle. A cliff ridge hangs over it so no one will be able to see us there."

Catriona led Robert along the passageway until he felt the warmth of the sun on his face. He took in a deep breath. Overhead a gull cried against the sound of the incoming waves. It was the first time he had been outside since arriving at Rosmorigh. He closed his eyes and tilted his face upward against the salty breeze.

"You can have a seat here on this outcropping," Catriona said, helping him to sit.

Robert suddenly realized she could very well leave him here, abandon him where no one could see him, where no one knew he was, and he would never know how to find his way back. With anyone else, even with Forbes, he might be concerned. With Catriona, somehow, he wasn't.

"Hundreds of years ago," she said, "the people of Rosmorigh kept boats hidden here in order to escape in the event of an attack by land."

"Sound reasoning."

"You might think, yet in the end it did them more harm than it did good. An invading clan learned of the beach and the boats and the caves. They attacked from both sides, the land and the sea, virtually trapping the

poor people of Rosmorigh in the caves beneath the
castle. They might have even found a means for escape
then, but for the lack of time. You see, most of the
caves are tidal; they fill with water twice a day. The
poor people could do nothing. They were trapped. On
the outside they would be mutilated, so instead they
chose to drown and their bodies were washed out with
the sea. It is known around this part of the Highlands as
'the Dawn of the Sorrows.' Afterward, the next laird of
Rosmorigh, who inevitably regained the castle, had
another passageway dug through which wouldn't fill
with the tide leading out yet a different way so the
same sort of attack couldn't be repeated."

"And this other passage, it is how you manage to
come and go so undetected?"

Catriona smiled. "I happened upon it quite by accident. Much of the area surrounding Rosmorigh is
moorland and when I was a young girl I used to walk
the moors searching for the *fraoich geal.*"

"I beg your pardon?"

"That is the Gaelic translation of *white heather,* a
rare Scottish flower, purported to bring good luck to
whoever finds it."

"And have you ever found it, this white heather?"

"No, but my mother did when she was young. She
used to send me out to look for it in the tussocks when
I was a girl, although I think it was more to get me out
from under her skirts than for any other reason. Still, I
was determined to find this fabled white heather. I
never did. One day about six months ago I found
myself near to Rosmorigh. The heather was in bloom
and I stopped to search again just as I had when I was a
girl. It was then I discovered the entrance to the cave.
Actually I fell into it, and then I wandered through the
caves, trying to find a way out. I discovered the stairs
that lead to the library and a door hidden in the paneled
wall. When I found the switch that opened that door, I
thought I had emerged into a dream. I had never seen
so many books before in my life. There was so much to

read about and I could come and leave without anyone ever knowing. I've been coming to Rosmorigh ever since."

"And you've never been discovered?"

"No. The previous laird, your father, only came to Rosmorigh occasionally. And your factor Abercromby comes when it is time to collect the rents, of course, but otherwise the castle stands empty. Until now."

The wind picked up then, swirling around them. Catriona looked out over the sound and noticed a dark grouping of clouds moving toward the shore.

"It looks as if we'll be getting some rain soon," she said. "The tide will be coming in and this beach will be underwater in another couple of hours. Shall I begin reading your letters to you now before it grows too late?"

Chapter Eight

Lord Cheveley wasn't able to offer anything further when I met with him last evening at White's. He said he had questioned Father a while ago on the frequency of his absences, but that Father wouldn't divulge anything to him. However, he did say that when Father returned to Devonbrook after his most recent journey to Rosmorigh, he told Cheveley he was on the verge of a success and would soon checkmate Kinsborough permanently in the collecting game.

Robert listened closely to Catriona as she read to him his brother's words. It was the last of the letters he had given her, the first having been from his solicitor Quinby, the second from his aunt Amelia in Suffolk, inquiring after his well-being. This last letter, however, had been the most telling.

He thought back on Noah's words. *Checkmate.* And it amazed him he had never considered it, for it should have been his foremost thought. Wallace Burnett. The Marquess of Kinsborough. His father's biggest rival.

Other than what he had learned of him through the collecting circles—and even that was precious little since the marquess rarely came out to the auctions himself, having nearly all his business handled by his agent—Robert knew little of the man. He knew he held an estate of considerable size in Yorkshire, he wasn't prone to the usual vices of gaming or drink, and he was spoken of well among his peers as a generous man, an exemplar amid society. The only point of any notoriety attached to him was his well-known rivalry with Robert's father, and even that was considered by most to be naught but humorous sport between gentlemen.

But there was nothing humorous in the way Robert's father would speak of the man with noticeable bitterness in his voice. Robert remembered once asking his mother, the duchess, the reasons why the two men opposed one another so fiercely. She had just shaken her head, telling Robert that the past was better left alone and that whatever had brought on this mutual enmity had occurred many years before, when Kinsborough had attended Cambridge with his father. Apparently it was there at the university that the two men had first met, there that the spark of fierce competition between them was struck, a competition the likes of which would last a lifetime.

A competition which in the end, Robert then reminded himself, hadn't lasted a lifetime after all.

Could Kinsborough have set the fire in order to finish the battle between the rivals once and for good? Having the Devonbrook collection gone would certainly elevate Kinsborough's own collection to a position of some distinction among society in Town. From his father's records as to where the various pieces had been housed, the majority of the collection had been at Devonbrook House, and thus had been destroyed by the fire. Kinsborough, too, had known the role Robert played in his father's passion. Could he have begun circulating the rumors of Robert having been the one responsible for the fire in order to pull attention, and suspicion, away from himself?

Robert thought again of what Noah had written, of his father having told Lord Cheveley how he would soon checkmate Kinsborough. What had his father been hinting at? It had been a part of their agreement that Robert held sway over all acquisitions for the collection. Anything of that nature would have been handled by him. Still, the duke could have pursued a piece without discussing it with Robert. Had he somehow learned of something so extraordinary that he'd gone after it without first involving his son? And could

Kinsborough have learned of it, too, deciding that the competition between university comrades had finally gone too far?

"Is that all my brother writes?" Robert asked then, realizing Catriona had grown quiet.

"No. He goes on a bit more." Catriona continued.

I have sent along the latest newspapers giving what is known of the situation in France, thinking Forbes might read them aloud for you. Tolley writes that the mood in Brussels is that of jubilant expectation. There are balls each night and the boys are dancing till dawn, never knowing when they might be called to fight. Napoleon is yet in Paris and has failed to open negotiations for peace with the Allies. Peace! Can you believe his gall? The Allied Nations await his next move, which will surely be an offensive one. Wellington stands ready to defeat him and will make certain he cannot return to power a third time. The suspicion here in London is that the fight will be shortly won and then they can all return to Paris for their long-awaited holidays. I will forward any further correspondence I receive from him. Hoping all is well with you, and awaiting your reply. Your brother, Noah.

Robert was silent for a time, contemplative. He knew well that feeling of waiting, the anticipation of the coming fight, yet not knowing when or where it would emerge. The desire to be with Tolley and his countrymen on the Continent filled him, yet the fact that he would be able to do little more than get in the way remained. Robert prayed Wellington would emerge victorious even while he told himself he must not focus on it. He was a part of the events taking place in France, yet he was distinctly removed from it. Instead he could but sit. And wait to hear from Tolley. And hope.

Until then, he must take his attentions away from the Continent, and the only way for him to do this would be to concentrate all his efforts on uncovering the truth of the fire. Given Noah's letter, Kinsborough's possible connection seemed a likely place to look into.

"I am assuming since you read so well you also can write?" he asked.

"Yes, of course," Catriona answered.

"Would you be willing to transcribe my dictated reply to my brother?"

"Certainly. Although it is getting too late to do so today. Tomorrow, perhaps?"

Robert nodded. It would give him the night to consider his next course of action. "Tomorrow would be fine."

"I shall come at midday so that I might afterwards do some reading. After midday, then?"

"I will be expecting you."

Robert was standing at the window in the library when Catriona returned the following day. He had spent the night after she'd gone marshaling his thoughts, considering every possibility which could have led to the fire. Through all his musings, two things in particular seemed always in the forefront. The Marquess of Kinsborough and Rosmorigh. Just how the two were connected to his father he had yet to discover, but he would. He was determined to.

Robert turned when Catriona came into the room. She stopped, noticing immediately he did not wear his spectacles.

"You are by the window," she said, smiling.

"The pain lessens." He stepped away, toward her more, stopping at his chair. He placed both hands on the back of it. "A fortnight ago, I would not have been able to stand before an open window like that without cringing. But now, there are actually times when the pain is nearly tolerable." He paused. "Surely that is a good sign, and I have only you to thank."

"Me?"

"Yes. If you hadn't taken me out beyond these walls yesterday, I would have stayed here locked away in the dark, behind my black lenses the rest of my days. I never would have known the touch of the sea air or the warmth of the sun against my face again. I never would have known how much I could miss having things like that in my life. It is astounding, really, the things we take for granted when they are always present. It is when they are gone that you realize how important they really were."

Catriona suspected he was speaking of more than the sun and the wind against his face, and she wasn't certain how she should reply. She had never been able to give anything of any significance to anyone. Flowers she had picked in a field for her mother. A hatband she had fashioned out of the MacBryan plaid for her father. But this—to know that she had given someone who had been lost the hope of something better, and to have given it to *him*; it gave her a sense of true elation.

"You said you wished me to draft a letter to your brother?" she said, moving to sit behind the striped wood desk. She took up the quill.

"Dear Noah," Robert began. "Your letter has given me a thought which I should like you to pursue at the earliest possibility. The Marquess of Kinsborough. You can enlist Quinby to assist in any way. Look into the state of his finances, his whereabouts during the past several months, especially the night of February 22nd, and anything else you can think of that might be of consideration. I will wait for your next post and will continue my own work from here. Your brother, Robert."

Catriona dusted the letter to dry it then folded it. "Have you a seal?"

"My father should have one in the desk. Top drawer."

Catriona opened the drawer. It was empty inside except for a small, flat wooden box pushed far against the back. She pulled it out. "Oh," she said upon opening it.

"What is it?"

"I had thought a box which I found inside the drawer might contain your father's seal, but it instead holds a quantity of papers."

Robert came around the chair, making his way slowly toward her. "Papers?"

"Yes." Catriona quickly scanned the topmost sheet. "Written pages. It looks as if it might be a descriptive discourse of some sort. In fact it is even titled here on the second page. 'A Narrative Journey through the Highlands of Scotland written by His Grace, James Edenhall, the fifth Duke of Devonbrook.' Was your father perhaps planning to write a chronicle detailing his holidays spent here at Rosmorigh?"

"I wouldn't know," answered Robert. "I wasn't even aware of Rosmorigh's existence. Although, it could serve to account for his numerous visits here."

Catriona read on, skimming through the pages. "With each section of the discourse, he seems to choose a particular setting nearby to the castle, then describes it, giving his own estimation of it, similar to that which Boswell published describing his tour through the islands with Johnson." She giggled then as she began reading the first part of the chronicle.

"What is it?"

"It says here your father went to see the Widow Gorrie early on in his excursions. The widow is a tenant at Rosmorigh and his description of her is both amusing and accurate. He writes, 'The woman living in this croft is most curious. Her skin has a most unhealthy color to it unlike anything I have ever before seen. She offered me her chair to sit and take a rest, but I politely refused, given her peculiar perfume.' "

"What is so peculiar about her perfume?"

"Mostly that she wears none. In fact, she rarely bathes at all because she believes it is the Devil's way of reaching one's soul through the skin. Even more so to ward away *auld Clootie* as she calls him, she rubs her skin with a preparation she makes from a mixture of plants. One of the plants she uses has given her her nickname—Valeria. It is the valerian plant she uses that gives her a most unusual smell and what is worse, using this mixture as she does without bathing has turned her skin quite blue!"

Robert smiled, amused. "Is she mad?"

"Not truly. Just a bit confused sometimes." Catriona looked through the next few sheets. "It looks as if your father undertook to visit all of Rosmorigh's tenants on his journeys. He writes of each one, as well as the places he stopped while out and anyone he encountered along the way." She quickly flipped through to the ending pages of the script. "It looks as if he wrote clear through to the last time he came here."

The last time he came here. A thought struck Robert then. "Catriona, would you be able to take me to these same places? The ones described in my father's journal? I would like to go where my father went and have you read to me his description of each place. It might help me to understand, to discover what brought him here so often. I need to know why he came here and why he never told anyone about it."

The desperation in Robert's voice was so prevalent. Without even thinking first, she asked, "Robert, what happened to your father?"

Robert's face instantly went still, and a look most frightening darkened his features. Catriona expected him to refuse to answer her. In fact, she realized she shouldn't have asked at all. "I'm sorry."

He shook his head. "It is all right. I have tried shutting it out for so long now, refusing to think of it, and never speaking of it. Perhaps the time has come now to admit what really happened."

He began slowly. "There was a fire, it was at my family's seat in Lancashire. Most of my family were killed, my father, my older brother, Jameson, and his wife and young son. And Pietro."

"Pietro?"

"He was my valet." Robert hesitated. "Actually, he was much more than that. He saved my life once." He tightened his jaw as he fought against his emotions, his hand clenched tightly in a fist at his side. Catriona waited, sensing Robert had more to say. And he did.

"I first came across Pietro when I was on the Peninsula years ago. I had been apprehended by a French unit out on patrol. They'd locked me in a storage closet in an abandoned farmhouse while they tried to decide whether I was the Spanish courier I'd claimed, or the English soldier I really was. My explanation of having taken my red uniform jacket off a dead Englishman hadn't done much to convince them. They were on the verge of ending the debate, having decided to kill me, when Pietro freed me by picking the lock on the closet door."

"He took great risk in helping you."

"The risk mattered nothing to him. Pietro hated the French. They had killed his family—his mother and his sisters—when they had invaded his village, leaving him at sixteen with no means of survival. After he helped me to escape from the closet, I appointed him my batman. He went everywhere with me, and then after the war I brought him back with me to England to give him a better life." Robert closed his eyes. "And instead I took his life away. If I hadn't convinced him to return with me, he never would have been at Devonbrook House that night when the fire broke out. It is something I shall never forgive myself."

Catriona felt a terrible chill pass through her. She reached out and took his hand. "You never could have known."

Robert just shook his head.

"Your sight," she said then, suddenly realizing the

one thing Robert had neglected mentioning. "You lost your sight in the fire, didn't you? That is why you came to Scotland, to grieve for your family and your friend?"

"I came here for them, yes, but not solely to grieve. I came hoping to find the truth." He took a slow breath. "The fire was not accidental, Catriona. It was set deliberately."

"And you believe it is in some way connected to Rosmorigh?"

"I know it is. My father had never told anyone about this place or his visits here. I only learned of the property upon receiving the details of my inheritance from my solicitor after his death. That was most unlike my father, for he had never been a secretive man. After learning of Rosmorigh, I wondered if it might have something to do with his death. I came here to find out for myself. I came to search for the truth."

Truth. The conversation she had heard that night, the things Forbes had said about Robert. It started to make sense to her now. "Your servants believe you set the fire, don't they? That is why you wish me to read your letters to you. That is why you do not trust them."

Robert frowned. "It is generally believed by my servants and by most everyone in London as well that since I was the only survivor of the fire and would benefit the most by it, I must have set it deliberately in order to inherit the title which was to have been my brother's. I never wanted the title. My God, my brother and his wife and son died in the fire, too. And Elizabeth was with child. What sort of monster do they believe me?"

Robert closed his eyes tightly, trying to take hold of his emotions. But Catriona could not help the tears that were now falling down her own cheeks. To have lost his sight in the fire was terrible enough, but to have been accused of purposefully murdering his own family. It is no wonder he'd come to Scotland.

Robert hadn't come to search for the treasure. What he sought was something far more precious than any case of gold.

Robert had come to find the person responsible for killing his family, and now she was going to help him.

Chapter Nine

Catriona turned as Robert walked out onto the inner courtyard to join her. It had been a peaceful morning, cool, but now that it was nearing midday, the skies were clear and the sunlight was shining down on them through the crenellated parapets of the tower that rose high above them. A slight wind ruffled Robert's dark hair above the standing collar of his dove gray waistcoat, his full white sleeves billowing in the wind. His top boots crunched on the graveled walkway. She noticed he wore his spectacles against the light. Forbes, having seen to the task of his master's direction there, turned to leave, moving without a word back to the castle.

"Are you ready?" Catriona asked.

"A moment, please." Robert stood still, the sounds of the sea and the soaring gulls echoing around them in the secluded bailey. "Describe to me what it looks like."

Catriona looked around them. "We are in the center courtyard. A gatehouse leads out to the landward side and is covered thick with ivy on one side. The main tower is tall, standing above the cliff side and looking out onto the sea. The cries you hear are the kittiwakes who are nesting in the eaves and watching us now from the battlements above. I've always thought Rosmorigh the most beautiful castle ever built."

Robert was silent a moment and then he nodded. "We can go now."

"Have you a horse?" Catriona asked.

Robert frowned. "I had thought we would be walking."

"The journal indicates your father set out on horseback. It is a rugged landscape and most of the places he traveled to would be too far and too difficult to reach on foot."

Robert had not considered that they would need to ride; he hadn't been on the back of a horse since before the fire. Anywhere he had gone had been either on foot with someone's assistance, or riding in a carriage. He had, however, brought his stallion Bayard with him from London, hoping, perhaps foolishly, that he might regain his sight and be able to ride once again.

"I do have a horse, a stallion. Bayard is strong, though a bit spirited. Perhaps if we both were to ride him, you could direct him to where we need to go, and I could help to keep him under control."

Catriona agreed and Robert called for the groom to bring Bayard. Once they had both mounted, Catriona took Robert's arms around her waist and set his hands over hers on the reins, then she touched her heels to Bayard's sides and they started off.

Robert was surprised at how easily he was able to acclimate himself again to the back of his horse without his sight. From the tension on the reins he could feel when Bayard was lowering his head to snatch a bite of grass, or when he was stretching out his neck, readying to start on a run. He kept him at an easy canter, rolling with the smooth gait in the saddle.

It was the nearness to Catriona which was disconcerting him more.

His arms held her, his legs brushed against hers with every movement of the horse, and after they'd ridden awhile, she began to grow relaxed. Soon she was leaning back against him, her back pressed into his chest, her head resting gently against his shoulder. Robert wondered if she even knew how soft her hair was as it blew across his cheek. More than once he found himself turning his face into the silken strands, taking in its sweet scent, and had to school himself to turn away.

Robert realized he had been fighting an attraction to her from the very beginning, even while he told himself a man like him who had been so ruled by his sight before could never be tempted sexually by someone he had never even seen. Before his blindness, one of his greatest pleasures had been watching women, how they moved, fluid, graceful, so differently from men. He hadn't the slightest notion what she looked like, yet every time Catriona came near him, he only wanted to be closer to her, to feel her skin, to know her softness. And even as he denied this attraction to himself again now, sitting on this horse with her perched before him on the saddle, moving close against his hips, he could not help but want to know her completely.

They had come through some trees now, for the breeze was again blowing freely across his face, the sunlight warm. In the distance, Robert could hear the sound of water softly trickling. There was a smell of fresh earth and moss in the air. Catriona pulled Bayard to a slow halt.

"This is the first place your father came to in his chronicle," she said. "It is a small burn which runs into Loch Linnanglas and then further on into the sound. He spent some time sitting on a grouping of boulders beside it while he wrote of it. Shall we dismount and I will read to you what he has written?"

Despite that he was reluctant to move away, Robert

thought it certainly the wisest course, especially since
deny it as he might, their closeness and the intimacy
of their contact was beginning to bring forth a physi-
cal reaction from him, one she would no doubt notice
very soon.

" 'It is a chilly morning this day,' " Catriona began reciting once Robert was sitting at the edge of the
burn, " 'but I could not pass this sight without first
stopping, both to water my horse and to take in this
tranquil place. It is autumn and the leaves are a brilliant orange and yellow, splashed beneath which is the
green glen floor. I think I should like to have it painted
someday for my collection. The waters of this brook
are fresh and clear and I could not resist the urge to
take a drink myself. I find myself staring in wonder at
the place, which looks so untouched by man, and the
history which it no doubt has seen.' "

Robert didn't need to have his sight in order to visu-
alize this scene, his father had described it so vividly.
He could imagine the duke sitting on this very rock,
scribbling in this journal, and somehow he felt close to
him by being here. He took off his spectacles, setting
them beside him. He closed his eyes against the instant
shock of pain the sunlight brought to him and tilted his
face upward toward light, drinking in its warmth. On
impulse, he stood and moved toward the sound of the
water.

"What are you doing?"

"I'm thirsty and I'm taking a drink." Robert knelt
down on the mossy bank, reaching outward until his
fingers dipped into the cool liquid.

"You should be careful, Robert. It is slippery at the
edge and—"

Even before she could finish, Robert lost his footing.
With a resounding splash, he plunged face first into
the burn.

"Damnation!" he shouted as he rose, trying to find his
way back toward the bank. His boots had filled and his

feet were heavy as he dragged them through the water. Each time he reached the burn's edge, he only slipped again on the mud-slick surface, and each time his frustration mounted. Finally he just stood, knee-deep in the middle of the burn, his hair dripping over his unseeing eyes, wishing he could slam his fist into something hard.

"Robert," Catriona called to him from the edge, "reach out and I will take your hand."

"No!" He slapped his hand against the water, spraying it outward. "I am grown, not a child who has yet to learn to walk."

"Then stop acting like one, Robert," Catriona threw back at him. "And stop using your blindness as a means for hiding your grief."

Robert's anger exploded into rage. "I am not using my blindness! And I will not be pitied like some poor helpless wretch! I am a man. I have scaled the sides of buildings inches from enemy patrols. I have infiltrated French camps where no one even suspected who I was. I have fought men and I have killed men when it meant my life or theirs. So I can certainly take a drink of water from a brook without requiring the assistance of a bloody nursemaid!"

Catriona was silent for a long time before she said, frighteningly calm, "Then since you are so capable, you can certainly find your way back to Rosmorigh on your own."

Robert must have stood nearer the edge of the burn than he'd thought. He knew this because seconds later she pushed him. Hard. And having been unable to see it coming, he fell back into the water like a felled oak.

He floundered, shocked, then managed to stand, water dripping now from every inch of him as he listened to the sound of Catriona walking away, her skirts rustling over the tall grass. He had deserved it. He realized that even as he'd been shouting at her like an idiot.

He deserved for her to be angry with him. He deserved for her to leave him there until nightfall, standing and soaked to the skin. He deserved to catch the devil of a cold and spend the next two weeks sneezing his fool head off.

Why had he come at her like that? Catriona was the one person who didn't treat him as if he were an oddity, an invalid for his blindness. She refused to accept the limitations of it, and merely found ways around it. More, she didn't make him feel as if he were less than an entire man for not having his sight.

And knowing this about her, he realized that she wouldn't have left him there to find his way back to the castle alone.

His eyes burned painfully and his head pounded from the exposure to the sunlight. And he had no idea where he'd left his spectacles. He felt every inch an ass. He called her name, but she didn't answer, further prolonging his humility.

"I am sorry, Catriona. I shouldn't have yelled at you like I did. It was wrong of me."

Still no response.

"Certainly, you aren't planning to stand idly by and watch me bloody my nose by walking into a tree?"

"Of course I wouldn't. And there are no trees in the burn."

Robert turned in the direction of her voice. She was standing closer than he would have thought, just a few feet away from the edge of the burn. "Will you help me to find my way out of here? Please?"

Catriona hesitated and then finally said, "If you but step forward and to the right a little, there is a place where the grass grows down into the water. You should be able to find solid footing there."

A fine teacher, Robert thought, for she was going to make certain her lesson was truly learned. It was a few moments later when Robert was standing on the grassy bank, humble and dripping wet. He held out his hand. "Can we call it a truce?"

He felt her hand slide into his. "It is all right for you to need someone sometimes, Robert. It doesn't make you pitiful or helpless. It only makes you human."

Need. Robert couldn't remember having ever really needed anyone since he'd been a boy. It was a thing he had always prided himself on, his self-sufficiency. With Jameson having been heir to the Devonbrook title, Robert had had to find his own way of making a living on a younger son's allotment. The customary occupations of law, medicine, or the Church held precious little interest for him. It was through his own cunning and accomplishment that he'd finally made his place and his fortune in the acquiring and selling of art. And since that time, need was a weakness to him, a vulnerability he had always and steadfastly refused to forfeit himself to. But this resistance, this refusal to accept anyone's help had always pertained to his father or his brother. Not to this slip of a Scottish girl.

Robert stood still as Catriona step closer beside him. She reached up and softly pushed back his dripping hair from his face, wiping the wetness from his cheek. She replaced his spectacles, slipping them gently over his eyes. "You do not have to be alone, Robert, if you would but allow it."

Robert felt something change inside him, a tightness that began slowly to loosen. He should be cold, for he was soaked through and the wind carried a definite chill with it. He should be frustrated and angry, or even abjectly ashamed, but it wasn't anger or shame that had brought his body to feeling as if it were on fire. All he knew at that moment was wanting. And all he wanted was her.

Without a further thought to logic or what should have been, Robert reached out and took Catriona, pulling her close against him. She didn't say a word. He touched the side of her face with his hand and lowered his mouth over hers slowly, kissing her gently until any trace of anger at his inability to see had vanished. He wanted, needed to feel like a man, a complete man. And this woman was the one person on earth who would allow him that freedom.

He could feel the touch of Catriona's breath warm against his lips when he lifted his mouth slightly from hers. His head was still bent close and he wished he could see her face, to look into her eyes, to know her reaction. Neither of them spoke. They had no need to. The birds chirped in the trees overhead. The breeze moved over them, wrapping them in the scent of wildflowers. No garden was ever more like Eden.

A grumbling of thunder murmured in the distance then, and the spell, that strange and wondrous magic which had wound around them from the moment Catriona had come up beside him at the bank of the burn had gone.

"There are clouds gathering off the coast," she said. And then immediately after, "Remove your shirt and your boots."

Robert stilled. "I beg your pardon?"

"Your shirt is soaked and your boots are filled with water. It is fast growing cold. I will at least wring the water from your shirt so you don't catch a chill from this wind. There is a rock behind you where you can sit."

Robert sat down, silent as a stick, and pulled off his boots, handing them to Catriona.

Catriona turned. Her heart was pounding furiously as she walked back to the burn to empty Robert's boots, and she wasn't quite certain why. She wondered how she could have gone from wanting to cosh him on the head in one moment to wanting nothing more than to be in his arms, kissing him again the next. She was glad he hadn't been able to see the true affect he'd had on her, how she had lost all strength in her knees and truly believed she'd just stumbled into a dream. She knew that it was his frustration with his blindness which had driven him to kissing her, just as it had made him lash out like he had. They both had been acts committed without thought.

It had been the same such reaction when she'd pushed him into the burn. Catriona rarely got angry. It just wasn't in her nature. But when Robert had compared her to a nursemaid, something inside of her snapped like a twig. She still didn't understand it. But she did know she must never let him affect her that way again. It was foolish. And even more, it was dangerous.

She finished emptying his boots. "I'm afraid these will still be a bit soggy, but at least you won't slosh when you walk. Now, let me see that—"

Catriona turned toward Robert to retrieve his wet shirt, and when she did, she froze.

He was standing before her, his shirt off, his dark hair damp and glistening in the ebbing sunlight. *My God,* she thought staring at him in mute astonishment. *He is beautiful.* The sight of him uncovered, his chest muscled and bare, stunned Catriona more than had his kiss. He was magnificent, more magnificent than any painting could ever be, his muscles defined, his stomach flat and planed, his shoulders broad and strong. He was everything she would ever imagine a man to be, everything she had imagined him to be before she had met him, when he had still been only an image in a portrait and a dream in her head. Her heart was racing now and she let out a slow breath in a failing effort to calm it.

"Is something wrong?" he said then.

"No." She swallowed. "Here, let me take that shirt and see what I can do to make it a little less waterlogged."

Catriona handed Robert his boots and took the shirt, quickly turning away. But as she twisted the sodden fabric in her hands, she glanced back at him, wondering what it would feel like to run her fingers over the solid length of him. His skin looked smooth, like a statue, but warm, where marble was cold. Good God, had she gone mad? What was she thinking?

This man was a duke. He was nobility, a peer. He had vast property and wealth beyond her imagination. She was naught but a poor crofter's daughter with a whimsical fantasy of buried treasure and knights in shining armor.

Catriona flipped the wrinkles out of his shirt with a sharp snap. "I've gotten this as dry as it will get. We had better start back for Rosmorigh. We can head back out on the morrow and resume following your father's journal. The clouds are coming in quite fast. It looks as if we are in for rain."

Rain it did.

No sooner had they left the guarded, tree-shrouded glen near the burn and were out on the open moors then did the skies above them open with a resounding clap. Heavy drops showered down upon them, pelting them. It was astounding. The gentle breeze which had lifted Bayard's silvery mane as they had walked along the small trail that led through the wood now whipped through the tall broom grass and heather in the moor fields like an icy unforgiving hand sweeping away everything in its path.

Bayard had begun to grow skittish at the first thunder and was now dancing about, jerking his head as Catriona struggled to keep control of him. The smell of his fear rose from his rain-slick skin. When a crack of thunder exploded just above them, he lifted his front hooves from the ground, bunching up his hind legs, readying to bolt, and would have had Robert not quickly taken up the reins, tucking the horse's head tight against his chest.

"Is there any place nearby where we might find shelter?" Robert asked, shouting above the near-howling wind.

"Yes." Catriona squeezed her fingers into Bayard's thick mane, hugging her knees tightly around his girth. "There is a crofter's cottage just a short distance away. We should be able to reach it before the wind grows much worse."

It took them some time to make any distance, for Bayard continued dancing about, ready to tear off at any given moment. The wind and the increasing rain were making it difficult to see, and it seemed as if the storm might overtake them when Catriona finally made out the outline of the cottage ahead. As they drew close, she dropped from Bayard's back. She waited until Robert had slid down after her, then yanked the frightened horse forward, taking Robert's arm with her free hand.

She pounded on the heavy door, calling out, "*Hoo!* Mr. Allan! 'Tis Catriona MacBryan! Can you shelter us from the storm, sir?"

When no response came, she pounded again. "Mr. Allan? Are you there?"

The rain began to fall harder, the din it created drowning out Catriona's voice. Lightning shot through the dark sky above them, causing Bayard to rear up in response, his eyes wide and frightened. Catriona had to let go of Robert to maintain her hold on the reins.

"Catriona!"

"It is all right. I've got him," she shouted and pulled the frightened horse back toward the cottage door. She quickly covered his eyes with her tartan shawl. "I do not think Mr. Allan is here. Do you think you can break the door free?"

Robert flattened his hands against the rough wooden door. Stepping back two paces, he lifted his foot and kicked it hard. The second time he tried it, the door sprang open.

"Come on," he shouted and he moved with her inside.

Catriona struggled to lead Bayard in behind them. Once inside, sheltered from the wind and rain, the horse calmed down immediately. Catriona fixed the damaged door shut with a sack of oats set nearby.

Inside the thick and sturdy fail and divot walls of the tiny cottage, the sounds of the storm seemed another world away. Catriona lit a candle and led Robert to a chair before taking Bayard further inside, keeping his head down so he wouldn't brush it against the low ceiling.

"Mr. Allan won't be angry at our intrusion?" Robert asked.

"If he were to find out what had happened, that we had been caught in this storm so near his stead, he would be more offended if we hadn't sought shelter here. He is a good friend of my father's."

"And Bayard, does Mr. Allan's hospitality extend to horses as well?"

Catriona laughed softly. "Of course. If he wasn't away kelping down the coast, Mr. Allan's own flock would already be inside. He's just taken them off to be tended by someone while he is away."

"Mr. Allan sleeps under the same roof as his animals?"

"Most Scots bed down with their animals. It is a custom long practiced, starting from the days of the reivers when they brought the flocks and herds inside to keep them from being stolen. And a good thing it is, for now there is feed for Bayard. I'll see about getting us a fire started and perhaps something to eat. The storm shows no signs of letting up, so we may be here awhile."

Within a half hour Catriona had a good blaze burning in the stone hearth. A short time later she had dishes of hot porridge and mugs of warm heather ale set out before them on the table.

"It's not the tastiest of meals, but it will fill us and keep us warm," she said.

They chatted while they ate, and Catriona nearly

forgot about the storm raging outside. Occasionally a jagged streak of lightning would blaze through the sky, which had quickly darkened black as the night, flashing through the two small windows set in the walls. Soon the storm was right above them, its fierce report shuddering through the tiny cottage.

"The thunder reminds me of when I was in Spain," Robert said, sitting back.

Catriona put on a kettle to boil. "I had read of the wars in several of the news sheets that your father would leave behind after his visits to Rosmorigh. Many of the neighboring crofters have older sons who served in the Highland regiments, and who went back after the news had reached them of Napoleon's return."

Robert nodded. "In Spain they call this kind of storm *el tempestad*."

"In Gaelic it is called *gailleann nan sliabh*."

"*Galeen-an-sli*," Robert attempted uncertainly.

"Not exactly," Catriona said. "It is in how you form the words with your mouth." She took his hand. "Come closer." He did, and leaning forward, her face near to his, Catriona pressed his fingertips against her lips. Softly then she repeated, *"Gailleann nan sliabh."*

It was the most seductive touch Robert had ever known. He did not move even after she released his hand. He couldn't. He kept his fingers pressed close to her lips, trying to take control of the kindling emotions inside of him.

Neither of them spoke for some time. The storm roared outside. The fire crackled in the hearth. Catriona's heart was pounding. She watched Robert's face in the firelight, the hesitance, the uncertainty. She didn't move. When he came forward and replaced his fingers with his lips, she melted against him, taking his kiss and returning it with her own. It was as if they had been swept away by a furious current, the two of them riding out the storm that had begun between them, a storm more fierce, more potent than the one raging outside.

When he finally pulled away, Catriona couldn't move. Words were beyond her. She had promised herself she wouldn't allow herself this bliss, and that promise had already been broken. She wanted to say something, but could think of nothing. The heavy silence between them might have grown awkward had the posset Catriona left simmering over the fire not chosen that precise moment to boil over.

She hastened from her chair, grabbed a pot hook from beside the hearth, and lifted the cauldron away from the flames.

When she returned to the table, Robert was frowning.

"I'm sorry," he said. "I shouldn't have done that."

"I'm not sorry," she answered. "Not at all."

When he didn't respond, she stood and moved to the window. "The storm still doesn't seem to be letting up and there won't be enough peats to last through the night. It looks as if we will have to sleep here before the fire."

"Your family. Surely they will be worried."

"Yes, they no doubt will, but they also realize I know how to shelter myself. Your people at Rosmorigh, your servants, they will be the ones to worry. They will most likely think I lured you from the castle and then did you in."

"If that were so, they would rejoice."

"Then they are cruel as well as foolish." Catriona lifted the lid on a large wooden trunk set against the wall. "Mr. Allan lives here alone. There are but two blankets and it will get cold during the night, but we can spread out these rush pallets on the floor in front of the hearth to keep warm."

As she unrolled the two pallets and positioned them in front of the hearth, Catriona wondered how she'd ever manage to fall asleep beside him.

Robert listened as she began setting out their make-shift beds, wondering the very same thing. He determined that moment that he wouldn't touch her.

Even if it killed him.

Chapter Ten

The sun was shining through the windows, dappled and new, beaming inside the small cottage when Catriona first heard the voices coming from outside.

"If she's not here, I canna figure where else she could have gone to."

Boots crunched heavily on the gravel pathway. A dog sniffed at the door and whined, scratching at it. Catriona stirred on her pallet, shielding her eyes from the bright morning light.

"The door looks to have been broken. She must be inside."

It took a moment for the voices outside to register to her sleep-hazed mind. And in that moment, the door pushed opened.

Ian Alexander stood frozen on the threshold. Despite that she still wore her shift, Catriona instinctively pulled the blanket up over her breasts to shield her. *Her shift.* Good God, she thought, looking beside her to where Robert had just begun to awaken.

"Catriona?" Robert said, almost simultaneously with Ian.

Robert's voice was confused, sleep-dulled.

Ian's was distinctly angry.

"She's there then, is she, Ian? Thank the Lo—"

At the sight of her father materializing behind Ian,

Catriona wished she could sink into the ground, hoping against hope that she might wake and find this all a terrible nightmare.

"What the devil are you about?" Angus shouted, shoving past Ian with the swift look of murder in his eyes. It was no nightmare, but it was close. It was her father and he was staring not at her, but at Robert, who had risen from his pallet and was standing beside her, his bare chest exposed above his breeches. Catriona wondered which of the two of them Angus would kill first. From the look of rage in his eye, she determined it would likely be Robert.

She took a step toward her father. "Da, please, it is not what you think."

"Not what I think, you say, lass? You're lyin' here in naught but your smalls next to a half-naked stranger who looks every bit a Sasunnach and you're for telling me 'tis not what I think? D'you take me for a fool, Catriona MacBryan? I should have known 'twasna just the books that took you to sneakin' off like you do. And I'll tell you what I think, lass. I think I'll be seein' this bludey Sasunnach swingin' from the nearest tree afore the noontime!"

"No, Da! You cannot! He is the laird!"

Catriona wondered if her father might simply erupt where he stood, so red did his face become then. "The laird, is he? So that English duke finally decided to get rid of this piece of empty land, did he, sellin' it to this young buck? Or did he lose it in a game o' chance like the last bludey good-fer-nothin'? Well, no matter, for he may own the land and think on it only when he fancies to, but he certainly does not own the people who have worked it for longer than his ilk ever laid claim to it. He can rape the land, and he can rape us crofters with his increasin' of the rents, but he'll not be rapin' my daughter, too—"

"Da! Stop it," Catriona said, trying to position herself between her advancing father and Robert. "He has done nothing." Angus shook her off. She grabbed his arm, pulling hard. "Listen to me, Da. We were caught in the storm last night. We'd no place else to go for shelter. Our clothes were soaked. See—they are there by the hearth to dry. There weren't enough peats to last the night, so we had to lay close by the fire to keep from catching cold."

"If I might add a word." Robert stood facing Angus. From the moment he opened his mouth to speak, he immediately silenced all conversation. Catriona was grateful Robert couldn't see the look of hatred that darkened her father's features. "Mr. MacBryan, I can well imagine your anger at finding your daughter here. But despite appearances, I assure you nothing inappropriate has taken place."

"And you expect me to believe that, Sasunnach, when my daughter stands afore us all wearing but a stitch of clothing over herself?"

Robert looked at once confused. "I am sorry, sir. I was not aware . . ."

"What do you mean by sayin' that?"

"I mean I did not know of Catriona's state of undress. I swear to you—"

"Do you think me an idiot? She's standing right afore you, isn't she?"

"Yes, but—"

"No real man could look at her and not want to—"

"Da!" Catriona shouted, cutting him off before he could finish his thought and mortify her completely. "Stop it! He cannot see how I am dressed or not dressed. He cannot see anything. He is blind!"

The room fell absolutely silent. Angus looked from Robert to Catriona, uncertain whether he believed her. Ian stood at the door, his eyes fixed on Catriona.

Catriona reached out to touch her father on his arm. "It is the only reason I would have removed my wet clothing, Da. I would never do anything to bring you shame. It was only because we were soaked to the skin and it was cold and I knew his grace could not see me."

Angus's face went pale. He stared at his daughter

and suddenly looked as if he had just swallowed a rock. "Did you say 'his grace'?"

Catriona nodded. "Yes, Da. He is Robert Edenhall, the Duke of Devonbrook and new laird of Rosmorigh."

The MacBryan stead was located nearer to Mr. Allan's croft than Rosmorigh, so it was to there the motley party traveled after leaving the cottage. No one spoke a word during the cheerless journey. Angus walked in front, leading the way, his white hair gleaming in the morning sunlight. Ian trudged sullenly behind him, his sheepdog Mackie following at his feet. Even Bayard seemed to sense the grim mood as he plodded along behind Catriona and Robert, his head drooping, his hooves nearly dragging over the damp muddy ground.

At the sound of their approach, Mary MacBryan came rushing from the cottage. She was followed after by Mairead, and the two of them stopped abruptly when they saw what awaited them outside.

"Catriona," Mary said, eyeing Robert curiously, "we've been worried half to death over you."

"We were caught in the storm, Mam," Catriona said, kissing her mother on the cheek. She turned to tether Bayard to the tree. "We were too far to make it home so we had to take shelter at Mr. Allan's croft for the night."

Catriona could well imagine what her mother was thinking as she took in the sight of Catriona's hair wild about her face in rusty chestnut waves, her wrinkled skirts, and Robert's equally disheveled appearance. Still, whatever Mary's thoughts, she kept them well hidden. Mairead, on the other hand, looked at Catriona and shook her head in abject dismay.

"Mam," Catriona said, leading Robert forward, "this is Robert Edenhall, the Duke of Devonbrook. He is the new laird of Rosmorigh."

"It is a pleasure to meet you, Mrs. MacBryan," he said.

Mary came forward, wiping her hands on her apron, her eyes wide. Robert had put on his spectacles and the sight of him standing there, coupled with the shock of learning who he was, had to be bewildering for her.

"Your grace." Mary extended her hand to him in greeting, then looked curiously at Catriona when Robert didn't immediately take it.

"He cannot see your hand, Mam," Catriona explained. "The duke is blind."

Robert reached out and Catriona took her mother's hand, placing it in his. Robert bowed over it politely. "I apologize for having worried you over the safety of your daughter. Catriona had been kind enough to take me about the lands surrounding Rosmorigh yesterday, and we were caught in the storm."

Mary smiled. "There is no need—"

"Let us go inside now." Angus stepped in between them, moving for the door. "No doubt his grace is hungry this morn after spending the night in old Eideard Allan's shabby croft. The only thing he keeps to eat in that place is ale and kail. Knowing my Mary, she's got us a feast awaitin' inside."

Catriona took Robert's arm and started leading him inside. She turned when she saw Mairead heading behind her and away from the cottage. Ian had begun to walk back the way they'd come, leaving with Mackie close by his side. Mairead had stopped him and looked to be trying to convince him to join them for breakfast when Catriona turned again to go into the house.

"His grace will sit here," Angus said, motioning to his own chair at the head of the huge oak table. Mary looked at Angus as if he'd grown a second head, for no one except Angus was ever allowed in that chair, but Catriona knew well her father's reasons for offering the honored place to Robert.

Despite his innate distrust of the English, Angus could not ignore the fact that Robert was a duke and laird of the land he lived on and as such was to be given both his respect and his warmest hospitality. It was the way of the Scots and had been for centuries. And beyond that, evictions were becoming more common, an ever-increasing threat to the tenant crofters, for sheep farming had been found to bring more of a profit to the landholders, a steady income without the ever-present risk of a bad crop yield to prevent the rents from coming in. No one could afford to allow their personal emotions and Scottish pride to rise above their primary responsibility, that of keeping a roof over their families' heads. Not even the Scots-proud Angus MacBryan.

"Well, wife, let's not stand there looking all muddled in the face like you are now. Get you us some food for the laird."

Catriona went to Mary and together with Mairead, who had just come in with Ian, they began setting out dish after dish of food.

Angus had been right. Mary had prepared a feast, no doubt rising before the dawn and working through the morning until she had heard them approaching. Mary always baked whenever she was worried, making far more than they would be able to consume in a week's time, and leaving Catriona and her sister to take what remained to the neighboring crofters.

As she took the basket of oatcakes to the table, Catriona glanced over to Ian. He was sitting at the far end of the table, a part of the assembly, yet still somehow removed. Tall, even handsome in his way, with sandy brown hair and eyes the color of the summer sky, he had a manner that was both quiet and unobjectionable. He would someday make a fine husband, but not to her, for even without Mary's objections to it Catriona knew she could never wed him.

She cared for Ian, yes, but cared for him as one would a friend or a brother, for hadn't Angus always treated Ian like the son he'd never had? Ian's father Callum had been Angus's closest friend, and when he and his wife had left Scotland for America, they had left their fourteen-year-old son behind to stay with his grandmother until he could be sent for. Angus had promised to take care of Ian, to watch over him until the day when he would join his parents in the new land.

But that day hadn't come, for the Alexanders had never arrived at the New World they had risked so much for and had dreamed of bringing their son to. They had succumbed to sickness during the journey over in the disease-ridden, overcrowded transport hulk, the one on which they'd used every bit that they had to pay for their passage.

Angus had been good to his word. He'd seen to Ian's education and then, when he had come into his twentieth year, he'd brought Ian into the trade, a trade that was both risky and uncertain—the smuggling trade.

Catriona hated that her father involved himself in such a dangerous undertaking, for he was ever on the lookout for the landguard who were known to fire first before asking any questions. At the same time, though, she could not help but feel proud, for it was because of Angus they and their neighbors were able to obtain the necessities they could no longer afford to buy from Scottish merchants, necessities which were too heavily taxed by the English government. Whenever Angus returned from the coast, he always brought back with him quantities of salt for curing, tea, and tobacco, even sugar, risking his freedom, and his life, to give them all these precious things. He'd become a hero among the crofting community, a hero at a price that might one day prove too costly.

Catriona often heard her mother up late during the nights when Angus was away, pacing the floor in front of their box bed. But that would change, Catriona knew, when she found the cask containing the lost gold from the Bonnie Prince's treasure. Angus would no longer have to involve himself in the smuggling. He would be safe and they would never have to worry over paying the rents again.

And Rosmorigh was the key to it all. Somewhere in that vast, book-filled library lay the answer to the

mystery. Catriona had to find it, and somehow before
Robert learned of it first.

For as much as she didn't like it, it was a deception
Catriona had no choice but to play.

No real man could look at her and not want to . . .

Those words alone had occupied Robert's thoughts
since the moment he had returned with Catriona to
Rosmorigh.

He swallowed down what remained of his second
glass of brandy, numb now to the burning it had brought
to his throat. What Angus had said when he'd first discovered them in the cottage that morning, finding his
daughter alone and unclothed with a stranger, had cut
deeply. In those few words Angus had quickly summed
up exactly what Robert had lost in the fire, beyond his
family and his ability to see. And it didn't matter that
Angus had never finished his thought before Catriona
had cried out for him to stop. It was those first three
words which bore the undeniable truth that Robert was
faced with; and no matter how he tried, he could not put
them aside.

No real man.

Robert had never been the sort of man given to indis-
cretion in his private life. His mistresses had been rela-
tively few when compared to his peers, always lovely,
and always quite willing to share his bed. Robert
appreciated them. He loved looking at them, loved the
way looking at them made him feel. Potent, sensual,
virile. He had never been a hurried lover, or selfish in
seeking his own pleasure before first bringing pleasure
to his partner. Their enjoyment had only heightened his
own, adding to his fulfillment. It wasn't vanity or nar-
cissism. Just simple maleness. A thing far more heady
to him than anything else he'd experienced in life.
None of the women he had known could have said with
any honesty that he was less than an attentive lover.
And because of this he knew he would never before

have spent a night alone lying beside a scantily clad young woman, completely oblivious of her.

Certainly not a woman like Catriona.

The times when Catriona wasn't with him had begun to stretch on into eternity, filled with nothing but thoughts of her, images of what she must look like. That was the worst part of it. Robert thought of the hundreds of paintings he had seen during the course of his life. Such remarkable creations, so captivating one dared not look away for fear never to behold such a thing of absolute and marvelous beauty again. He had seen images so real they had made his heart pound in awe for the artist's skill. Yet somehow Robert knew none of them would compare to Catriona.

He knew this—and he hadn't even seen her.

A sudden thud on the floor in front of him, close by to where he knew Catriona sat reading, drew Robert from his thoughts.

"What is it?"

"There is a coal," Catriona said. "It has fallen from the fire."

Fire.

Panic shot like an arrow straight through him.

Robert stood, moving for her, but only knocked the table over, and with it the brandy bottle. It smashed near his feet, but he barely noticed it. He could not see Catriona. He could not hear her. Just like the night at Devonbrook . . .

"No!"

Catriona came to him, taking hold of his arm. "It is all right, Robert. The coal is out. I'm sorry to have alarmed you. There wasn't any real danger."

Robert didn't say a word. He just reached for Catriona and pulled her tightly against him, holding her until his frustration and anger—and fear—had gone.

"I'm sorry," she said softly against his shoulder.

"What do you possibly have to be sorry for?"

"I'm sorry for what has happened to you, Robert, for

the loss of your family, and for the fire, and how it has taken your sight. I can only imagine how you must feel."

Robert released her and reaching behind him, found his chair. He lowered into it. "I only hope you will always imagine, Catriona, and never truly have to know."

Catriona stared at Robert, feeling his pain and realizing she could do nothing about it. He was right. She would never know how he felt, how he hurt at what he had lost. She could imagine and she could condole with him, but she had never known the horror of losing someone she loved to the murderous hand of another.

She thought of his father's discourse. If only she could help him discover who had taken the lives of his family, perhaps then he might allow himself to heal, to live, to seek the future. Perhaps, also . . .

"I should head back for home now," she said, turning to leave. "I will come back in the morning and we can continue with following your father's discourse if you would like."

Robert had turned his face away from her. He was still shaken, frustrated, angry. Catriona waited a moment more, but he remained silent.

"Good night then."

Robert listened as Catriona left the room. After she had gone, he pulled his spectacles from his face and with an anguished cry, he flung them across the room. He then turned his face directly toward the light of the fire, the only light in the room, bright and blazing, and forced himself to look at it.

Pain shot through his head, a pain so intense he had to clench his jaw, biting down hard against it. But he would not close his eyes against it. The pain grew the longer he looked, crippling, sharp, raw. He fought it, refusing to be a casualty to his blindness any longer.

After a short time, the pain slowly began to even out. Shadowy shapes materialized through it, hovering dark and light before him. Nothing was discernible to him, as if his vision was out of focus, muted by a blurred and impenetrable mist. Robert froze his sight on a place where light met dark, trying to ignore the pain of protest in his eyes. He stared at it, screaming at himself in his head to focus, forcing his unseeing eyes to find some sense of recognition in the contrasting shades.

What was it? What lay there just beyond the haze and the blur of the pain? It was something, something moving, rhythmic, steady, the light and the dark switching slowly from side to side. He couldn't discern what it was, couldn't make out even its outline, but it was definitely *something*.

Robert did not move. He feared even to blink, lest the small bit he had, the light and the dark something, might vanish, never to return. Finally, when he could bear the pain no more, when it threatened to bring him down completely, he closed his eyes, dropping his chin to his chest, and let out a heavy breath of frustration.

And then he drew in another breath. A deep and slow breath. A healing breath. A breath of determination. He opened his eyes again.

He would not give up. He would see again. He would sit at this chair and he would stare at that same place, hour after hour, day after day, until he could discover for himself what it was. Light and dark. Forward and back. Something was there. He just had to find it through all the darkness and the shadows, and he would.

And when he did, when he finally saw that something, he would move on to another, something else, and he would concentrate on it until he knew what it was, too. He would continue working at it, each day, until he knew what every object was that was contained in this room, from the largest furnishing to the smallest notion.

He would overcome this. He would not spend the rest of his days living as a blind man, an invalid who was to be pitied and whispered about. He would have his sight back, he would see again, for above all else, he knew he could not leave this life without first seeing Catriona.

Chapter Eleven

Mary MacBryan peeked out the cottage window as she took up her basket of mending from the cupboard. She smiled, catching sight of Catriona beneath the stalwart limbs of the beech tree she had climbed as a child, kneeling over the wooden tub where she was washing out Angus's shirts.

One by one she took them from the murky water, wringing them out before spreading them over the low rock fence by the byre to dry in the early morning sun. The small iron pot of soapwort root Mary had boiled earlier for scrubbing the shirts with sat on the ground beside the tub.

Catriona stood, pressing a dripping hand to the small of her back to ease the twinge which had no doubt come about from her awkward position. Her skirts were covered with dark wet blotches and her sleeves, which she had pushed up on her forearms, were soaked to the elbows, leaving Mary to wonder which of them, Angus's shirts, or Catriona, was the wetter. Her back was to Mary, and Mary could see the rusty-colored wisps of her hair which had come loose from the snood Catriona tried failingly to confine it to. Little bits of it were damp and curling at the back of her neck as she stooped to the tub once again.

Mary turned. She glanced back.

Looking closely at the fence this time, she noticed that several of the shirts had dropped from the fence and were lying like downed soldiers on the grassy ground. One still clung to it desperately, barely hanging on by an arm. Yet another was in danger of being trampled by the stirk, for it had fallen just inches from where the shaggy red beast was grazing. Catriona, meanwhile, was moving back to the tub and—

Mary yanked the door open just in time.

"Catriona!"

Catriona halted inches before she would have tumbled headfirst into the knee-high tub. She turned in the direction of her mother's voice and it was then Mary noticed that the upper half of her face was obscured by the cloth she had fashioned around her head.

"Yes, Mam?"

Mary made her way across the yard to her. "What in heaven are you doin', lass?"

Catriona lifted the cloth from over her eyes to peer curiously at her mother. "I'm putting Da's shirts out to dry." She motioned behind her without turning. "See?"

"Yes, I do see," Mary said, smiling, "and obviously more clearly than do you."

Catriona turned to view her handiwork. At the sight of the fallen shirts littering the ground, she looked back, smiling at her mother. "Sorry, Mam. I'll wash them out again."

The front of Catriona's blue homespun skirts were even wetter than the back. Mary waited, sitting on a low stump while Catriona went to collect the fallen shirts and tossed them back into the tub to soak. Mary already knew, even before asking, what the answer to her next question would be. "Catriona, what were you doin'?"

"I'm washing Da's shirts, of course."

"No, lass. I'm meanin' with that cloth you've got tied 'round your head."

"Oh, that." Catriona reached up and removed the

cloth from where she had pushed it to her forehead, looking at it as he said, "I wondered what it would be like to be blind."

Mary waited a moment in her response. "Because of the young laird, his being blind and all."

Catriona came to Mary, abandoning the shirts to the washtub. "Robert becomes so frustrated when he cannot do things for himself. And after seeing the results of my own efforts, I can begin to understand more his reasons why."

Mary stared at Catriona. "You've feelings for this man—this Robert—do you, Catriona?"

"Why would you think that, Mam?" Catriona said, looking at her mother, surprised at her words, and perhaps even more surprised that something she thought she had hidden so well was really so obvious. Of course she had feelings for Robert. She had loved him in his portrait even before she'd known his name. And now that she knew him, she loved him even more. He'd lost his family to a terrible tragedy and he had been wrongly held up as the one responsible. Robert, this man who had been her guardian, her knight, all the times she'd gone to the castle, keeping her safe, protecting her. And now it was he who needed the protecting. But she couldn't tell anyone that part of it, she knew, for it was foolishness for her to think there would ever be anything more. And her mother surely would agree.

"Catriona MacBryan, I've known you since you came squalling into this life. You're taken with the young laird. I can see it in your eyes. And who wouldna be? I'll say he is a handsome one, this duke." She smiled softly, adding, "This Robert. And if you dinna care for him, you wouldna be out here with this silly cloth tied round your head ready to tumble yourself into a dirty washtub."

Catriona sat down on the stump beside her mother, kicking at a pebble and talking to her toes. Mary MacBryan had never been an easy one to fool. Even when Catriona had been a child, Mary had always known when her daughter had sneaked away a cup of her precious cream for some stray cat, or when she had forgotten to gather blueberries for preserving and had instead spent the day listening to the Colonel's yarns about Jacobite days. And because of this, Catriona knew it would do her little good to try and hide the truth any longer.

"Oh, Mam. I do care for him, yes, but what does it matter? Robert is a duke. He is nobility. And what's more, he is English. He has no use for someone like me. We come from different worlds. Very different." She looked at Mary, adding, "I fear too different."

Aye, Mary thought, but not so different after all. She thought back to a night some twenty years earlier. A dark night. A fateful night. Despite the time which had passed, it was as vivid to her as if it had been yesterday. The heat. The blood. The horrible fear that had later come true. Mary closed her eyes, pushing the nightmare memories away and remembered the tiny babe she'd first held that night while now looking at the woman she'd become.

On the wind which ruffled her woollen skirts over her worn leather shoes, she would have sworn it sounded as if a voice whispered to her then.

'Tis time, Mary.

Mary tried to push it aside, but it was a persistent wind, determined.

She must know. . . .

Mary opened her eyes, realizing the wisdom of the wind's prophetic words. The time for secrets was passed. Now was the time to tell her daughter the truth. "Catriona, there's something—"

"I certainly cannot change that I am a Scottish crofter's daughter," Catriona said, silencing Mary's next words. "Nor would I ever want to. You, Da, and Mairead, you are everything to me. Even if Robert cared for me as I do him, I would never fit into his life, the only life he has known. Just as he would never fit into mine. Splendid dress balls and silk dresses tied off with satin bows—I know nothing of them, Mam. And even if he should ever want me with him, I would be naught but an embarrassment to him, an oddity. I will not do that to him, or to myself either. I cannot."

Mary tempered her tongue from letting go the words she had begun to say. "But the laird knows what you are, Catriona. You brought him here to this cottage."

"Aye, Mam, he may know what I am, but he cannot *see* what I am. Do you ken the difference? I would never know if he would look on me differently were he able to see me, truly see me for who I am, where I come from. Scotland is as foreign to him as London would be to me. Until he can see me as the person I am, I could never hope to . . ."

Catriona never finished her sentence. There was no need for her to. Mary understood more than she cared to admit. She just wished she knew what to do about it.

Then came the wind again.

The time has come.

Catriona stood, returning to the washtub and Angus's shirts. Mary thought a moment longer.

"What if you could give the laird back his sight?"

Catriona looked at her mother. "Mam?"

"You said you would need to know if the laird returned your feelings after he saw you for what you are, aye? What if he could regain his sight?"

"But his sight was lost from injuries in a fire, Mam. No one can say if he will ever see again. The barest light pains him fiercely and he has said his physicians tell him that with there being no change by now, he most probably will never see again."

Mary smiled. "Aye, Catriona, but some cures can only come from the heart. Not the head." She stood. "Come with me, lass."

Mary took Catriona's hand and led her back to the cottage. "Why don't you make us each up a wee *strupag* of tea while I go to fetch something," she said once they were inside, leaving Catriona at the huge oak table as she disappeared into one of the two backrooms.

Catriona set the kettle on the fire to boil, taking out two tin cups and the tea box. Mary returned a short while later, just as Catriona was pouring the water. She held a small wooden box in her hands.

"You must tell no one of this," she said, setting the box on the table. "Not even your sister." She played with its fastening and opened it, removing a smaller one from inside.

She looked at Catriona, placing both of her hands lovingly against its top. "When I was a young lass, no more than nine years of age, my grannam called me to her one night. She was very ill and said she must tell me something afore she would die. You see, my mother had birthed six daughters afore she had me, and another two after. My grannam had also birthed lasses, eleven of them; my mother the seventh of them. Grannam said that this made me the seventh daughter of a seventh daughter, something which haidna occurred in our family for five generations. She said I would be blessed by this and then she gave me this box. My *ciste àraichdeil* is what she called it, and she told me I was to pass it down through each generation to follow until there was another like me, a seventh daughter of a seventh daughter."

Catriona leaned forward in her chair, listening raptly. "And you now wish to give this box to me?"

"Aye, lass, I do, but it is not so much the box that I wish to show you now. There is something which it contains I wish you to see."

Mary lifted the lid, which was carved and polished and looked very ancient indeed, removing something from inside. It was small, fitting into Mary's palm and wrapped in a light cloth. "In this cloth is what will give the young laird his sight again."

She held it out to Catriona.

Catriona took the cloth, handling it carefully. Slowly she unwrapped it. Inside, she found a small sprig of a

plant. Its leaves and petals had turned brown with age,
dried and brittle. She peered at it closely and then she
looked up at Mary, her eyes wide and bright and filled
with fascination.

"This is the white heather," she said, her voice soft
with awe, as if she had just uncovered an ancient secret
long hidden by time.

Mary smiled. "Aye, lass. 'Tis the *fraoich geal.* 'Tis
old and withered now, but when it was abloom in the
field where I picked it when I was a young girl like
you, 'twas as pure and white as the newest snow."
Mary touched Catriona's hand, looking into her eyes
with her most serious face. "You must hearken to me,
Catriona. This flower is a very special thing. It holds
magic within its brittle petals. You must take the
heather and when the moon is full and white in the sky,
you must go with the young laird to Linnanglas."

"Loch Linnanglas?"

Mary nodded, eyes wide. "Aye. You must go there
and sit at the bank of the loch and you must crush these
dried heather flowers into your hands. Then you must
let them scatter on the wind over the young laird, the
healing wind of the moon. After you have done this,
the laird must then go into the loch. The mystical
waters of Linnanglas will restore his sight to him."

Mary squeezed Catriona's fingers then, and added,
"But you, too, must go into the waters with him, Catriona, lest a kelpie come upon him and snatch back his
sight afore it is restored to him, then all would be lost."

Catriona at first looked doubtful of the tale, but as
Mary went on, telling her again of the legend of the
white heather and its magical powers as she had when
she'd been a child, playing on Catriona's own fancy for
the mystical, she soon saw she was winning her over.
She could read Catriona's thoughts clearly—*If the tale
wasn't true, then the laird would be no worse off, but if
it were true . . .*

It wasn't a chance Catriona was willing to take.

"But what if I cannot convince Robert to go into the loch?"

Mary shook her head, eyes wide. "Oh, you must, lass. You must. 'Tis the only way the power of the *fraoich geal* will work for him. But you canna tell him what you are about for if he were to learn of the heather, and of what you were doing, his sight wouldna come back to him. Then all your work would be for naught."

Catriona stared at the dried heather sprig for some time, holding it as if it had been spun from the finest gold. Carefully she considered Mary's words before she then placed the heather back inside its protective cloth, wrapping it inside. She looked at her mother and her eyes were dark blue with wonder, like the midnight sea, like another young lass who had once listened to Mary's tales of wonder. Like her mother, Lady Catherine.

"I will do it."

Catriona took the cloth-wrapped heather and walked from the cottage without further word. Mary sat and watched her go. Catriona would need to decide on a way in which she would convince the laird to go out to the loch in the middle of the night, much less how she would convince him to immerse himself into its icy waters. Mary smiled to herself, imagining the thoughts which were no doubt running rampant through Catriona's keen mind.

But Mary knew Catriona would somehow find a way to bring the plan into being, despite any obstacles that might fall in her path. Whenever that lass put her mind to something, she did it. She was like her mother that way.

And someday Catriona would learn of that part of her life, but not before she was certain that the young duke cared for her, for who she was now, the Scottish crofter's daughter, before he could care for who she would be.

Mary had realized the truth of that when Catriona

had voiced nearly the same opinion. In order for Catriona to be certain of the laird's feelings for her, he must reveal them to her before any of the past, her past, could be told. Otherwise, she would always wonder who he had truly wanted. And until that happened, until Catriona knew in her heart that the laird returned her tender feelings, the truth must still be kept a secret, if only for a little longer.

Mary thought back on the wonder in Catriona's eyes when she'd first recognized the heather. Ever since she'd been a wee lass, when Mary had first told Catriona about this legendary Scottish flower, Catriona had been obsessed with finding it on her own. It was an obsession which Mary had nourished throughout Catriona's childhood with tales of magic and lore.

If it had been anything else contained in that box, a box which had indeed been given Mary by her grandmother to pass to her daughters, Catriona might not have believed in it. But if there was one thing in particular Mary knew, and truly loved about Catriona, it was her tendency toward all things whimsical.

For Catriona, it would be like living one of those leather-bound tales she slipped away at night to Rosmorigh to read. Two young people, alone in the night, beside the moon-kissed waters of a misty loch. The worlds, those very different worlds they each came from, wouldn't matter a whit. And they certainly would be no match for the inevitable.

The Scottish moon had a special sort of magic all its own. Sprinkle it with a dusting of white heather and any manner of things might occur.

Mary was depending upon it.

"Well, lass, have you come to tell me you've found the book at Rosmorigh that will lead us to our treasure?"

The Colonel was waiting for Catriona outside his cottage when she arrived to visit him later that day. Sitting in his chair, his whiskey bottle beside him, he puffed quizzically on his clay pipe. Mattie was curled, snoozing at his feet in the sunlight.

"Still nothing, I'm afraid, Colonel."

The Colonel stared at her closely. "When you haidna come about these past days, I thought you might have found the text and had gone off on your own to find the treasure without my picture map."

Catriona reached down to scratch Mattie behind her furry orange ears. "Actually, I haven't had much opportunity to search through the library these past days."

"You hinna, you say? Ah, lass, but I know you're still goin' to that castle e'ry day. Now, if you're not tryin' to scare off the young laird, and you're not searching through those books, then what're you doin' up there all this time, lassie?"

Catriona looked at him. Sometimes she wondered if the Colonel was some sort of seer, watching over everyone's doings through some sort of Arthurian crystal. He always seemed to know what everybody else was about. "I tried to scare him off, Colonel, but he's like his father. You remember he didn't believe I was a ghost either."

"Aye, but he dinna stay at the castle for long either."

"I can still search for the text. The duke said I could come to the library whenever I wished to. He has asked me to read his correspondence and write his letters for him."

The Colonel opened his bloodshot eyes wide. "Did he, now? Then you can tell me what he's doin' here all this way from London, aye? You can tell me if he's lookin' for our treasure for himself?"

"He knows nothing of the treasure, Colonel, nor do I think he would care if he did. He has come here for a different reason entirely. There was a fire and most every member of his family was killed. The fire had been deliberately set and the duke thinks somehow it is related to his father's visits here."

The colonel nodded. "And you've offered to help him find this out?"

"Yes."

He shook her head. "Och, lass . . ."

"It is the only way, Colonel. Can you not see that as soon as the laird can determine Rosmorigh had nothing to do with his father's death he will leave? And if I help him, then that will certainly hasten his departure."

Catriona looked at him, hoping he would believe her reasoning, reasoning that had precious little to do with the truth.

The Colonel rubbed his bearded chin. "And how is it you can be so certain Rosmorigh dinna have anything to do with the former laird's death?"

Chapter Twelve

Catriona reached her hand into the small tidal pool, tugging at the limpet which clung stubbornly to the side of the half-submerged boulder. The water was cool against her legs, her toes squishing into the sand and seaweed along the bottom. She hardly noticed that her skirts had become soaked and crusted with sand at the hem as she tossed the limpet into the small pail with the others she had gathered for her mother's stew.

She turned. Robert sat away from her, leaning against a grassy dune close by to where her slippers and stockings lay piled. Bayard munched happily on the tuft of marram grass beside him. It was warm, so Robert wore no coat, just a tan waistcoat and his white linen shirt, the sleeves of which were rolled back over his forearms. He'd been so quiet, she wondered if he might have dozed off, for his eyes remained hidden behind the dark lenses of his spectacles. Until he reached over to pat Bayard's neck when the horse moved nearer to him.

"Would you like to help?" she called, but Robert only shook his head.

"If you will recall, I tried that once and ended up facefirst in a burn," he said. "I think I'll keep myself to land this time."

"All right, but you'll have only yourself to blame for missing out. It really is quite fun."

Robert listened as Catriona went back to her limpets and seaweed, his thoughts turning to the letter she had read to him earlier that day. It had come from Noah, and in it his brother had reported that he'd finally managed to confirm Lord Kinsborough's whereabouts during the time of the fire. The news wasn't favorable.

The marquess, he wrote, had apparently been at a ball in London, far from Lancashire, until late into the evening the night of the fire. There was no question of it, either, for the well-known society matron who had hosted the affair assured Noah that Kinsborough had indeed been in attendance that night; she had even allowed him to peruse her guest list as further proof of it.

Robert hadn't been pleased by this for it meant that his suspicions about Kinsborough had been wrong, that he hadn't had any hand in the fire after all. At least it would have seemed so at first, had Noah not then gone on in the letter, describing to Robert a curious visit he'd received just that morning from none other than Kinsborough himself.

The marquess had come to Noah with an offer, an offer which he wished him to relate to Robert, since no one in London seemed to know where his brother had vanished to. Kinsborough told Noah he had heard it being bandied about the ballrooms that the fire had left the Devonbrook estate in financial straits. But his offer, while cloaked in samaritan concern, was really quite self-motivated. He wanted to purchase any and all pieces that remained from the Devonbrook collection. He didn't indicate any particular interest, only the bulk of what remained, what had been held safely in the London town house or at any of the other properties. And the price Kinsborough offered was generous. Too generous. It was a price which would have tempted many, and this only led Robert to wondering even more what the man might be about.

Every time he tried to reason it out, the result was the same. He kept coming back to the journal. Robert could not deny the inkling he had that it had something to do with the fire. On their last outing, just three days before, he and Catriona had followed the duke's discourse to a small cave hidden deep in the side of a rocky, windswept hillside. There they had eaten a picnic lunch of Mary's barley bannocks and cold mutton while Catriona read to Robert from the journal, describing how his father had come to the place one frosty day in December.

No explanations, no hint at why he'd chosen that place in particular, but from Catriona's description of the cave and its secluded setting, it didn't seem likely his father had simply stumbled upon it. Somebody had to have told him of it. He had gone there with a purpose in mind, although he never alluded to what that might be in his journal. That particular entry, however, had been dated just three months before the fire.

Robert had been so lost to his thoughts, he hadn't even heard Catriona approaching until she had plopped down beside him on the sand.

"Giving up on the limpets already?" he asked.

"I think I have enough for the stew, and even a spare few for the Colonel. Besides, I suspect you are more interested in journeying to the next place in the discourse, than in sitting here while I splash about in tide pools."

Robert would have liked to have seen her. And, God willing, he soon would. In the past days, he had filled nearly every waking moment attempting to recover his sight. The day before, he'd spent an hour concentrating on an object on the desk, rewarded finally by a brief glimpse of what he felt certain was an inkwell before he'd had to close his eyes against the pain. But the pain grew less with each session. The images were beginning now to take on dimension and color, even if only for a brief moment's time. Soon, Robert told himself, soon he would regain his sight and be able to look into Catriona's eyes and see the smile that he knew accompanied her captivating laughter as she skipped along the sand.

Catriona had picked up the journal and started skimming it to see where they would journey to next. "From the next entry in the journal, it looks as if your father moved inland now toward . . ."

Her voice dropped off.

"Catriona? What is it? Is something wrong?"

"What? Oh, no, nothing is wrong. I was just reading something your father had written here about there being a forked tree close by to where he stopped. Shall we be off then?"

Three quarters of an hour later, they came to the location of the duke's next journal entry.

Catriona's heart was pounding. Standing in front of them on the path that was nearly hidden beneath the overgrowth of bracken covering the small hill, was a huge oak tree whose curving branches extended upward toward the very heavens. It must have been standing there for centuries, the body shaped in a perfect *V,* looking as if it might have been cleaved in two by a giant, for it sprung from two very distinctive trunks. Catriona was awestruck. This was the one, the same forked oak referred to in the Colonel's picture map. She thought of the other images so crudely drawn on the aged parchment. A winding burn. An isolated cave. And now a forked tree.

The journal.

Robert's father had gone to similar places, and in direct following with their placement on the map. Had he perhaps known of the treasure?

"We are there?" Robert asked, pulling Catriona from her thoughts.

"Yes. If you'd like we can sit here on this hill and I'll read to you what your father wrote."

*Today I discovered the forked tree where local legend
has it Charles Stuart, the Bonnie Prince, hid himself
for three days and nights from the English soldiers
who were scouting the area in search of him. I sat on a
bluff above the tree and tried to picture the young
prince concealed by the leaves of this majestic oak,
unable to move or perhaps even breathe lest he be discovered. It is a vista that should be committed to
canvas. I wondered at how he must have felt, looking
down to Loch Linnanglas and the French frigate which
reportedly awaited him there to take him off to safety.
As I listen to the stirring whisper of the breeze through
the leaves, I could almost feel the heartache the young
prince must have felt at knowing he could not alert the
French to his position and then watching hopelessly as
the frigate finally withdrew, leaving him behind.*

Setting the journal aside, Catriona scanned the
horizon.

Somewhere out there a treasure awaited. She could
feel it. And so obviously had Robert's father, the duke.
But how? Had he found the book containing the text
which told of the treasure's whereabouts in the library
at Rosmorigh? She thought of what Robert had said
about his father and his passion for collecting rare and
unique things. The prospect of a treasure such as this
would have been quite a find to a man with a mind for
collecting such as the duke. Had he known what it was
that awaited him at the end of his journey when he had
written of it, and sought, with this journal, to forever
commemorate his search for it? Or, she thought further, remembering his words regarding the tree and its
history, had someone told him about the treasure?
Someone who knew all the Jacobite stories, someone
such as . . .

. . . Colonel MacReyford.

Catriona remembered something else then, something the Colonel had said to her the last time she had
gone to see him.

He had asked her how she could be so certain Rosmorigh hadn't had anything to do with the death of Robert's father..

It was nearing nightfall, bare traces of grayish dusk lighting Catriona's way. The small secluded cottage lay like a slumbering dog at the base of a creagan scoured bare by glaciers thousands of years before. The windows were dark and as she drew near, she spotted the tall polished staff the Colonel used when he went out on walks, leaning at its place beside the weatherscarred door. Coming closer, she noticed something small and white and square sticking out from the door; it was a letter addressed to the Colonel.

Catriona put down her pail and took the letter. She then opened the door, knocking softly. "Colonel?"

There came no response. The cottage inside was dark. Too dark. Catriona pushed the door open further, allowing the dim light from outside to shine in. She noticed immediately there was no fire burning in the central hearth. Catriona couldn't remember a time when she hadn't seen a fire there, the Colonel's favorite posset simmering in its crock, and sometimes a trio of herring hanging from the *slowrie* above; two of them for the Colonel and the other for Mattie.

Catriona went in and found the tinderbox in its place atop the cupboard near the door. She lit the candle that always sat beside it and turned to look about the toosilent chamber.

The first thing she noticed was the uncommon visibility. The dense peat smoke which usually clouded the inner rafters, swirling about for want of a *lum* to escape through, was gone. The fire had been out for some time. She saw the Colonel's wooden rocking chair near the window where he would watch for visitors and passersby. It was empty, his footstool where Catriona would always sit faithfully before it. A half-empty whiskey bottle stood on the table. Everything was there in its proper place, except for one very unusual thing.

The Colonel's red Jacobite coat which he never removed lay folded atop the wooden storage chest beside the chair.

Catriona walked slowly to the far side of the chamber where the Colonel's ancient box bed stood filling the corner. The bedding was rumpled but not unmade, as if someone had recently sat upon it. She reached underneath the bed's frame to where the Colonel kept the small pouch that contained the picture map of Prince Charlie's treasure. She felt a chill pass through her when she found that, like the Colonel, it was gone.

A rustling noise came then from outside, from somewhere on the straw-thatched roof. Catriona blew out her candle and listened closely in the darkness. The sound came again, nearer to the door this time. Silently she padded over and peeked outside.

A figure came flashing past, close by to Catriona's face. She cried out, startled, until she saw Mattie's glowing green eyes peering at her in the twilight.

"You frightened me nearly out of my shoes," Catriona said to her, rubbing her behind her ears. "Where is the Colonel, Mattie?"

Mattie let out a plaintive meow and began pendulating back and forth, quite unusual for the creature who barely ever gave Catriona a second's attention. Her ears were pricked anxiously forward as she peered at the pail of limpets Catriona had left by the door, mewing again. Catriona looked down to the small tin dish outside the door, where the Colonel usually put out Mattie's food. It was empty but for the few stray leaves which had blown into it.

The poor thing was starving.

Catriona picked her up. "You can come home with me tonight. Then, tomorrow, we'll try to find out where the Colonel went off to."

It was late by the time Catriona arrived back at her family's cottage, the moon peeking its glimmering white light out over the tops of the distant trees. A single candle was all that burned atop the table inside, but it cast enough light for Catriona to see that her father had come home again. The weathered traveling satchel he used for carrying his clothing and necessaries was sitting just inside the doorway.

"Catriona."

Mary was sitting beside the hearth fire, darning one of Angus's stockings. She wore her new gown, made of a lovely sea-colored muslin which Angus had brought, along with others for Mairead and Catriona, back with him the last time he'd come home from the coast.

"Hello, Mam," Catriona said, dropping Mattie onto the chair. "Have we any cream?"

Mary nodded toward where her cup and teapot sat on the table beside her. Catriona took the cream, placing it on the floor before the hungry cat. Mattie set to it with enthusiasm, burying her face inside the small wooden cup.

"What'd you bring that creature here for?" Mary asked, inspecting the line of stitches she'd just finished on Angus's woollen stocking.

Catriona took up an oatcake, nibbling reflectively. "Have you seen the Colonel today, Mam?"

"Nae. Not since the day afore yestreen when Mairead went wit' me to take him some of the crowdie."

"I stopped to bring him some of the limpets I gathered today, but he's not at his croft and it doesn't look as if he's been there for a time. The hearth is cold and there was even a letter stuck in the door for him."

Mary stopped sewing and looked over at Catriona. "Dinna get yourself all taken with worry, lass. He's probably just gone off to see ol' Valeria Gorrie. You know how he is always askin' after her." Mary smiled. "I'm beginnin' to think he might be taken with her."

Catriona was still uneasy. Perhaps her mother was right, but what about the map? Unless of course the Colonel had taken it with him so as not to risk anyone finding it at the cottage while he was away. But what if he hadn't gone visiting at all? What if the same person who had learned of Robert's father and his journal had also learned of the Colonel's picture map?

Mary must have read Catriona's concern on her face for she said, "Dinna fret, Catriona. I'll send your da out to look for the Colonel first thing on the morrow. He'll find him."

Catriona nodded, knowing she could do nothing more that night. They would have to wait until morning. Removing her brown woollen cloak, she hung it on the peg set high in the wall. "When did Da get home?"

"Just after nightfall," Mary said, narrowing her eyes as she scrutinized her stitches further. "Dinna e'en eat his supper, he was so tired." A rumbling noise sounded from their bedroom then. "Snaggerin' like a bull, he is, and smells like the bottom of an ale keg, too. Thought since I winna be gettin' any sleep myself this night, I might as well make use of the time and be doin' this darnin'."

Catriona sat down on the floor in front of her mother, resting her chin on her bent knees. "Your gown, it is a fine one, Mam."

"Och, Mairead makes a finer stitch than I can." She motioned to where the gown that was to be Catriona's hung on the wall. "Mairead says you're to be putting on your own gown to make certain it will fit you afore she stitches it complete."

Catriona stood and took the gown, stripping down to her chemise before slipping it over her head. Angus had brought them a looking glass once which had been part of a landing. It had been damaged during transport, the right corner of the glass broken off, but Catriona could still see every inch of the lovely bright blue gown Mairead had fashioned for her.

It fit her like a glove, hugging her snugly to her waist, the skirts flaring softly over her hips to drop in folds to her ankles. The elbow-length sleeves were dec-

orated with a small trace of snowy lace, another bit of
the booty from one of Angus's excursions. The neckline, which was square and hugged tightly to her
bosom, was finished with a strand of lighter blue
ribbon and Mairead had taken a bit of a tartan, fash-
ioning it into an overskirt of sorts that draped softly
around the waist. The tartan, which had been woven by
Mairead, was made of the MacBryan colors, dark green
and navy blue, striped with white. It set off the blue of
the gown beautifully.

"It is perfect," Catriona said, turning to look at the
back of the skirts as they swirled gracefully about her
ankles.

"Mairead has a talent for stitchin' like I've ne'er
seen afore." Mary paused a moment, smiling over her
sewing as she said, "And come the morrow night, your
young laird will think you're a sea siren come to mortal
life."

Catriona turned, staring at her image in the glass.
Her hair had come loose from its snood and was
curling about her face, one thick tress of it hanging
down over her shoulder. Her cheek was smudged with
dirt and her fingers were colored black from having
drafted Robert's letters that afternoon. She rather
thought she smelled a bit like Bayard, too.

If Robert were to see her as she was now, the first
image since losing his sight to the fire, he would surely
wish himself blind again.

"More likely he would think me a sea monster," she
said glumly, and slipped her new gown off, hanging it
again on the wall peg. She walked over to the basin by
the window, pouring some cold water in it to wash herself with. When she turned, Mary was no longer sitting
in the chair by the hearth, but was standing right
behind her.

"Mam," Catriona said, startled at finding her there.

Mary held something out to Catriona. "Here. This is
a cake of heather soap I've been savin'. You go to the
burn early on the morrow, afore Angus awakes, and

have yourself a swim like you always do. This soap will make your skin look like cream and smell like a field of flowers. I think Mairead e'en has a bit of the ribbon left from your gown. We'll thread it through your hair so you truly will look like a sea siren come to life when the laird gets his sight back."

Catriona hugged her mother to her tightly. "But, Mam, what about Da? I didn't think he would be home so soon this time. I know he allows me to go to Rosmorigh to read Robert his correspondence, but won't he be angry if I am gone so late at night?"

Mary smiled, touching Catriona softly on her cheek. "Dinna worry yourself about it, lass. You just leave your da to me."

Chapter Thirteen

The dawning sun was barely peeking over the eastern horizon when Catriona left the cottage and started for the burn. Night lingered high above her, the air crisp, so crisp her breath fogged on it as she walked barefoot over the dewy glen floor. She wore her night chemise and even though it was summer, the morning was brisk, the grass wet and cold against her feet. Her toes tingled from the cold. She knew the water would be even colder.

She ducked under a tree branch and came out into the clearing. Tonight she would take Robert to the loch and with the white heather sprig her mother had given her, she would give him back his sight. Sleep had eluded her all through the night before, but she wasn't tired, not at all, for her thoughts were filled with wonder of what Robert's reaction to her would be once he saw her. Would he dislike her? Would he think her ugly? Would he realize the hopeless differences between them? And when he no longer needed her to be his eyes, would he send her away?

Catriona sat down on a moss-shadowed rock set away from the sylvan burn, laying her gown, stockings, and shoes on the ground near her feet. It was a peaceful morning and a swirling mist clung to the quiet water

and to the dense wood behind her, surrounding her,
shielding her, protecting her. Above, perched on a fir, a
brown-and-white song throstle chittered his morning
melody, while further out, two red deer picked their
way cautiously through the heather and sedge tussocks
toward the shelter of the trees.

Catriona loved coming here. There was a bend in the
burn where the water slowed, forming a natural pool
that was both deep and clear. She often came here to
bathe when the season was warm, rather than in the
back room of the cottage, knees bent to her chin as she
sat in her mother's washing tub.

Slipping her chemise over her head, Catriona walked
to the edge of the water and dipped in her foot. The
crispness of the icy water stunned her a moment before
she stepped in with her other foot. Taking a deep
breath, she dove into the shallow pool. The shock of it
was both astounding and invigorating, the cold bringing every nerve to tingling. When she surfaced, she
gulped in another deep breath of the chilled morning
air before plunging under once again.

When she surfaced again, the cold had lessened to
where she barely noticed it any longer. She skimmed
the water, gliding slowly across the surface to the
grassy edge, taking up the soap cake and scrubbing her
goose-pimpled arms. The scents of the soap and the
morning mingled on the gentle breeze that came whispering over the glen. Pink sunlight crept over the surrounding hills, filtering down through the treetops and
reflecting on the water's glassy surface.

Catriona lathered the rich soap in her hair, drawing it
through the sleek strands and then leaning her head back
in the water to rinse it. It was as she leaned her head
back a second time that she thought she heard the snap
of a twig come suddenly from the wood behind her. She
dipped down so that only her head was above the
water's surface. Her eyes darted about, searching for
something, anything through the heavy mist. The deer
had gone and a stillness had come upon the place which

should have meant nothing, but which filled her with
alarm. The wood was never this quiet, not in the early-
morning hours when the birds were usually trilling and
flitting about the trees. Why had everything suddenly
gone silent?

Catriona waited. When the throstle began its song
again, she eased a bit and quickly finished rinsing the
soap from her hair before moving back across the
water to where the towel she'd brought lay waiting for
her. She would have liked to have stayed in the water
longer, indulging in this simple treat, but her uneasi-
ness had made her decide it best to return home.

Away from the burn, hidden beneath the sheltering
boughs of a low-limbed oak, Ian Alexander watched as
Catriona rose from the water to dry herself. He sucked
in his breath at the picture she presented, gloriously
naked, water dripping from her, glistening on her pale
skin in the early-morning sunlight.

She looked like an angel.

He had come upon this blissful scene as Catriona
had first leaned back in the water to rinse her hair.
He'd been instantly mesmerized at the sight of her, her
breasts rising from the water, rose-colored nipples taut
from the cold, peeking just above the surface. Even
thinking on it now, his erection pushed against the
heavy wool of his kilt.

Ian had always thought Catriona a comely lass, so
much more finely boned and delicate than her sister or
any of the other Highland lasses. He'd never considered what lay hidden behind the woollen skirts, billowing chemise, and confining snood, the inches of
white skin and that hair. He wanted to wrap the length
of it around his fist and drag her hard against him. He
wanted to look down at her, into those blue eyes, and
know that she was his.

Ian stared at her, watching as she stood at the side of
the burn, her belly flat, her hips nicely flared, the nest
of dark curls between her legs stark against her white
skin. He bit his lip against a trembling that came over

his body, the blood beginning to pound in his ears, his eyes moving again to gaze at her exquisite breasts. He stood frozen as she raised her hands above her head to dry her hair with the cloth. This time he bit down on his lip so hard, he drew blood.

Full and perfectly rounded, he knew her breasts would fit into his hands perfectly. He tightened his fingers into fists, fighting against the urge to go to Catriona, pull her against him, and knead her lovely flesh in his palms. Catriona turned then, her hair trailing in wet springy waves to just above the line of her buttocks. He swallowed against the sweetness he knew he would find at suckling her. He wanted her so badly it hurt. He knew it would be utter heaven to have her.

Ian had never been with a woman, had never known the soft touch of skin kept hidden behind layers of woollen skirts. He had seen a man and a woman together once when he had mistakenly opened the wrong door at an inn where he and Angus had stayed on one of their journeys down the coast. The pair of them hadn't even noticed him standing there, fascinated at their mating, watching as the man grunted and groaned, thrusting himself into the woman who lay panting beneath him. Her legs were raised up and clasped tightly behind the man's back as she begged the man to give her more. But Ian had felt nothing for that woman. That woman had been coarse and fleshy. And dirty. Catriona was different. Catriona was clean. Pure. Untouched. Ian had always known she would be beautiful, his angel, his swan. He just couldn't have imagined how truly pure her beauty would be.

Ian knew Catriona felt for him as a brother, that she had never considered him to be anything more. Certainly not a lover. But once he had her, and had shown her what awaited her in a marriage bed, he knew she would think on him differently. He was glad he had refrained from falling into the iniquity of other men who wasted their seed on whores and women who were otherwise impure. When he finally gave himself to a woman, it would be only to the purest.

It could only be to Catriona.

Ian waited in the trees, hidden by the mist, until Catriona had taken up her things and had started back for the cottage. He closed his eyes, committing the sight of her to his memory, thinking with vivid anticipation of the time when he would have her for his own. And he would have her, he knew, for he'd been promised it.

Ian walked slowly over to the edge of the burn where Catriona had bathed in the clear water. She was gone from it now, but the suds from the soap she had washed herself with still floated on the still surface, drifting to the edges of the pool with the breeze.

He spotted something white in the grass near his feet, a single woollen stocking which Catriona had dropped. He took up the cloth, cloth which had touched his angel in forbidden places, and lifted it to his face, inhaling its essence. He closed his eyes and envisioned himself on top of her at the edge of this burn, lying on the soft grass, thrusting himself into her warmth as she cried out his name, telling him that she loved him, begging him never to leave her. He pictured her then, her belly no longer flat, but swollen with a child. His child. They would have a dozen children, he decided, for he knew he would never grow weary of mounting her, and he would never miss a chance to fill her woman's place with his seed.

Ian's brow was beaded with sweat when he opened his eyes again. The wood was quiet except for the chirping of the birds. Peace reigned outside while within him a storm raged, a storm of desperate, animal need. He had Catriona's stocking clenched in his fists and stretched out taut between his two hands in front of him. The muscles in his legs were rigid and tense. His erection stood stiff from his quivering body. Blood seared through his veins, intense and hot, until finally he could stand it no more, and taking hold of himself, he relieved his painful discomfort the only way he knew how.

Catriona looked up at the night sky as she came to the top of the last rise before Rosmorigh. The moon was fat and white and full, surrounded by an ethereal bluish glow, suspended in the midst of the blackness and the twinkling of countless stars. She could feel it in the soft breeze that blew over her and she could smell it in the wildflowers that surrounded her. It was a glorious night. A special night. It was a night for all things magic.

In the pocket of her gown lay hidden the sprig of white heather, wrapped in its protective cloth. Her heart thumped with excitement and her belief that Robert would have his sight again soon.

She wore her new gown, the gown which Mairead had worked all day to finish, and Mary had woven a single sky blue ribbon in her hair, which was loose and hanging down her back in thick, twisting waves. The ends of the ribbon trailed softly around Catriona's ear.

Robert was sitting at the desk when she came into the library, his face lowered closely to a small statuette atop it.

"Robert?"

He sat up quickly, too quickly, knocking the statuette onto the floor and shattering it.

"Oh, dear," Catriona said, crossing the room. She picked up the pieces of what was once a figure of a horse. "I fear it is ruined."

"Leave it," he said. "Forbes will take care of it. He is getting rather used to cleaning up after my clumsiness. "I'd given up on you," he said then, drawing her attention away from the figure. "I had thought you would be coming earlier today. You didn't."

He sounded displeased. She looked at him. "I had planned to come earlier, but there was something I needed to do at home. It took a bit longer than I had expected."

There had been something she'd needed to see to and Catriona had waited all day for her father to return. He'd been gone searching for the Colonel and still hadn't returned when she had left well past nightfall. She hadn't wanted to leave at all, but finally her mother had convinced her she must go, assuring her Angus would find the Colonel and what a great chuckle he would have over the worry he had caused her. Catriona prayed her mother was right.

"I remembered reading that your father had gone to this next place in his discourse at night. I thought we should do the same, in order to accurately recreate his observations there."

Catriona hated lying to Robert, but it was the only way she could think of to get him to get to the loch with her. She wondered what she might tell him to convince him to go into the water once they arrived there. Her compunction at her deception was eased by knowing he would soon have his sight again. Catriona reached down and touched the cloth that held the heather sprig. Soon, she told herself, soon everything would be different.

She wondered how long it would take once they had gone into the loch for Robert to regain his sight, for only after she was certain the spell of the white heather had done its work would she tell him the truth of the treasure. She knew she should have told him the moment she had realized his father had been on the trail of the treasure as well. It was what he'd come to Rosmorigh for, the truth. She hadn't told him, though, because she realized that when she did reveal the truth, Robert would leave Rosmorigh. He would return to London and he would find a way to prove Lord Kinsborough's guilt. And when Robert did return to London, she wanted it to be with his sight, so no one would dare to mock him again.

"Your father went next to Loch Linnanglas. It is too far to reach walking, so I stopped at the stable before coming up and saw to Bayard's bridling since your groom was already abed. I left him awaiting us in the courtyard."

Robert sat at the edge of the desk, his hands flat against its top. "Since you have already gone through the trouble of arranging for the horse, then we can certainly go. If you would though, before we leave, I received a letter today from Tolley in Brussels."

Now Catriona understood why he'd seemed so anxious at her arrival. He'd been waiting all day to hear the news of Bonaparte. "Of course." She broke the letter's seal quickly, reading it to him.

I am soon for London. It is over, Rob, and once again Bonaparte has been defeated by us. The last decisive battle took place just two days ago at a place called Waterloo. It was a difficult fight, with casualties on both sides, but in the end Wellington's boys were victorious. And now the council must decide Bonaparte's fate. Many are calling for his execution, but it is more readily believed he will be exiled once again, only this time permanently. I'm for Paris now. I plan to remain long enough to find out what will be done with him before I continue on to London. I haven't received anything from you since your letter of mid-May. I'm holding the hope that you will see me in Town. Best regards, Tolley

When Catriona finished reading, she looked over to Robert. His eyes were closed and his head was lowered, his chin resting on his chest. "Robert?"

"I wasn't at all certain he'd be coming back this time." He lifted his head. "I thank God he is."

Catriona reached for his hand and Robert searched for her. The low light from the fire was playing shadows across his muted vision, and through the distorted images he tried to find her. He stared hard, focusing, trying to find something real amid the blur of scattered colors. And then he saw something, a flash of blue, the color of sky, before it was gone.

In the weeks since he had known Catriona, Robert had come to wonder what he'd do if he ever lost her. She'd come to mean so much to him. Before the fire, he'd always taken the people in his life for granted, assuming they would always be a part of his life. He knew now how wrong that had been. And he knew now he would never do it again.

The rapping at the cottage door startled Mary as she was spooning the haggis from the crock onto the supper plates set out before her. She made to answer it, but Angus put out a hand to stop her.

"I'll be for it, Mary. I'm knowing who it is."

Of course, she thought. It had to be the Colonel.

Angus hadn't found him that day, not at the Widow Gorrie's, nor back at his own cottage later that night. No one he had asked had seen the Colonel about either. The letter Catriona had found in his door had come from the Colonel's sister Margaret, who lived in London. She had asked him to come to her and beseeched him not to ignore this letter as he had all her others. The MacBryan's hadn't even known the Colonel had a sister; he'd never spoken of her, even to Catriona. From her words it appeared Margaret hadn't seen or heard from him in some time, and after reading it they had thought perhaps he might have gone off finally to see her. But hearing his knock on the door now, Mary realized they had been mistaken. Wherever he had gone, the Colonel had returned now and having found his cat missing, knew Catriona would have brought her here. Catriona would be sorry she had missed him.

Angus opened the door, but it wasn't the Colonel after all. It was Ian Alexander who stood waiting on the other side.

"Good e'ening, Ian," Mary said, turning as Angus began pulling on his heavy boots. They were the boots he wore whenever he was leaving, the boots he wore when he was going to meet a ship bringing another load of smuggled goods. He hadn't said anything to her about his going off for a landing. He hadn't even packed his bag. "Angus?"

"I'll be back by the morn," he muttered, pulling on his heavy greatcoat and shoving his hat on his head.

Perhaps he had asked Ian to help him search further for the Colonel. "But what of your supper? You have to eat. And, Ian, you come sit here and have a bit as well."

"Nae, Mary," Angus said. His voice was low and grave. "We've a landin' to make."

Mary stared at him. "So close to home?"

"Aye. Excisemen kept us from landin' this load at Mallaig. They're keepin' close watch on the coast there, so I had it brought up the sound to land it 'ere. I had no other choice left to me."

Mary looked at Angus, her mouth set in a grave frown. He never brought in a load close to home, for the risk of capture was too high. If the landguard came upon them, they would search every house within miles to find them. They would tear apart every place where smuggled goods might be hidden. And they would arrest anyone they thought might be harboring information. "But where can you land it?"

"I dinna know that just now. The ship is waitin' off the coast. I'm to send it a signal by lamp when I find a place where 'tis safe to bring it ashore. I'm to meet with the others afore at the cairn crossing so we can try to decide on a landing site."

Angus turned, preparing to leave. He took up his satchel and the lantern that hung on a hook by the door. As he tossed his coat across his wide shoulders, Mary warred with herself, with the consequences her words would bring, before finally blurting out, "You can land the load at Rosmorigh."

"Are you daft, wife? The laird is there."

"Nae, Angus. The laird is away this night. He winna be back till the morn."

Angus turned slowly to look at her.

"You can land the load on the shore beneath the cliffs," she said. "No one will see you there and then you can stow the load in the caves under Rosmorigh till 'tis safe to take it off."

Angus narrowed his eyes on his wife, staring at her closely. "How is it you're knowing the laird is away this night, Mary MacBryan?"

Mary glanced quickly at Ian, then peered back at Angus. "Dinna ask me that, husband, for I canna tell you of it."

Angus didn't have to ask her. He shifted his eyes to the only empty chair at the supper table. Catriona's chair. Mairead remained wisely silent.

"I thank you for your thoughts, wife. You've saved me a heap of trouble from the landguard." He yanked the leathern ties on his satchel shut with a snap. "And as for the rest of it, I'll be takin' that up with you when I return on the morrow."

Chapter Fourteen

Linnanglas was a small loch, fed by the River Linnan and sheltered on its northern side by a high and narrow glen. Where its farther shore was rocky and barren from centuries of vulnerability to the harsh wester winds, the north was a verdant and rich brae secluded from the ancient droving road they had followed there by a dense wood of elm and oak trees. In daylight, when one could see the stark contrast of the two sides, it was a striking picture. At night, the effect was purely magical.

Bayard came to a sluggish halt at the edge of the loch. Catriona's heart began to pound.

"We are here," she said, sliding from Bayard's back. She dropped the reins after Robert had dismounted, allowing the horse to graze on the sweet dew-damp clumps of clover growing nearby.

As she turned to look at Robert in the moonlight, she wondered how she would avoid the subject of his father's journal. She might mislead him, but she could not lie if he were to ask her what his father had written. And she still would need to find some way to get him to go into the loch. *Distraction.* She needed something, anything to keep him from thinking of the journal. But what could she possibly do to distract him away from it? She struggled to think of words to say.

"When I was a young girl, I would come here and pretend to be a mermaid," she said, leading Robert to a small haugh which was thick with daisies and speedwell. She lowered herself onto her knees while he sat, legs stretched out in front of him beside her. "There is a little island which sits in the middle of the loch. It is called Eilean na . . ."

Catriona hesitated when she noticed Robert staring at her. Because of the night and the darkness, he had left his spectacles at the castle and something was different in his expression tonight. Very different. She couldn't quite place it, but his eyes were staring at her, staring hard. For the first time, they looked as they had in his portrait, penetrating, alive, and Catriona realized then that it was because he was focusing on her face, not simply in her direction. Almost as if . . .

"What is it, Robert? Do you want me to tell you what the loch looks like?"

Robert didn't answer. Instead he slowly reached forward with both his hands and cupped the sides of her face. His gentle touch sent an immediate thrill racing through her. Catriona kept herself still, drawing in a slow, measured breath.

"No, Catriona," he said. His voice was low, wrapping around her. "I do not want you to tell me what the loch looks like. I want you to tell me what *you* look like."

"Me?"

"Surely you have seen yourself."

"Yes, of course. I just never . . ."

"Catriona, paint me a picture of you with your words."

She was silent a moment, studying him before she said, softly, "My hair is brown and my eyes are blue."

"No one's hair is simply brown. Is it dark, like sable, or lighter like sand?"

"My father used to call it a rusty brown when I was a . . ."

Slowly Robert curled a strand of it around his finger. ". . . girl," she finished. What was he doing?

"What color are your eyes?" he asked, and as he did, he ran his fingertips over the arch of her brows and then softly, like a feather, over her eyelids, sending a shivering sort of sensation down her spine that wasn't caused by the chill of the night air. There was no chill, only a warmth that was fast growing hotter.

"Blue," Catriona breathed out slowly when his fingers traced down her nose to her mouth, his thumb rubbing over her lower lip.

"Blue like the color of the storm sky?" he asked.

"Yes." He could have said anything and she would have agreed. Catriona had closed her eyes when his fingers moved along her cheeks, brushing past her ears to touch her hair.

"And is that all there is to you, then? Hair and eyes and nothing else?"

"Everything else is much the same as anyone. I have two ears and two eyes, a mouth . . ."

"Yes, you most definitely have a mouth." His thumbs traced over her lips and Catriona held her breath, wanting him to kiss her so badly she thought she'd die from the waiting. Her heart was pounding. She was afraid to move lest the feeling his touch was creating would vanish. A warmth which had started in the center of her melted exquisitely outward through every inch of her body.

She tried to go on. "My nose is . . ."

His fingertip came to rest on the tip of her nose. "Perfect." Robert traced his finger down to her mouth again. Catriona swallowed nervously.

"Allow me to finish." He lifted her hand and splayed her fingers open, placing his own against it, palm to palm.

The heat created by this intimate contact was beyond intoxicating. Catriona knew she should move away, stop this from going any further. This wasn't why she had brought him to the loch . . . but God help her, she just couldn't utter the words that would make this feeling go away.

"You have small hands," Robert said. "I can nearly close my fingers over yours." He took hold of her fingers with his own, then moving them, placed one finger between his own and his thumb, caressing softly. "Fine, delicate, soft skin."

Robert lifted Catriona's hand to his lips and kissed the tips of each finger with painstaking slowness, lingering over each one. She thought she would surely ignite from the heat of his mouth on her skin. She remembered the kiss they had shared the day by the burn, and again, later that same night when they had been caught by the storm. She wanted to feel Robert's lips on hers, to know again the excitement and the fire. All those times she had stared at his portrait, wondering what it would be like. . . .

What would it matter if she had just one more kiss?

Taking her fingers from his hand, Catriona reached for Robert, and drew him to her.

Robert accepted her silent invitation, bringing Catriona closer against him. He hurt with the need to have her, this woman who accepted him so completely and unconditionally.

He felt Catriona slacken against him, splaying her hands against his chest as he deepened the kiss, his tongue moving into her mouth. She was a willing pupil, instinctively mimicking his movements with her own, completely unaware that she was driving him beyond all sense and reason. She clung to his shoulders as he lay her back on a bed of soft grass and wildflowers. Never in his life had it felt so right to be with a woman, here under the moon and the stars and the heavens. Never in his life had a woman felt so right as Catriona.

Robert moved his mouth downward, tasting the sweetness of her neck, the softness of her earlobe, as he searched for the fastenings of her gown, fumbling in his haste to have her naked beneath him.

"Here," she whispered. "Let me help you." And seconds later he felt the fabric loosen. He pushed it down over her, sliding his hands around to her back. Then slowly he lowered his mouth over her breast.

Catriona drew in a quivering breath as his mouth found her, and Robert continued his silken seduction, teasing her nipple to hardness, sucking, pulling at her, flooding her with the same building and intense heat which threatened to overtake him. He felt her squeeze her fingers through his hair, arching her back, her woman's instinct telling her how to move against him. He wanted to take her, to take her right then and ease the sweet burning that was consuming him, but he wouldn't allow himself to hurry this night. Not for him. And not for her.

Robert lifted Catriona up against him as he leaned above her and pulled her gown over her hips, sliding the fabric over her legs, and off of her. Unable to see her, he memorized her in his mind through his touch as he ran his hands over her, her velvet-soft skin. The unknowing was far more sensual than if he had been able to see her before him.

He felt her fingers at his shirtfront, unfastening the buttons and then pushing the fabric back over his shoulders. He took her against him, her breasts pressed to his chest, their bodies warm against the coolness of the night.

Robert moved his hand over her, sliding it slowly between them, searching. Catriona jerked when he found her, but as he started moving his fingers over her, coaxing her, arousing her, she soon clung to him in desperation. He could feel her swelling beneath his touch, moist, hot, swaying against him, seeking that release which she had yet to know but that every impulse within her told her she would find. If only she waited . . .

Catriona gasped against his ear, clutching at his shoulders, clinging to him tightly until, finally, she found that unknown release and Robert felt her body rocking against his hand, trembling with the newness and the wonder of her climax.

Laying her back, Robert freed himself quickly from his breeches and moved over her. He felt himself against her, felt her parting her legs to take him. When he felt himself parting her, entering her moistness, his body spasmed in response. He had never known such wanting, such need for one woman. He had to have her, to know her, to take her, but she was an innocent and knew nothing of what was happening between them.

"Catriona, I—"

"Please, Robert, please do not talk. Just show me."

It was all the reassurance he needed. Gathering her to him, Robert pressed his hips forward until he felt the resistance of her maidenhead. Covering her mouth with his, he buried himself inside of her.

Catriona stiffened against the shock, but did not cry out. Robert felt her stretching to take him, holding him tightly inside. It was nearly his undoing. He kissed her forehead, her face, her ear. Slowly he moved then, fighting to maintain the tenuous hold he had over his desperate need. Catriona lifted her hips, opening, yielding, seeking to take more of him, and in that instant, he lost what little possession he had over himself. He thrust against her twice, surging into her sweetness with a muffled cry of release, before he rocked with the force of his own climax.

They lay there clasped together for several long, blissful, silent moments. Afterward, when he had collected himself, Robert withdrew from her. Catriona sat up slowly before him and touched the side of his face in the moonlight.

She had never known such complete happiness. Having Robert, feeling him within her, it was more wonderful than she could have ever dreamed. She welcomed the weight of him over her, the sense of oneness their joining had brought. He was magnificent. He was her knight. Her guardian. And she loved him more than she had ever thought possible.

"Are you hurt?" he asked, taking her hand and pressing it to the side of his face.

"No." Catriona looked at his body, so prefect, so beautiful. In the moonlight, she noticed that her gown, which lay crumpled beneath where they had lain, was littered with the tiny dried petals of the white heather. It had slipped from inside her pocket and was strewn all about them and beneath where he now lay.

The heather. She closed her eyes. She was supposed to have scattered it over him, *on the wind,* her mother had said. Instead she'd completely forgotten about it. She thought of the rest of her mother's words. *You must crush these dried heather flowers into your hands. Then you must let them scatter on the wind over the young laird, the healing wind of the moon.*

What if the heather's power had been lost? What if now it wouldn't bring back Robert's sight? Catriona took some of the petals in her fingers and let them fall softly over him, tiny flecks of it scattering like snowflakes through his dark hair. She watched them swirl on the night wind, hoping it wasn't too late as it drifted over his skin, across his belly to . . .

"Robert, there is blood. On you."

"I know. It is all right, Catriona. It is your maiden's blood."

Catriona looked down at herself and saw the splotches that colored the skin of her inner thighs. "It is on me as well."

He stood and reached for her hand. "Can you lead me to the loch so we can wash it away together?"

Catriona walked with Robert to the water's edge, moving into it slowly until the surface was at midthigh. Turning toward her, Robert took Catriona into his arms and kissed her tenderly in the moonlight. She felt his hands on her body, sliding with the water over her skin. Distantly she recalled of the rest of Mary's words.

After you have done this, the laird must then go into the loch. The mystical waters of Linnanglas will restore his sight to him.

Catriona smiled softly as Robert pulled away from their kiss. She touched a bit of his hair which had fallen over his eyes, thinking she hadn't needed to lure him into the water after all.

Neither of them knew that standing at the edge of the trees, frozen and angry to the point of hatred, Ian watched his swan, his angel as she ran her hands over the Englishman's nakedness.

"Row us 'round that bit of cliff wall there, lad," Angus said to Ian. He was sitting across from him in the small, crude skiff. The moon was out, bright, full. It was not a good night for a landing. Angus pointed toward the shoreline, bobbing a half a cable's length away. "The strand there aneath Rosmorigh should be close to it."

Ian silently pulled on the oars, directing the boat through the swirling current toward the shadowed shore. Behind them, three other boats followed in the darkness, pitching silently over the black water, the occasional splash of an oar on the water's surface the only confirmation they were still with them.

The men in these boats made up Angus's landing crew, crofters whom he had known all his life. They were men he trusted, men who would receive the goods from the cutter and later, when they were certain the landguard no longer posed any threat, would transport the goods inland for delivery through a system of secret contacts hidden across the Scottish countryside.

Angus slipped out of the skiff a few moments before they touched land, cutting his bulk through the calf-high water and hauling the small craft hard onto the sandy strip of shoreline which lay beneath the rocky cliffs of Rosmorigh. The sodden wool of his kilt slapped against his legs as he walked. He looked up to the castle standing high on the cliff wall, its dark outline silhouetted in the moonlight.

Angus didn't like landing the load this close to home. It posed too great a risk, and he knew he took even greater risk in using the caves to stow the contraband, for in addition to the revenuers, he now risked detection by the laird. Breaking the laws of an English king was dangerous enough, but breaking the age-old trust between laird and tenant, despite the fact that the laird was English, was closely akin to betrayal.

Still, he'd had no other choice. If they had tried landing the load anywhere else on the coast, they would have risked being seen on the open moorland which ran on either side of the Rosmorigh cliffs. Down here, secluded by the rocky walls and the darkness, the revenue officer and his dragoons would never be able to find them.

"We wait here for the signal," Angus said as the other boats landed, the men who rode inside spilling out onto the beach. He noticed that several of them were sharing a bottle, booty from their last landing to keep warm against the chill wind blowing in off the sound. They laughed among themselves at someone's muttered quip, passing the bottle round once more.

Angus frowned. The longer they sat waiting for the cutter and drinking, the louder the men would become, increasing their risk of capture. He scanned the water for sign of the French ship bringing in his load, even though he knew he would never see it.

The captain, a burly tar called *Le Poisson* for the way in which he skirted capture by the revenuers, was a master at concealment. It was said he'd once passed within a league of a revenuer undetected; he was even known to have painted the hull of his craft, *Le Caméléon,* sea green in order to better avoid capture on the water in the daylight.

Angus spat in the sand, noticing Ian half-hidden in the shadows beside him. "I thought you might have been taken by the landguard when you dinna return from your croft to meet wit' me and the others at the cairn crossing."

Ian didn't answer him, just stared out at the water. In

the moonlight Angus could see that he was slowly clenching and unclenching his jaw.

Something was different with the lad tonight. Something wild and fierce in his eyes.

"I thought you said you were just goin' to fetch a tinderbox to light the lamp with," Angus went on, trying to draw it out of him. "What were you doin' so long, lad?"

Ian's mouth was set sullenly as he went on staring out to the sea. "I couldna find it. That's all."

There was a change in him. When he had first come to get Angus, standing at the cottage door, Ian had had the light of adventure in his eyes, as if he were preparing to do battle this night against the force of His Majesty's excisemen. But now, since rejoining the party, coming upon them just as they were preparing to shove off without him, he seemed restless, even agitated as he yanked suddenly at the rope tied to the small boat, turning to walk more into the shadows with the other men.

Angus watched as Ian took the bottle, guzzling a good dose of it down while the others laughed and urged him on. He told himself it was just nervousness. It would not be much longer now, the waiting.

Within a quarter hour, Angus spotted the blue flash of light flickering through the darkness, indicating the arrival of *Le Caméléon*.

"There she is," he said, taking up the spout lantern he'd brought with him for giving his return signal. Fashioned for him by the local blacksmith, its only opening was through a long sleeve attached on one side of the lantern housing, assuring that the light would only be seen in the direction Angus pointed the spout. Setting the lantern in the crook of his arm, Angus placed his hand over the spout opening, then removed it for a moment before covering it again. He did this a second time, indicating to the cutter that the coast was indeed clear. He then awaited the responding signal.

"They are comin'," he said, setting the lantern aside.

The men around him abandoned their drinking and conversation and immediately sprang to action. Two of them pushed off the shore in the first skiff to meet *Le Caméléon*'s approaching tub boat. They would bring to him a costly cargo this time, far more costly than was usual. Kegs of brandy and port from France roped in pairs, silks and laces from Spain, tobacco from America, and tea and spices from the Dutch East Indies compressed in waterproof packets. These would be sent to places throughout the kingdom, some as far away as Edinburgh, even York, wherever the venturer Mr. MacAfee had found someone willing to pay his price.

Only after the load had been successfully dispersed would Angus receive his payment and the payment for his crew, from MacAfee's agent, the bagman named Drum who dressed as a man of the cloth in order to move about unmolested by the landguard.

The first of Angus's crew was already returning to shore, the small boat riding low in the water, weighted down by a number of heavy kegs.

"All right, lads, pass the kegs on up to me at the cave and I'll start stowing them inside." Angus looked about for Ian to help him. "Douglas," he called softly to the man nearest to him, "do you ken where young Ian's gone off to?"

"Nae, Angus," said Douglas, a considerable man who came to Angus carrying a keg on each massive shoulder. "I hinna seen the lad since just after we landed."

Angus looked to where he had last seen Ian before hoisting up one of the kegs and taking it inside the cave. He could not stop now to look for him, not when they needed to get the load stowed quickly so they could leave before the cutter might be spotted anchored as it was off the coast.

Once inside the caves he opened the small door at the side of his spout lantern to light his way through the narrow passages. He glanced around the shadowed passageway. He had never been in the caves himself, but he had heard of them from Catriona.

Catriona. Angus thought fleetingly of Mary, his wife, and the guilty look that had shadowed her eyes when she had revealed that the laird would not be at the castle that night. Angus knew from that look that wherever the laird had gone, Catriona was with him. And wherever she was, she was with him alone.

He shoved the thoughts away, knowing he needed all his attentions focused on the load. Any sound or movement might mean a revenuer was approaching. Likely that had been Ian's thought as well, and he had gone off to keep watch while the rest of them stowed the load.

Angus came from the cave, heading back for more of the load and watching as the second boat was shoving off now to retrieve the rest of the load when the silence was suddenly split by the report of a pistol.

Chapter Fifteen

"Dragoons!" Douglas cried, abandoning the large chest he carried to the sand at Angus's feet. He turned, rushing back to fetch the rest of the load before the landguard could reach them.

Angus peered out beyond the beach, but could see nothing, for the moon had moved behind a stretch of clouds, shrouding the shadows in darkness. But he wasn't worried. It was doubtful the guard would be on the water, for they would have heard them approaching. And since they would need to pick their way down the rocky cliff wall to reach them, Angus and his crew would still have ample time to finish stowing the remaining load before slipping back onto the water to escape.

Angus was inside the caves, stowing the chest, when he heard the popping of gunfire and the surprised shouts of his men outside. He went to the cave entrance and was stunned to find that the dragoons were already on the beach. There were scores of them and they were already running for his scattering men. They couldn't have come down the cliff wall that quickly. Not without someone seeing them first. It could only mean they had been waiting for them, hiding in the dark recesses of the rock wall along the beachfront.

And that could only mean they had known beforehand the location where the load would be landed, a location that had only been decided that night.

Angus dropped the chest, shoving it quickly against the cave wall. All was not yet lost. The dragoons couldn't have been hiding closely enough to see where Angus and his crew had been directing the load to the caves. Had they been, Angus would have seen them, would have known they were there. Enough of the load still remained on the high part of the shore for the guard to think that the crew had planned simply to leave it there until they could transport it inland later. Angus couldn't risk discovery by running out to retrieve more. The cave opening was dark and obscure in the cliff wall, and even if they did find the entrance to it, the kegs and chests he'd already brought in were stowed far enough back into the shadowed niches which ran along the passage walls. The guard would never find them.

While they might lose the rest of the load, they still could escape arrest. Angus's crew knew well what to do when faced with the landguard. It was one of the first things he had taught them. They would scatter as best they could, pushing off in the skiffs, or swimming far enough from shore to escape, if needed. And Angus, he would simply move further into the caves and wait for the landguard to disperse in pursuit of the others.

"Mary! *Hoo,* Mary MacBryan! Are you there?"

The thundering voice was accompanied by a loud and insistent pounding at the cottage door.

Catriona rose quickly from her bed. She had only returned from leaving Robert at Rosmorigh a short while before, having already shared with him the slumber of lovers wrapped in his arms beside the loch. Beside her, Mairead was just waking, rubbing her eyes in the near darkness as she made for the kitchen.

Mary was at the door when they came out, holding a

candle high in her trembling hand. "Who is there?" she called.

" 'Tis Douglas, Mary. Douglas MacKansie. I've come to ask if you've seen Angus this night."

Mary yanked open the door. Standing in her chemise, her hair loose from its braids in ripping waves about her shoulders, she barely reached to Douglas's chin. Behind him, the sky was still dark with the last remnants of the night and the first inklings of the coming dawn. "What do you mean, Douglas? Wasna Angus with you last night?"

Catriona and Mairead stood back, watching as Douglas MacKansie's hulk filled the low doorway.

"Aye, he was, Mary, but there was a bit o' trouble with the landin' at Rosmorigh. Did you na hear of it?"

Rosmorigh? Catriona came forward. "Da arranged for a landing last night? At Rosmorigh?"

Mary turned troubled eyes to her daughter. "Dinna be angry at your da, lass. I knew the laird winna be there at the castle last night. Yer da was in a terrible state. He needed a safe place to bring in his load. 'Twas my doing that they stowed it at Rosmorigh. I thought 'twas the safest place since yer da said the guard was watching at Mallaig. I dinna think they would be watchin' at Rosmorigh, too."

"Lying in wait, they were," Douglas said then. "Bludey English dogs. They knew somehow that we would be landin' there. They had to, for they were already on the shore, hiding in the rocks when we started stowin' the load in the caves."

Catriona looked at him. "In the caves?"

"Aye, lassie. When the guard come upon us like they did, that's where your da was, in the caves. We were stowin' the load inside till we could come back later to fetch it. The lads and me, we all scattered when the guard came runnin' at us from the shadows. I dinna see Angus come from the caves though. I thought he would go back inside to hide till the guard left, then come home afterward."

"Angus dinna come home last night," Mary said. Her voice had grown heavy with her fear. It was a risk they'd always known existed, but one which they had prayed against every time Angus went off on his ventures. Even when the guard had come close any number of times before, he had always managed to escape. This time, though, it seemed his luck had run out.

Everyone fell silent, wondering what might have kept him from coming home.

"Oh God, no!"

All eyes turned on Catriona at her sudden outburst. She had one hand pressed over her mouth and her eyes were shining with terrified tears.

"What is it, lass?" Mary said, taking a step toward her.

Catriona clutched at her mother's hands. "The tide, Mam. The tide will have already started to come in. If Da is there inside the caves, he will not know before it is too late. He will be trapped inside the caves!"

Angus hadn't realized how much time had passed while he sat in the caves waiting, allowing time for the revenuers to have gone, until he started back the way he had come and sank to the ankle of his brogues in water and sand.

The tide had started to come in.

He continued on along the passageway until he could go no further, for the water had filled the lower part of the cave, swirling and churning so that he could no longer see the direction out. Unable to proceed, Angus turned and went back the way he'd come, taking the path which seemed to climb upward inside the cliff belly. Higher and higher he went through into the darkness, for he'd had to leave his lantern behind when his progress had grown difficult. He grabbed onto the cragged handholds, setting the toe of his brogue into a footstep until he found he could climb no higher. The path he followed had ended at a rocky halt.

Angus started down again. He became a little alarmed to find that the water level had climbed now to midthigh. He moved down another of the numerous passages, only to be made to turn back when this one, too, ended abruptly. Time was passing quickly. None of the subsequent passages he took led to any place other than an uncompromisingly solid wall.

His heart had begun beating faster each time he made his way back after another failed attempt. The water had risen to his chest now. He was having difficulty distinguishing which passages he had already tried and which remained. His lantern, which he had set high above him, jamming it into a rocky inset in the wall, was dangerously close to being doused.

Angus peered around him. At least one of the passages had to lead out in another direction. Hadn't Catriona said as much? But Angus hadn't listened to her, thinking it more of her bookish nonsense, like the forty thousand stars and such.

Which one to take? The water was cold and Angus's teeth began to chatter reflexively. He bit down to stop it, refusing to fall prey to his fear. From the speed with which the surf was coming in, he calculated that would only have enough time to try one more passageway. Perhaps two. After that, the water level will have risen too high, preventing him from coming back.

From what he could determine, three passageways remained untried. He studied them, wondering which would lead him to safety. Following any of the passages would take time. If he chose the wrong one, he might manage to duck down through the water to try one of the other two. But his light would be gone, leaving him to search in total darkness. He would never find his way out, much less back through along the uneven cave wall.

He called out "Hoo" to the passage nearest to him, listening for an echo that might indicate it went further than the others. But the sound of the rushing water and his own pulse beat thrumming in his head made it nigh

impossible to hear anything but his growing fear. He
had to choose. Time was fast passing him by. But
choosing meant that he could do nothing to change
what would happen afterward. Which passage should
he follow? He couldn't decide.

Until suddenly the light from his lantern went out,
leaving him in total darkness. He moved for the passage nearest to him.

The sun was rising by the time Catriona spotted the
lone tower at Rosmorigh peeking over the horizon, its
pink-orange lights glowing against the bottoms of the
clouds which stretched across the morning sky.

She was nearly there.

Her sides ached from running and her throat was raw
from gulping in the crisp morning air. She hadn't
stopped to rest since leaving the cottage, not even after
she'd fallen on a rocky incline, scraping her knees and
tearing a hole in one stocking.

Pausing now, her chest felt now as if it were afire
and she took in measured breaths in an effort to calm
her fast-beating heart. But she could not stop, she told
herself. She had to find her father.

Catriona had almost made it to where the cave
opening lay indiscernible to the unknowing eye, hidden amid a field thick with heather and gorse, when she
heard the sound of horses approaching at a hurried
pace behind her. She turned. just as five riders galloped thunderously up the hillside, pulling to a halt
several yards in front of her. Four of the riders lingered back while the one who seemed to be leading the
party urged his horse, a great black stallion whose nos-
trils puffed and steamed in the crisp morning air, close
to her.

"Good morning, miss. I wonder if I might trouble
you a moment—"

Catriona lifted her head to him.

He wasn't a man who was by any means large, but
dressed as he was in a fine black cloth greatcoat, set

over a rich blue frock with gold trimmings at the front, he took on a formidability most others lacked. His white breeches were spotted with mud above his polished Hessians, his hair, a light sandy color beneath his tall beaver hat, windblown from his ride. He stared at her and his eyes were blue, vivid blue, darkened somewhat by a peculiar look.

He urged his horse closer to her, staring still. His nearness caused Catriona to take an instinctive step backward. And when she did, her movement seemed to break him from his momentary hypnosis.

"May I ask what are you doing on Rosmorigh land?"

His directness coupled with the authority in his voice, made her wary. "My family are tenants of the laird of Rosmorigh. I was going to the castle."

"Tenants at Rosmorigh." The look in his eye darkened then. "And you, why are you going to the castle? You are employed there?"

"Have I done something questionable, my lord?"

His stallion whipped its head upward suddenly, shaking the reins and pawing anxiously at the ground. He tightened his hold on the beast. "We came upon a band of smugglers last night below the cliffs at Rosmorigh. We apprehended several of them. We are looking now for the others."

Catriona's face grew flushed in the chilled air. He was a revenuer. She prayed they hadn't found her father even as a small part of her wished they had, for at least she would then be certain he hadn't been caught inside the caves by the incoming tide.

"Have you seen anyone about, miss?" the man asked, still staring at her, only now the look in his eye chilled her. Why did he continue staring at her so queerly?

"No, my lord. I have seen no one. I—"

A faint shout came from the distance, hoofbeats pounding on the damp ground as another rider quickly approached. He pulled up beside the man on the black stallion.

"Caught us another of them smugglers, Lord Dunstron. He fired on young Robbie with a carbine and nicked him good in the arm. Got him cornered, but he's saying he'll kill the next Sasunnach dragoon that comes near him."

Lord Dunstron. Catriona recognized the name. He was a landholder and laird of Castle Crannock, an estate which lay several miles northeast of Rosmorigh. She had never seen him before but she remembered her father once saying Lord Dunstron was a cruel and uncompromising laird. He had once evicted a tenant of his, a woman past her seventieth year, viciously tossing her out wearing nothing more than her nightclothes to watch as they burned down her cottage before her. It had been winter then, a harsh and bitter one, and the woman had expired from the cold when she had been unable to find any shelter.

Lord Dunstron turned to regard Catriona again. She couldn't keep herself from frowning. "Seems I must leave now," he said, "but I hope we might have the occasion to speak again soon." He tipped his hat to her, his gloved hand black against the morning sky. "Good day, miss."

Catriona watched as Lord Dunstron wheeled his stallion around and shouted for his men to follow as he galloped back down the incline, tossing up clumps of earth behind him. Catriona hoped the poor man he was pursuing managed to escape. Considering what Angus had told her about him, there was no telling what Lord Dunstron would do once he captured him.

Catriona waited until the riders had vanished before she slipped through the hidden opening to the caves. In her haste she had forgotten to bring a candle, so she was made to move slowly along the passageway, feeling her way with her hands pressed flat to the wall in the blackness. It slowed her progress. She turned at one point, taking another passage which branched off to the right, instead of the one she usually took, the one leading to the library at Rosmorigh.

As she moved along, she called out to her father, but

there was no answer. Only silence, broken by the sounds of her footsteps. She went on further still, moving toward the opening which would eventually lead onto the beach. There was no indication of Angus or anyone else having recently been there.

Catriona swallowed back a lump in her throat when she felt the ground grow soft beneath her slippered feet. The walls of the cave were slick, the smell of seawater filling the air. The tide had indeed come, and had already begun to recede.

Perhaps he had found his way out, Catriona told herself, even as she continued onward, going further and further along the rocky cavern passage. That must be it. Angus had slipped away and was hiding out somewhere else, making certain the revenue officers were gone before returning to the cottage. Angus would never allow his smuggling activities to bring danger to his family. There was naught to worry. He had to be safe. He just had to.

Catriona saw a faint light ahead of her on the passageway, indicating that she was coming to the place where the caves opened out onto the beach beneath the castle cliffs. She had to stop just before the cave opening, for the water was still high enough that the waves splashed sluggishly inside.

Angus was nowhere to be seen.

It was then Catriona spotted the wooden chest half buried in the sand and shallow water near to her feet. It had been part of the load her father had been landing. A terrifying shudder took her when she noticed a piece of cloth twisted beneath it, drifting on the water's shallow surface.

Catriona reached down and pulled the cloth from beneath the chest. It was her father's tartan, the ancient MacBryan colors of rich green and navy and white, the plaid that he always wore crossed over his proud chest. She took up the dripping cloth and held it tight against her as tears fell softly down her face.

Chapter Sixteen

A knocking drew Robert away from the small desk globe he was trying so hard to focus on as he was sitting at the desk in the library. He took a sip of his coffee, cold beside him now on the long-abandoned breakfast tray. A moment later, Forbes came into the room, announcing the arrival of a visitor to Rosmorigh.

"Sir Damon Dunstron of Castle Crannock, your grace."

Robert's vision had improved now to the point where he could see the blurred outline of the man, tall, though not overly so, who came to stand before him. The shifting and shadowy shapes of a number of others lingered on the fringes of the room. Robert remained seated, waiting until Forbes had come to stand beside the desk.

"Good day, Sir Damon," he then said, motioning outward. "Won't you have a seat? Can I have my man offer you something? Brandy, perhaps? Port?"

Sir Damon stood before the desk, silently refusing Robert's offer of the chair. "Thank you, your grace, but I have not come making a social call. In fact you might say my reasons for coming here are somewhat related to your choice in refreshment." He paused, and when Robert didn't respond, he added. "I have come because

I have recently learned of smuggling activities which have taken place close by to Rosmorigh."

Already Robert didn't like the man's manner, for he spoke as if he believed himself far above his present company, contempt, even disdain resounding in his voice. Robert waited a moment before responding, staring directly as he said, "I assure you, Sir Damon, the brandy I offer to you is not any form of contraband."

Sir Damon's voice was noticeably more congenial in his response. "Of course I never intended to imply that you were at all involved in these activities, your grace."

Had Robert been capable of seeing the man clearly, he somehow knew Sir Damon's mouth would be turned in a superficial and placating smile then. "Of course."

"Had you been aware of these activities," Sir Damon went on, "I am quite certain you would have notified the authorities at once. The people who are involved in this rampant lawlessness are not men of like social caliber to you or I. They are rabble, common criminals who are ruled by the depravity they practice against His Majesty's laws and against those who seek to enforce them."

Robert didn't much appreciate the man's efforts to couple them similar. "It is my understanding, Sir Damon, that oftentimes this depravity is a direct result of the strict poverty brought on by those same laws."

"Perhaps, but a man's social status does not exempt him from abiding by the law of the land and paying his due tax."

Robert offered nothing in response. This wasn't the first time he'd heard this sort of opinion coming from a member of the upper classes. Unfortunately, it was a belief held by many, a belief which even the terrible events surrounding the recent revolution in France had not served to dispel. Robert decided against a disputation—such arguments were rarely if ever productive—and simply waited for Sir Damon to arrive at his reasons for coming there.

"In truth, your grace, I have come here to inform you

of a landing which was made last evening on the small stretch of beach that lies just beneath your castle cliffs."

Something about the way this man spoke, his words so carefully rehearsed, made Robert instinctively wary. "Indeed? A landing? Here at Rosmorigh?"

"Yes. I would have thought you had heard the gunfire which was exchanged between my men and the smuggler's crew."

Robert said nothing. His whereabouts the previous night were none of this man's concern.

"Perhaps you did not," said Sir Damon. "In any case, we have successfully apprehended several of the parties involved, and they are indeed naught but common criminals, as I earlier said. They will be dealt with and duly punished, however, there are still a number of others we continue to pursue. Which brings me to my reasons for coming here. There lies the possibility that the parties involved in this enterprise include individuals believed to be your own tenants."

"And these tenants, Sir Damon, I would assume you have their names?"

Robert was focusing on something shiny which Sir Damon held before him, a somewhat large object that appeared to be square in dimension. A book, perhaps?

"No, your grace, I am afraid I do not have any names. However, I do have with me the likeness of one individual whom I suspect is involved, or might have information that could lead me to these men. I am attempting to track her whereabouts. I was wondering if you might chance to recognize her."

Her? Sir Damon placed the object he held on the desk in front of Robert. It wasn't a book, nor merely the likeness Sir Damon had declared. It was a portrait and it was framed in gold. Of the painting, Robert could see little other than a distorted blend of colors, yellow, blue and black, before his eyes. He looked toward the waiting Sir Damon.

"I am afraid I can be of no assistance to you, Sir Damon. You see, I am—"

"Your grace," Forbes suddenly said from where he still stood beside Robert. "The woman in the portrait. It is Miss MacBryan!"

"I would think not, Forbes," Robert said.

The valet went on. "But it truly is her. Although the hair is darker than Miss MacBryan's and the clothing is of course far richer than her own, the eyes and the face are nearly identical. I have no doubt that it is her."

"Forbes—"

Sir Damon cut in then. "My good man, what did you say her name was?"

"MacBryan, and her family are indeed tenants of his grace here at Rosmorigh."

Robert wanted to smash his fist into Forbes's damnably blathering mouth. The man hadn't spoken as many words in the months since the two of them had been thrown together as he just had in the space of a moment's time. Still if the portrait did resemble Catriona that closely, then something clearly wasn't right. Why did this man, the pompous Sir Damon, have in his possession a portrait framed in gold of someone who looked like Catriona, but obviously was not? And why did Robert gain the distinct impression that Sir Damon's pursuit of these smugglers was secondary to his pursuit of the person in the portrait—Catriona? He thought of the words Sir Damon had used. He'd said he'd been unable to *track* her whereabouts, like the dog pursuing the proverbial fox. . . .

While Forbes and Sir Damon went on comparing the similarities between the portrait's likeness and Catriona, Robert stared down at the swirl of colors before him. If he could just focus on the face, this face which was said to look so like Catriona's. If he could only see her . . .

Shutting out the images and the voices surrounding him, Robert concentrated on a blurred patch of blue set near the center of the portrait. He stared at it, willing his eyes to see the image clearly. The pain in his head immediately rose up in response, growing, throbbing, and he tried to ignore it, until it burned behind his eyes with an unbearable fire. And then, for one brief instant, before he'd had to squeeze his eyes shut against the pain, he would have sworn he clearly saw what appeared to be two lovely blue eyes, large on a pale and delicate face.

Eyes the color of the storm sky . . .

Robert lowered his head and waited for the throbbing in his head to pass.

Despite what Sir Damon implied with his reasons for coming there, Robert was the one person who could say with all confidence that Catriona had not been involved in any smuggling activities the previous night. He knew this because she had been with him at the loch, wrapped in his arms until the moonlight had ceased to shine upon their slumbering bodies in the earliest hours of the morning. He could still feel the softness of her skin against his, the heat of her as she took him willingly and eagerly into herself. Catriona didn't have an ounce of deception in her. But what if . . . ? What if Catriona had known of the landing and had taken him away purposely because of it? Smuggler? Criminal? It was something any number of the women in London might have done, but he just couldn't sit with the belief that it had been Catriona's intention. Not when she had been an innocent.

And while Sir Damon might very well be a revenue officer in pursuit of suspected smugglers, Robert didn't need the ability to see clearly to realize his reasons for wanting Catriona were quite separate.

And, therefore, were also quite questionable.

Robert stood, frowning at Forbes in a final effort to stem his rattling tongue. His gesture succeeded. The idiot valet immediately fell silent beside him. "Thank you for your insight, Forbes. I am certain you have been quite helpful to Sir Damon." He turned to regard his guest once again. "I assure you, Sir Damon, I in no manner seek to hide anything from you. I did not recognize the woman in the portrait because quite frankly I cannot see it. I am blind. I will, however, check into the matter of Miss MacBryan and any part she might have in these smuggling activities which occurred here last night. You may rest assured I will report to you anything I chance to learn. I am, after all, a man who lives by the law. Forbes will see you and your men out. Good day, Sir Damon."

Sir Damon stared mutely at Robert before muttering an anger-tinged "Good day" in response. Grabbing up the portrait, he turned to follow his men out the door.

Forbes returned a short while later. "Your grace, if I might make a suggestion that Miss MacBryan's access to Rosmorigh be stemmed until—"

"No, Forbes, you may not make any suggestions. You have done enough already. Have my horse saddled immediately, Forbes. And have a mount readied for a groom to accompany me. I've a call to make this morning."

The wind blew as restless and unsettled as Robert felt, whipping across his face and tugging at the edges of his greatcoat, as he made his way across the moors toward the MacBryan croft. The sense of unease that had come upon him the moment Sir Damon had come into the library that morning remained with him still, and he knew the only way he might rid himself of it would be to find Catriona and resolve the questions running through his head. Blind or no, he knew once he spoke with her, questioned her, he would learn the truth.

He had asked one of the younger grooms, a lad of eight or nine years named Willie whose mother worked in the kitchens at Rosmorigh, if he knew where the MacBryan croft was located. Willie assured Robert that he did, for his ma and Mrs. MacBryan liked to chat over tea sometimes. He was more than willing to take Robert across the estate to it.

Having ridden out with Catriona on their numerous

outings to follow his father's journal, Robert now had the confidence he needed to sit his horse alone without yet the full ability to see. Still he missed the presence of Catriona sitting on the saddle in front of him, the way her head would ease back until it was resting on his shoulder, her hair blowing across his face.

They had ridden for some time when Willie finally slowed his horse to a halt.

"The MacBryan croft lies just ahead, your grace."

They came to where Robert could see the outline of the cottage standing a short distance away in front of them. The smell of baking filled the air, reminding him of the first time he had come, after Angus MacBryan had found him alone in the cottage with Catriona after the storm.

Robert dismounted and handed Bayard's reins to Willie. "Wait here. I will be back shortly."

Robert could make out the darker form of the door against the weathered white-gray of the cottage walls as he approached. He blinked and he could almost see what he thought were flowers growing along the side of it splashed in a blurred symphony of colors before him. In his rush to find Catriona, he had forgotten his spectacles, but oddly, he felt no terrible pain from the sunlight this morning. It was more a dull aching.

He walked to the door and knocked on it softly.

"Your grace . . ."

It was Mary MacBryan and she quite obviously hadn't expected to see him standing at her door this morning.

"Mrs. MacBryan," he said. "May I have a word?"

She hesitated. "Of course. Please come in, your grace."

She took his hand and led him inside the cottage to a seat at the table in the center of the room. "I made some bannocks this morning and was just boiling some water for tea. Can I make up a cup for you?"

"Thank you, madam."

A few minutes later Mary was setting out a cup in

front of him, directing it to his hands. She took the chair across from him. "I would assume you've not come makin' a social call, your grace."

Robert took up his teacup for a small sip before answering. It was a strong, clean blend, not the Bohea that he might have expected, but a Hyson customarily taken by the upper classes. It certainly wasn't a tea he would have expected to find in a crofter's cottage in the remote Scottish Highlands. Unless it had been brought in somehow . . .

Robert thought of his visit from Sir Damon that morning.

"I was hoping to speak with Catriona this morning, Mrs. MacBryan. I had expected her at Rosmorigh early this morning to attend to some of my correspondence, but she did not come."

Mary remained quiet. Robert decided to go on.

"I did, however, have a visit from a nearby land-owner. I became concerned because he was questioning me about some activities which have recently taken place nearby, and he seemed particularly concerned with Catriona."

Mary nearly dropped her teacup. "Catriona?"

"Yes. His name was Sir Damon Dunstron of Castle Crannock. Do you know him?"

"Aye, I know of him." Her voice had grown soft, almost frightened sounding.

"What I found especially odd is that he had a portrait with him. He asked me if I could identify its subject, which, of course, I could not, given my blindness. However, my valet Forbes identified the portrait's subject. Strangely, he claims it is a likeness of Catriona."

"Sweet Lord, he has seen her." Mary rose from the table, pushing her chair back abruptly. "Your grace, you do not understand . . ."

"I am aware of that, Mrs. MacBryan. That was my purpose in coming here."

She paced behind him for several moments, wringing her hands, he guessed, quite obviously agitated by what he had just told her. "Mrs. MacBryan, Sir Damon informed me of a landing which was to have taken place on the stretch of shore beneath Rosmorigh. Given the excellent blend of tea you just offered to me, I am assuming your husband is most probably involved. That is not my concern. My concern now is for Catriona. I find it odd that Sir Damon would have a portrait of someone who looks nearly identical to her, dressed in fine clothing, when I know very well that Catriona is the daughter of a crofter. I find it even stranger that under the guise of pursuing dangerous smugglers, Sir Damon seems more concerned with locating a young Scottish woman. There is something more to this than smuggling, isn't there?"

Mary returned to her chair. She sat for some time, considering her response to everything Robert had just told her. Finally she spoke. "Your grace, I trust your word that you've only Catriona's safety in mind. I believe you care for her, care for her beyond that of a laird to his tenant. I must tell you something which even Catriona dinna know, something I'd not planned to tell her until I felt I needed to."

Her voice had started to break and she paused to collect herself. "I have managed to keep her safe these years, and perhaps I have grown careless after all this time. I should have known the day would come when he would see her. And I should have thought that when he saw her, he would certainly know. They look so alike."

"I assume by 'he' you are speaking of Sir Damon?"

"Yes, your grace. I know well of this man. When I was Catriona's age, e'en afore I was wedded to Angus, I lived with my family on Crannock land. We were tenants there. The laird then was a kind man named Sir Charles Dunstron. My father always thought him a fair and just man and everyone knew he treated his tenants well. I'd worked at Crannock as a chambermaid for a time until I went to be a ladies' maid to the laird's young wife. She was expecting a child when the laird's grandnephew Sir Damon came to visit, having just finished his university studies."

Mary paused to take a sip of her tea. Her voice had grown calmer. "I knew from the first time I saw him that he had the devil in him."

"Sir Damon?"

"Aye. 'Twas because of him that I was made Lady Catherine's maid. He'd tried to force himself on me once when he had come upon me changin' the linen in his chamber. Lady Catherine happened by and heard my struggle with him. I dinna wish to think o' what would have happened to me if she'd not come outside that door when she had. But when Lady Catherine brought the matter to Sir Charles's attention, Sir Damon said 'twas me who had initiated the relationship."

"Quite often that is the excuse used in such situations," Robert said.

"Aye. Sir Charles was put in a troubling place. He warned his nephew to keep himself away from the servants and then told Lady Catherine I could stay wit' her since she was increasin' and would be drawin' close to her confinin' time. I'd helped my mother when she'd attended at some other birthings. It was naught but a fortnight later when Sir Charles was dead."

"Do you mean to say Sir Damon killed him?"

"I canna prove it, but 'tis what I believe, and 'tis what Lady Catherine believed, too. The physician said Sir Charles had succumbed to a fever, but I believe Sir Damon poisoned him. I also believed Lady Catherine's life was in peril as well."

"I would assume that since the heir was not yet born, Sir Damon would become the heir should Lady Catherine deliver a daughter."

"Aye. Once Sir Charles was gone, Sir Damon treated Lady Catherine most terrible. I knew it was due to me, because of her havin' interfered like she did when he'd come at me. Moved her to a chamber, he did, that was no better than a tollbooth cell. Started ordering her food prepared for her, but I winna have her eat anything he brought to her. I brought her my mam's cookin' and we kept to ourselves, me and Lady Catherine. It was me that attended her at the birthing of her son."

"So she did deliver an heir."

"Aye. Delivered him and then lost her life a short time afterward. 'Twas a terrible birth for her, your grace, but she was so happy when she knew she'd had a laddie. Until Sir Damon come and took the bairn right from my arms. I never saw the lad again."

Robert concentrated on her words. "You are saying you believe Sir Damon brought harm to the child?"

"Killed him, he did. I am certain of it. He dinna e'en allow Lady Catherine to hold the bairn in her arms. Left us sittin' in that burnin' hot chamber without even a cup of water to ease poor Lady Catherine's sufferin'. Now, though, I know 'twas a good thing, his taking the bairn away like he did. For if he hinna take the lad, he would have been there when Lady Catherine delivered her second bairn that night. Her daughter."

Robert suddenly fit all the pieces together. Of course. Who else could it have been? "Catriona."

"Aye. They were twins. Catriona was a strong lassie bairn, but her poor mother winna see her past but a few moments after she was born. Lady Catherine already knew what Sir Damon would do to her son. She dinna want the same fate befallin' her lassie. Before she died, Lady Catherine made me promise to take Catriona away from Castle Crannock and raise her as my own, so Sir Damon could not bring her to the same harm he would bring to her brother that night." She paused. "There's something more."

Mary stood and left the table, returning a few moments later. She took Robert's hand and pressed something into it. "She gave this to me to give to Catriona when 'twas time to tell her the truth. There is this and a handkerchief that 'twas Lady Catherine's. 'Tis all I have to prove what I say to you now."

The handkerchief. Robert had never returned it to Catriona. The *C* stitched upon it. It hadn't been meant to signify Catriona. It had been intended for her mother, Lady Catherine.

Robert took up the gold chain in his fingers. The pendant it held twisted in the light of the peat fire, a glimmering blur before his unfocusing eyes. Robert needed no further proof from Mary. Her words, the way she'd spoken them with such fear and pain and grief told far more. The secret she had kept so long had played heavily upon her. "Did Lady Catherine have any family?"

"She talked of a brother, but I ne'er knew Lady Catherine's birth name. I dinna e'en know where in England she was from."

"Lady Catherine was English?"

"Aye, she was. Sir Charles brought her back wit' him after he had gone to London. He was besotted with her, and she adored him. And that devil, he took them both . . ."

"And he will be punished for his deeds, Mrs. MacBryan, I assure you of it. Where is Catriona now?"

Mary stood again. "Oh, dear, I was so busy telling you about Lady Catherine, I forgot about Angus." She hesitated. "I'm sorry to tell you, your grace, that Angus was part of that landing party last night aneath Rosmorigh."

"I had already come to that conclusion. I must ask you though, was Catriona also part of that plan?"

"Your grace?"

"She took me out and away from Rosmorigh last night. Was it so that I wouldn't be there when Angus was down on the beach beneath the cliffs?"

"Oh no, your grace," Mary said. "Catriona dinna know a thing of it. 'Twas my suggestion to Angus that he land it there, because I knew you were away wit' Catriona. I'm sorry for it. I know I canna expect you to understand." She hesitated, obviously troubled. "He's not a criminal, my Angus. He lives by the law of God and does what he must to see his family cared for. Last night, when he was stowing the load in the caves, the landguard come upon them. He went into hiding, but when he dinna come home by this morning, Catriona feared the tide. She left first thing this morn to look for Angus in the caves. When she dinna come right back by midday, I sent Mairead out after her. But it's been too long now. They should have come back. Oh, your grace, what will I do if that devil has already found her?"

Chapter Seventeen

The ride back to Rosmorigh was slow, too slow for Robert's patience. He tried not to think of Sir Damon and the chance that he could have already found Catriona, of what he could be doing to her, but the images came unbidden regardless, filling his mind and making his frustration mount. If the blackguard dared to harm her, blind or not, Robert would kill him by his own hand,

Bayard must have sensed Robert's urgency for he was tugging at the bit, dancing about and trying to break from his slow enforced trot. He wanted to race and Robert would have liked nothing better, but he could not, not without his sight. Instead he was left to clutching the reins tight in his gloved hands, saying a silent prayer that Damon hadn't yet found Catriona, that she was safe and searching for Angus in the caves, or even awaiting him in the library at Rosmorigh. And that only made his frustration mount higher.

If what Mary had told him were true—and Robert had no reason to doubt it—then Catriona was in very real danger. And the worst of it was that she knew nothing of her past and thus she could have no notion at all of just how much danger she was truly in. Sir Damon was a man without conscience, without morals, without heart. He had committed a sin worse than any other, killing not only Lady Catherine, but with her, her newborn son, an innocent. He had taken a life which had barely begun, committing the most unforgivable of sins. And then afterward, a true testament of his character, he had kept in his possession a portrait of the woman he'd so abused as some sort of macabre memento of his terrible deeds.

And it was because of this Robert knew that what Mary feared was true. Had Sir Damon known of Catriona's existence before now, there was no doubt he would have killed her. And he would surely try now, if given the opportunity.

Only Robert would make certain he never found that opportunity.

Back in the library, Robert made his way immediately to the wall that opened onto the caves. He tried to remember the numerous times Catriona had taken him there, when they had gone down onto the stretch of beach beneath the castle to read his letters. What had she done to release the door? There had to be a switch hidden there that would trigger the wall to slide open. But where? He could, he supposed if he needed, ask Forbes or one of the other servants to help him search for it, but he didn't want them involved in this further. Forbes had already done enough to worsen matters with his rattling tongue. There would be no telling what more he might do, given the chance.

Robert felt along the edges of the wall panels, running the flat of his hand against the smooth, polished wood. He traced his fingers against the floor, and then high above, feeling over the carved scrollwork that decorated the surface. Still he could find nothing.

He was contemplating forcibly kicking at the wall when the clock beside him chimed softly three times. Its gentle bell sound broke him from his near-panic. He turned to it. In the light of the candle branch set on the mantel beside him, he could nearly make out the movement of the clock's mechanism spinning before him in a glimmering blur.

A memory struck him then, the memory of the first day he had met Catriona, when she had asked him to help her find the mechanism hidden in his father's desk. He hadn't thought he could find it, but she'd told him something which had made him think perhaps he might.

Try to rely on what you have, not what you are lacking. . . .

Compelled by the memory of her words, Robert reached for the hearth and pushed against the carved and pitted stone. He tested every crevice, running his hands against the underside of the mantel until finally he found a small place against the wall where the stone wasn't truly fixed. He applied a small amount of pressure to it. A rush of cool air swept against his face as the wall slid easily back.

Darkness yawned before him. Cold. Uncertain. But all he could think of was that Catriona might be there.

Taking up the candle branch, Robert placed his free hand against the rough and pitted wall and started slowly down the narrow cave steps.

The sounds of the sea called to him, distant, leading him, and he followed the passage which seemed to follow in its direction. He calculated that it had been nearly nine hours since Catriona had gone in search of Angus that morning. He didn't know the tides and so had no way of knowing what awaited him at the end of the passage. He only knew he needed to find her.

The sounds grew louder, echoing around him. Robert set the candle branch on a ledge he felt cut from the stone wall, thinking he would go on a little further in search of her. He decided he would leave the light as a makeshift beacon so should he need to turn back, he would be able to find it to guide him through the darkness of his shadowed vision.

Robert moved slowly along the passageway until he felt the water splashing against his boots. He hadn't yet made it to the beach outside the caves where Catriona had taken him so many times before. Already the water was ankle-deep. He thought of the story Catriona had told him of when the people of Rosmorigh had been drowned in these same caves after they had been trapped by the tide. He remembered her words. . . .

Their bodies washed out to sea . . .

Robert shouted her name, his heart beating faster. *What if . . . ?* He wouldn't think of it. He shouted once again. His voice echoed deep within the wandering and endless tunnels, lost against the crashing of the waves on the shore beyond. He moved further still along the same obscure route until he felt the water rising to his knees. The sea had grown louder, lapping against the cavern wall, drowning out the sound of his heart beating hard against his chest. Where could she have gone to? She had to be in the caves somewhere. There was no other place she would have gone. Unless . . .

Robert could feel the water swirling frantically around his legs, tugging, pulling at him as if already wanting to take him with it. Again he shouted Catriona's name. No response. He moved yet a little further along the passageway, bracing himself with his hands pressed flat against the rocky, uneven wall.

When the water was close to his waist, Robert realized his own time was running short. He could go no further, for the water had come too high. He had no choice left to him. He would need to turn back until the tide receded, then return to search for her again later.

As Robert turned to look behind him for his guiding candlelight, his boot slipped on the damp cave floor, sending him crashing into the swirling surf. He surfaced, disoriented as he thrashed about for a handhold. He braced himself against the wall and searched for the candle beacon through his blurred vision, but he could not find it. He could see only darkness, could hear only the sound of the water rushing in to fill the small chamber. Having lost his direction, Robert had no way of knowing how to retrace his steps. Faster, louder, the water came in around him, threatening to overtake him inside the hollow chamber even as he tried to think of what he should do next.

He had been a fool. How could he have thought he would be able to find Catriona on his own? He should have brought Willie with him, for despite his improving vision, he was still for all intents and purposes blind. He told himself he should have known better. During the wars, when he would place himself time and again in dangerous situations, he had always first considered the outcome, every possible result which might occur, and what he would do should he find himself faced with any one of them. In that way he had always been prepared. Ready, able to face what might come to him. But this time, when he truly needed to have followed that course, he hadn't. His concern for Catriona had completely filled his mind and his only thought had been to find her before Sir Damon, not to what might happen to him if he didn't. And now he'd likely drown for his foolishness.

Fear began to rise up inside of him. He thought back to the first time he'd seen battle on the Peninsula, when his fear had grown so that he felt certain it would choke him. He had closed his eyes, shutting away the images and the sounds of the men who had been dying close to him, concentrating every thought and effort on what he must do. He did that again now. He had to get out of this place. But how?

"Robert?"

Catriona's voice came from somewhere behind him, distant, soft, dreamlike. Relief flooded through him, stronger than the surging tide. Once again, his guardian angel had come to his rescue.

"Catriona, I am here."

"Do not move from where you are," she said. "I will come to you."

Robert remained where he was braced against the cavern wall, water swirling at his chest as he listened for her approach in the din of the incoming tide.

Finally he heard her threading her way through the water to him.

"Take my hand," she said, touching him on his shoulder. "I will lead you out."

Catriona brought Robert onto a dry passage that was set up from the lower cavern. "You will need to duck your head. The ceiling here is low for a space, until we reach the inner chamber."

Robert knew when they had arrived, for the air had grown noticeably cooler and the sounds of their footsteps echoed softly around them. The sea suddenly seemed miles away. The chamber was quiet, still. Robert lifted his head. The glow from the candles Catriona held fluttered with the shadows before his eyes. He searched for her but he could not see her in the muted light.

"What were you doing down here?" Catriona asked. "If I hadn't found your candle branch in the passageway, I never would have known you were here. Do you know you could have drowned in the tide?"

"I was just coming to that realization seconds before you called to me." Robert paused when he felt her hand warm against his. She was here. She was safe. Damon couldn't touch her now. The tide couldn't take her. Only then did he allow himself to acknowledge the peril they had both been placed in. He took her into his arms and pulled her against his chest. "I had come to look for you," he murmured into her hair. "I didn't know where you had gone. This was the only place I could think of to look."

Catriona was silent and her fingers were clutching tightly to Robert's arms. Her body was trembling, shivering really, though it wasn't from any cold.

"Catriona? What is it?"

"My father, Robert," she said, her voice muffled against his chest. "I fear he is gone."

"Gone to where?"

She pulled away, her hands resting on his forearms. "I believe the tide took him. I found his tartan in the cave and his lantern was nearly buried in the sand on the beach. Oh, Robert, it is all my fault. He didn't know about this chamber. He could have no way of knowing it is the only one that doesn't fill with sea-water when the tide comes in. I should have told him." Her voice broke then and she shook her head hope-lessly. "He couldn't have known where to go when the water came in."

Robert took Catriona into his arms again, tucking her head beneath his chin. "Perhaps he found a way out before the tide came fully in. He might even be at the cottage now, waiting for you to return."

Catriona closed her eyes, murmuring, "I hope so, Robert, but it will be hours before we can go back. By now the lower cavern is filled. We are trapped here until the tide goes back out."

Mary stirred the ruddy, glimmering embers in the hearth with an iron poker, bringing up the fire to ignite the peat she'd just placed upon it. She watched it catch before setting the crock on to simmer, knowing Angus would be hungry when he returned, for he hadn't fin-ished his supper the night before.

There would be plenty for him to eat when he came home. She had spent the past hours since Robert had left preparing whatever she could lay her hands on, anything to keep her mind from thinking. And wor-rying. Fresh oat bannocks which she'd baked on the *greideal* over the fire and a sweet-smelling gingerbread were already set out on the table to cool, filling the cot-tage with their comforting scents. The limpet stovies she'd just hung on the crook over the fire would simmer for another hour, and she would need to fetch some additional peats before she could set to shelling the mussels Angus had brought her the previous day for the brose.

Mary looked about the empty cottage. She hoped the girls would return soon. Mairead had returned a short time after the duke had departed, without Catriona, and

Mary had sent her off to the Colonel's to see if he might have returned, and then off in search of Ian, thinking perhaps the lad would know if Angus were hiding out somewhere. Mary knew if her husband suspected any trouble he would keep himself away, hiding for weeks if need be, doing whatever he could to prevent danger from coming to his family's door. And then there was Catriona. How she prayed the laird had found her and was at that moment bringing her safely home.

Mary thought of her visit from him that morning. The duke was a good man. She knew he would never allow that devil Sir Damon to harm Catriona. And Mary was glad to have told the laird the truth of Catriona's birth, to finally let go of the burden of the secret she'd kept for so long.

Only one person other than herself knew of the truth; Mary's husband, Angus. She thought back to when she had brought Catriona, the tiny infant, home with her that long-ago night. Mary had been young then, seventeen, and though promised to Angus, she was not yet married. Her parents, while knowing she had done the only thing she could have in taking the child, were concerned. Angus had been courting her, but had wanted to have set up his own croft before taking a wife. Mary loved Angus too much to expect him to raise someone else's child. So she had gone to him that night to tell him she could not be his wife.

But Mary soon found she had underestimated her man.

Angus had refused her exemption. MacBryan blood was rooted in the ancient clan traditions, traditions where oftentimes generations earlier, the sons of the great chiefs had been fostered with the lesser clansmen as a means of building a loyalty to the *clan* and not simply to a *chief*. It was an ancient tenet of the Scots, the unity of the whole, not just an allegiance to the one. Therefore the idea of fostering the daughter of Sir Charles, the laird they had all loved and respected, wasn't an obligation to Angus at all. It was an honor.

Staring into the fire, Mary made a final silent prayer that her family was safe before setting the poker against the hearthstone. She went to the small closet at the back of the cottage where the wide wooden bin Angus had built for storing the spare peats was kept. She was bent over it, removing the chunks of foamy earth from inside when she heard the door to the cottage open. She eased; the first of her prayers had been answered.

"Mairead?" she called, "is that you? Any news of the Colonel? Did you find young Ian?" She grabbed up the peat basket and headed for the kitchen. "I was just fetchin' some peats for the—"

Mary halted in the doorway, frozen, her words forgotten as she looked at the person standing there. It wasn't Mairead. Nor was it Angus. Mary stared at the man who awaited her, his rich clothes looking so out of place among the humble cottage surroundings.

He had aged, but the time that had passed had done nothing to dim the wicked gleam in his devil's eyes. It was a face she had prayed never to see again. She felt as if the wind had been knocked from her when he smiled, a sinister grin that sent a shiver of fear tracing along her spine.

"Hello, Scots witch. Did you think I wouldn't come for you?"

Mary didn't answer. Instead she dropped the peat basket and ran for the back of the cottage.

The candle branch flickered softly beside where Robert and Catriona sat, glowing against the dark and shadowed cavern walls. Already two of the four candles had burned down, guttering before going out completely. Catriona stared at the glimmering light, the dancing of the flames upon the two candles remaining. Soon they would be left with nothing but the darkness, the darkness and the sound of the coming sea.

The sea that had taken her father.

Tears began to fall and an emptiness filled her

inside. Her father had only wanted to give his family an adequate living, modest, but decent, not the struggling one of so many of the crofters, marked by poverty and want. Had there been any other way, he would have surely chosen it. But he'd done the only thing he could think of, the only way he could find to give his family the things they'd needed, and now he could have died for it.

Robert could not see her tears, but he must have sensed her sadness, for he reached for her, touching her softly on her cheek. Catriona took his hand, holding to it tightly. She needed to know something other than the horrible sadness that was making her feel so utterly hollow inside, the tumult that made her want to crumple to her feet and scream until she didn't feel this way any longer.

What she needed more than anything else was to feel alive.

She whispered softly. "I need you, Robert."

Catriona reached for him, clasping her hands around his neck and pulled him to her, kissing his mouth as she sought to find a way to bring him yet closer to her. She wanted to bury herself against his strength, his warmth, his hardness. Robert returned her kiss, realizing somehow her feelings, knowing the need, the desperate desire to feel and forget and lose oneself in something other than the unbearable grief.

He knew because he'd been buried in his own grief for so long, he'd nearly forgotten what it was like to feel anything other than pain and anger and frustration. Until Catriona had come into his life.

Catriona pulled away from their kiss. "Oh, Robert," she said, her voice strangled and sad. She choked on a sob.

"Shh, my love," he whispered to her, smoothing a hand over her head. "Let us not think of what awaits us on the outside. We are here and we are together. Let us just be what we should, what we each of us needs the other to be."

He took her to him once again and kissed her deeply, moving his tongue into her mouth, tasting, touching, knowing her. His hands were strong, holding her as he lay her back onto the ground. He released her only long enough that he might slip his shirt over his head and then bunch it into a cushion which he placed beneath her head.

Catriona stared up at Robert in the glowering candlelight. The muscles lining his flat belly and chest were shadowed, defined, as he stood above her. He was so beautiful. She lifted her hand and held it to him, beckoning him to come to her once again.

Robert lowered himself beside Catriona slowly and took her into his arms, leaning over her. Catriona reached for him, caressing the sides of his face with her hands, running her fingers through his hair and down over his broad and muscular shoulders. His body felt like fine marble beneath her touch, hard, perfect, magnificent. She closed her eyes as he ran the tips of his fingers upward along each of her legs, drawing down first one, and then the second of her stockings.

The lingering of his gesture, the slowness, was exquisite.

Catriona closed her eyes and took each sensation he gave her as he slowly unfastened the small buttons that lined the front of her gown, peeling way the layers of clothing until he at last found the prize he sought. Catriona felt the coolness of the air outside brushing against her bare skin and she lifted her hips so that he might slip the gown from her.

She lay naked, listening as he stood from her. She opened her eyes, quietly watching as Robert shucked away his breeches and was standing over her as naked as she. The curve of his buttocks glowed in the ebbing candlelight as he turned to face her once again. He knelt beside her and drew her into his arms, crushing her mouth beneath his.

Catriona stroked her fingers over him, his back, down his stomach, seeking, exploring, and then finally knowing when she found him. She closed her fingers over his hardness, stroking the hot and velvety skin. She heard him suck in a sharp breath. It pleased her to know she could make him feel as wonderful as he did her. Instinctively she moved her hand, tightening and loosening her fingers over him. Robert's breath was coming fast against her ear, hot, desperate, until he reached for her hand and stilled her.

"Not so fast, my love. We've all the time in the world."

Robert lifted himself over her once again and kissed her forehead, her eyelids, her ears, nibbling tiny bites along the sensitive skin of her neck, sending tingles of awareness racing through her. Catriona arched against his mouth when he found her breast, drawing on her nipple, bringing it to tautness. Within her a fire began to smolder, a fire which grew, building to flame as his mouth moved lower and lower still over her belly.

When she felt Robert's breath brushing against the insides of her thighs, she drew in a slow and anticipating breath.

At the touch of his tongue on her, parting her, teasing her, she nearly came undone. It was foreign and different, this way in which he was loving her, but it felt so wonderful she dared not ask him to stop. He seemed to know exactly where to touch her, how to bring the sensations within her alive, fueling that inner fire until she was clenching her hands in his hair and lifting her hips upward, seeking that most excellent release.

And then the release came upon her, showering over her in a million different sensations, passing through her in waves of wondrous pleasure. And his mouth kept on with its sweet and sensual assault, his tongue delving inside of her, teasing her until she could bear the pleasure no more and was begging him to stop.

Robert drew away from her, leaving her struggling to regain her breath. But only long enough for him to maneuver between her legs. She felt his hardness pressing against her moistness, stretching her, filling her slowly, so slowly, until he was buried so deep within her it truly felt as if they were one.

There was no pain this time, only sweet, exquisite fire. It was a feeling like no other, and Robert drew back his hips until he was filling her again, thrusting into her. Over and over he came into her, rocking against her, fluid, smooth, until his movements became erratic and he was gasping out her name and she was his, and then with one final powerful thrust she felt his release spasming deep inside of her. He was clutching her tightly against his chest, his face buried in her neck, every muscle in his back rigid with his climax.

Robert relaxed after a spell and threaded his fingers softly through her hair. Slowly he drew himself from her, stretching out his length beside her on the cave floor. Catriona rested her head against his chest and listened to the sound of his slowing heartbeat close to her ear.

She loved this man, loved him with everything she had within her to give, and dreamed of a life they could spend together even as she thought it surely would never be. Robert could never love her, not the way she loved him, for despite the magic and wonder they shared as lovers, he was and would always be a duke, and she would always be a Scottish crofter's daughter.

And so it was she, Catriona MacBryan, who whispered softly what she so longed to hear from him, and what she daren't reveal to him in words he could understand.

Tha Gaol Agam Ort. The Gaelic phrase which means *I love you.*

Chapter Eighteen

Catriona opened her eyes. It was dark and quiet and still, so still she could hear the whispering sound of her own breathing. Her cheek lay softly against Robert's chest, the touch of his skin warm and comforting against her. His arm was turned protectively against her shoulder and he was yet asleep, peaceful in the serene darkness. The lingering scent of their lovemaking surrounded them.

Catriona lay still for several moments, just listening to the steady beating of his heart against her ear, the soft rush of his breath as it drifted against her forehead. Until she realized she could no longer hear the sound of the sea, not even faintly.

She sat up, instantly awake, and in moving, she roused Robert.

"Catriona? Is something wrong?"

"No." She was already standing. "The tide has gone out again. We can return to the cottage now to see if there has been any word of my father."

She felt beside her and found her gown lying on the cave floor, where it had been tossed along with the rest of their clothing. She hesitated. Even though she was anxious to get home again, she was reluctant to leave this place. It had been their haven, their sanctuary, where no one could touch them and where the differences between them no longer mattered. Here they ceased to be laird and tenant, and were nothing more than they should ever be. Man and woman. Lovers. But outside, beyond these protective rock walls, she knew the rest of the world wouldn't allow them to remain that way.

Catriona slipped on her gown and then found Robert's shirt and breeches. "Here are your things," she said, pressing them to him.

They moved slowly along the pitched black passageways, for despite the fact that the tide had gone out, the cave floor was slick with the water and seaweed which had been left behind. Catriona led Robert through and a short time later, they were at the foot of the steps leading up to the library.

Catriona released the catch on the sliding door. It was dark in the library, night had already fallen, and Catriona left Robert at the door, feeling along the hearth mantel for the tinderbox. She struck a flint and touched a sulphur match against the glowing tinder, found a spare candle inside, and lit it.

"Catriona."

"I'll just see if I can find another candle branch here somewhere," she said, starting across the room.

Robert grabbed her arm suddenly. She turned.

"Catriona."

She looked at him and peered into eyes which were staring into hers. He didn't look at her as always he had, his eyes merely directed at her. Robert looked at her now as if he could truly see her and he was smiling at her, a smile that she had never seen before. It was a smile that lit his face, reaching to his eyes and bringing them alive with golden brown lights. It was a smile of recognition. She returned the smile.

His voice was soft. "Even in my dreams I never would have imagined you this beautiful."

"Oh, Robert, you can see."

Elated, Catriona threw her arms around his neck, and

in doing so, promptly snuffed out the light of her candle.

Robert laughed into her hair. "Don't take the light away now that I can truly see you."

Catriona released him and grabbed up the tinderbox with trembling hands. It took her several attempts to relight the candle, but when she had, she turned and looked at Robert standing before her.

Robert would have sworn he was dreaming if not for the throbbing he felt behind his eyes. But the sight of Catriona was worth ten times the pain. Her hair was loose and tumbling about her shoulders, disordered from their lovemaking, and it was indeed a coppery brown that shone burnished in the candlelight. She was small, her features delicate, but she had a strength to the way she lifted her chin. And her eyes, he could never have imagined such expressive, glimmering, exceptional eyes. Now that he could see them, stare into them, he would never want to look away. "Your eyes truely are the color of the storm sky."

He took her to him and folded her into his embrace. Finally, he could see her.

"It was true," she said, smiling, when he released her moments later.

"I beg your pardon?"

"I didn't want to tell you earlier in case it wasn't true, but . . ." she paused, choosing the words to tell him carefully, ". . . last night, when we were at the loch, I took you there to give you back your sight."

Robert looked confused. "I see . . ."

Catriona laughed at his unintended pun. "Yes, you do see, and it is all because of the white heather."

"The flower you searched for as a young girl?"

"Somewhat. You see, my mother gave me a sprig of white heather she found when she was a girl. She'd kept it all these years. She told me to take you to the loch. She said that if I sprinkled the white heather over you and then took you into the waters of the loch, you would regain your sight," She laughed aloud. "And you did."

Robert listened to Catriona, her belief, her absolute conviction in what she was telling him. He had never told her of his improving vision, of the exercises he had practiced in his efforts to restore his sight. He hadn't wanted to tell her until he was certain he had been successful. And now that he was, he wouldn't tell her, because one of the things he truly loved about Catriona was her untarnished outlook on the world. She had a belief in the goodness of life, of its inexplicable magic, and she shared that magic, shining it on everyone she touched. He wasn't about to take that away from her now.

So instead he just smiled and said, "I will be certain to thank your mother properly when we see her."

The sky was cloud covered and it was therefore pitch dark as they made their way on horseback over the windswept moors to the MacBryan cottage. The faint glow of firelight flickered through the front window as they started down the incline toward it. They were just approaching the door, leaving Bayard at the enclosure, when the door opened suddenly and a tearful Mairead appeared on the other side.

"Oh, Catriona . . ." was all she managed before she grabbed her sister to her and pulled her into a tight and desperate embrace.

"What is it, Mairead?" Catriona asked. "What has happened?"

Mairead could but sob incoherently, unable to tell them anything in her present state.

But Robert already knew. As he looked beyond Mairead inside the cottage, he could see the overturned chairs, the scattered and broken crockery. A spinning wheel lay in pieces by the hearth. The small colorful curtain framing the window had been rent nearly in half. The scene had all the ingredients of violence.

And he immediately knew.

Sir Damon Dunstron had been here.

" 'Tis how I found it," Mairead gasped out, turning as Robert stepped past her inside. In the light he could see that her eyes were red and badly swollen. It had been some time since she had come home to find this horror.

"I thought perhaps it had been someone looking for Da." Mairead hesitated, choosing her words carefully in front of Robert. "Because of last night . . ."

"It is all right," Catriona said, staring about in bewilderment at the dreadful melee. "Robert already knows the truth about Da and the landing at Rosmorigh last night."

"But then, I found Mam . . ."

"Mam?" Catriona's voice grew small, almost child-like with fear.

Mairead pointed to the doorway at the back of the cottage. "She is there. I managed to get her to the bed. I have tended to her as best I could, but I know not what more to do for her."

Catriona started forward, but Mairead grabbed her arm. "Nay, Catriona, you mustn't see her."

Catriona yanked away from her sister. "Of course I must see her. She needs me . . ."

Robert took Catriona's hand. "Catriona, let me go to see Mary first. Mairead needs you more right now."

Catriona didn't want to do as he asked, but she also realized the truth of his words. It was obvious to anyone looking at her that Mairead was in a state of shock. Her eyes were wide, but they were seeing little other than the horrific scene she had undoubtedly found when she'd returned to the cottage. She was twisting her skirts desperately in her fingers, murmuring something softly against the bunched-up cloth. She needed tending, the reassurance which only her family could give her. Robert would not be able to do so.

"You are right," Catriona finally said and she took Mairead's hand, leading her slowly to the table. She picked up one of the overturned chairs and set it aright, helping Mairead to sit before sitting herself across from her. She covered Mairead's trembling hands with her own and whispered soothing words to her as Mairead began to rock in her seat, chanting over and over, "What will we do . . . What will we do . . . What will we do . . . ?"

Robert left them, walking slowly to the back of the cottage. The chamber there was small, fitting only the box bed and a crudely fashioned wooden chest with a washing bowl and pitcher set atop it. It took his eyes a moment to adjust to the dim light. He heard a faint wheezing sound coming from the bed. He started over to it. Nothing could have prepared him for the sight which met him in the light of the single candle burning there.

Mary's face had been beaten past recognition. Both eyes were swollen closed and bruised a sickly blackish purple color. Her lower lip had been split and blood dripped from the corner where her jaw sagged brokenly. Her nose looked as if it had been crushed. Her chest rose and fell in uneven, struggling breaths, indicating to Robert the probability of broken ribs. He didn't want to wonder at what other horrors were concealed beneath the woollen blanket that covered her frail body.

Robert had seen men come from battle who looked better than this. This wasn't simply a beating. It was a desecration. And looking at her, he knew she would not live to see the morning.

"Mrs. MacBryan?"

The candlelight glimmered at the slits of her eyes, indicating that she was attempting to look toward the voice that called to her. A pained groan sounded from behind her swollen mouth.

"Y-your grace . . ."

When she opened her mouth even the slightest bit to speak, Robert could see that she was missing one of her front teeth. He took a deep breath to rein in his anger. "It was him, wasn't it? It was Sir Damon who did this to you."

Mary attempted to move her head in a nod, but the pain was too much for her. She whispered, "Aye."

"He will not get by with this. I will see that he has—"

"P-please . . ."

Mary lifted a weak and trembling hand to him. Her fingernails told of the struggle she had given against her attacker, for they were broken and had the slight coloring of blood beneath them. Sir Damon would be marked. Robert took Mary's hand in his and knelt down beside the bed to listen to her.

"Y-you m-m-must tell Cat"—she swallowed convulsively—"Catriona the tr-truth. What I t-told t-to you . . . about the p-past. I cannot tell her of it n-now."

Robert nodded. "I will."

"And y-you m-must give her th-this . . ."

Robert looked down at where he held her hand. A gold chain was entwined in her fingers and she was pressing it into his palm. Robert took the chain, lifting it up so the small gold locket it held twisted in the candlelight.

"P-please k-keep her s-s-safe . . ."

"I will. I promise you I will."

A small tear fell from behind her swollen eye and her mouth turned slightly in a weak smile. "You m-must bring her to m-me."

Robert shoved the locket and chain into his coat pocket and moved to the door.

"Catriona, will you please come here?"

When she came near, he took her hands and looked solemnly into her eyes. "Your mother has been hurt, Catriona. She has been very badly beaten."

She gasped, her eyes already filling with tears.

"You must remember," Robert said, squeezing her hands, "no matter how you feel when you see her, you must stay strong. For her. She needs to see you now. You must prepare for the worst."

Catriona stared at him a moment and then slowly nodded before unclasping her hands from his and walking slowly into her parents' room.

She squeezed her eyes tightly closed when she first saw her mother, trying desperately to take hold of her turbulent emotions. But seeing her mother so broken, so helpless, the tears came unbidden. She took in a slow, deep breath and choked out, "Mam."

"C-Catri . . ." Mary lifted her hand. Catriona knelt beside the bed, taking her mother's fingers and touching them to the side of her cheek.

"Oh, Mam, who did this to you?"

"It will be all right, l-lass . . ." She took in a wheezing and laborious breath. "I have done what I w-was meant to do. W-hat your m-mother asked . . ." She closed her eyes as if keeping them open were beyond her capabilities.

Catriona struggled to understand her. "What do you mean, Mam? I do not—"

Mary took in another struggling breath. "The laird will t-tell you. You must trust him. He w-will see to you now—"

Mary's words faded and her head slumped slowly to the side. Her hand, which Catriona still held tightly in her own, went suddenly limp. Catriona's eyes blurred with tears of fear and sadness and heartache. "Mam? Mam, please . . . please . . ."

Catriona felt Robert's hand on her shoulder as she lowered her head to the blankets and wept, clutching Mary's hand tightly to her while Mairead sobbed in the doorway.

Chapter Nineteen

Catriona opened her eyes. Soft sunlight, hazy and pink, touched her face, beaming in a myriad of rainbow colors through gleaming windows which stood as tall as she across the immense room. She lay in a bed that was far bigger than any she'd ever seen, so big it could have easily slept Mairead as well as Mattie with her. Set high from the ground, she'd had to use the small steps that stood beside it to climb into it the night before. Cherubs and birds had been carved into the polished mahogany, hangings of rose and pale blue-colored silk draping softly overhead. Like everything in the room, the bed and even the pillows which cradled her head smelled of flowers and spice.

Catriona looked to the windows again and the colorful play of the sunlight streaming through. *Rainbows.* She recalled that day when she'd first met Robert and how she had described the same sight to him. It felt as though that had been years ago now, for everything was different and the terrible events of the past days had now cloaked all the colors of her rainbows in mourning black.

Catriona tried, but could not recall precisely when they had left the cottage the night before. Mairead had told them of where she had gone that day, searching but never finding the Colonel or Ian. From what she'd been able to learn from the other men who made up Angus's crew, it looked as if Ian had likely been one of the men captured by the landguard that night, for no one had seen him since.

Robert had brought Catriona and her sister, exhausted and numb, to Rosmorigh. Mairead was still in a puzzled state of disbelief. To Catriona it all seemed so illusory, images far too ghastly to comprehend, her worst night-mares realized. How could both her father and her mother now be gone? They had just been there, Angus grumbling over his ale mug, Mary smiling that gentle smile as she tended to her family. If only it truly were a nightmare, but waking among such peace and beauty and sweet scents only confirmed the heartrending and naked truth of the past days.

"Good morning."

Catriona turned to see Robert standing in the doorway through the haze of her tears. She hadn't heard him come in. "Is it?"

Robert came forward and sat beside her on the bed. He put his arm around her and Catriona sagged against him, dropping her head onto his shoulder. The sunlight through the windowpanes played across the floor at their feet. Outside a new day was dawning. Neither said a word for some time.

Finally Robert spoke. "Are you hungry?"

Catriona shook her head.

"You must eat something, Catriona. You haven't had much of anything to eat in two days."

"I care little for food right now. I only want to find out who did this."

"You will need your strength—"

"How could I possibly eat when the person who killed my mother is out there somewhere running free? I have to find out who did this, Robert. I need to."

"You needn't worry over it." Robert looked at Catriona. "I already know who did this."

Catriona lifted her head. "What? You know? Why haven't you told me before now? Who is it?"

Robert took a deep breath. "Catriona, there is much we need to discuss, you and I, and Mairead as well. Your sister is awake and is in the dining room awaiting us. Like you, she is too upset to do much of anything, but I told her, and I am telling you, I will not begin to discuss anything until you have both eaten a decent meal."

Catriona just stared at him, angry. He would not relent. She knew that. And she was just too tired to argue. Giving up the fight, she stood and walked from the room. She'd made it halfway down a corridor that ended at a stone wall before she realized she had no idea where she was going.

Robert came up behind her and took her hand. "Come, Catriona. I will lead you to the dining room."

She almost laughed at the irony, and would have if she hadn't been crying right then. How many times had she led him when he had been unable to see his way? How odd that he was now doing the same for her because she was so blinded with her grief and her anger that she could no longer see beyond them.

The dining room was situated a floor below the bed-chambers, on the western side of the castle's main tower. It opened through wide double doors, one entire wall made up of tall windows which faced onto the sea. Skye rose through the mist beyond, obscure, mys-terious. It would have been a stunning view at any other time, but Catriona barely gave it notice. A huge stone hearth filled the far wall and a table that would easily seat thirty stretched across the center of the long room. Tapestries and ancient war weapons decorated the stone walls.

Mairead, who sat looking so small and bleak at the far end, turned when Catriona and Robert entered the room. She tried valiantly to summon a smile, but only managed a crooked grimace.

As Catriona took the seat nearest to her, a footman came immediately forward, bearing a covered plate. Upon removing the cover, Catriona found several different varieties of cheese cut into small, bite-sized pieces. Some sort of egg dish and scones already spread with preserves sat beside it. A small china pot of tea was then placed beside her on the table, the steaming brew poured for her into a matching cup. Like platters of food and teapots came before Mairead and Robert, and Catriona saw that her sister was looking to her as if awaiting instruction as to her proper response to such finery. Neither of them had ever been waited on this way and Mairead did not quite know what to make of it.

The footman came forward, holding out a small plate with two bowls, one filled with the whitest sugar Catriona had ever seen, and the other fresh milk for her tea. Catriona did the only thing she could think of. She thanked the footman who stood beside her. He simply nodded. She waited for him to leave the plate and take himself off, but he didn't. He stayed at her side, still holding the plate with the sugar and milk.

Finally Robert said, "Do you take sugar or milk with your tea?"

"Sugar, please," Catriona said to Robert, then watched as the footman served her a small bit. He then moved on to Mairead, who equally as uncertain, watched as the footman ministered to her tea.

Robert sat, sipping at a cup of coffee while the two women ate their meals. The sisters consumed precious little of the feast, though, nibbling on tiny bites. The mood in the room was solemn. Robert asked the footman to clear the table and bring a fresh pot of tea for the ladies. Once done, he then asked that the doors be closed and they be left alone.

It had taken every bit of will Catriona possessed to calmly eat what she had of the meal when she wanted so desperately to do something—anything—to find who had killed her mother. She was glad now for

Robert's insistence, though, for the food had indeed replenished her and had offered her the chance to regain her rationality. She would need it for what she was about to hear.

Robert stood. "Firstly, I would like you both to know that before your mother died, she told me who it was who had beaten her."

"Who?" asked Catriona immediately.

Mairead remained silent, staring into her teacup.

"It was Sir Damon Dunstron."

"The revenue officer," Catriona said.

"You know him?"

"Yes. He is the laird at Crannock. He stopped me yesterday morning when I was going to the caves to search for Da."

"After which Sir Damon came here to Rosmorigh to see me. He had a portrait of someone whom he asked if I recognized. He said he suspected this person of having been involved in the landing at Rosmorigh." Robert looked at Catriona. "The portrait was of someone who looked remarkably like you."

Catriona looked puzzled. "Me?"

"I, of course, didn't recognize you, I couldn't even see it at the time, but Forbes did and he communicated his opinions to Sir Damon. I did not quite trust the way Sir Damon was questioning me about you, particularly about your identity."

"But how?" asked Catriona. "How could Sir Damon have a portrait of me?"

"I wondered the very thing. Something didn't seem quite right, so after Sir Damon left, I went to your family's cottage, hoping to ask you. Only you weren't there. It was then your mother explained everything to me."

Robert stood with his back to the windows, the brilliant sunlight shining in behind him.

"Catriona, your mother, Mary MacBryan, was not your true mother, in blood."

Catriona looked at him, silent, stunned, and at once furious. "Why would you say something like that?"

"Because it is the truth. Mary raised you as her own at the request of your true mother before she died after giving birth to you and your brother."

Catriona shook her head, refusing to hear anything more. "No. This is not right. I do not have any brother. There is just Mairead. You are lying."

"Catriona, you must listen to me. Your mother was not Mary MacBryan, at least not by blood. The woman who gave birth to you was Lady Catherine Dunstron. She was the wife of the laird of Crannock, the previous laird before Sir Damon assumed the title. Her husband, your father, was a man named Sir Charles Dunstron, who died several months before you were born. Sir Damon was Sir Charles's grandnephew and depending on the outcome of Lady Catherine's pregnancy, he would, or would not, be the next laird. Mary had attended to your mother, Lady Catherine, during her lying-in when she gave birth to a son. Sir Damon took that son from her the very night he was born. The child was never seen again. But what Sir Damon did not know was that Lady Catherine had given birth to a second child that same night. A daughter." His voice lowered. "You."

Tears were streaming down Catriona's face so that she could no longer see Robert standing before her. She shook her head from side to side. This could not be. It just wasn't possible. Dear God, when would she wake from this wretched nightmare? "I do not believe you."

Robert sat beside her. "Catriona, I know this seems too incredible to be true, but it is. I have no doubts as to what Mary told me. I swear to you I am telling the truth. After you were born, your mother, Lady Catherine, asked Mary MacBryan to take you and leave Crannock before Sir Damon could learn the truth of you. She feared for your life. She asked Mary to raise you as her own before she died from complica-

tions of the birthing, complications in which Sir Damon played a significant role."

Mairead jumped in suddenly. "Why wouldn't Mam tell us of this before now? And why would she tell you of it first?"

"Your mother never told anyone the truth because she feared for Catriona's safety should Sir Damon ever learn of her. And then, yesterday, when she realized he had discovered the truth after seeing Catriona that morning, she told me of it so I could protect Catriona against Sir Damon. We assumed Sir Damon would be out searching for Catriona. I left Mary at the cottage so that I could find Catriona before he did. I never thought he would have come for Mary and would have done what he has, else I would have insisted that she come with me to Rosmorigh, even though she wanted to stay and wait for Angus, and you," he finished, looking at Mairead.

Catriona was sitting still and gravely silent. Too silent. Robert took her hand. In his other hand, he held the golden chain and locket which Mary had given to him to give to her.

"This was your mother, Lady Catherine's, necklace, Catriona. She asked Mary to give it to you when the time came for you to learn the truth."

Catriona took the locket into her hand. It was round and flat and engraved on its front were the initials *C* and *T,* and the year *1789.* Her fingers trembled as she released the tiny clip which held it closed. Inside were two small painted miniatures of a young man and a young woman. Although the hair was fashioned in a coiffure that had been stylish decades earlier, the resemblance was certain.

Small realizations suddenly became clearer. How different she had always looked from both her parents and Mairead, smaller, darker-haired, her blue eyes so unlike the MacBryan brown. Catriona had always wondered why her mother had sent her to live with her Aunt Lizzy during all those many years as a child, why she hadn't been able to stay with them in the Highlands. Knowing what she did now, all of it made sense. Mary had sent her away to protect her, to shield her from the truth, to keep her alive.

"You have had Sir Damon arrested, have you not?" she said suddenly, looking up at Robert.

"No, Catriona, I have not."

"What do you mean? He cannot be allowed to get by with this. He has killed someone, Robert."

"I realize that, Catriona. And it is not the first time he has killed, which means he would not hesitate to do so again, given the opportunity. I have thought about it through the night and I have come to what I believe to be the best solution for us all. As soon as we can see matters settled here, we will, all of us, travel to London."

"London? But Sir Damon is here!"

"Which is precisely why I wish us to leave. Mary told me that Lady Catherine was English. Obviously she was of the gentry, perhaps even the nobility. It could very well be that she has family in England still. We will go to London and see if we can discover just who Lady Catherine Dunstron was."

Robert stood at the windows in the library staring out at the island of Skye, its rugged coast barely visible against the darkness of the night.

Now that he could see the sight of it for himself, it wasn't at all difficult for him to understand why his father had refused to sell this place. Even when he'd been unable to clearly see its beauty, Rosmorigh had had a quality that had drawn Robert to it. The ancient and ivy-covered stone walls that made up the keep, the untamed countryside that surrounded it on its landward sides, Robert knew he would never let it go.

It possessed a magic that made a person feel as if anything might happen here, even a miracle such as a blind man recovering his sight. He thought of Catriona's innocence, her unquestioning belief in the white heather flowers and their part in the recovery of his sight. Perhaps, he thought, lost to the magic which surrounded him, perhaps they did have something to do with it, after all.

Even if it was just a little bit.

Whatever it was that surrounded this place, this mysterious aura, it had done far more than restore his sight to him. It had given him Catriona. And it had returned to him another part of his life, as well, a part he had thought lost to him forever.

The surge of recognition still thrummed through him, as it had the very moment when his eyes, his *seeing* eyes, had noticed that first painting. Placed in the dining hall, it had been one of the first pieces Robert had ever acquired at auction. At the time, he hadn't even known the artist, but the piece had intrigued him, and he would never forget the feeling of triumph he'd found at having taken it at the auction.

And there were the others, countless others, all of which Robert had acquired through the years. They were his personal favorites, pieces he'd purchased for their investment potential, or simply for the fact that they'd appealed to him in some way. He had thought them all lost in the fire at Devonbrook House, for there were no records to indicate they had been housed here at Rosmorigh instead. But they had been here all this time, hidden safely from the fire, and because of his blindness, hidden from him as well.

It was all so very clear to him now, the reasons why his father had left Rosmorigh to him. The duke had chosen the castle specifically, and then he had sent here the pieces he knew Robert cared most about, to remain until the day when Robert would come to live here as laird.

There was but one piece though which the collection still lacked, that final acquisition which the duke had been seeking, the one he had written about. What he had been searching for. The acquisition which had ultimately taken his life.

And Robert knew he would not rest until he had uncovered the mystery behind it.

He turned when he heard someone come quietly into the room.

"Oh, I did not know anyone was still awake."

Catriona stood in the doorway, her bare toes peeking out from beneath her nightgown. She looked lovely, her hair falling down her back in waves of copper fire. Only there was something missing, something that when he'd been blind somehow he had still seen. It had been in her voice, in her laughter, in her touch. It was the smile, the light that had shone through the darkness to him. And now it was gone.

Robert hadn't had the opportunity to talk to Catriona since telling her the truth of her birth that morning. He knew she'd been shocked, and that she hadn't wanted to believe what he'd told her. He'd seen the pain in her eyes, the fear, and he had wanted nothing more than to reassure her, tell her that he would take care of her, protect her, see to her. He saw the sadness which had taken away that special light, and he wanted somehow to bring it back.

He remembered feeling quite the same when first told of the deaths of his family after the fire. No amount of words had been able to take that pain away, a pain that had run so deep he thought never to be without it again. It was a trauma which Robert had needed to overcome himself, in his own time. And Catriona would need to do the same.

Only when she had, could they then think of the future. Their future. Together.

"Was there something you needed?" Robert asked her, for she still stood, looking lost in the doorway.

"I was just coming to find a book to read." She paused. "I could not sleep."

Robert came across the room. "I was going to have a glass of port before retiring myself. Would you care to join me with a glass of sherry? My mother used to say sherry was a great help to her on nights when she could not sleep."

Catriona shrugged and crossed the room. While Robert poured the glasses, she stood before the book-shelves, searching through the titles. Her eyes fell on the Malory and she instinctively removed it.

"You have a fondness for King Arthur?" Robert asked, taking the seat beside her.

She took a small sip of the sherry, pleased with the way it made her feel warm inside. Anything to ease the chill which seemed ever within her now. "I like to read the chivalric romances, *Sir Gawain, Arthur,*" she paused, looking at the book she held. "I am particularly fond of the Grail legends."

He smiled. "I once attended an art auction where there was a chalice reputed to be the true grail. It looked quite ancient indeed and my father was deter-mined to have it at any price. Until it was discovered just before the piece came up for bidding that it had really been crafted as a hoax. He always said he would one day find the true Grail and have it for the collec-tion." He shook his head, taking a sip of his port. "Per-haps it was that which he was searching for here at Rosmorigh."

Catriona looked at him. She realized how unfair she'd been to him in keeping from him his father's search for the Jacobite treasure. "Robert, there is some-thing I must tell you." She hesitated. "I know why your father was coming to Rosmorigh. I know why he was writing the journal. You were right when you said you believed he was searching for something. And you were right in saying he was not the only one searching for it. I was searching for it, too."

Robert looked at her curiously. "Go on."

"I did not know of your father's intentions. When he would come to Rosmorigh, I would stay away until he left again." She stared at him, searching his face in the candlelight. He was frowning. She stumbled on.

"There is a man, Colonel MacReyford, who is a tenant here at Rosmorigh. He had information of a Jacobite treasure, gold which had been sent from the French to Scotland to aid Bonnie Prince Charlie during the '45. Legend has it that it is hidden somewhere near Rosmorigh."

"You mentioned information. What sort of information does this colonel have?"

"He has a map which shows in images how to locate where the treasure is hidden, but it is vague and from looking at it alone, one could likely never realize what it led to. You see, there is another part to the map which tells in words how to find the treasure. It, too, is too vague on its own. It is only when the two of them are together that the location of the treasure can be discerned."

Robert was listening to her carefully. "And this other part of the map, the one which tells the treasure's location in words, where is it?"

"I do not know. The Colonel only knew that it was inserted somewhere within the text of a book, and that book was reputed to be here at Rosmorigh."

Robert's frown deepened. He considered what she'd told him over a sip of his port. "That is why you were coming to Rosmorigh, isn't it? To search for this book."

"Yes, but not only for that reason. Searching for the book also gave me an excuse to come to read."

Robert considered this for a long moment. "How long have you known my father was searching for this treasure, Catriona?"

"It wasn't until after we had found the journal, and even then, it wasn't until the day we went to where the forked oak was."

"Why didn't you tell me of this then?"

"I wanted to, Robert, but I needed to speak to the Colonel first. I suspected he might know more of your father's involvement than he was letting on to me. So I went to see him that same day after I'd left you, but he was gone. And with him his picture map of the treasure. Oh, Robert, don't you see? What if the person who set the fire at Devonbrook House has now brought some sort of mischief to the Colonel as well?"

Robert swallowed down the rest of his port. "I have every intention of finding that out, Catriona, as soon as we arrive in London."

It was a sennight later when Catriona and Mairead boarded the small packet boat Robert had arranged to take them down the coast to Oban and then on further still to Liverpool. From there they would then travel by land, and it would take them over a fortnight to reach London. Catriona would need every moment of that time to prepare herself for her uncertain future.

Robert had been wonderful, really. He had made arrangements for Mary to be interred in the graveyard at Rosmorigh, and although his body had never been found, a gravestone had been erected beside Mary's for Angus. Afterward, Robert had gone to retrieve what few possessions they would keep from the cottage, sparing Catriona and her sister that heartrending task. Since that night, Robert hadn't spoken of the treasure, and now it seemed as if he had set that mission to the side, instead concentrating all his efforts on Catriona and her safety.

Robert had written a letter to his brother Noah, informing him of their impending arrival and asking that he contact the Devonbrook solicitor Quinby to request that he begin making inquiries—discreet inquiries—as to who Lady Catherine's family might be and if there were any relations still living.

Catriona still found it difficult to think of anyone other than Mary as her mother, even though the locket offered ample proof to the contrary. It had been Mary who had always been there, comforting her, caring for her, loving her. Mary had been the one who had fostered Catriona's love of reading, encouraging her in her dreams of adventure, perhaps somehow knowing of the grand adventure she would one day face.

That same adventure she was now embarking on.

Chapter Twenty

The draperies opened with a snap and the maid turned, gasping with a start when she noticed Catriona sitting up at the edge of the bed, awake and watching her.

"Oh, goodness, miss," she said, looking at her queerly. "I hadn't expected ye'd be awake 'ere in the dark all alone like that. Would ye be takin' tea 'ere in yer chamber, or down in the dining parlor with his grace and the other miss?"

Catriona watched as the girl picked up the gown she had worn the night before when they'd first arrived, eyeing it as if fearful it might move.

"Thank you. I will go down with the others," she said, staring down to where her feet dangled over the side of the tall bed. All her life she had slept in low box beds whose mattresses had been stuffed with straw and heather. She wondered if she'd ever grow accustomed to lying on soft down or on a bed so high that she couldn't sleep for fear of falling from it at night.

She realized then that the maid was staring at her. "Shall I be stayin' to help you to dress then, miss?"

"No, thank you. I can manage."

The maid looked at her, puzzled, then laid the dress beside her on the bed, turning to leave the room. Catriona waited until she was gone before she slid from the bed to stand.

The maid hadn't woken her. She had been up since before the dawn, or at least since the noises of the city had convinced her that even the fitful sleep she'd slept through the night would no longer be possible. The city was something she was not accustomed to. She had expected there would be an adjustment, yes, but everything was so vastly different. Mornings at the cottage had issued in softly with whispering breezes off the sound and the faint echoing call of the capercaillie from the mist-shrouded Highland hills. The London morning was made up of the clip-clopping of horse and carriage, the closing of doors and the murmur of conversation throughout the house as servants began seeing to their duties, dogs barking, and the occasional shout from somewhere below the slanted rooftops.

Slipping on her gown, Catriona padded her way barefoot down the narrow corridor until she found the stairs leading to the lower floors. She remembered very little of their arrival the night before, for it had been late and dark and she'd been exhausted from their journey. Now, as she walked along the thick padded carpet, she could but stare at the numerous paintings, framed in gold, that filled the walls, the gleaming side tables set with marble busts and various other decorative objects, the richly adorned chambers she spied through open doorways.

This place was even grander than Rosmorigh and Catriona had never felt so out of place in her life. Even the draperies which framed the tall windows wore fabrics far richer than any she'd ever had. While she may be tied to this sort of a life by blood, her heart remained rooted in the Highlands. Realizing this, Catriona couldn't help the nagging feeling that she'd made a terrible mistake in allowing Robert to bring them here.

Things had been different even while at Rosmorigh. Though foreign in its splendor, the castle was also a familiar place to her, set on familiar land, among familiar people. Here, in London, Catriona felt as though she had just stepped into a separate world, and indeed she had.

And, indeed, she longed to go back.

Once Catriona located the dining parlor, after mistakenly entering two other chambers—one an intriguing library and the other a storage closet filled with spare furnishings—she found Robert inside, sitting in the far chair. She halted just inside the doorway, watching him as he read a newspaper. How exciting it must be for him, she thought while he hadn't yet realized she was there, reading again after his long spell of seeing nothing.

He looked handsome, exceptionally so, for his attire was more formal than that which he'd worn at Rosmorigh. He wore a rich burgundy coat, gray waistcoat, and black breeches. A starched white neckcloth twisted fashionably about his throat and gleaming black boots cut just below his knees. He had a look of strength, a look of nobility—the look of the duke that he was.

Catriona glanced down at herself, her colorless homespun gown with its worn linen chemise underneath and cringed. She wondered if she might just turn around before he saw her and—

"Good morning," Robert said, immediately quashing that thought.

"Good morning," she answered quietly, left no choice but to move through the room to sit in the chair beside him. The footman, who stood waiting in his bright yellow-and-blue livery, came forward instantly to pour her a cup of fragrant tea. As he poured, she noticed him glancing at her bare feet beneath the table.

"Did you sleep well?" Robert asked.

"Yes," she lied, "quite well."

Robert folded his newspaper and regarded her closely. "I would have allowed you to sleep through the morning, but there are matters to which we must attend and I thought we should set to them right off."

Catriona nodded, sipping her tea and tucking her feet further under her chair as he went on.

"Mairead should be joining us soon and—"

As if on cue, Mairead came into the room just then, smiling a bit timorously and muttering her greetings. Catriona noticed the caution she used when taking up her teacup, as if fearful she might break it. Mairead, too, was obviously overwhelmed at the surroundings.

"I have arranged for a seamstress to come later this morning in order that we may properly outfit you both."

"A seamstress?" asked Catriona. "But we have our own clothing, Robert."

"Yes, you do, but there is precious little of it. You will need clothing more fitting for town life, and if you are to be attending social events, you will need—"

"Social events? But I had thought we had come to London to find out about Lady Catherine?"

Catriona still couldn't bring herself to refer to anyone other than Mary as her mother.

"We have, but even more importantly we must also protect you from Sir Damon. I have come to a plan that I believe will be our wisest course. From his past actions, there is no way to predict what Sir Damon might do next. He is quite obviously capable of anything. I have considered the situation carefully and it is my belief that the best way to protect you is to bring you out into society."

"But I know nothing of society. Would it not be wiser to remain hidden until we can find out more of Lady Catherine?"

"Not really. Knowing that we would want to protect you, Sir Damon would expect us to remain hidden. Through my years in the Peninsula, I learned that the best way to confuse the enemy is to do what he least expects. We will bring you out as Miss Catherine Dunstron of Castle Crannock in Scotland."

What had he called her? Catherine? Already Catriona, the poor crofter's daughter, ceased to exist.

Robert went on. "In this way, too, we will be able to easiest learn of any relation your mother, Lady Catherine, might have, since Noah hasn't yet had much success in discovering her name before she wed Sir Charles. My sponsorship will assure your acceptance in the highest circles, for despite what people may believe of me, I am still a duke. Your lineage will do the rest."

Lineage? It all sounded so very rigid. Catriona was trying desperately to digest all he'd just said, when he went on.

"Which brings into attention another matter I would like to discuss with you." Robert glanced briefly at Mairead. "In private, if you would excuse us for a moment, Mairead?"

Mairead simply nodded, hands clasped in her lap, looking afraid to so much as move.

There was nothing that could not be discussed in front of her sister, and Catriona nearly voiced those feelings, however, there was an odd look in Robert's eyes that made her hold her tongue and take his arm as he stood to escort her from the room.

Robert took her to the library she'd mistakenly entered earlier and closed the door behind them.

"Catriona, there is one final element of my plan which I have not yet brought up. I have spent the past fortnight since we left Rosmorigh doing nothing other than considering what I am about to ask you, so do not think I have come to this lightly."

She stared at him as he stood above the chair where she'd sat and nodded mutely.

"Catriona, I would beg the honor of your hand."

She blinked. Twice. Had he just asked her to marry him? Surely not. Surely she must have heard him wrongly. "Excuse me? What did you say?"

"There are a number of things I have come to consider, all of which have led me to my now asking you to become my wife. Firstly, there is the matter of your safety which is foremost in my mind. As my wife, I could see to your protection far more thoroughly than as an acquaintance. Married there would be no questions, no assumptions placed on our being together."

Protection? Was that his foremost consideration? What of his regard for her, his affection, his love? Or was what had transpired between them merely an "acquaintanceship" to him, so insignificant as to not merit mention?

"Secondly, and more pressingly, there is the matter of what we shared together."

The small lump that had begun to form in her throat lessened somewhat. He did have feelings for her, feelings which she shared, but which she had been reluctant to reveal for the fear he did not return them. "Oh, Robert, I—"

"That being the possibility of a child."

Catriona's words clogged in her throat and the lump instantly grew to the size of a walnut, effectively stopping her from finishing what she'd been about to say, that she loved him with everything she had and wanted nothing more than to spend the rest of her life with him. She had expected him to declare his feelings for her, to tell her he cared for her as much and as deeply as she cared for him. But he hadn't. She lowered her eyes so he wouldn't be able to see the bleak glimmer of deferred expectation shining there in the beginnings of her tears.

"You have not had your cycle since the time when we were together, have you, Catriona?"

She shot her glance upward at his candid question, and in doing so immediately confirmed his suspicions. Nay, she had not bled, not even after she should have.

"I had thought as much," he said. "This will necessitate a bit of exigence in our timing."

Exigence? Timing? Why did it sound as if Robert were disappointed in the possibility of their having conceived a child? And why did he sound so blasted literal? She had just told him she could likely be carrying a child, their child, and his first response was to fret over the timing? What had happened to the man she had loved in the Highlands?

Catriona struggled to maintain her composure as the realization hit her full force. Robert was asking her to wed him, yes, what she had dreamed about but dared not believe might ever happen. But he was not asking for her hand because he loved her, and not because what they had shared together had affected him quite as deeply as it had her. Robert was asking her to wed him because he felt it his responsibility.

Catriona considered what Robert must be thinking, placing herself in his position. He was an honorable man, raised in the noblest of families, and his honor had been called to question after the fire and the deaths of his family, wrongly, yes, and that had stung him deeply. And with the possibility, nay, probability of her true mother, Lady Catherine, having come from a family of even somewhat gentle breeding, he could not chance having that honor called to question again by the birthing of a bastard.

A burning settled deep in Catriona's heart that left her feeling raw inside. Questions whirred through her mind—Would Robert have asked her to be his wife had he not known of her true parentage? Would he have wanted her even if she still were naught but a poor crofter's daughter?—questions she could not give voice to, for her pride wouldn't allow her to acknowledge what she knew would be his response. She wouldn't, she couldn't reveal to him her feelings, for she didn't want him feeling responsible for them as well.

"We will need to get you out and introduced into society as my betrothed as quickly as possible. The more people are aware of you, the safer you will be should Sir Damon decide to come to town and stir up any trouble. I have arranged for my Aunt Amelia to come stay here. You will meet her later this afternoon. She will act as your companion when you are out, providing the proper chaperonage when necessary. She is known and well thought-of and her sponsorship will also help to assure your acceptance. As well, she can school you on the particulars of moving about in society. I will be leaving this house today and will spend the nights at the other Devonbrook house in town, where my brother resides, so there will be no question of any impropriety. The staff here will be at your full disposal. Mairead is here to keep you company. And while you are with the seamstress this morning I will see to the printing of the announcements in the papers, that is . . ."

Robert suddenly realized what Catriona had already been thinking while he'd been dictating his plans for her aloud. While he'd been standing there, rattling off all his defenses, he hadn't acknowledged one very vital detail. Catriona had never actually accepted his proposal.

"You haven't yet answered me, Catriona. Will you be my wife?"

A knocking came to the door barest seconds after he finished speaking. A butler poked in his head, interrupting before she could respond.

"Your grace, the modiste has arrived."

Robert never took his eyes from hers as he answered quickly, "Show her to the morning parlor, Wiggin, and ask Miss Mairead to await Miss Catherine there."

Again he'd called her by that name, *Catherine*, as if Catriona weren't quite good enough for London society. An anger began to fill her, a resistance for all this change, this unwanted change.

"You still haven't answered me, Catriona," Robert persisted. "Will you be my wife?"

Catriona looked at Robert squarely, trying both to calm her growing anger and soothe her wretchedly aching heart. "Yes, Robert, I will be your wife. What choice have I? However, answer me one thing." She stood, this time pleased by the sight of her bare toes peeking out boldly from beneath her skirt. "Who is it you are asking to wed? Catriona MacBryan or Miss Catherine Dunstron?"

Robert watched Catriona walk slowly from the room then to join her sister and the modiste in the parlor, too stunned to offer a single word in response.

Chapter Twenty-one

Catriona stood back from the mirror and looked at the image which gazed back at her from the other side. It was the image of a stranger, the image of *Miss Catherine Dunstron.*

The fallacy was now under way, the transformation nearly complete. And standing here now, she barely recognized her former self. Her hair, which when it hadn't been bursting from the confines of her black net snood, had always fallen free about her shoulders in a riot of waves, was now crimped and curled with heated tongs. Pinned upon her head and wound with cording in a rather Grecian-looking arrangement, it looked far too artificial for her liking. Circling and preening, the maid, Sally, assured her that this particular coiffure was the latest rage among the *ton*; Catriona, however, thought it merely looked silly.

Her face looked different as well, she thought, even though it had been left free of addition. Sally had assured her that "natural" beauty was quite the thing and that she should be grateful hers was truly natural, for *oh!* the cosmetic lengths some of the young ladies would go to in order to look fresh-faced. . . .

Catriona's attention wandered away from the chittering maid as her gaze traveled down to inspect the gown that floated over her.

Made of the darkest blue silk which the modiste, Madame Davenant, had tried earnestly to dissuade Catriona from, earnestly—and unsuccessfully. Madame, Catriona learned during the course of the more than six hours the woman and her diminutive assistant Marie-Anne had spent with her, had come to London after the outset of the Reign of Terror. She had dressed the highest French nobles, even the tragic queen Marie Antoinette. Now, having fled her native country, she catered to a select London clientele, bringing to them the latest of the most sought-after designs from Paris. And the latest and most sought-after, she had assured Catriona, were the light and filmy fabrics chosen by every other fashionable miss in town.

Catriona stood firm, insisting on this particular fabric for the first of her ball gowns, a cloth which Madame Davenant had intended for use instead as lining for a pelisse. But Catriona didn't care, for the effect was exactly what she'd hoped for.

The small bodice, which felt especially foreign to her in the way in which it hugged her breasts, was cut exceedingly low and bound snugly beneath her bosom with a wide bit of pale lace trimming. That was until Catriona had set Mairead to the task of altering the thing soon after it had been delivered, finished that morning straight from Madame's shop. The lace had been the first thing to go and skillfully inserted in its place was a swatch of colorful tartan, the MacBryan plaid of navy, green, and white which Angus had always worn so proudly. Another measure of it draped shawl-like around Catriona's shoulders. Mairead had then proceeded to remove the frilly flounces Madame and her seamstress had added along the gown's hem, as well as the pretty little bows which had peeked out from under her skirts on the toes of her satin slippers. With this, the last of Catriona's alterations on the gown were complete.

Catriona stepped back, surveying the entire costume. The finished product was indeed far more to her liking.

Dark in respect for mourning her parents, the rich silk shimmered in the candlelight, uninterrupted by laces and flounces, and bringing to attention more the adornment of the colorful tartan. Added to this was the locket which Mary had given her, proof of her true beginnings. It hung suspended from its long twisted golden chain, reaching nearly to her waist and glimmering in the soft candlelight. But it was the tartan one noticed first, and that was precisely the way Catriona had wanted it, for while she might be the daughter of Sir Charles and Lady Catherine Dunstron, in her heart she was, and would always be, a MacBryan.

A soft knocking at her door pulled Catriona from her critical study. She turned just as Mairead came into the room.

Even her sister looked differently now. The heavy homespun and woolens had been replaced with light muslin, not nearly as splendid as Catriona's, but far finer than any Mairead had ever worn before. The delicate design of the gown brought out an elegance in her, nearly transforming her, and the glow which had come into Mairead's eyes at the clean and lovely fabrics had taken away just a bit of the sadness that seemed ever shadowing them since leaving the Highlands.

"Catriona, you are truly bonnie," Mairead said, staring at her. "If Da could see you now . . ."

Mairead's voice softened and her eyes misted over.

"It was you who made the gown so lovely," Catriona said, hoping to ease the awkwardness of the moment.

" 'Twill be a dream for you," Mairead said. "Dancing in that ballroom with all those noble people . . ."

"They are no better than any of us."

"Aye," Mairead went on, "perhaps to you, but you're one of them, Catriona. I would never belong in this life."

Catriona looked at her sister. "I am no different from you."

"But you are, Catriona. You always have been, even before we learned the truth of you. Crofting and such never was the life for you. And now to think you're to wed a duke. Do you think his grace will want me to return to Scotland after you're wed?"

Catriona frowned. "Why would he?"

Mairead spoke up. "He owes me nothing, Catriona. You belong here, but I am not of this life. And he has already been so good to me. He's given me new clothing finer than anything I've ever had before and he's given me a bed to sleep in, but once you become his duchess he may . . ."

"I am no different than I have ever been," Catriona said, her voice rising. "Nothing will change that. No matter what may happen, I will always be a MacBryan, and I will always be your sister."

Mairead smiled softly and hugged Catriona to her. "And I wouldn't want any other."

Sally, having slipped out, suddenly bustled through the door. "His grace and Lady Amelia are awaiting ye at the door, miss, and the coach is outside ready to take ye to the ball."

Catriona turned to her sister. "You are certain you will be all right here tonight?"

Mairead nodded. "I've still some alterations to finish on the other gowns and though I would like to be with you, I really would rather remain here. You will be fine. And you will have a wonderful time of it. I know you will, and his grace will be there with you to make certain of it."

Catriona smiled, wishing she could share her sister's enthusiasm. "Well, then, I guess it is time for the charade to begin." She took a deep breath, turned, and walked from the room.

Robert was indeed waiting for her and when he turned from the door at hearing her descent on the stairs, he was stunned, too stunned to do anything more than stare.

From the moment he had first really seen her, that day in the library at Rosmorigh, Robert had thought Catriona beautiful. It was not a conventional beauty, for she was different from any other woman he'd ever seen. Her hair, indeed a coppery brown just as she'd described to him, had fallen about a face that was intriguing, outwardly curious, with eyes that were a bottomless brilliant blue. Seeing her now, though, her hair pulled back to reveal the truly classical structure of her face, the pale skin along the slender line of her neck, he thought her the goddess she had been styled to resemble. Burnished bronze ringlets danced about the nape of her neck. Whispering silk draped against her slender body as she moved. From beneath the deep rounded neckline of her gown, her breasts rose softly, immediately making him want to draw her to him and crush her against his chest. Looking at her, Robert knew that from the moment she was introduced into society that evening every man present would want her, and every woman would envy her.

She had been standing before him sometime before he realized he was still staring at her like a besotted schoolboy. He drew back a space and took her gloved hand. "You look lovely." He glanced at the tartan then. "I would assume that bit of your ensemble wasn't Madame Davenant's idea?"

Catriona's hand stiffened in his. "No. It was mine."

"It is perfect," he responded, noticing her reaction. In the past days he had come to understand the response he'd received from her that day when he had asked her to wed him. It hadn't been difficult, for all he'd had to do was place himself, figuratively, in her place to know what she had been thinking that morning. Everything Catriona had ever known in life had completely changed and overnight she had become someone else, someone totally different and totally foreign to her. It wasn't a change she had particularly wanted. Robert had had little trouble in understanding her feelings, for the fire and his blindness had done the same thing to him not so many months earlier. The tartan was her way, her public way, of stating to one and all that despite what had happened, she was still the same person. She had always been.

"I would like to give you something to wear this evening," Robert said, drawing forward a small wooden box from the side table. He opened it and took something from inside.

Robert then turned to Catriona. "This belonged to my mother. It was given to her by my father as a wedding token, and given to my grandmother by my grandfather before them. I would be honored if you would wear it."

Robert placed the bracelet around Catriona's gloved wrist, deep blue sapphires set off by glittering diamonds and pale creamy pearls. Catriona looked up into his eyes, touched that he would give her so personal an heirloom.

"Thank you," she said, uncertain of what else she should say.

Robert spared her. He introduced his aunt Amelia Edenhall to her. She was older, short, and somewhat plump, and her gown had more lace on it than Catriona had ever seen. Her face, and especially her soft brown eyes, displayed a kindness about her and she embraced Catriona with sincere enthusiasm, touching her softly on her cheek as she stepped back to regard her. "I am so pleased to meet you, my dear Catriona. We will have such fun together. Do you play piquet?"

Catriona smiled, a little surprised at the question. Of everything she had expected this woman to ask of her, who she was, where she'd come from, this had not been one of them. "No, I'm afraid I do not know the game."

"Well, then, I shall have to teach you." She hooked her arm through Catriona's, leading her to the door as she went on, "My dear, by the time I am finished with you, you'll be taking Lady Darlington's pin money just as easily as I do. It really is quite fun."

Catriona liked her immediately.

* * *

Every ounce of Catriona's confidence lagged the moment they stepped into the crowded ballroom. The footman announced them, and it seemed as if every head in the room turned to stare at them as they stood atop the few steps leading down to the crowded floor. Immediately the ladies whispered into their fans and the men murmured into their starched cravats.

Catriona clearly read the thoughts of everyone there: The Duke of Devonbrook had returned, and he had brought himself back a misfit.

If Robert noticed the reaction—how could he not?— he certainly didn't allow it to show. Setting his hand protectively at Catriona's elbow, he steered them slowly through the crowd. Amelia flanked Catriona's other side, smiling to every acquaintance they passed. Robert merely nodded his head, acknowledging a few with a muttered "Good evening." Most just stared openly, and once, when Catriona tried to lower her eyes away from the questioning gazes, Amelia leaned toward her and whispered softly, "You've nothing to fear, my dear. It is they who are the strangers."

Her words gave Catriona courage so that, like Amelia, she could actually return some of the stares with a polite smile—and without fearing that Sir Damon Dunstron's would be the next face she'd look upon.

They had nearly traversed the room when a young man stepped toward them, instantly taking Robert in a familiar embrace.

He stepped back. "I'd thought your letter a jest when I received it." He smiled at Robert. "I'm glad I was mistaken."

He had to be Noah, Catriona thought, detecting the slight resemblance between them, and even to Amelia, in the set of their eyes and their smiles. However, the differences between the two men were easier to note, for Robert was darker, his appearance impeccable, while Noah had hair that was more umber brown and green eyes that looked out from behind his spectacles. And his cravat did indeed, as Robert had once

described him, look as if it had once been used as a
signal flag in battle.

"Noah," Robert said, turning to her, "allow me to
introduce Miss Catriona Dunstron."

She instantly realized he had termed her Catriona,
and no longer Catherine. It made the use of her new
surname far easier to accommodate. Catriona smiled.
"It is a pleasure to meet you, Lord Noah."

Noah bowed cordially. "It is my greatest pleasure,"
he said. "As it is likewise to welcome you to our
family, as I'm certain Aunt Amelia already has. Miss
Dunstron, allow me to say that you are as lovely as
your penmanship." He kissed her hand. "And I thank
you for keeping me in communication with my brother
while he was away at Rosmorigh."

"I was happy to have done it."

Noah turned back to Robert. "It is splendid to have
you home again, Rob, although I can see now why you
were so long in the Highlands."

Robert nodded, turning when a voice sounded
behind him suddenly.

"Your timing is impeccable, Devonbrook. You just
won me a wager worth the thirty guineas Sir Henry
Porter staked against your returning to Town before the
New Year."

Robert laughed, rich and deep. It was a sound Cat-
rionaa had never heard, and one she liked immediately.
"It is good to see you, Tolley," he said, shaking his
friend's hand. "And I mean that in the most literal
sense of the word."

Catriona had never seen a man so colorfully dressed,
though his costume wasn't at all garish or overdone.
Every aspect of it, from his finely tailored holly green
coat to his buff-colored breeches and polished boots,
even his striped waistcoat, everything came together in
a symphonic presentation.

"Ah," he said, turning to her before Robert could
make the introductions, "I would have little doubt as to
who you are, my dear. No doubt this is Miss Dunstron.

Even without his sight, Robert finds the lovely ones."
He bowed over her hand. "It is my greatest pleasure to
meet you, Miss Dunstron."

Catriona smiled. "Thank you, Lord Sheldrake."

"Please, I am Tolley to my friends, and I hope that
we will be just that." He turned to Amelia. "And who
is this lovely creature?" he said, his eyes smiling at
her. He peered animatedly through his quizzing glass.
"Surely not Lady Amelia Edenhall? I must warn all the
dowagers at the gaming tables to beware." He looked
to Catriona once again. "Do not allow her genteel
appearance to fool you, my dear. Beneath that lacy
veneer lies a shameless cardsharp."

Amelia slapped him playfully with the sticks of her
fan. "You are an insufferable tease, my lord."

The musicians began tuning their instruments and
Tolley still hadn't relinquished his hold on Amelia's
hand. "You will favor me with this first dance, won't
you, my lady? We shall cut the most splendid figure
together."

Tolley had really given her little choice in the matter
as he immediately led her out onto the floor.

Catriona turned as Robert came up beside her. They
stood watching the dancing for several minutes when
Catriona noticed that most of the people standing
nearby weren't watching the dancing at all. They were
instead staring at Robert as if he were the devil incar-
nate, whispering to each other and shaking their heads
in disapproval. From the frown that etched deep on
Robert's mouth, Catriona knew he noticed the attention
he drew as well. She became instantly angry. This was
"polite" society? Robert was, after all, a duke, and was
to be afforded the respect of his title. He had lost his
family. How could they be so cruel?

When she heard the distinct word of "murder" amid
all the murmuring, she finally could bear it no longer.
The musicians were moving on to another dance. She
turned to Robert. "Would you care to dance?"

Chapter Twenty-two

If Robert was surprised by Catriona's invitation, he didn't readily show it. In fact his face didn't change its expression at all as he answered cordially, "You might do well to remember it is customarily the duty of the man to ask such things."

Catriona was undaunted. "Then why do you not ask me?"

Robert glanced once more at the assembly, surveying the crowd. "I wouldn't think that a particularly good idea, Catriona. I draw enough attention as it is."

"Then at least you could offer them something of merit to talk about. I mean right now they have nothing but their own stupidity." She took his hand, refusing him further argument. "And after all, you paid Mr. Wilson to teach me to dance. You should at least make certain you got what you paid for.

"I believe they are preparing for the waltz," Catriona said, turning to him as they arrived on the dance floor.

"Indeed," answered Robert wryly, the corner of his mouth quirking as he clasped her about the waist.

"Can you follow the steps? Mr. Wilson tells me it can be rather difficult, especially for men. Larger feet and all."

"I shall endeavor to try."

The music started and at first Catriona tried to see

the reaction from the ring of onlookers, tried before Robert whirled her around preventing her from getting a closer look. The second time he turned her, his hold on her waist tightened and he pulled her nearer to him. When she looked up at him to ask him what was the matter, the words died on her lips. He was staring at her intently, his golden brown eyes flashing recklessly at her in the candlelight.

"Have I told you how exceptionally lovely you look tonight?" he asked, whirling her around.

All she could manage was a soft "Oh."

Suddenly the onlookers and their murmuring didn't matter so much any longer. Her heart was racing, rejoicing, her feet barely touching the floor as he spun her through the gliding steps of the dance. It was the same feeling she'd had when she'd been stranded alone with him in the cave, away from the troubles of the outside world. She felt quite as if she'd entered a dream. A glimmer of hope settled deep within her. Perhaps Robert could come to love her. . . .

She had thought of little else since the morning when he'd asked her to marry him. She'd wondered if she had expected too much. Was there truly anything that could compare to the loves she had read about all her life? Perhaps they were only to be found in the pages of books, not to be lived. She thought of Angus and Mary. They had certainly loved each other, but had it been the passionate, live-or-die sort of love, or one based on something entirely different?

Angus had always told her that her head was filled with whimsy and dreams that could never be. Catriona knew Robert, and he was not the sort of man who allowed himself to need. He preferred to be the needed. And she had loved him even before she'd ever met him. Maybe in time things could be different. Catriona thought of the moments they had shared in each other's arms, the magic and the passion they had brought to one another. Surely Robert must feel something for her, to give himself to her so completely.

It was that hope which she clung to as they moved across the floor in delightful harmony. And the way he was looking at her only caused that hope to grow. Catriona was so lost to his eyes as he stared at her, never looking away, that she couldn't have noticed that the floor had cleared and it was just the two of them left dancing. She reveled in the feel of his hand as it held her waist, his other hand clasped to hers. He was a wonderful dancer, effortless, so that even she forgot the need for concentrating on her movements.

Robert didn't release her, not even after the music had ended. He stood there in the midst of the dance floor, still holding her tightly, staring at her. She watched him and her heart was pounding. And then he drew her upward, slowly lowering his mouth over hers for a kiss.

The collective intake of breath from the crowd barely registered to Catriona's swirling senses as he kissed her deeply, passionately before the entirety of London's elite society.

When he finally pulled away, Catriona's head felt adrift.

He smiled down at her. "Pray tell me, my lady, was that of sufficient merit for others to talk about?"

Catriona couldn't answer him. In fact, it was all she could do to manage a bewildered stare as he smiled at her and then said, only loud enough for her to hear, "That, my dear, is what Thomas Wilson, Dancing Master, would call 'ending with a flourish.' "

Robert took Catriona's gloved hand and walked her from the floor, quite like she had taken his only minutes earlier. Every pair of eyes in the room was upon them, some with heads shaking, others just staring as if they couldn't quite believe what they had just seen. Even Catriona wouldn't have believed it, if it hadn't happened to her.

As they proceeded toward the edge of the floor, Robert suddenly halted. He'd had no choice but to, for a man had stepped directly in his path, blocking his way.

"Devonbrook," he said. "I hadn't expected to see you in attendance this evening."

He was an older man, wide in the girth, with a mouth too small for his teeth and a head too large for his ears. He placed particular emphasis on the *S* sound when he spoke, as if trying to indicate that what he had to say was of grave importance. He glanced at Catriona, giving her as much consideration as he might a midge, then stared up at Robert, who stood nearly a head taller than him, awaiting a response.

Robert's expression revealed little. "Good evening, Lord Kinsborough."

Kinsborough. Catriona could but stare. This was the man Robert believed had been responsible for the fire. How angry he must feel, standing there before him. But Robert masked his feelings behind indifference. Catriona would do the same.

"I trust your brother brought to your attention my offer to purchase the pieces left from your father's collection," Kinsborough said.

"Yes, he did. However, you are a bit mistaken regarding the ownership of the collection, my lord. The Devonbrook collection is mine. And it is not for sale."

Kinsborough narrowed his eyes. "Don't be a fool, Devonbrook. Your finances are in no position for you to set aside such a generous offer."

Robert's jaw twitched slightly, otherwise he remained stone-faced. "Whatever my financial position, I can assure you, Lord Kinsborough, I am no fool. But allow me to enlighten you. You would be pleased to know that my father had the foresight to transport a great number of the collection's rarest pieces away from Devonbrook House before the fire. From what I can gather without having seen the records, it appears as if, excepting the personal pieces, most everything remains intact. And in honor of my father and his vision of the collection, I feel compelled to inform you I am even more committed to it than he."

Tightening his fingers around Catriona's hand, Robert pushed past Lord Kinsborough, leaving the man to stare at his coattails.

They moved toward the far wall, the only space vacant in the now filled-to-near-bursting room. Robert left Catriona for a moment to fetch them some refreshments. Catriona was watching him as he cut his way through the others, completely unaware of the man's approach to her right.

Until he spoke.

"Good evening, cousin."

Catriona turned, taking in a startled breath. Sir Damon stood close beside her, taking her hand in his and kissing it politely. But there was nothing polite about the way he was staring at her, as if she were a tasty morsel on a plate set before him. Catriona glanced in Robert's direction, but he had disappeared into the crowd. "What do you want of me?" she said quietly.

He smiled, refusing to give up his hold on her hand. "Nothing more than a dance, my dear. Is it too much to ask of someone who is family?"

Catriona decided against drawing attention by protesting or trying to pull away. She remembered what Robert had told her. Sir Damon could do nothing to her in this room filled with half of London society. He obviously had something to say to her—having been responsible for the deaths of Lady Catherine, her brother, and Mary, he should have—and quite honestly Catriona was more than just a little curious to hear what it might be. The musicians were preparing for another waltz, giving the least audible and most visible opportunity for them to speak.

Sir Damon's hand was tight on her waist as he positioned himself before her. The touch of his hands on hers, the hands which had done what they had to Mary, gave her a repulsed shudder. Catriona steeled herself and looked up at him, staring straight into the eyes of a murderer. He waited to speak until the music began.

"You look exactly like her, you know," he said, his eyes glimmering with something—regret?—in the light of the candles burning above them.

"I wouldn't know," Catriona answered. "I never knew my mother."

"I knew I should have had that MacBryan woman arrested for what she did to poor Catherine that night, but the boy had looked so sickly. I wanted to get him to his wet nurse immediately. And when I came back to the chamber, she was gone and Catherine lay dead."

So he was going to try to feign innocence. Catriona decided to play along. "Is that why you killed Mary? Because of what you believed she did to my mother that night?"

"She died, did she?" Damon's jaw tensed. "She deserved far worse than my beating for stealing a child straight from its dying mother's womb. When I learned who you were, that you actually existed, I was overcome. To think that you, my dear cousin, have lived within the space of a few miles of me all your life and I have never known you. The time that we have lost. The memories we could have shared. It pains me now even to think of it. That Scots witch will burn in perdition for what she has done."

Catriona tried not to show her disgust for him, although she nearly winced as his fingers tightened painfully around hers. She glanced toward the edge of the dancing floor, searching for Robert. She could not see him.

"Why did you leave for London without first coming to see me at Crannock, Catherine? It is your home now. You belong there. You have always belonged there with your true family."

Catriona had to wonder if he would have seen her quartered there with her other family members, buried in the ground by his own hand.

"I would have explained everything to you, if you

had only but given me the opportunity," he went on, pulling her from her thoughts. "Why did you leave?"

Catriona didn't answer him. Instead she asked, "What happened to my brother?"

Damon's eyes darkened. "As I said, he looked so sickly when he was born. I took him to the wet nurse but I'm afraid it did little good. He did not last the night."

"Did you not send for a physician?"

"I saw no need. Crannock is remote, it would take days for one to travel there, and the child had expired before the dawn. And when I returned to Catherine's bedside to see to her care, she was already dead. That MacBryan witch left her lying in a bed soaked with her own blood. If I had but known of you, Catherine, I would have scoured the countryside searching to get you back."

"Pray, Sir Damon, why do you think Mary MacBryan would have done it? Taking me away like that while my mother lay dying."

"One can only hazard a guess. Perhaps she hoped to gain something from having you in her possession. Your father, my great-uncle Charles was indeed a wealthy man."

"Indeed," echoed Catriona. "Yet she never sought a ransom."

"Perhaps she came to realize the gravity of her actions and could not see her intentions through."

Catriona nodded in agreement. "One would think murder would prey on a person's soul."

Damon looked at her. If he realized the veiled accusation, he certainly didn't reveal it. "One can only hope, cousin. Nonetheless, I know of you now and I plan to make up for all the time we have lost. I have arranged for a coach to take us to Liverpool, then a packet boat from there to Crannock. We can be back at home by month's end."

"I cannot just leave. I have Mairead with me and—"

Damon's hold on her waist tightened. "My dear

cousin, the MacBryan girl is a peasant. She is not your true family. I am your family now. These people have benefited enough from having had you in their lives, especially given the circumstances of their association. They are naught but common crofter folk. You never were one of them."

Catriona was having a difficult time of it concealing her distaste. To think that this man was related to her by blood. No matter the differences in the connection, she would always consider Mairead her sister.

"I'm sorry, but I still cannot go with you."

"Why ever not?" he asked, his voice deepening.

"Because I am to marry."

Damon smiled, a gesture that chilled Catriona deeply inside. "Surely you cannot mean Devonbrook?"

Catriona frowned at him. "Robert has asked me to wed him and I have agreed."

Damon proceeded to chuckle, his eyes narrowing on her. "Catherine, as your cousin I must advise you against it. Devonbrook is a man with title, but without the means to support it. He lost everything his family had in the fire, a fire which I must inform you most everyone else in this ballroom believes he is responsible for. He is pursuing you for your fortune, using you to regain a position in society. You do not have to believe me, either. Ask Lady Anthea Barrett. She was Devonbrook's betrothed at one time, only she was fortunate enough to realize what a grave error it was before the vows were exchanged. Do not condemn yourself to the fate she was wise enough to avoid. We can pay a visit to Brewster, my London solicitor, and ask his assistance in extricating you from your betrothal promise."

Catriona wondered if Sir Damon realized just how much he had revealed to her while he had been engaged in his assault of Robert's character. She would need to delay him long enough to confirm her suspicions, without giving rise to his own.

The music ended and as they turned to leave the dancing area, they found Robert waiting for them.

"Catriona, come here." His face was set and he was staring at Damon with a predatory light flickering dangerously in his eyes. "If you so much as . . ."

"Robert," Catriona cut in, taking his arm and smiling. She noticed that several of the people standing around them had begun to take notice of the brewing confrontation. "I believe you have already met my cousin Sir Damon Dunstron. He was kind enough to ask me to dance while you were away getting our refreshments. He has explained some things to me and has given me much to consider."

Robert was still staring at Damon coldly. "Did he, indeed?"

"Yes," Catriona replied. "Everything is quite all right now." She forced a cordial smile. "Thank you, Damon. We shall see each other again soon."

Damon grinned at her. "I'm looking forward to it, dear cousin."

Catriona felt as if she might scream.

Anything to break the infernal silence in the house.

She looked out the window to the street. There was still no sign of Robert, nothing to indicate he had yet returned. What was taking him so long? She prayed nothing had happened to him. She didn't know how much longer she could wait.

After the ball the previous evening, Catriona had told Robert everything Damon had said, his explanation of Lady Catherine's death, her infant son, even how he had accused Mary of orchestrating the entire plan. Robert had pointed out that since there was no one to refute Damon's allegations against Mary, there would be no way to see him brought up on charges for the crimes. Even Mary's death could not be vindicated, for again there was nothing to prove Damon had beaten her.

In relating everything to him, Catriona also told

Robert how Damon had let slip the name of his solicitor, and his reference to Catriona's inheritance. Together they came to the decision that Robert should pay Mr. Brewster a visit. It would be perfectly acceptable for him to do so, for if there were any fortune that would be hers, as her betrothed Robert would certainly have an interest in it.

Robert had left early that morning and hadn't returned since. It was now nearing midday. Mairead was in her room, closeted away since Catriona had asked her if she would agree to make her wedding gown. Mairead had been at once shocked that Catriona would want her and not Madame Davenant to design such an important gown, and elated that she had asked her. Robert had gotten her a bundle of fashion publications—*La Belle Assemblée* and *La Miroir de la Mode,* among them—and she hadn't emerged from her chamber since first delving into them. She was showing quite a modiste's talent, and Noah reported that a number of women at the ball the previous night had approached him asking who had fashioned the particularly striking tartan favored by Catriona. Amelia, who had moved her things into the town house as well, was herself napping, having danced through a goodly portion of the previous night with Lord Sheldrake.

A knocking at the parlor door brought Catriona quickly around from the window.

"Miss Catriona?"

It was Sally, the maid. "Yes, Sally?"

"I found this when I was emptying your trunk." She held out what appeared to be a letter. "I thought you might be wantin' it to put with your personals."

Catriona took it, reading the Colonel's name across the front. It was the letter she had found the day she had discovered him missing. Intuitively she glanced over to the armchair where Mattie lay stretched out and sleeping, her furry red-orange body filling the seat. Robert hadn't even hesitated in granting her request to bring the cat along with them when they had left from

Scotland, and Catriona found having her helped to alle-
viate the homesickness she sometimes felt. She also
found she slept a sight better when the feline was
curled against her in the crook of her legs. "Thank you,
Sally."

Catriona peered again at the signature that flowed
across the bottom of the page in rounded, carefully
penned script.

*Margaret Reyford, Number 23, Upper Cadogan
Place, Cadogan Square, London.*

An idea seized her, something she should have
thought of doing sooner. "Sally?"

The maid reappeared around the door. "Yes, miss?"

"Could you please ask Wiggin to arrange for a
coach?"

Sally looked puzzled. "A coach, miss? For you?"

Catriona nodded to her. "Yes, Sally, of course for
me. I think I would like to take some air."

Chapter Twenty-three

The coach pulled to a slow halt before a small brick house that faced out onto a square. It was shaded by graceful elms whose leaves whispered with the breeze, on a quiet street, with pristine boxes of flowers splashed beneath every window at street level. The air here was fresher and everything seemed cleaner than that in the city which lay away from them in the distance.

"This is it?" Catriona asked the coachman.

He was a jovial man named Calder who hadn't batted an eye at Catriona's request for a ride, unlike Sally, who'd spent a quarter of an hour before leaving and most of the journey there trying to convince Catriona otherwise. Sally now sat on the squabs beside her in the stylish landau, mouth set in a dour frown, obviously less than pleased at being there.

Catriona didn't care. It was a pleasant day and Calder had folded back the roof, entertaining her along their ride with humorous snippets about each place they had passed. He pointed out the city's landmarks, places Catriona had only read about in books, and as he tooled them along the crowded streets, he told her of other things, too, his comments focusing mostly on members of society—Lord So-And-So having fought a duel with Lord Whoever here, and Lady What's-Her-Name gambling away twenty thousand pounds of her husband's money there. Calder seemed to know everything there was to know about everybody in the city.

"Aye, miss," Calder said, handing her down. " 'Ere she is. Number twenty-three. Now don't ye fret none over cuttin' yer visit short. I'm just goin' to pull the boys o'er 'ere under this fat tree and take me a snooze in the shade. I'll be waitin' fer ye when ye're ready to go."

Catriona thanked him, then turned toward the house. It was a quaint dwelling, Georgian in design with an upper terrace that looked out onto the street and the center green on the other side. Boxes of colorful geraniums were set beneath the windows, which gleamed in the afternoon sunlight. A shallow birdbath stood just inside the gate, crusts of bread scattered about for the sparrows to pick at.

Catriona approached the door and knocked softly with the shiny brass knocker.

A maid opened the door. "Yes, ma'am?"

"Hello. Does a Miss Margaret MacReyford live here?"

The maid looked at first confused. "Mrs. Margaret Reyford lives here. May I ask who is calling, please?"

Catriona wondered if she'd heard her right. "Yes, please tell her my name if Catriona MacBry—, Dunstron. Miss Catriona Dunstron. I am an acquaintance of her brother, Colonel MacReyford."

The maid's face registered a moment of surprise. "I'll go and see if she can visit with you." She motioned to a place just inside the door. "If you would please wait here . . ."

Several minutes later, the maid showed Catriona to a small parlor set at the back of the house. Double doors opened out onto a back garden which was filled with various brilliant flowers. It was a most peaceful setting, birds trilling, the sunlight filtering softly down through the trees and tall bushes. A figure sat in a wicker-backed chair, facing away from Catriona. Her hair was white and covered by a lace-trimmed mob cap. Despite the summer warmth, a blanket covered her shoulders.

"Miss Reyford?"

The woman turned to look at Catriona. She was well advanced in age, her eyes nearly hidden behind small rounded spectacles. Her face bore the wrinkles of many years.

"Yes, child," she said, her voice as frail as she appeared in body. "Do come and sit here with me. Lucy will pour you some tea, yes?"

She waited until Catriona had taken the dainty china cup. "Lucy says you are acquainted with my Bertrand."

"I have never been told his first name. I know him only as 'the Colonel.' "

Margaret Reyford smiled. "That is Bertrand. So proud of his rank, he was. Even wore his uniform on our wedding day."

"Wedding?" Catriona replied. "But I had always thought his wife was named Matilda."

The woman smiled. "He used to say the name Margaret reminded him too much of his mother, the first Mrs. Margaret Reyford. He called me Mattie instead."

He had never called his cat anything but Mattie. Catriona had just always assumed it meant Matilda and he had never corrected her. "The Colonel was not your brother then?"

"Oh no, my dear. Although he may as well have been. He went off to fight against the Jacobites not a fortnight after we were wed. I never saw him again."

Catriona was fast growing confused. "Do you not mean to say he fought with the Jacobites? Colonel MacReyford was Scottish."

"I'm afraid you are mistaken, child. My Bertrand was an English soldier, at least he was when he left me to go off with Cumberland against the clansmen."

"With Cumberland? But he told me he had fought at Culloden."

"And he did. It was at Culloden that I lost my

Bertrand forever." She moved her hand from under her blanket, holding something out to Catriona. "Here, this letter. It is the last I received from him."

Catriona took the paper from the woman's trembling hand. It was ragged along the edges and yellowed from age. Some of the words had faded to where they were nearly illegible. The page was dated in the year 1746.

My Dearest Mattie,
I cannot believe the horrors I have seen this day, the unprincipled massacre of humanity. My hands are still red with the blood of the men I have seen killed, redder still with the blood of the men I myself have slain. It is over now, but I cannot come home to you yet, my love, for the shame and the sin that darken me must never be allowed touch your innocence. I feel I must attempt to rectify some of the evil I have brought to this land and these innocent proud people. I know not how nor do I know how long it will take me. Only when I feel I have done this will I be able to return to you. Until then, I must beg you to wait for me.
Your devoted husband, Colonel Bertrand Reyford

Catriona closed the letter and looked to Margaret. "He never came home."

"No. I wrote to him every day at first, then every week. The past several years it has fallen to monthly. He never answered me, not once."

"But how did you know where to sent your letters to him?" Catriona asked.

"After the fighting, and when Bertrand did not return for many months, I sent my brother north to search for him. I knew not if he was dead or alive. My brother looked for four months before he found Bertrand living alone in a cottage, he said. William tried to convince Bertrand to come home, but he could not. He said he had not yet done enough to heal the wounds the English had inflicted there. Oh, Bertrand, he lost so very much. He never even knew his son."

Catriona's eyes were filled with tears. She had talked with him so often. He had been the best friend she'd ever had. How could she have never known this about him? "The Colonel has a son?"

"Yes. He is named for his father. He is a good boy, my Bertrand. He comes to visit me every few days to bring me sweetmeats and cream for my tea."

"She took Catriona's hand with her own. "Perhaps you could convince my Bertrand to finally return home."

"I am so sorry," Catriona said as she handed the letter back to her. "Shortly before I left Scotland for London, the Colonel vanished. No one has been able to account for his whereabouts since. I found your letter at his cottage. It was how I was able to find you. I fear for him."

A single tear fell down Margaret's wrinkled cheek.

"Forgive me," Catriona said, reaching for her hand. "I didn't mean to upset you with telling you this. Perhaps, I should be going now."

Catriona squeezed Margaret's hand and stood. She watched as the woman clasped the letter the Colonel had written her so long ago tight to her chest, then turned to walk slowly from the garden.

When Catriona arrived back at the town house, Robert was waiting for her, standing atop the steps at the front door like a sentry.

"Where in perdition have you been?"

Catriona skipped down from the coach. "Robert, hello, wait until I tell you—"

"You haven't answered my question, Catriona."

He was angry with her, glowering at her even as she came to stand before him. But once she told him what she had done, what she had learned, he would understand. "I was bored beyond reason here waiting for you to return so I asked Calder to take me for a ride to—"

They had walked into the house and Robert had immediately ushered Catriona into his study, closing the door loudly behind them. He turned to face her, frowning down at her like a fierce storm cloud. "I already know that much. Wiggin told me. Do you know the danger you placed yourself in?"

"I am fine, Robert, as you can see. There is no need to—"

"London isn't the Highlands, Catriona. You cannot go running off on a whim without telling anyone first."

She was beginning to realize just how far away Scotland was more each day. "I did tell someone, Robert. I told Wiggin, and Sally came along with me."

"Sally had no idea where you were going. She told Wiggin so. Now she'll be fearing for her position, thinking I'm going to dismiss her for allowing you to leave."

Allowing you to . . . Catriona tried to remain calm. "Robert, be reasonable. Calder never left me. And Sally was with me the entire time I was—"

"That is beside the point. From now on, you will inform me when you wish to take the air and I will accompany you. If I am unavailable, then you will wait for me to return. Do you understand?"

Catriona didn't like the way he was talking to her as if she were a misbehaving child. She didn't like it a bit. All the way home she had looked forward to seeing him and telling him about her visit with Mrs. Reyford. Now she didn't even think she wanted to tell him. "By what you are saying, am I to understand that by making me your wife, you intend to place limitations on my every movement?"

"If it keeps you from danger, yes. And what of the child you possibly carry. Had you stopped long enough to consider the danger you might be placing it in as well?"

The child. Catriona drew a slow breath. "I have no intention of living like a prisoner the rest of my days, *your grace.* If that is what marriage is to you, then perhaps we should both reconsider your proposal."

Robert's face grew rigid.

Catriona turned to leave before he could see the tears that were coming to her eyes. Blinking them away, she had just reached the door when she heard him say, "Catriona, before you make that decision, I think you should listen to what I have to say, to what I have to tell you about my visit with Brewster today."

She stilled, her grand exit cut short. She turned. And waited.

Robert motioned toward a chair. "Will you please sit?"

Catriona walked slowly to the chair. She sat, back rigid and straight, staring at him stonily silent.

Robert drew a deep breath before beginning. "As we already knew, your father, Sir Charles Dunstron, was a baronet and he held the lairdship over Crannock. What we didn't know was that when your father learned your mother Lady Catherine was with child, he wrote to his solicitor in London setting up the conditions of inheritance should he pass away. His solicitor was Johann Brewster. His letter indicated his wish that if the child were a son, he should inherit the entire estate and would assume the baronetage. In absence of a male child, this would, of course, revert to his closest living male relative, in this case, his grand-nephew, Damon Dunstron. However, in the case of a daughter, he set up an entirely different set of stipulations."

Robert watched Catriona closely. She was listening to him now. And at least he knew she was safe.

When he'd seen her pulling up in front of the house so carefree and unaware, he'd been ready to throttle her. She had given him quite a scare, leaving as she had, and all he'd done since returning from Brewster's office to find her gone was pace the carpet, watching out the window, imagining every sort of trouble she could have found out alone.

And if only she had known the degree of trouble that truly awaited her . . .

"Sir Charles stipulated that in the case of a daughter, where no male child of his own would inherit before her, the bulk of his wealth would fall to her after she had passed her twenty-first year." Robert paused. "And only if she were wed."

Catriona looked at him. "And if she were not?"

"Then the monies would revert to the next in-line male. More specifically, your cousin Sir Damon Dunstron. You would be allotted a portion, but it would be managed, supervised, and the amount set by the heir."

"Damon," Catriona added, frowning.

"Yes."

Catriona sat for a moment, considering the news. Finally she stood and faced him. "Well then, it would seem there really is no choice in it. I will have to marry you, after all."

"Catriona, I—" His words were cut short as she turned to leave. Robert watched as she walked from the room then, her backbone so stiff she looked as if she might snap. Robert frowned.

She could have no idea of the seriousness of her situation. She couldn't because he hadn't told her everything. He hadn't told her of how just before he had left Brewster that morning, the solicitor had called him back into his small, paper-strewn office.

"One final thing," he'd said, peering at Robert from over the document he was perusing. "We will, of course, require proof of Lady Catherine's identity before her inheritance can be assumed by her."

The first thing Robert had thought of was the likelihood that Sir Damon would simply paint Catriona as an imposter. He'd already found a way to explain away his actions of twenty years ago, laying all the responsibility of the deaths of Catriona's mother and brother in the hands of Mary MacBryan, who was now dead, unable to defend herself. He would thus stop at nothing to ensure Catriona wouldn't inherit. He might even consider killing again before any proof of her identity could be found.

Their only solution was to find Lady Catherine's family. Robert had realized this and had immediately set Noah and Tolley to the task. It might take some time, and until then, he would simply have to keep Catriona safe.

But after the events this day, he wondered how he was ever going to manage it.

Tolley arrived for supper at eight. The rest of the party were sitting in the parlor when Noah arrived at a quarter past.

"Where is Catriona?" Tolley asked. "I want to make certain she is here before I make my grand announcement."

Robert looked out the hall and saw Catriona just coming down the stairs. It was the first he'd seen her since their altercation in the study earlier that day. She walked in quietly and sat beside Aunt Amelia on the settee, avoiding his eyes at all costs. Mairead had decided to take her supper upstairs. She had begun work on Catriona's wedding gown and rarely emerged from her chamber except to eat with them occasionally or to ask Catriona's opinion of some aspect of the design.

"Wonderful," Tolley said, standing. He took a deep and impressive breath. "To celebrate my successful return from the Continent and Boney's last capture, and in honor of the coming marriage of my good friends, Robert and Catriona, I am hosting a house party at my seat in Kent. Everybody in Town will be invited, of course. No one will be permitted to miss it."

Tolley was detailing the events he had planned when a knocking came from streetside. Wiggin appeared at the door moments later.

"There is a gentleman to see Lady Catriona. He says it is most urgent."

Catriona looked at Robert. "Do you think it is Sir Damon?"

"I wouldn't think him so bold. Even if it is we are all here, so he cannot do anything to you."

Catriona stood and walked to the hall. Robert followed after.

An older gentleman, looking to be nearing seventy, was standing by the front door, his hat in his hand. He smiled when he noticed her approaching. "Hello, my lady," he said politely to her, nodding in Robert's direction. "Your grace."

"Do I know you, sir?" Catriona asked.

"No, but you came to visit my mother earlier today."

Catriona's face broke into a wide smile. "Mr. Reyford!" She shook his hand. "Won't you please come into the parlor and join us?"

"No. I've got to be going on home now. My wife worries something terrible if I am late." He pulled something from inside his coat. "My mother asked me to give this to you. It came with a letter she received just today from my father. It is the first she has heard from him since he left. She said after your visit to her today, she just knew he would write to her again. This letter was inside. It is addressed to you. I think after you read it, you'll understand more why my father went away like he did."

Catriona took the small square of paper into her hand. "Thank you, sir."

"Good evening to you," he said, turning to go.

"Mr. Reyford," Catriona called. "Will you please wait here just one moment more? There is something I should like to give to you."

Catriona went quickly up the stairs, returning but a few moments later, carrying a red garment draped over her arm. "This was your father's jacket. I'm afraid it's a bit ragged. I don't think a day passed that he didn't wear it. I think he would like you to have it, until he can wear it again."

Mr. Reyford smiled at her, his eyes growing moist, glistening in the candlelight. "Thank you, miss."

Mattie came around the corner then, giving her low, scratchy meow. "Mattie!" Catriona picked her up. "This was the Colonel's cat. He named her Mattie, for your mother. He will be very worried about her. Perhaps your mother would like to keep her until—"

"No," Mr. Reyford said, shaking his head. "I think my father would like it better if you were to keep her right now. Thank you, miss." He bowed his head. "Your grace."

He slipped through the door.

"But how did you know where to . . ."

He was gone before she could finish.

Catriona set Mattie down and opened the letter quickly.

My sweet lassie,

If ye're readin' this then you know I've gone and you know I wasn't quite what I said I was. I hope someday you will be able to forgive my deception, just as I hope someday my Margaret, who waited for me all these years, will forgive me for ne'er returnin' to her. And don't be makin' the same mistake with the laird that I made with Mattie in lettin' the world come atween you and the one you love.

Now, lass, 'tis time for me to leave this life. You were always frettin' o'er my cough, but a man knows when 'tis too late. My time on this earth has run short. I didn't want you spendin' yer days watchin' me die, so I went off to make my peace wit' the Lord for the things I did. I'll not have you weepin' o'er me, lass, so dry those tears right now. You're a good girl and you made an old man's days far better than they should have been.

Keep care of my Mattie. She'll keep yer feet warm at night. I'm sendin' along something for you. It is yours now. You know well what to do with it.
Your friend, Colonel Bertrand Reyford

Catriona turned to the second page of the letter, knowing even before she saw it that it was the Jacobite picture map.

The legend of the treasure continued.

Chapter Twenty-four

The coaches began arriving at midday, circling around the front of Tolley's Kentish manor house. By two o'clock, there was a line of them waiting to let off their passengers that stretched down the white gravel drive, vanishing from sight around the bend through the trees.

Scores of guests had come from London, sleek barouches gleaming in the sunlight, two-wheeled curricles driven by tigers, their distinctively striped coats showing bright against the landscape, and fashionable phaetons pulled by matched teams of six. The occupants of these stylish vehicles were just as remarkable. Bedecked in ostrich plumes and pristine silks, they had all come to the Sheldrake seat for a weekend of country frolic.

The estate, Drakely Manor, stretched over the countryside like a slumbering landscape painted on canvas. The house Catriona would learn, was small by nobility standards, but it looked like a palace to her. It had been built by his grandfather, Tolley had told her while taking her about on tour the previous day, an eccentric fellow who had apparently been exceedingly fond of ducks. And it was evidenced wherever one chanced to look.

Above the front door was a coat of arms bearing a brilliantly colored pochard wearing a crown and surrounded by a laurel wreath. Statues of them carved in marble adorned the lower gallery, and a number of the chambers had been named for them. Mallards, mergansers, eiders; they were even carved into the woodwork and painted on the molded stucco ceilings wherever one chanced to look.

Mairead would have been in awe, Catriona thought, had she not instead remained behind in the city. Catriona had worried over leaving her, but it had been Mairead who had eventually decided it.

"I want you to be the loveliest bride London has ever seen," she had said. "And having you all gone from the house will give me the opportunity to get a great deal of work finished on your gown."

Catriona had consented, knowing since she would have Wiggin and the other servants with her, she would be quite safe.

Given the numerous guests expected, Catriona would be sharing a chamber with Amelia, which was quite agreeable to her, since the bed in the room they'd been given could have easily slept five.

Amelia had a way of putting Catriona entirely at ease whenever faced with the members of society. She would say something utterly outlandish, whispering it to Catriona so that no one else might overhear, such as when they'd gone out driving on Rotten Row and Catriona had wished she might sink into the coach seat to avoid the speculative glances they were receiving. Amelia had noticed this and had asked Catriona to consider what one particularly pompous man might look like wearing naught but the corset she knew he sported beneath his frock coat before snapping the reins so that they might pass him while Catriona giggled at the image she'd summoned.

Standing at the window of their chamber now, Catriona looked out over the back garden, which was dressed brilliantly with flowers in glorious bloom. A labyrinth formed out of high-standing hedges filled the lower part of the garden, and from where she stood

Catriona could see to the green further out, where several of the guests were playing at bowls. One of Tolley's sisters was showing her children how to play off to the side and she could see them dancing about as they managed to topple several of the pins.

Watching the scene, Catriona's hand moved instinctively to her belly, laying flat against the tiny life nestled there. She hadn't yet told Robert of her certainty now of their child, perhaps foolishly thinking he might yet prove her wrong, tell her it wasn't only because of the child, because of the responsibility he felt for her, that he wanted her for his wife. It was absurd, she knew, clinging to this desperate hope like she did. But a part of her just wouldn't allow her to abandon all hope.

Catriona looked down when she heard a familiar meowing near her feet. "Hello, Miss Mattie," she said, picking her up and holding her close, rubbing her soft fur against the side of her face. "I'd have thought you away in the garret or in the cellar hunting in the shadowy corners for mice."

Since that night when she had read her last letter from the Colonel, learning of his reasons for leaving as he had, knowing she would never see him again, Catriona had kept the cat close by her. Tolley had graciously agreed that Mattie should come along for the weekend in the country. Mattie slept with Catriona at night and curled in her lap while she was reading, serving as a constant reminder to Catriona of her quest. She looked forward to the day when she could return to Rosmorigh and resume her search through its library for the book which held the treasure text. Even though she no longer needed Prince Charlie's treasure for monetary reasons, her commitment to finding it remained ever as strong as it had been before.

And she could take encouragement in knowing she would have a confederate in her quest, for Robert was just as compelled as she that they should complete the journey separately begun by his father and the Colonel, only they would pursue it together.

But before they could set out on their quest, before they could leave to return to Rosmorigh, Robert would need to finally put to rest the questions of the fire. And this weekend might just present him with the opportunity.

Lord Kinsborough would be among the many guests traveling to Drakely Manor. Tolley had arranged it rather adroitly, letting it be known Robert would be there, squiring his intriguing betrothed. It would give the marquess the best opportunity to again press Robert to sell the collection, and Robert the opportunity to search for the proof of Lord Kinsborough's guilt.

The weekend would also serve another purpose entirely, that to redeem Robert in the eyes of society. From Tolley Catriona learned that she had come to intrigue the glittering *ton*. It seemed rather silly to her, the list of requirements he'd told her she had completed in order for her to be considered an "original" by them.

She was unknown to all except her small, tightly knit circle, a mystery and thus a sensation in the making. She was engaged to wed a scandalous duke, a man she had rescued from exile, her unquestioning belief in him having already begun to change the minds of his previous accusers. And the last of her accomplishments was her wearing dark colors which went against the current fashion, but which thanks to Mairead's skill with her needle, had a notable style all their own. And whatever she wore, be it a delicate ball gown or the riding bonnet perched aslant upon her head, it was always complemented by what had become her trademark, the MacBryan plaid.

In the short time Catriona had been in London, she had made it fashionable to be a Scot. Tartan wraps had begun to adorn milky shoulders and bonnets trimmed with plaid were set atop elegant coiffures. Even now, as she gazed down at the groups of guests standing on the lawn below, she could see more than a couple of gentlemen wearing plaid waistcoats beneath their coats. It only displayed society's frivolity and before turning from the window, she wondered fleetingly if any of them would dare to don a kilt.

Catriona started when she saw Robert standing in the doorway. "Robert."

"I had come across something that I thought you might like to have."

He held out something small in his hand, white and square. Catriona took it, recognizing the handkerchief she'd lost the night she'd tried to frighten him away from Rosmorigh. She looked up at him.

"You knew it was mine?"

"I knew from that night in the library at Rosmorigh, but I never said anything to you. When Mary told me everything about your past, she mentioned the handkerchief. She said that it had been your mother's— Catherine's. I thought knowing that, you might like to have it back."

Catriona stared down at it. He had known all this time, known that it was she who had tried to frighten him off that night, and he had never said anything to her. But he'd kept her handkerchief with him. That seed of hope inside of her began to grow. "Thank you."

"Actually, the handkerchief wasn't the only reason I came here. I was hoping to speak with you privately before the festivities for the weekend begin."

"Of course." Catriona lowered herself into the chair behind her, waiting.

"Catriona, I know you are feeling as if your life has fallen out of your hands. And I am sorry for making you feel that way. I hope you will always know that I would never do anything to hurt you. I only wanted to keep you safe. It is what husbands do. I never meant that you should live as a prisoner in our home."

Our home. Catriona looked at him, peering at his eyes.

"Do you think we might make another go of it?" he asked.

It was a start, she knew, and she latched on to it tightly. "Of course, Robert."

He came into the room then, smiling at her. He sat at the foot of the bed, facing her. "Tolley has challenged me to a race on the south lawn. He is determined he should finally beat Bayard with the new bay he just bought at Tattersall's. I thought you might like to come."

Catriona stood, setting Mattie on the chair. The emptiness she had felt already began to lessen. "Of course."

A crowd had gathered just below the house on the stretch of lawn where Robert and Lord Sheldrake would race. Tolley was checking the fastenings of the saddle on his horse, a beautiful stallion, dark brown with black points. Bayard stood, equally as impressive, his dappled gray body striking against the verdant background of the green, waiting for Robert.

"Are you ready to face defeat, my friend?" Lord Sheldrake said to Robert as they approached.

Robert chuckled. "You would do well to keep your mouth closed, my lord, lest the clumps of dirt thrown up by my horse find their way inside and choke you."

The crowd laughed at the raillery and the number of lookers-on began to swell.

Tolley mounted, his horse dancing about anxiously as he swung into the saddle. "Terms?"

Robert, too, swept onto Bayard's back, glancing at his friend with a wry grin. "One hundred guineas."

The crowd emitted a low and lengthy "Oooh."

Tolley shook his head, chuckling. "Come now, my friend. Surely you can do better than that. Say, double?"

Side wagers were already circulating through the crowd, the odds evenly split. Catriona looked about, and it was then she noticed Lord Kinsborough standing on the outer fringes of the throng. He was staring directly at Robert.

"I accept your terms, my lord," Robert said. He executed a gallant salute. "And to the victor goes the spoils."

"Splendid!" said Tolley. "Then let us be off." The two horses came side by side at the far edge of the milling crowd. "The course of the race is as follows." Tolley pointed outward. "Across the lawn, over the fence at the far side, around the pond, through the brook, and then back."

"Looks simple enough," Robert said, peering outward.

"We shall see if you still think so after I've beaten you." He sat up in the saddle. "Are you ready then?"

"Are you?"

They positioned themselves and awaited Noah's starting gunshot.

"Wait!"

Catriona pressed through the crowd to Robert. She removed a strip of the tartan she had knotted on her gown. "You should wear this for good luck." She reached up and tied it to the topmost button hole in Robert's coat.

"My lady's colors for her knight as he rides off to adventure?" he asked quietly.

She smiled.

He took her hand, kissing it. "I shall take my lady's favor with me into battle."

And with that, Robert reached down and plucked Catriona effortlessly from the ground, seating her before him on the saddle. Her dark green silk skirts fluttered over his legs in the gentle morning breeze. "A kiss shall seal my fate," he said, and before Catriona could respond he covered her mouth with his.

Catriona barely heard the sound of the onlookers around them, for her head was spinning, her heart pounding, while Robert kissed her.

When he pulled away, she was clutching at the front of his coat, dazed.

"You'll crumple my lady's token," he said, then

gently lowered her back to the ground. Her feet were at first unsteady beneath her.

"I shall be back to claim the victor's kiss shortly."

Catriona stood back, preparing to watch the race. She barely even noticed the report of the starting gun when it fired.

They were off, tearing across the rich lawn at full gallop, clumps of dirt and grass flying out behind the thundering hooves. Robert hugged his legs tight around Bayard's girth, leaning low over his neck when they cleared the rock fence. He could hear Tolley riding close to his side, but ignored the urge to turn and look.

It felt beyond exhilarating to be astride again, the wind whipping across his face, a powerful beast churning like the storm beneath him. They rounded the first curve of the placid duck pond and it was then Robert first noticed that Tolley was pulling ahead. He murmured words of encouragement to Bayard as they came around to the second turn.

Once they were on a stretch again, Robert gave Bayard his full head. He could feel the surge of the stallion, his legs pulling at the ground beneath his pounding hooves. As they neared the brook, Robert thought to pull him back a bit. But he didn't. Tolley's horse slowed, hopped uncertainly through the water and with a powerful snort Bayard sailed clear, spanning the brook and breaking for the finish with a mad gallop.

They were closing in for the finish when Robert felt something whiz by him suddenly, close to his ear. The second shot grazed his shoulder, coming from behind.

He pulled Bayard up. Noticing his abrupt halt, Tolley did the same, wheeling his mount around to join him. They were just ten or more yards from the finish.

This time Robert heard the shot. It fired into the ground near Bayard's front hooves, spitting up dirt. Bayard reared in alarm.

"Someone is firing!" came a shout from the crowd.

"There is no hunting hereabouts to my knowledge,"

Tolley said. "There!" He pointed west to the top of the hill. A figure was there, astride a horse, standing like a shadow against the sunlight. "Let us be after him!"

Robert and Tolley dug in, starting for the other rider, who spun about, making quickly for the trees. Several of the guests who were mounted on the outskirts of the crowd joined in the pursuit, thundering after them.

Catriona watched, fear knotting her stomach as Robert disappeared over the horizon.

The waiting was interminable. Given the lead Robert had had on Tolley at that point in the race, there was little doubt that the shots had been meant for anyone other than Robert. Several of the ladies standing nearby came to Catriona, offering her words of comfort. Amelia squeezed her hand reassuringly. "He will be all right. They will find who did this."

Who did this . . . Catriona turned, looking through the crowd to where Lord Kinsborough had stood. He was gone.

Suddenly someone called from the crowd. "There they are!"

Catriona watched as a group of riders came racing down the hill toward them. When she saw Robert among them, she closed her eyes and let go a heavy breath of relief.

Everyone began talking, asking questions at once. Who had fired? Where had he gone? Catriona barely heard Tolley say that the rider had appeared to be a man and that they had lost him in the wood. She moved quickly to where Robert was just dismounting. She walked into his arms, resting the side of her face against his chest. She closed her eyes.

"I am all right," he said.

Catriona opened her eyes. She saw her plaid still tied on his jacket through the blur of her tears, but something wasn't quite right about it. Something was on it, red against the blue and the white and the green.

"Robert, you are bleeding."

"I am fine. The shot just grazed me. It is nothing."

Catriona pushed back the front of his coat. She hadn't seen the wound right away, for the dark navy of his coat had hidden the injury from her. But upon opening his coat, Catriona saw that it was certainly more than *nothing*.

Catriona gasped at the blood, bright and red, that had soaked through his shirt where the bullet had entered just below his shoulder.

The doctor Tolley had sent for arrived nearly an hour later. Catriona had already gotten Robert to the nearest open chamber, the library, and had begun to remove his shirt, unfastening the buttons at his throat, when Robert reached up, grabbing her hand.

"Catriona, the doctor will see to it."

"Nonsense, I can clean the wound at least. But we must get this shirt off and—"

"Catriona," Robert said, his voice dropping low, "we are not yet married."

He glanced to the doorway, where outside in the hall most every person present stood watching.

The doctor stepped in, effectively ending the disagreement. "Miss, I know you are worried over his grace, but I assure you he is in capable hands. I have pulled more than my fair share of shot from the local hunters. But the wound will likely not be very pretty and it wouldn't do for you to faint."

Faint? Catriona had never fainted in her life. She had always been the one who had stood by watching when her mother had stitched up Angus's leg after he'd sliced it with a scythe. Still, she peered to the door and the interested eyes that awaited her there. She decided they had supplied quite enough to society conversation. "I will await you in the parlor."

Catriona was sitting with Tolley and Amelia when the physician came to see them nearly an hour later. Noah stood at the windows behind them. They had been discussing the possible suspects, and had narrowed it down to the likeliest two: Lord Kinsborough and Damon.

"Lord Sheldrake," said the physician at the door, "a moment if you please so that I might discuss the duke's condition."

Tolley looked at Catriona. "I believe his grace's betrothed is the one to whom you should speak."

The doctor nodded, motioning toward the door. "Miss?"

"You may speak freely here, Doctor," she said. "We are all Robert's closest friends and family."

"Very well. The shot entered the fleshy part of the duke's shoulder, barely missing the bone. It took some effort for me to remove it. It was not without some trial on his grace. The wound has been cleaned and bandaged and I have dosed him with laudanum for the pain. I have asked two of Lord Sheldrake's footmen to remove him to a bedchamber upstairs. He will need to rest tonight. Tomorrow he can take the air and walk about the grounds, perhaps, close to the house and nothing more strenuous."

Catriona nodded. "I will see to it, sir."

The doctor handed her a bottle. "Here is another dose of laudanum should he need it. I will come back in the morning to check the dressing and clean the wound again."

Chapter Twenty-five

Catriona opened the door to Robert's bedchamber slowly so as not to make a sound. It was late, well into the early hours of morning. She had waited impatiently in her chamber until she had heard the last of the guests retire before leaving to come. Oddly enough, it had been Amelia who had helped her, keeping watch in the hall.

Amelia knew Catriona was beside herself with worry over her nephew, and knew too that she wouldn't have slept a wink had she stayed. Catriona would have spent the night pacing the floor, keeping Amelia awake with her. She wanted to be with Robert should he need her. She needed to be certain he was well, for despite Tolley's assurances that he was, she wouldn't believe it until she could see for herself.

Catriona wondered if Tolley had told Robert yet that they hadn't found any clues as to who could have shot at him. Lord Kinsborough had been found later and hadn't known a thing about the incident, for he and another of Tolley's guests, an earl whose reputation hovered far above reproach, had been in the parlor playing whist the entire time. Without him, Damon was left as the most likely suspect. And that, of course, meant that he'd followed them to Kent, and could at that moment be anywhere.

The candle Catriona carried threw a halo of light about Robert's sleeping face as she looked down at him in bed. He was sitting up, several pillows propped behind his head. His chest was bare, his left shoulder wrapped with bandages. Setting the candle on the table by the bed, she dropped into the chair beside it, setting Mattie in her lap, the book she'd been reading clasped in her hands.

Robert had given her the book before they had left London, after having taken her to a place called Hatchard's, where she had browsed freely through the book-filled shelves while Robert had sat reading the latest newspapers. They had spent three hours there. The book he'd given her was an adventure story, he told her, a modern Grail of sorts, set in the Highlands of Scotland. Its authorship was apparently somewhat of a mystery. Written anonymously, the book was at the center of a great deal of wagering among the *ton*. Though many believed they knew who had written it, despite the novel's huge success, no person had come forward to claim the distinction. It had already gone through numerous printings, and certainly would still, yet the publisher steadfastly refused to reveal the mysterious author of the book called *Waverly*.

Catriona opened to the place where she had last left off. She tried concentrating on the words, but found her eyes constantly straying to Robert. She remembered the light which had shone in his eyes when he'd given her the book, charging her with uncovering the identity of its author. Her new "quest," he'd told her, hoping it might keep her occupied until they could return to Rosmorigh to resume their true one. If she guessed the author correctly, he'd promised she would decide what should be done with the treasure after they found it. If she didn't, then the decision would be his.

Catriona preferred thinking of Robert as he had been that day at Hatchard's, teasing her, challenging her, rather than when his face had been so pale, the blood on his shirtfront so stark. The time she had passed sitting in the parlor, waiting while the doctor had been with Robert had given her the chance to consider a lot of things. She loved Robert. She loved the man he was. And the thought that she had come so close to not having him in her life had filled her with a fear unlike any she had ever felt before. She wanted him in her life. Forever. And even if he didn't love her as she did him, perhaps someday he would. Or perhaps he just couldn't. She no longer cared. She just wanted to talk to him again.

"You know, I've been reading this book you gave to me," she said softly to him. She realized the laudanum would prevent him from hearing her, but she needed to do something other than stare at him in fear. "I cannot understand why there is such controversy over who wrote this when it is so obvious it is Sir Walter Scott. Who else could have written it? You shall be sorry you wagered with me for it."

She looked at him. His eyes were still closed, his chest rising and falling softly. She moved from the chair and knelt beside the bed. She took his hand with hers, resting her face against it. What if he fell to a fever this very night and never awoke again? What if Robert never knew that she carried his child?

"Do you know that I loved you even before I met you?" she whispered then. "I used to talk to you, to your portrait hanging there in the library at Rosmorigh. I thought you were magnificent. I still do. And now I have your child inside of me." She lowered her head, resting it against his leg. "Oh, Robert, I wanted to tell you. I tried to tell you, but it just never seemed right. I never wanted you to feel you had no choice, that you had to wed someone like me because of the child. I know you do not love me, not the same way I do you. But you care for me, and that is enough. I was wrong to expect that you should love me, too. Some marriages are based on far less. But I will make you happy, Robert. I promise. I will love you enough for both of us."

"No, you will not."

Catriona lifted her head. Robert's eyes were open, lucid, alert. He was awake. How much of what she'd said had he heard?

He touched the side of her face. "Catriona, I have been a fool. You once told me it was all right for me to need someone. I had fallen into a burn and I had treated you badly. When you said that to me, I didn't believe you. I thought needing someone would make me weak, dependent. But I was wrong. Needing someone has only made me stronger. I do need someone, Catriona, and it is you. I should have known it from the first day when you came to Rosmorigh and brought your light to my dark and angry world. You were the one person who didn't treat me as if I were an oddity. You were my eyes when I could not see and you were my heart when I did not care. And now you carry a child. Our child, yours and mine. How could you wonder at my regard for you? Care for you? Those words could never adequately describe what you mean to me. So I will tell you in words that I know you will understand, words you once spoke to me, only I was too stubborn to really hear what it was you were saying. *Tha Gaol Agam Ort.* I love you. I love the woman who pushed me into the burn, Catriona MacBryan. And if it takes me the rest of my life, I will show you just how much you mean to me."

Catriona wondered if she could be dreaming. Only when she felt Robert pulling her toward him and he was kissing her was she certain she couldn't have imagined it. And she returned his kiss with all the love, all the fire that she felt for him to her soul.

"I need you now, Catriona," he said, nibbling at her ear, her neck, burying his face in her hair.

"Your shoulder," she said, even while she prayed he didn't stop.

"You can love me, Catriona. You can make love to me tonight."

Catriona nodded against his mouth. "Show me how to love you, Robert."

Catriona stood at the edge of the bed and slowly removed her nightgown, dropping it to the floor. Robert watched her intently, his eyes moving over her, looking at her closely as he had dreamed of doing so many times, at all the places he had touched her. "Come to me, Catriona."

He held his hand out to her and led her over to sit next to him. He kissed her, her mouth, her neck, suckling at her breasts. Catriona felt as if her body had caught fire. Every nerve ending tingled, every touch of his lips on her skin made the need within her build, filling her, taking her higher until she thought she could stand the waiting no longer.

Robert guided her over him so that she was straddling him. His fingers found her, readying her, teasing her until she was moist and trembling against the movement of his hand. She lowered her hips over his, guiding him inside of her, until he was filling her completely. He touched her deeper than she ever thought possible. Following his movements, she lifted her hips before taking him within her again. Robert's fingers were on her, making the burning inside of her build. The more he continued to stroke his fingers over her, the faster her movements became until she felt she was rocking over him, her head thrown back, searching for her release.

And when that moment came, Robert grabbed her hips and pulled her over him one last time, burying himself deep inside her heat. The waiting was over and the need within her shattered into a million tiny waves of pleasure. And at the same time she knew this exquisite wonder, she could feel Robert moving inside of her, releasing his seed. It was the sweetest feeling she had ever known.

Still holding him within her, Catriona lay herself over his chest, and listened as his heartbeat slowed, his breathing grew even, and his heated skin began to cool, knowing a feeling of complete happiness.

* * *

The morning of the last day of the weekend dawned pleasant and sunny, a gentle breeze blowing in through the stirring leaves of the tall birch trees. Breakfast was served on the outside lawn that morning, the footmen having moved the huge oak table from the formal dining hall, and another one from the smaller dining parlor where the family usually took their meals. Trays of food were being brought out continuously, Tolley's French chef having risen before the dawn to prepare the marvelous feast. And Tolley had spared no expense in arranging for the most exotic of menus.

Westphalian hams, buttered eggs, a number of different types of fish served with a variety of complementary sauces, even Jamaican bananas were included with the platters of exotic fruits. Yet despite her curiosity Catriona couldn't bring herself to sample the reindeer tongue which the young lord sitting across from her was consuming with zeal. In fact, her stomach was feeling rather queasy. She found, though, that if she avoided looking at everyone else's plate, it wasn't so bad, so she simply sipped at her tea and nibbled on a plain biscuit.

"How fairs the duke, Miss Dunstron?"

Lady Sheldrake, Tolley's mother, had come up behind her. In her hand she held a plate of kippers with a sausage swimming in a fruity-smelling sauce alongside. From the way she was standing, when Catriona turned, the plate was positioned right under her nose. She felt her stomach lurch and quickly moved, swallowing hard against her rising nausea.

"I haven't yet seen him this morning, my lady. I believe he will be abed yet today."

Nobody was more surprised than she when Robert came walking through the double doors to join them mere seconds later. A white sling held his arm in front of him, contrasting with the dark green of his coat. A number of people came forward to greet him and it took him some time to reach Catriona, where she was sitting at the table. He smiled, taking her hand and kissing it gallantly.

"Robert," she said.

"Good morning, my dear. The good doctor came this morning to check my shoulder and change the bandages. He said I could take to my feet as long as I kept my arm immobile with this sling. I told him I couldn't chance that you might find someone else with which to pass the time in my absence. He quite understood. I trust you slept well?"

Catriona could not help but grin in response to his obvious reference. She had but left him a few hours before, after making love to him one more time as the dawn had begun peeking through the curtains. "Yes, your grace, I slept quite well indeed. Thank you. And you?"

"Very well. I feel quite restored. I'm not at all certain, but I suspect the laudanum must have affected my senses for I had the most unusual dream . . ."

"I am glad to see your injury is not impeding you from enjoying the day's activities," Catriona cut in, throwing him a warning glance.

Robert smiled, quite enjoying her discomfort. "Not at all." And then he bent to whisper in her ear. "Nor the night's activities either."

Catriona smiled, feeling the flush come to her face. She looked around, certain everyone sitting at the table knew exactly what had occurred the night before. It was then she noticed the blond woman staring at her quite openly.

She was sitting at the far end of the table and had obviously been watching the entire exchange. Her eyes moved from Robert to Catriona, at whom she stared, her mouth pinched in a frown, as if she had just walked in wearing the same gown. Noticing Catriona, the woman stood from her chair then and turned, disappearing into the house.

"Who was that woman?" Catriona asked Robert. A footman had brought him his plate.

"Lady Anthea Barrett," he answered.

Damon had mentioned her the night he'd taken Catriona onto the dance floor. "Were you not once betrothed?"

"I see the gossips' tongues still carry old tales." Robert set down his fork, which was a good thing, for the sight of the puffy eggs atop it was turning her stomach. "Yes, I was betrothed to Anthea, briefly. She broke off the engagement after the fire when she learned I was blind."

Catriona looked back at the door. "It would appear from the look on her face she regrets her decision."

She took a sip of her tea, glancing at Robert's plate. He certainly had his appetite this morning. She reached down to remove a pebble which had found its way into her shoe. When she lifted her head again, Robert was holding out a heaping forkful of the most noxious-looking substance she had ever before seen. He fixed it right before her nose.

"You must try the jugged hare, my dear. It is quite delicious."

And to that Catriona promptly responded by casting the contents of her stomach into his lap.

Catriona lay on the bed, a wet cloth soaked in vinegar pressed to her forehead, staring out the window at the billowing clouds and wondering if she could feel any more humiliated than she did at that moment. She still couldn't believe she had done what she had, even though having Amelia sitting before her, fanning her softly, was surely proof enough.

She had thrown up on Robert, at a breakfast table filled with half of London's most elite society. Tolley, bless his shoe buckles, had immediately blamed the hare, ordering his servant to "toss the rubbish out" and cautioning his guests not to swallow another bite. And then Amelia, sweet Amelia, following Tolley's lead, declared that she felt quite sick after she had eaten the hare as well. Plates were collected and pots of herbal tea were brewed to calm the growing number of upset stomachs. But despite their well-intentioned ruse meant to avert attention away from her, Catriona knew the true reason for her malaise. And it certainly wasn't the hare.

And now most everyone else knew it, too.

"You're carrying his child, aren't you?" Amelia said from the chair beside the bed, easily reading Catriona's thoughts.

Catriona simply closed her eyes.

" 'Tis nothing to be ashamed of, my dear. Children are a blessing." Amelia patted her hand. "Can I get you some tea?"

Catriona offered her a weak smile. "No, thank you, my stomach is feeling much better now." She took a deep breath. "Oh, what must everyone think?"

"You have given my nephew so very much. I will be forever grateful to you. As for the others ... some shake their heads and cluck their tongues and whisper of it over their tea. They say it is unfashionable, the open regard you and Robert have for one another. Meanwhile their husbands are sneaking away to meet a lover in the stables. If they have guessed the truth of the child, they will forget it just as quickly after you and Robert are wed and return to Rosmorigh and another bit of gossip comes about more scandalous than yours. Others have said it is refreshing to see a man and a woman so obviously in love. You have restored Robert in the eyes of society, dear Catriona. They no longer talk of the fire and the part they at one time believed he'd had in it. They begin to believe in the healing powers of love, the truly magical thing it is, for surely your love restored Robert's sight to him. And no one should ever be made to feel ashamed for something as beautiful as that."

Catriona heard laughter coming from the parlor as she reached the bottom of the stairwell. She approached the door, still unable to believe the hour was so late.

After the disaster that morning, she had decided to take a nap to restore her spirits. She'd woken to learn she had slept through supper.

At the parlor door, she paused, surveying the crowd of guests inside. There were tables set up for card play, and a number of gentlemen stood at the hearth sipping wine and conversing. Ladies were reading quietly or stitching samplers, while another group surrounded the pianoforte and the woman who was playing there. It was a comfortable setting and Catriona easily slipped inside. It took her a moment to find Robert, who was sitting in a chair near the far corner. Tolley, Noah, and Amelia sat close by. It was from their small group where the laughter was coming.

Tolley was speaking as she drew near.

"It should be a novelty this time, traveling to Paris for once without a war going on around me."

Robert spotted her then. "I was beginning to worry that you might sleep through the remainder of the weekend." He smiled. "Are you feeling better?"

"Much," she answered, taking a seat beside Amelia on the settee. Tolley continued on, detailing his plans for his trip, on which he would be leaving within the month. Robert teased him, suggesting that he had found a French *amour* during his last stay there. Tolley merely smiled, attempting to reveal nothing, when instead he all but confirmed Robert's assumption.

A butler came in then and bent toward Tolley, whispering something in his ear.

"Splendid!" Tolley responded. "Seems this is to be a night of surprises!"

He stood and left the room, only to return moments later with a man, older and quite distinguished-looking.

"Catriona," Tolley said, coming first. "There is someone here I would like you to meet."

Catriona stood. The gentleman stepped forward slowly. "Catherine?"

She peered at him curiously. "I beg your pardon, sir?"

The man was staring at her as if he were looking at a ghost. "Of course you cannot be her, but the resemblance is uncanny."

"Are we acquainted?"

"Catriona," Tolley said. "This man is Christian Talbot, Viscount Plimlock. He is your uncle."

She looked at Robert. "My uncle? How? My father had no brothers, for they would have inherited before Damon could have."

"No, he is your mother's brother," Noah said. "Her twin brother, actually. I was able to discover your mother's maiden name through Brewster. He did some searching and found that she was Catherine Talbot before she married your father. I then did some searching to see if she had any living relatives and found Lord Plimlock."

Catriona looked immediately at her locket. The initials, *C* and *T*. "The young man pictured here. It is you?"

Lord Plimlock looked at the locket and smiled, nodding. "Our mother gave that to Catherine when she was a girl. Seeing you, and that locket, I know now there is no doubt. I admit I was skeptical when first told that Catherine had a daughter, but after hearing of Sir Damon, it began to make sense. Catherine's death just never sat right with me. There were too many unanswered questions."

"You were twins," Catriona said, "just like . . ."

He nodded. "I understand you had a brother."

"Yes. He died at birth."

Catriona had been thinking quite a lot lately about her infant brother who had not lived long enough to know he'd even had a sister. When she had first learned the truth about her beginnings, Catriona had somehow pushed the knowledge of her brother away. She hadn't been prepared to face that part of her life, having lost Mary and Angus so recently. Even her mother Lady Catherine hadn't come to her thoughts, but had stayed there with her brother, hidden away until she would be ready to reflect on them.

But since discovering that she carried a child, thoughts of her brother and Lady Catherine had come to her more often. What would he have been like today? Would he be tall? Would he look like her? How would her life have been different had the both of them lived? Learning now that her mother had also had a twin brother made it seem as if the pieces long lost from a puzzle were finally set into place.

"You will have much to talk about," Robert said. "We will allow you your privacy."

When the others had gone, Christian moved to sit beside Catriona on the settee.

"Did you know my father?" Catriona asked.

"Yes." Christian looked out over the room. "I was against their marriage, not because I thought Charles wouldn't be kind to her. He loved Catherine quite madly. It was obvious to anyone who saw them. But I thought he was too many years older than she. She was so young. He had been married before and had lost his first wife in childbed. If I had only known . . ."

Catriona reached out and touched his hand. At first he looked surprised at the contact, then he smiled.

"You must have loved her very much," Catriona said.

"We were very close, at times it seemed as if we were one. But after she married Charles, I was a fool. I was angry with her for leaving me. We had so many adventures yet to take." He closed his eyes, taking a deep breath. "I know now that is why I was so against her marrying Charles. Because she was leaving me, and perhaps somehow I knew I would never see her again. She wrote to me, scores of letters begging me to come for a visit. I never answered them. Later, after Charles's death, she wrote of Damon, of her fear of him, and I simply ignored her pleas for help, telling myself she had brought it on herself." He looked at Catriona, his eyes moist with unshed tears of regret. "I could have saved her. Catherine could be alive today if not for me, both she and your brother. Why? Why was I so selfish?"

Catriona looked at him. "No. It was not your fault. There is only one person to blame and that is Damon. He must be made to pay for his deeds. And if it takes me the rest of my life, I will find a way to see that he does."

Chapter Twenty-six

Catriona and Christian spent the better part of the following day together, and during that time discovered they shared a number of common interests. Love of reading seemed to be a Talbot trait, as was a fondness for adventure.

Her mother and Christian had been the only children of their parents, both who were no longer living. Christian told her that his mother, Catriona's grandmother, the first Catherine, had only recently passed on, succumbing to an ague she'd suffered from for some time. She would have loved knowing Catriona, he'd said, for it was from her that they had all acquired their love for reading. It was from Catriona's grandfather, the first Viscount Plimlock, they had gotten their love for adventure. Christian told her of how the man had once tried to fly off the upper story of their family seat, Lockwood, with wings he'd made from feathers he'd woven together with string. Instead, he'd only ended up breaking his leg in the fall.

While Catriona passed the time with her uncle, Robert set out on his own bit of business. He was standing now in the Sheldrake gallery, admiring the works of art collected by Tolley and his ancestors, and waiting. He was staring at a painting of a mallard in flight when the Marquess of Kinsborough came into the room to join him.

"I trust your summons here indicates you have reconsidered my offer," he said, frowning as he came to stand beside Robert.

Robert never took his eyes from the painting, never turned to acknowledge the marquess. "You know, I find now that whenever I look at a painting, or a statue, or even outside at the landscape, I am reluctant to close my eyes for fear that I might open them and find myself blind once again."

Kinsborough regarded the painting. "Quite a thing," he said, "your having gotten your sight back."

"Yes, isn't it?" Robert hesitated. "Unfortunately, the injuries suffered by the rest of my family from the fire were far more severe. Death is a rather difficult thing to recover from."

Kinsborough was already beginning to look uncomfortable. "It was a tragedy."

Robert turned to look at him, his expression casual. "Do you know that Jamie, my brother's son and heir, would have turned five years old this month?" He looked again at the painting. "He was quite the artist, Jamie was. I endeavored, of course, but my talents lay in the acquisition, not in the creation. But Jamie, he could have become extraordinary, if only he'd been given the time. And who can say what the child my brother's wife was carrying could have become? We will never know."

"I'm very sorry for what happened to your family, Devonbrook," Kinsborough said, his voice growing agitated. "Your loss is obvious, both emotional and financial. That is why I have offered to purchase what remains of the collection, to help you recover and move on."

"The irony of it is, my lord, the collection remains mostly intact. I could not know this, of course, until I had recovered my eyesight, but my father had had most of the pieces sent to his Scottish estate. They were not at Devonbrook House when the fire broke out, so they were kept quite safe. The collection was my father's obsession. He had devoted his life to it. I do not believe it would be serving his memory any respect to part with a single piece of it now. Thank you for your offer, my lord, but I simply must refuse."

Robert turned, walking down the long gallery wall, gazing at the artwork displayed there, leaving Kinsborough behind.

"Devonbrook."

Robert had thought him gone. When he turned he saw that Kinsborough still stood where he'd left him. His eyes were filled with desperation. "I must appeal to your honor, as a gentleman."

"Gentleman?" Robert smiled sardonically. "But I am no gentleman, my lord. Do you not recall? I murdered my entire family for a title."

Kinsborough lost himself and began to sob into his hands. "It wasn't supposed to happen that way. It was an accident. The worst sort of accident. I never wanted them to die."

Robert stood, listening to every dispicable word as the marquess wailed on.

"He was only supposed to find the painting and destroy it. But he hadn't found it with the others. He thought it might be in your father's chambers. The candle fell. The draperies caught quickly. Too quickly. There was no hope of putting it out. But that coward, he simply ran to save himself. He left your father, the others, to die. Oh God, if I could have taken James's place, I would have. I swear to you I would have. We were at university together. All those years. I never hated him. I envied him. He had Louisa. He had everything I ever dreamed of having. And then he had the painting . . ."

"What painting, Kinsborough?"

Kinsborough looked up from his hands, his face red, his eyes swollen. "It was my wife. She took a lover. He was an artist. He painted her, unclothed, stretched out

for all to see. For all to recognize. I thought I had
finally gotten the thing. Traced it to a dealer in France.
It took me ten months to locate it. A man called
Charleton had it. I sent him an offer. He accepted. But
then somehow your father learned of it. He'd paid a
maid who worked in my household to report on my
business to him. He bought the painting from under
me. He was going to put it up for everyone to see. At
your sister-in-law's ball. The *ton*. Everyone would see
her. Everyone would see my wife. Like that. And
everyone would know."

Robert listened carefully to him. He just couldn't
believe what he was hearing. "My father bought an
indiscreet painting of your wife and told you he would
display it to society? Knowingly?"

Kinsborough shook his head. "He did not know it
was her. He hadn't yet seen the painting."

"Why wouldn't you have simply told him the truth?"

"I could not. He had taken Louisa, your mother,
from me all those years before." He laughed, a dry, hu-
morless sound. "Taken. Louisa had never been mine.
She'd always wanted your father instead. I was too
ashamed to tell him the truth about my wife. I should
have. I know that now. But I thought to get him back
with his own scheme. I learned about the maid. He'd
hired her to spy on me. I shouldn't have done it. I
should have just gone to him and told him the truth.
Too many years of competing. Too many losses to him.
I just could not do it."

Kinsborough's voice began to grow louder, and then
suddenly he stopped and was falling to the floor,
clutching at his chest. His face was red, almost purple
in color. He didn't appear to be breathing at all. Robert
ran to him and knelt, feeling for a pulse.

"Kinsborough!"

His heartbeat was racing madly. The marquess
was fighting to breathe. To live. Robert loosened
his neckcloth and started undoing the buttons of his

waistcoat. A servant came to the door, having heard the disturbance.

"Run!" Robert shouted. "Get Lord Sheldrake! Get a doctor! Hurry!"

Kinsborough grasped onto Robert's coat. "I must tell you . . ." He gasped for air. "I am sorry . . . so sorry . . ."

"Save your strength," Robert said. "You must calm yourself."

A short while later, Tolley came running in with the doctor who had tended to Robert.

"I had come to have a look at your shoulder," he said, kneeling beside Kinsborough.

"Tend to him, Doctor. Forget my shoulder."

Robert stood and watched, hearing the marquess's words over and over again in his head.

Accident . . . I am sorry . . . so sorry . . . so sorry . . . so sorry . . .

And then something else he had said came to him.

Get him back with his own scheme . . . supposed to find the painting and destroy it . . . there was no hope . . . coward . . . he simply ran to save himself.

And, suddenly, it all made sense.

Forbes.

Kinsborough had hired him to act as his father's valet in order to get the painting and destroy it before it could be displayed at Elizabeth's ball. Kinsborough hadn't been the one to set the fire. Kinsborough hadn't wanted the collection destroyed. He'd only wanted the painting of his wife, and Forbes had bungled it, then turned around and laid the blame for it all on Robert.

Well, no more.

Robert left the room when it looked as if the marquess was out of any danger. His face had returned to nearly its normal color and he was breathing calmly into the small balloonlike sack the doctor had pulled from his bag. As he made his way through the house toward his chamber, Robert rehearsed what he would say when he confronted Forbes with the knowledge that he had been the one responsible for the fire. That he had been the one to murder his family.

He had made it to the lower hallways when a maid came upon him, stopping him.

"Excuse me, your grace, but the lady asked me to give this to you."

She bobbed a curtsy. Robert took the note and read it.

"Robert, there is something I must discuss with you about our wedding. Privately. It is most important. Please come and meet me in the garden."

Robert's first thought was to wonder what was wrong. And what part Sir Damon Dunstron had in it. Catriona wasn't the sort to write a note. Unless . . .

Why in perdition had he left her alone?

Forbes would have wait, just a little longer.

When Robert arrived at the garden entrance he looked all around for Catriona. No one was about the center fountains or the rose beds in bloom. There were but two places she could be. The cherry orchard which stretched to the right of him, or the maze at his left.

"Robert?"

Robert looked toward the direction of Catriona's voice. "Catriona? Where are you?"

"I am here. In the maze."

Robert entered the tall hedges, wondering what game she was playing. He rounded the first bend, where he saw the copy of *Waverly* he'd given her lying on the ground, pages flipping in the breeze. He picked it up. "Catriona?"

"I'm here," he heard ahead a moment later.

He continued on. When he got to the center of the labyrinth, he spotted her. Her back was to him, her face hidden behind the rim of her straw bonnet. He came up slowly behind her and pulled her against him. "So, lady, tell me what trick do you play?"

He looked down. It wasn't Catriona's stormy blue eyes peering up at him from beneath the bonnet's rim. These were green and catlike eyes. Familiar eyes. Betraying eyes. "Anthea?"

He let her go quickly as if she'd stung him.

"Robert."

"What are you doing here?"

She lifted her chin. "I wanted to speak with you. Alone. But you are never alone. You are always with her."

"You wrote the note?" Robert looked around the maze. "Where is Catriona?"

"She is not here." She smiled then. "She had other things to attend to."

Robert stared at her, frowning. "What are you talking about, Anthea?"

"I've been asked to inform you that Miss Dunstron has had a change of heart. She has decided she will marry someone else."

None of this sounded real. Not at all. "And she told you this herself?"

"Yes. She asked me to convey to you her heartfelt apologies. She has gone off to wed her cousin, Sir Damon Dunstron."

"Like hell she has," Robert said, fast growing impatient with her. "Where is she, Anthea?"

"Oh, Robert, do you not see that now we can be together again? It will be like it should have been before. You wanted me then. We can be married now. Nothing has changed."

"Everything has changed, you foolish idiot." Robert grabbed Anthea by her shoulders, shaking her. He lowered his face to where it was inches from hers. "Now tell me where Catriona is."

Anthea's face went white, her voice shaking. "He has her. He took her out the other end of the maze."

"Where, Anthea? Where is he taking her?"

"I do not know. I swear to you . . ."

She started to go limp in his arms, as if in a faint. Unwilling to waste any more of his time, he released her and turned to leave.

"Robert, wait!"

He started down the path and turning once, found

himself at an impasse, a wall of ten-foot-high hedges standing in his way. He retraced his steps, only to meet another hedge wall through another passage. His frustration was growing, for he knew the longer he took, the greater the chances of Damon bringing harm to Catriona. He didn't want to think of the possibilities. When he came to his third impasse, he looked to the clouds and shouted, "Damnation!"

A voice came to his head, a gentle voice that had offered him help once before.

Rely on what you have and not what you are lacking . . .

Robert looked down. The grass inside the maze was tall and damp, showing his footprints. He followed them back to the center of the maze, from where Anthea had suddenly vanished. He looked around at each opening from the center. He noticed one where it looked as if several people had trodden. He followed the footprints through every twist and turn of the labyrinth of hedges until it led him through to the other side. A service path that ran behind the main house was there. It bore the mark of fresh wheel ruts. They were riding in a carriage.

Robert followed the service path back to the house. Noah and Tolley were standing on the terrace. Robert ran to them, trying to ignore the growing pain in his shoulder.

"Where does that service path lead to?" he asked Tolley.

"To the south road. Why?"

"Damon has taken Catriona. They are in a coach. I need a horse. Now."

"You cannot ride with your shoulder in a sling," Noah said.

"Rob," Tolley said, his eyes focused on Robert's arm, "your wound has already opened."

A small red patch of blood had come through the white fabric of the sling. "I do not care. I have to get Catriona back."

"Then let's hurry!"

As they came around to the front of the house, they spotted a coach driving down the drive toward them.

"A late arrival?" Tolley questioned. "But the weekend is nearly over."

"I don't care who it is," Robert said. "I'm taking that coach to find Catriona."

Chapter Twenty-seven

Catriona was frowning. While the landscape of the Kentish countryside was whizzing by the window, she was sitting in the coach that was taking her farther and farther away from Drakely Manor.

And farther and farther away from Robert.

She wasn't scared. Not at all. She was just angry.

She looked to the coach seat across from her, and the two men who sat there. She couldn't resist the urge to shake her head like a mother faced with two misbehaving children. "I would have expected this of Damon, but not of you. I would have thought better of you."

Ian Alexander quickly looked away, avoiding any communication with her eyes.

Damon noticed the reaction and quickly cut in. "Do not listen to her, Ian. This was the only course we could take to ensure our success. There was no other choice."

Catriona glared at Damon. "I know well why you have done this. You must try to protect yourself from the punishment you rightly deserve. But you, Ian? What could have brought you to this? This man is a murderer. He killed my mother. He killed my brother just barely out of the womb. What sort of man could kill an innocent child?"

"Shut up!" Damon yelled. "Ian will not listen to any more of your lies. He knows it was not me. He knows that it was that woman, that MacBryan witch, who killed Catherine and the child, and then sought to blame me."

"And so you killed her, too," Catriona finished.

Ian obviously had not learned that much. He looked at Damon, the shock of disbelief coloring his face. "You killed Mary?"

"He did not tell you that part of it, did he?" Catriona went on. "Mary did not kill Lady Catherine and her child. You knew Mary, Ian. Do you truly believe her capable of it? She always treated you so well, Ian, as if you were family. You were family. Do you know what this man does to his family, to anyone who gets in his way? He kills them, and when he tires of you, he will certainly kill you as well."

Damon pulled back his hand and slapped Catriona, hard across the mouth. It stung, but Catriona refused to cower. She lifted her head and stared at him, touching her mouth where his hand had struck her.

"You dinna have to hit her," Ian said. He looked at Catriona, his eyes filled with genuine concern. "Are you hurt, Catriona?"

"I am fine, Ian, for you see contrary to what he may believe, Damon does not frighten me. I know that Robert will come for me and when he does, this man will finally be made to answer for his crimes."

"Ah, yes," Damon said then, smiling. "The good Duke of Devonbrook. Ian knows him well, quite well, indeed. Perhaps when he comes for you, Ian can finish the task he failed at the first time and have his shot hit its mark right."

Catriona looked at Ian. "You? You are the one who tried to kill Robert? It was you who shot at him? Why, Ian? Why would you do something like that?"

Ian's mouth turned in a grimace, as if he'd just swallowed something truly unsavory. "I had to do it. He soiled you, Catriona. I saw him. On top of you.

Sticking his rod in you. You were my angel, my pure, sweet untouched angel. You never should have gone to him."

"Ah, yes, he did plow her, and on more than just the occasion you saw them," Damon said, seizing the moment. "Even now the Englishman's child grows in her belly."

Ian looked down to where Catriona's hands rested instinctively against her middle.

Damon chuckled. "Go on, dear cousin. Dare to deny it. Tell this besotted idiot that you are not the Englishman's whore."

Catriona simply stared at Ian, remaining silent.

"Are you, Catriona? Are you goin' to have the duke's bairn?"

Catriona nodded softly. "Yes, Ian, I am. Robert has asked me to wed him. I'm sorry if I have hurt you. I do care for you very much, but I love Robert. I always have."

"That is where you are mistaken," Damon said. He removed a pistol from his coat pocket and aimed it at Catriona.

"You ne'er said anything about killin' her!" Ian exclaimed.

"What did you think I would do with her? Lock her in a tower so she could find some way to escape and see us both hanged? Yes, Ian, you would hang, too, for it was because of you that Scotsman, MacBryan, drowned in those caves."

"Angus wasna supposed to go into the caves," Ian explained to Catriona. "He was supposed to go onto the skiffs with the others. He would be arrested and Sir Damon would be commended for capturing the smugglers. Then I would get my pay. That is what the plan was. But it dinna work out that way."

Catriona stared at him, outraged. "Angus treated you as he would his son, Ian. He took care of you. He raised you after your parents died. How could you betray him like that?"

The coach veered to the left then, pulling off and away from the road. They jostled along for some distance over a bumpy field and then stopped. Damon opened the door, motioning with the barrel of his pistol for Catriona to move outside. "Get out. And if you think to run, you can be certain I will kill you."

Catriona stepped from the coach. They were atop a rocky windswept cliff which hung out over a high ravine. A curtain of trees sheltered them from sight of the road. Catriona knew why they had stopped, why they were here in this secluded setting.

Damon was truly going to kill her.

"Walk," he said, and then he pushed Catriona forward, the pistol aimed on her as he and Ian followed behind. She stopped when she reached the edge of the cliff and turned to face him. No matter what happened to her, she would not show her fear. She raised her chin and stared him straight in his murderous eyes.

"I hope you realize that no matter what you do to me, Robert will hunt you down. He will find you and he will kill you."

Damon smiled. "Once I have vanished on the Continent, he will never see me again."

"I would not be so confident." Catriona continued to stare at him. "Robert will not rest until he catches you." She frowned. "Why did you do it, Damon? Were the money and the title truly worth it to you? When you looked at my mother's portrait all these years, did it bother you, knowing what you had done to her?"

Damon's face seemed to change then, darkening with some hidden emotion—regret? "Catherine should have never refused me. I tried to convince her, after Charles was gone, that I would make her even happier than he had. He was an old man. He would have died soon . . ."

"Even if you hadn't killed him first?"

Damon frowned at her, narrowing his eyes. "Catherine was beautiful, but she thought herself better than I." He sneered and the look on his face changed to one of true evil. "She learned the consequences of her misjudgment, though, and now you, too, will learn the same."

He lowered the gun on her.

"No!"

Robert suddenly leapt forward from the trees, hurling himself against Damon and knocking the pistol from Damon's hand. They tumbled back onto the ground, rolling and struggling, nearly obscured by the dust brought up from their fight. They grappled, moving close to the cliff's edge. Ian stood, frozen, mesmerized.

Catriona spotted the gun then lying in a clump of grass by her feet. She ran for it, but just as she reached for it Damon managed to break away, closing his hand over it before she could. He scrambled to his feet, alternately aiming the pistol at both her and at Robert, who had stood and was standing not five feet from her.

Catriona looked at Robert. She wanted to run for him, to bury herself against him, but Damon still held the gun on them. She noticed a red blotch that was fast spreading across the white fabric of his sling. "Robert, your arm . . ."

"It is all right, Catriona," he said, but she noticed that his forehead was beaded with sweat and his jaw was tightly clenched.

"That is enough!" Damon shouted, waving the gun dangerously. "It matters little about his arm when you will both be dead in a matter of minutes."

"No, Damon."

Catriona turned to look at where Ian stood, staring at Damon with anger in his eyes.

"You will not kill them," Ian went on. "You will not kill anyone else again."

"You fool," Damon hissed at Ian. "Do you think she cares at all about you? She is a whore."

Ian advanced, his eyes dark and menacing.

"You saw her yourself," Damon went on, "flat on her back, rutting with Devonbrook."

Ian did not stop.

"You need me, Ian. I can give you things. Do not force me to kill you."

Ian closed in on Damon. A shot fired. Ian flinched, hit in the arm. A second shot fired. Damon turned, clutching at his chest, staggering backward slowly. He teetered a moment at the edge of the cliff before stumbling over the side.

There came no sound afterward. Only silence.

Catriona turned and saw that Robert had moved and was standing just behind the two of them, the barrel of the pistol he held still smoking. Noah had surfaced behind him.

Robert looked at her. "Catriona, are you hurt?"

"No, Robert, I am fine. Really."

The blood from his injury had soaked through the sling now. Catriona looked at his face, which had grown alarmingly pale. "Your arm."

"It doesn't matter," he said. "All I care is that I have you back."

"Catriona?"

Robert looked up, noting Ian standing a distance behind them. He started for him. "I will kill you for your part in this!"

"No!"

Robert froze at the unexpected shout which had come from behind them. Everyone turned, looking to where Mairead had suddenly materialized. She came forward, placing herself between Ian and Robert.

Catriona stared at her sister, wondering how she'd gotten there when she was supposed to be in London. She realized then there was also someone else, someone standing behind Mairead a space. It looked like . . . Could it be? It was . . .

Angus.

"Da!" Catriona ran for him and threw her arms around him. "Da, you are here."

Angus smiled down at her. "Aye, lass, I am. I've been following you since after you left Scotland, actually I've been following that bloody Dunstron. When I learned from the men what he had done to my Mary, and that you and your sister had gone, I knew he would soon be coming for you. So I followed him to stop him."

"Oh, Da, I'm so sorry about Mam . . ."

"I knew that devil had done it. I knew it and I swore I'd cross the world to find him and kill him for takin' my Mary." Angus looked down at her. "Mary only did what she had to protect you, Catriona. She loved you like you were her own. As do I. I always have. You must know that."

Catriona felt tears stinging at her eyes. "I know, Da. I know."

Angus looked over at Ian, his face set with his sad disappointment. " 'Tis a good thing your father isna here to see what you've done, lad."

"It isn't his fault," Mairead broke in. "Ian didn't know what he was doing," she said. "He couldn't know how terrible that man really was."

"Mairead, you knew?" Catriona asked. "About Ian and Sir Damon?"

Mairead nodded, staring at Ian. "I suspected the truth after the landing. I had seen Ian talking with Sir Damon the next day when I'd gone out looking for him."

Watching her sister, the way in which she stared at Ian so desperately, Catriona suddenly realized the truth. "Why did you never say anything?"

"Because . . ." Mairead hesitated. "Because I love him." She turned to her sister, tears of regret filling her eyes. "I know it is you he loves, Catriona, but I do not care. I love Ian. I have always loved him."

"But he helped to kidnap your sister," Robert said to her. "He would have killed her."

"No, Robert," Catriona said. "I do not believe Ian would have allowed Damon to kill me, even if you hadn't found us. He did not know everything Damon had done. He never could have known how deeply he had been taken in until it was too late. You saw what he did here, how he risked his life to help us. He would never have allowed Damon to harm me. I just know it."

Robert glared at Ian, unmoved.

"Please, Robert," Catriona said softly. "Don't do this now. Despite the mistakes he has made, Mairead loves him."

Robert looked at her, silent. Unwilling to argue further, he took Catriona's hand, staring at Ian coldly before turning back for the coach.

Epilogue

Catriona looked up from the letter she was writing. Robert, her husband, was across the room, stretched out on the floor while their son James Charles Robert Edenhall navigated his way along the edge of the settee. James was just learning to walk, his ten-month-old's legs still too uncertain to hold him alone, so he cut a path through every room using whatever furnishing might be closest by.

Catriona chuckled as he turned slowly, looking for his next handhold, his dark eyes wide with a child's wonder. Two fingers were all that remained attached to the settee, the side table bare inches from his other outstretched hand. And then those two fingers let go and he toddled two wobbly steps until he reached the table's edge.

"He took his first steps!" Robert exclaimed with all the excitement of a proud father. "Did you see that?"

"Now is when the mischief begins," answered Catriona, who had already abandoned the letter to join her boys on the floor. She took the wriggling James into her arms and pressed a kiss to his dark head.

Robert nuzzled her ear. "He's just like his mother, always off seeking new adventures."

"Yes, although his mother never was very successful at finding the one adventure she sought."

Reminiscing on that long ago treasure, Catriona glanced over to the scores of books which now lined the library walls, more than had ever been there before. In the past several months, Robert had had the surviving library at Devonbrook moved to Rosmorigh, where they would stay until the rebuilding of the house in Lancashire was complete. Catriona had gone through every one of those books, and still had never found the text map for the Bonnie Prince's treasure. She had come to the conclusion that it was lost forever.

As she turned her head, Catriona noticed that James had decided he preferred crawling to his walking and was making his way underneath the zebra wood desk's knee cubby where Mattie lay sleeping. And where Mattie wouldn't remain sleeping much longer.

Catriona stood. "I'll need to finish that letter to Tolley if I hope to make the next post. He is returning from Paris in a fortnight. In his last letter he said to tell you he's bought a horse that just might best Bayard. He is to bring him back to London, with Elise."

Tolley had indeed found himself an *amour* in France, and upon arriving in Paris he had promptly wedded her. She was the daughter of deposed French nobles. Her parents had lost their lives to the guillotine and when Tolley had first met her, she was living with her grandmother. Now he was bringing his new wife and her grandmother home with him to England, as well as his new horse.

Robert laughed. "Will he never give up?"

"Apparently he will not. He did write that he visited with Ian and Mairead while he was in Paris. Mairead has opened a shop on Rue Pavot and has already taken on quite a clientele. It seems a number of the ladies she made gowns for in London visit her there. Word has traveled quickly and now the French ladies are coming to her, begging for one of her designs." Catriona looked up from Tolley's letter at Robert then. "Ian is doing well with his transport venture."

Robert frowned. "I am not surprised. It is a vocation he seems particularly suited to."

"Robert, he did help you to get that painting you were pursuing."

"The man shot me, Catriona. He betrayed Angus and nearly was responsible for killing him. And do not forget he was in league with your cousin."

Damon. The mention of his name still caused Catriona a shudder. He was gone now, but he had left a legacy of grief behind him that would never be forgotten.

After returning to Rosmorigh, Robert and Catriona had traveled to Castle Crannock. She had inherited the estate at their marriage and upon Damon's death, and with its land Rosmorigh would grow to twice its present holding. But as she walked through the dark and forbidding hallways, Catriona could think of nothing other than the horror which had taken place there.

Standing in the great hall, the images of her parents hanging beside one another upon the wall, Catriona knew then what she must do. They had taken the portraits with them back to Rosmorigh, and then Robert had assumed the task of seeing to the castle's dismantling. When finished, he had left but a small bit of it remaining, the chapel beside which lay the graves of her mother and father, and the new and final resting place of her infant brother, whom they had christened Charles, and whose tiny body had been found wrapped in a blanket and buried in a vault beneath the castle's keep, the long-hidden secret now revealed.

And now Angus had begun building a house on that part of the estate. He would take over the supervision of the tenants, seeing to the long-needed repairs of their crofts, educating them in the best methods of raising crops in the uncertain Highland soil.

"Ian is changed now, Robert. Mairead writes that they are very happy together. She says he knows he was just very confused before."

"Not so confused that he couldn't fire a weapon."

Catriona stared at Robert.

He looked right back, taking a deep, impatient breath. "What?"

"You have forgiven Lord Kinsborough. You even sent him that terrible portrait of his wife so he could destroy it and be assured it would never be seen by anyone again. And Forbes, now that he is in prison, you can begin to put that part of our lives aside, as well. Can you not find some way to—"

A loud thud sounded from beneath the desk. Seconds later, James let out a wail.

"Oh!" Catriona reached down and picked up the crying infant, kissed the spot where he'd just bumped his head on the desk. "My poor boy." He quieted quickly, quite quickly in fact, for he began yanking on Catriona's locket necklace.

"That wasn't at all pleasant, now was it?" she cooed to him, removing the necklace and releasing it to his curious hands. It wasn't two moments later that he'd dropped it on the floor and was squirming out of Catriona's arms. She set him safely on the carpet and then turned to stoop and retrieve the necklace.

It was then she noticed something lying on the floor beneath the desk where James had been playing. Looking closer, she saw that it had fallen from a small hatch hidden under the drawer, another of the numerous compartments they hadn't yet discovered in the desk. James had released it when he'd bumped it with his head.

Catriona reached for the object, retrieving what looked to be a small book. She flipped it over to read its cover.

"Robert," she asked, "was your father fond of fishing?"

"I'm not certain. Why, my love?"

"Because I found this book, *The Compleat Angler*. It had been in the desk and—"

Robert started for her. "What did you say the title was?"

"The Compleat Angler."

Robert stood and leaned against the desktop, taking the book. A smile lit his face and he shook his head. "I should have known."

"Should have known what?" Catriona asked, watching as Robert started flipping through the pages.

"When Quinby first was cataloging my inheritance to me after the fire, he made mention that my father had written I should try my hand at angling. It was right after he'd written that I would find hidden treasures here at Rosmorigh. At the time, I couldn't have know what he'd meant." He looked at Catriona. "Would you care to place a wager that this is the book we've been searching for? That it was here, in this ridiculous desk, the entire time?"

Catriona's eyes were wide with excitement. "Forget the wager, just open it and see!"

Just as the Colonel had always said, if they hadn't been searching for it, they never would have found it.

The text had been inserted in such a way as to appear a description of the countryside, places best suited to angling. There was the description of the burn, the cave, the forked oak. "Where is the Colonel's picture map, Catriona?"

She moved to retrieve the small wooden box where she kept her most treasured things, the chest Mary had given her that long-ago day. Inside she kept the handkerchief that had once been her mother's, a ribbon-tied lock of James's dark hair, other small mementos. She removed the map from underneath.

"All right," Robert said, scrutinizing the two together. "Judging from this passage here, and following the places we have already gone to on the map, it would

seem the final place where the treasure would be hidden
is . . ."

"Loch Linnanglas!" Catriona exclaimed. "We must
go!"

She turned and stopped when she noticed that James
had crawled up beside Mattie on the settee and was
now peacefully sleeping beside her. "I'll have Sally
take him to the nursery while you have the horses
saddled."

An hour later they were standing on the banks of
Loch Linnanglas, reading out loud the final passage in
the book.

" 'There is a place where the trees grow thickly and
the grass is rich and green. In a pool there is a rocky
ledge where the fish bite quick and strong.' "

Robert and Catriona walked along the loch until they
found the small pool that was formed out of a scattering of boulders.

"A rocky ledge . . ." Robert said, and knelt along the
rim of the pool, searching.

"Be careful, Robert," Catriona said.

"Do not worry, my love," he said, removing his coat.
"I have no plans to go falling into the water again." He
stretched out on his stomach over the rock's edge.
Catriona took hold of his waistcoat.

"There is an opening beneath these rocks which goes
back a space under the ground. If you will hold my
legs, I should be able to reach inside and . . ."

Robert slipped over the side with a resounding
splash.

Catriona couldn't help but laugh. "Robert! Are you
all right?"

She tried to peer over the ledge, but could see
nothing. Finally she heard Robert shout, "I've got it!"

"You found the treasure?"

"It's a box and it's heavy as a boulder." She heard
him grunt and then watched as he pushed the box up to
sit on the ledge. Robert came around to the side and

Catriona helped him from the pool. His clothes were soaked and filthy and his face was smudged with dirt. Several soggy leaves were tangled in his wet hair. All in all, he looked incredibly handsome.

Robert retrieved the box and brought it back onto dry land. It was a small wooden chest, banded with steel, and was covered with moss and debris.

"It is locked," Catriona said.

"Yes, but the fixture is rusted from all this time near the water. I might be able to break it free with this rock."

Robert beat at the lock with the small stone. It took several strikes, but finally the lock sprang free. He turned and looked at Catriona, smiling at her from beneath the dirt smudges on his face. "I believe you should be the one to open it."

Catriona knelt beside the chest and freed the latch that held it. Then slowly she lifted the lid. Her eyes went wide and her mouth fell open in astonishment at what she found safely nestled inside.

Gold coins, hundreds of them, thousands of them, gleaming in the afternoon sunlight. Robert took out a handful, inspecting them closely. "They are certainly French."

Catriona could do nothing more than stare at the treasure for which she'd been searching so long. And as she sat there, she could almost swear she had heard the Colonel's cackling laughter as he whispered to her on the wind. *I knew you could do it, lassie . . .*

She finally turned when she noticed Robert beside her, removing his boots, and tossing his shirt atop them.

"What are you doing?"

"I'm filthy and it is a warm summer day. I am going for a swim."

Catriona kicked off her slippers and began pulling off her stockings. "Then I hope you won't mind if I join you."

Robert didn't object at all. He was too busy gathering his wife into his arms and making love to her on the grassy banks of Loch Linnanglas.

Where your treasure is, there will your heart be also.
—Matthew, 6:21

Author's Note

The legend of the Jacobite treasure is a true one, and one that persists even today. The French did send Bonnie Prince Charlie thirty-five thousand in gold louis to assist him in his fight to regain the English throne for the Stuarts. Brought on board the ships *Bellona* and *Mars,* it did arrive in Scotland shortly after the Jacobites had been defeated at Culloden. Of that there is little question. The mystery lies with the missing cask reputed to have been buried somewhere along the banks of Loch Arkaig in Cameron country, a legend bolstered in recent years by the finding of eighteenth-century coins stuck in the hooves of cattle which had been grazing in the area nearby.

Is the treasure real? Could there be a cask of gold buried just beneath the surface along the banks of that mysterious dark loch, waiting for discovery? Perhaps someday an antiquarian bookseller in Edinburgh might discover a map giving the location of such a treasure hidden in a dusty old book. It could be a picture map, yellowed and aged, or it could simply be written within the text so that no one except those who knew of the treasure would realize the truth. Perhaps that book might even be a ragged copy of Isaak Walton's book, *The Compleat Angler. . . .*

Being the dreamer I am, I would certainly like to think it could happen that way.

The story of my *Regency Rogues* will continue with Noah, Robert's brother, coming very soon from Topaz books. I hope you will look for it, and I hope you will write to me at P.O. Box 1771, Chandler, Arizona, 85244-1771, or visit my website located at *http://www.inficad.com/~jacreding*.

SIMMERING DESIRES

☐ **HALFWAY HOME by Bronwyn Williams.** When Sara Young's and Jericho Wilde's paths intersect at the Halfway Hotel, they're both in for a surprise—as passion ignites without warning. Now Jericho is torn between vengeance and caring . . . until he sees that death may come as quickly as this chance for love. . . .
(406982—$5.99)

☐ **THE WARFIELD BRIDE by Bronwyn Williams.** None of the Warfield brothers expected Hannah Ballinger to change their lives: none of them expected the joy she and her new baby would bring to their household. But most of all, Penn never expected to lose his heart to the woman he wanted his brother to marry—a mail order bride. "Delightful, heartwarming, a winner!—Amanda Quick (404556—$4.99)

☐ **WIND SONG by Margaret Brownley.** When a feisty, red-haired schoolmarm arrives in Colton, Kansas and finds the town burned to the ground, she is forced to live with widower Luke Taylor and his young son, Matthew. Not only is she stealing Matthew's heart, but she is also igniting a desire as dangerous as love in his father's heart. (405269—$4.99)

☐ **BECAUSE YOU'RE MINE by Nan Ryan.** Golden-haired Sabella Rios vowed she would seduce the handsome Burt Burnett into marrying her and become mistress of the Lindo Vista ranch, which was rightfully hers. Sabella succeeded beyond her dreams, but there was one thing she had not counted on. In Burt's caressing arms, in his bed, her cold calculations turned into flames of passion as she fell deeply in love with this man, this enemy of her family. (405951—$5.50)

☐ **HARVEST OF DREAMS by Jaroldeen Edwards.** A magnificent saga of family threatened both from within and without—and of the love and pride, strength and honor, that would make the difference between tragedy and triumph.
(404742—$4.99)

*Prices slightly higher in Canada

Buy them at your local bookstore or use this convenient coupon for ordering.

PENGUIN USA
P.O. Box 999 — Dept. #17109
Bergenfield, New Jersey 07621

Please send me the books I have checked above.
I am enclosing $_____ (please add $2.00 to cover postage and handling). Send check or money order (no cash or C.O.D.'s) or charge by Mastercard or VISA (with a $15.00 minimum). Prices and numbers are subject to change without notice.

Card #_____ Exp. Date _____
Signature_____
Name_____
Address_____
City _____ State _____ Zip Code _____

For faster service when ordering by credit card call 1-800-253-6476
Allow a minimum of 4-6 weeks for delivery. This offer is subject to change without notice.